MAKING LIGHT

MAKING LIGHT

Haydn, Musical Camp, and the Long Shadow of German Idealism

RAYMOND KNAPP

DUKE UNIVERSITY PRESS
Durham and London 2018

Printed in the United States of America on acid-free paper ∞
Designed by Jennifer Hill
Typeset in Scala by Westchester Publishing Services
Library of Congress Cataloging-in-Publication Data
Names: Knapp, Raymond, author.
Title: Making light : Haydn, musical camp, and the long shadow of German idealism / Raymond Knapp.
Description: Durham : Duke University Press, 2018. | Includes bibliographical references and index.
Identifiers: LCCN 2017033262 (print) | LCCN 2017044572 (ebook)
ISBN 9780822372400 (ebook) | ISBN 9780822369356 (hardcover : alk. paper)
ISBN 9780822369509 (pbk. : alk. paper)
Subjects: LCSH: Haydn, Joseph, 1732–1809—Criticism and interpretation. | Idealism, German. | Music—Philosophy and aesthetics.
Classification: LCC ML410.H4 (ebook) | LCC ML410.H4 K537 2018 (print) | DDC 780.92—dc23
LC record available at https://lccn.loc.gov/2017033262

Andreas Roseneder, *aH!–dyn #1*, 2007. Acrylics on canvas, 50 x 40 cm. Portrait of Joseph Haydn after Thomas Hardy 1791. Part of the exhibition series *Haydn Reloaded*, Esterhàzy Palace, Fertöd, Hungary, 2009.

For Ahuva Braverman

Contents

Musical Examples

Preface | Surviving Absolute Music

I began this book project with a fundamental intuition, that the specific kind of pleasure I derive from Haydn has something basic in common with many of the pleasures I find in musicals, and that those shared pleasures are not the same as those I find in most music of the nineteenth century and its extended traditions. With both Haydn and many musicals, fun and seriousness coexist easily, and are even superimposed on each other, in a way that I find particularly appealing. Often (especially in Haydn) this is the result of a sophisticated play with generic expectations that, however humorous or lighthearted, does not detract from the music's expressive potential. But with serious nineteenth-century music, encompassing the notion of absolute music and what historian William Weber has dubbed "musical idealism," gratification generally comes from a kind of immersion of the self into something larger, releasing a capacity to feel deeply. While Haydn and musicals seem to be more aware of the individual operating interactively with other individuals within a larger social environment, and to encourage a similar awareness in the listener, most concert, chamber, and operatic music from the nineteenth century seems designed to help one forget both self and others in favor of inwardness, contemplation, and submission to a deep, even overwhelming experience of the music.

Behind this intuition stand several aspects of my own progress as a scholar. Early on, I was much interested in eighteenth-century music, especially Haydn, who was the subject of four of my conference talks between the mid-1980s and early 2000s. But I held back from publishing any of this work because I was not ready to address the critical issues that Haydn advocacy must confront in our generation, which come down to the fact that very little of what attracts people to Haydn in the first place emerges in the now fairly copious literature on Haydn, where it is obscured by the august tone that such work so often assumes. (This was especially true in the early 1980s, if less true today.)

Meanwhile, I published much on the symphonic work of Beethoven, Brahms, Wagner, Tchaikovsky, Mahler, and others from the nineteenth century and its extended concert and operatic traditions, before being pulled into the quite different world of the American musical, which has been the main focus of my work for more than a decade. While I was fascinated in a self-reflective way by the obvious differences between these quite disparate traditions, I was also eager to apprehend the one in terms of the other, and to understand better why both attracted me as a scholar. It was not hard to find common ground; after all, both the nineteenth-century symphony and musicals are large-scale public works centrally concerned with issues of identity, often national identity. And the American musical, although primarily a creature of the twentieth century, also had deep roots in the nineteenth. But there was no getting around the fact that they went about their business quite differently, however related their aims and background.

As I was privately wrestling with these issues, having to do, I supposed, with my own divided self, I also took up the problematics of American musicals within the larger field of popular music studies, where (as it seemed to me) its fate was, like Haydn's, to be the square peg that none of the cool kids could be bothered to care much about, especially when you tried, a trifle too earnestly, to explain why they should care (which was, indeed, a lot like trying to fit those pegs into round holes). Several things started to seem especially relevant to me in this context:

1. US American popular music grew up primarily in theatrical contexts, including minstrelsy, variety, and operetta, all of which largely opposed the strictures of an emergent "classical music" culture that was based in German Idealism.
2. These origins and their significance for the emergence of popular music in the twentieth century have not been joined well by popular-music scholarship; indeed, advocacy for twentieth-century popular

music seems most often based on rationales borrowed from the very musical culture its forebears had rebelled against.

3. Camp—a hallmark of popular musical theater—has been particularly ill served by popular music's advocates. While this may be due in part to camp's association with gay subcultures, it probably stems more fundamentally from camp's fascination with the artificial, the contrived, and the theatrical—preoccupations anathematic to the cult of authenticity that has taken over popular music studies.
4. Camp itself has not been properly understood within historical contexts, perhaps because of a widespread insistence on understanding it as essentially gay, even though that association took hold relatively late and has been steadily eroded since Susan Sontag's "Notes on Camp" in 1964.

It was considering the tenacity of camp's appeal as it has since become mainstreamed, along with aspects of camp's mostly unexamined prehistory, that led me both to the intuition that what made Haydn matter for me was actually quite close to the mix of elements I have found so appealing in musicals, especially in the genre's camp dimension, and to the realization that therein lay a fundamental difference between "serious" music and the square pegs of Haydn and musicals. Both consistently make light of serious art even when taking that art seriously. And both do not "belong" within the round holes of German Idealist musical paradigms, the one owing to historical circumstance, and the other to its persistent undercurrent of resistance to idealist seriousness.

But having this intuition and testing it through argument and against the backdrop of history are quite different things. The latter requires some understanding of why German Idealism's impact on musical practices was so powerful and immediate, how music approached the absolute as it became idealized, and of why the vibrant receptive environment that originally awaited Haydn's music wilted under the new musical paradigms (chapter 1, "Idealizing Music"). It requires better understanding of Haydn's difference, of how Haydn's music played to its original audiences (chapter 2, "Entertaining Possibilities in Haydn's Symphonies"), and of how changes in musical culture altered the expectations that governed that environment, even if those changes were in some cases subtle and occurring only over time (chapter 3, "Haydn, the String Quartet, and the [D]evolution of the Chamber Ideal"). It requires a reconsideration of the origins and development of New World musical dualities, especially of how nineteenth-century theatrical music, particularly in the United States, originally opposed German Idealism's new musical paradigms, leading to the development of camp tastes (chapter 4, "Popular Music contra German Idealism: Anglo-American Rebellions from Minstrelsy to Camp"), and of how that opposition was eventually tempered by the desire of popular music's advocates to be taken seriously (chapter 5, "'Popular Music' qua German Idealism: Authenticity and Its Outliers"). And it requires that the kinship I intuited between camp tastes and Haydn's potential pleasures be carefully parsed, accompanied by an explanation for why that kinship has (so far) not left much of a scholarly or critical footprint (chapter 6, "Musical Virtues and Vices in the Latter-Day New World").

Each step in making this extended argument presents its own complex problems, all eminently worthy of extensive treatment. In chapter 1, the conditions that allowed music to emerge as the "highest of the arts," the intertwining of nationalism with music's new and still shifting paradigms, and a wide variance in the capacity for mutual accommodation between those paradigms and past composers, are all at issue. Crucial to chapter 2 is the question of tone, and the philosophical understandings that grounded Haydn's ability to entertain within Aristotelian virtues based on notions of human flourishing. Chapter 3 explores, within the historical development of the string quartet, how Haydn's approach to the genre, to draw auditors into a quasisocial space, was gradually displaced with a quartet dynamic that imitated and fostered the demanding intensity of German Idealism's inwardness, a process well under way with Beethoven and carried further by such figures as Brahms and Bartók. Particularly complex are the problems addressed in chapter 4, in which extended discussions of both minstrelsy and camp are obliged both to confront fully the intersections of each with disenfranchised groups—African Americans and homosexual men, respectively—and to probe, more centrally, their related but distinct engagements with idealism's aesthetic pretensions. Chapter 5 takes on "authenticity," a central category and criterion of value within popular music criticism both within and outside the academy, a category that forms alliances not only with German Idealism but also with Existentialism and various political issues, and which is itself highly problematic in its disregard both for the actual historical roots of US American popular music and for whole categories of music that are not only quite popular but also deeply valued. Chapter 6 probes the aesthetics of high camp through a modern case study ("Springtime for Hitler" in Mel Brooks's film *The Producers*), and by taking up the model of musical flourishing proposed by Mitchell Morris in his bracing essay "Musical Virtues," all in order to establish common ground—and common cause—between Haydn and musical camp.

But these and many other important strands have had to be worked out in some kind of balance against the more slowly unfolding larger argument of the book, which emerges fully only in the final chapter. Maintaining such a balance between the parts and the whole has seemed essential, since each provides necessary context for making sense of the other, and since only together might they adequately explain how we have reached our particularly problematic moment in music history. Of the various historical strands that I consider—each newly illuminated by the larger argument—minstrelsy was particularly hard to keep in balance. Because of minstrelsy's deplorable racial practices and their persistent afterlife, I hesitated before giving it as much emphasis as I do, but soon determined it to be crucial to the larger argument. Similarly considered, if somewhat less fraught, are the emphases I give to the philosophical underpinnings of Haydn, the prehistory of camp and the persistence of heterosexual camp even during camp's gay golden age, and the actually complex understandings that inform the category of "authenticity" in popular music studies.

In organizing the larger argument of the book into three parts, each successive part longer by a chapter than the previous, I provide space in the final chapter to revisit, and to some extent synthesize, key elements of the preceding chapters. Critically important to the larger argument is the final chapter's reengagement with the book's originary insight, particularly in detailing important philosophical differences between and among German Idealism, Haydn, and high camp. But the book's personal history has also led me to indulge an impulse to speculate in the final section of that chapter ("Bridging Persistent Dualities") about how a new musical culture might evolve to accommodate some of those differences. Such speculation is scarcely the main point of the book, which is not to decry those persistent dualities but rather to descry them more clearly, in order to understand better their nature, how they evolved, and how they have endured and even proven themselves useful. Nevertheless, such speculation seems to me necessary here, as an expression of the basic optimism that has long sustained musicology and related disciplines. After all, it is not just Haydn who may eventually be counted among the true survivors of absolute music, but us, as well.

Acknowledgments

I have been extremely lucky in my intellectual and musical associations, a great many of which have embedded themselves into the arguments of this book. These really began with Robert Rubinstein, whose enthusiasm and insights first led me to discover how unusual and dependably rewarding a composer Haydn was. George Parish, Howard K. Smither, and R. Larry Todd guided my early work on Haydn while still a graduate student, and much of their influence has filtered its way into this book. My UCLA colleagues Robert Martin, Elisabeth Le Guin, Tom Beghin, and Peter Reill, in association with the Clark Library at UCLA, were my collaborators on two exceptionally motivating symposia, in 1994 and 2001, that productively combined performance with scholarship, and which led to core discussions in chapters 2 and 3. Mitchell Morris, through his exciting work on musical camp and German Idealism, his unabashed focus on the pleasures that popular music affords, and his continued presence as an interlocutor par excellence, has been both an instigator and a sustaining spirit throughout. Steven Baur's work on the fold between popular and concert music in the United States during the nineteenth century was inspirational, and his continuing generosity in providing feedback for my own work in that area invaluable. Robert Fink's pioneering work on Gilbert and Sullivan, and continuing shared enthusiasm for their work, has been both energizing and helpful. The spirit of Elijah Wald's bracing reconsideration of the histories we habitually tell about popular music, and the many conversations we shared while he undertook that work at UCLA, hovers over much of the later stages of this project. Peter Broadwell's pioneering dissertation on musical pirates was a terrific spur to my related work in chapter 4, and he has been unfailingly generous as a consultant; indeed, even his resistance to my exhortations to include Gilbert and Sullivan's *Pirates of Penzance* in his dissertation proved a useful goad. And I would be remiss if I did not point out the obvious, that Susan McClary, in helping transform the field of musicology and, more particularly, UCLA's Department of Musicology, was essential to this project's inception and much of its early execution.

My more specific thanks go to Mitchell Morris, especially for his feedback regarding chapters 1, 4, 5, and 6, as well as extended discussions about nearly everything else in the book; to Elisabeth Le Guin for her responses to chapters 2 and 3; to Susan McClary and Mark Martin regarding chapter 1; and to Sarah Ellis, Sam Baltimore, Steven Baur, Stephen Pysnik, and Arreanna Rostosky for their crucial feedback on chapter 4. Members of the Musical Theatre Forum have also helped me shape some parts of chapter 4; among this stimulating group, I thank especially Stacy Wolf, Carol Oja, David Savran, and Elizabeth Wollman, for their encouragement and astute criticism. Over the years, I have subjected several of my seminars to parts of chapters 1 and 4, and I thank everyone for their thoughtful engagement with work then very much in progress; especially fruitful were the discussions in my "Musicals, Camp, and Musical Camp" seminar in fall 2013, which included Monica Chieffo, Wade Fulton Dean, Albert Diaz, Breena Loraine, Tiffany Naiman, Marissa Ochsner, Rosaleen Rhee, Anahit Rostomyan, Arreanna Rostosky, Schuyler Wheldon, and Morgan Woolsey.

I have with great benefit presented parts of this book at various conferences, including a Southeast Chapter meeting of the American Musicological Society (1983), the symposia at UCLA already mentioned along with later ones organized by Elisabeth Le Guin (2006) and *Echo* (2009), and conferences organized by Music in Gotham and Song, Stage, and Screen (CUNY Graduate Center, 2008), Music and the Moving Image (NYU, 2013 and 2014), the International Association for the Study of Popular Music–Canada (Ottawa, 2015), and Song, Stage, and Screen (London, 2015). Ronald Sadoff, Christopher Moore, and Philip Purvis provided useful feedback regarding the parts of this book that provided the basis for publications in *Music and the Moving Image* (2014) and *Music and Camp* (forthcoming), respectively. Ryan Shiotsuki and Patrick Bonczyk prepared the musical examples, and Patrick Bonczyk and Michael D'Errico, with the assistance of John Lynch and Tom Garbelotti at the Center for Digital Humanities at UCLA, helped prepare the book's website. The staff at UCLA's Music Library has been extraordinarily generous in their help throughout, including especially Gordon Theil, Stephen Davison, David Gilbert, and Bridget Risemberg. And the staff at Houghton Library at Harvard University and the Schlesinger Library at Radcliffe were helpful in securing some of the illustrative material in the book.

Among my colleagues not already mentioned, I wish to thank especially Roger Bourland, David Schaberg, Mark Kligman, Nina Eidsheim, and Jessica Schwartz for their sustaining support and sage advice, and above all Barbara Van Nostrand, who helped hold our prodigious but volatile department together through its turbulent second childhood. The Council on Research at UCLA, UCLA's Fiat Lux program, and UCLA's Herb Alpert School of Music provided essential research funds for the book at various stages of its development. And the Bogliasco Foundation supported me, in style, with the respite I needed to complete my draft of the book in fall 2015, in beautiful surroundings among many delightful people, including especially Ivana Folle, Alessandra Natale, and Ahuva Braverman (without whom I would never have applied), along with my stimulating cohort of fellow Fellows, Andrzej Adamski, Laura Colella, Philip Grange, Kathy Grove, Anna Huber, Kay Bea Jones, and Ayana Mathis. I have been fortunate, as well, in being able to work during the book's final stages of preparation with Ken Wissoker, Elizabeth Ault, and Sara Leone at Duke University Press, and to be buoyed by their sustaining enthusiasm for the project and extraordinary expertise. I thank Christine Riggio for her meticulous work in setting the artwork and musical examples, and Julienne Alexander for capturing the book's spirit so effectively in designing the cover. And my final revisions were especially well supported by careful readings of the manuscript by Todd Decker and Daniel Grimley, and the expert copyediting of Kerrie Maynes.

More personally, and for reasons they will remember more completely if I don't specify them here, I thank Dan Sallitt, Jon Hofferman, Bob Knapp, Judi Smith, Kyle McJunkin, Nancy Sokolow, Daniel Grimley, Carol Oja, Stacy Wolf, and, closest to my heart, Ahuva Braverman and my daughters Rachel and Genevieve (Zelda).

About the Companion Website

knappmakinglight.net

The author has created a website to accompany *Making Light*, which includes over 150 audio, video, image, and text examples to further illustrate or augment the discussions advanced in the text. To make this resource easy to use, each example is keyed to its appropriate place in the text, and numbered sequentially within each of the chapters that use this resource. For clarity, we've used the following notation (these particular indications would refer to examples 5–8 in chapter 4):

<AE4.5> (Audio Example 4.5)
<VE4.6> (Video Example 4.6)
<IE4.7> (Image Example 4.7)
<TE4.8> (Text Example 4.8)

To access an example, simply click on the appropriate icon on the website. Further help, if needed, is provided on the website.

PART I | APPROACHING THE ABSOLUTE

1 | IDEALIZING MUSIC

In an extraordinary moment during the performance of a piano trio at UCLA's Clark Library in April 2001 (part of an international conference on Haydn and Rhetoric), the cellist spontaneously laughed out loud in response to the pianist's droll delivery of a bit of composed abstraction.[1] Although some of those present clearly disapproved of this "extramusical" intrusion, the cellist's apparent lapse in concert decorum seemed eminently understandable to the rest of us. More than that, it seemed very *right*, given the particular quality of interaction cultivated by this group of performers, who vividly projected a mutually attentive interplay based not only on their embodiment of personae who speak and listen to each other but also on a clear sense that they had taken on these personae *so as* to speak and listen to each other, as performers. More abstractly, it seemed right because it coincided with a passage in which the mundane realities of music making already intrude—as they are wont to do in Haydn—into the "purely" musical discourse. It was an event that could have happened as it did only with Haydn, and only with performers as attuned to each other as these were—a moment, however unmusical it might have seemed to purists, in which performers, their adopted personae, and Haydn himself shared in equal measure.

In a more ordinary moment during that same conference, a leading Haydn scholar was asked whether he found a specific passage in Haydn funny. After deliberating briefly, he responded by precisely identifying the frequency with which he found it funny. While this response was clearly intended to be humorous, it was uncomfortably unclear where exactly the intended humor lay, whether in the affected precision, in the particular specified ratio (too high? too low?), or in his carefully weighed admission that he, at least sometimes, did indeed find the passage funny, even if his more typical or lasting response was more elevated, more appreciative of "deeper" musical value.[2] What made this moment so ordinary was that something like it might have happened in *any* discussion by countless musicologists who bring the standards and associated intellectual apparatus of German Idealism to bear on repertories that have little or nothing to do with those traditions. One might thus imagine similarly calculated responses to questions concerning the erotic dimension of much twentieth-century music: Do you find *Bolero* (or jazz, or Elvis, or the Beatles, or Madonna, or electronic dance music, etc.) sexy? Or, similarly, addressing the social dimension of many popular music traditions: Do you enjoy nightclubs with live jazz (or arena rock concerts, discos, or other venues in which music is performed but is not the only source of pleasure for most of those present)?

While one might well imagine that the impulse to honor Haydn through the scholarly activity of traditional musicology must be, at root, a response to his remarkable ability to create sites of joyous interaction among performers and listeners, little vestige of that joy survives in the rather juiceless fruit that such efforts tend to produce. Thus, the scholarly response to what should be basic questions to anyone working with Haydn—Do you find Haydn funny? How? Why?—spoke directly, and with unwitting pathos, to a peculiar sadness that often hovers over Haydn studies. Wishing sincerely to extend and share this kind of joy in their own work on Haydn, many Haydn scholars seem restrained from doing so by their own idealism, an idealism deriving from German Idealism and expressed, without apparent irony, through a desire to uphold an elevated standard of musical value.

But why is German Idealism the wrong context in which to place Haydn, and how did it come to pass that this context is now central to any developed appreciation of his music? What do humor in Haydn, and sexuality or sociability in twentieth-century US American popular musics, have in common, so as to place them out of the reach of a discipline grounded in the musical sensibilities and value systems fostered by German Idealism? What might we gain from taking different approaches to the study of Haydn and his music, in parallel to ongoing discoveries of alternative approaches to popular music? How might these alternative approaches be grounded, in philosophical terms? And what might these approaches tell us about the contentious questions that have seemed, since the nineteenth century, to have hovered perpetually around US American music more generally?

These are the principal questions I seek to address in this book. My first task will be to articulate as clearly as possible those aspects of German Idealism, and its correlative, the set of doctrines and practices known as "absolute music" (which William Weber terms "musical idealism") that negatively affect the specific context of Haydn reception.[3] As I will argue, this is not an abstract question, but rather one that addresses the precise historical circumstance that brought about Haydn's demotion, beginning in the nineteenth century and continuing even against the grain of the "performance practice" movement of the late twentieth century, from a master composer of the first rank to "Papa Haydn," a venerated fogy who helped make Mozart and Beethoven possible but whose music has not stood the "test of time" as well as theirs. As Bryan Proksch writes, "Seemingly the moment after [Haydn's] burial [in 1809], the musical world set about dismantling his reputation, coining one dismissive cliché after another. 'Roguish,' 'childlike,' 'naïve,' 'old-worldly,' 'dainty,' 'neighborly, and other terms . . . characterize Haydn . . . as some kind of cockeyed optimist shackled by his prerevolutionary birth and his employment as a naïve wig-wearing servant of the *ancient régime*."[4] Because it is important that Haydn not simply be seen as a special case, an isolated victim of this line of development—and because what happened to Haydn is directly relevant to many persistent dualities that have bedeviled US American music—I will then draw analogies between Haydn's situation and certain aspects of the flowering and mixed reception of US American popular music beginning in the late nineteenth century and continuing across the twentieth century. As I proceed, I will discuss specific Haydn repertories in which there has been a long-standing but steadily waning interest (mainly the symphonies and string quartets) in order to demonstrate how traditional approaches have missed out on the Haydn that so many performers and audiences (used to) know and love, and I will argue that our musical heritage, and our sense of what is valuable and virtuous in our culture more generally, has been sold short in the process.[5]

While attempting to reclaim Haydn and other musical repertories from German Idealist contexts, however, I am by no means putting aside, in toto, the rich musical legacy and practices that have drawn sustenance from that philosophical, aesthetic, and protonationalist basis. My own musical sensibilities, practices, and scholarly work have taken shape and thrived, in large part, within traditions and in venues that simply could not have existed were it not for German Idealism and its US American derivatives. Much of the music I value, perform, and write about was either born of German Idealism or enjoyed a richly textured rebirth owing to German Idealism, and my devotion to that music has not wavered. True, one of my principal tasks here will be to identify the disservices that German Idealism has done both to those musical practices for which it carries no sympathy and to some dimensions of those practices and repertories it has fostered, when they have seemed at odds with that basis. Moreover, in championing practices marginalized by German Idealism, I have little choice but to oppose its tendency to displace or cast into the margins all other standards of musical value. But mine is a carefully circumscribed opposition, comparable to that of a surgeon who must distinguish carefully between healthy and unhealthy tissue. To the extent that German Idealism has corroded the basis for otherwise healthy musical practices, it deserves to be cut away, but that does not mean that the grounding it provides for its core repertories need be devalued in the process. In any case, the surgery demanded here is in part restorative, involving not only a kind of philosophical amputation but also the functional revival of previously discounted components of human musicking, which may well pose an additional threat to German Idealism and its continuing sway over how music is performed, studied, and valued.[6]

THE DISTILLATION OF MUSIC IN THE NINETEENTH CENTURY

If you're not part of the solution, you're part of the precipitate.

This paraphrase of a familiar slogan by an anonymous chemistry student applies with surprising felicity to musical controversies that arose in Europe during the nineteenth century, particularly in the German lands, concerning the nature and understanding of music.[7] According to one way of thinking, which would eventually be identified with the phrase "absolute music," music was fundamentally different from the other arts

because it could not depict a readily identifiable subject; this inability was taken to be a defining characteristic of music, and became for some the basis for music's elevation to the purest—and thus highest—of the arts. As persuasively codified in Eduard Hanslick's 1854 monograph *Vom Musikalische-Schönen*, this solution to the problem of music pursued a process of intellectual distillation, through which "music," conceived in terms of its abstract essence, was separated from its nonessential accretions, such as description and expression.[8] Over time, even those who valued the connection of music to these and similar accretions would largely come to admit that they were, indeed, separate from music; thus, "describing" and "expressing" may be things music could *do* with varying degrees of success—or *seem* to do, for the more cautious—but description and expression were not a part of music *per se*.[9] In the solution of music, description and expression were part of the precipitate; one might choose to stir them back into the solution, but their established separateness would remain ineffably evident, making them seem, to purists, like a foreign substance suspended within an otherwise purely musical fluid.

Music's supposed accretions thus became widely recognized as a kind of noise, against which a variety of filters could be devised as needed, such as a listening strategy focused more on the music than on its potential for "extramusical" interpretation, or a preoccupation with musical forms and processes enforced through established methods of analysis. But not all such filters were solely the province of internalized reception, for music was being separated from the mundane realities of music making in a variety of external ways, as well.

The rise of the public concert as an institution in the nineteenth century, especially in the German lands, was a decisive step in the gradual separation of the audience from the mechanics involved in producing music.[10] One aspect of this separation was primarily intellectual, although it was encouraged by the setting; as music from the past was presented in an atmosphere that increasingly fostered a contemplative, even reverent response, music became detached from its original supporting context and rationale. Individual pieces that survived this process particularly well became part of a musical canon of seemingly autonomous works, each having stood the "test of time" by achieving a continuing vitality independent of its origins. Indeed, such works were prized particularly for their ability to withstand this kind of transplantation, reinforcing the notion that music could be—and, perhaps, *should* be—abstracted from the specific circumstances and meanings relevant to its inception. Thus, the history of a work, and the "extramusical" content associated with that history, were also part of the precipitate in the solution of music.[11]

And so also, in many ways, was the actual performance of a work. The concert hall separated audience from performers no less than it detached music from its earlier associative meanings. Even more pointedly, Wagner's removal of the orchestra from the audience's view at Bayreuth underscored what was rapidly becoming a guiding principle for nineteenth-century aesthetic sensibilities: however necessary performance might be for bringing music into physical existence, performance as such should not be considered music, and should be filtered out by the purist concerned with the autonomous musical work. Long before Milton Babbitt officially banished audiences from the concerns of the modern composer with his incendiary "Who Cares If You Listen?,"[12] performers were as effectively exorcized with an implied "Who cares if we look?," as audiences were encouraged to listen *past* the performers, to the music itself—a strategy that radio and recordings have since greatly facilitated.[13] In broader terms, and outside a Wagnerian context, a musical work was conceived to an increasing degree over the course of the nineteenth century as essentially independent of a particular performance, despite the potential for a given performance to alter, sometimes radically and permanently, a preexisting conception of the work.

It is difficult in the twenty-first century to reimagine the transactions between composer and performers, and between performers and audience, that would have been taken for granted during the late eighteenth century. Part of the difficulty is that they *were* taken for granted, and so were not often described in ways immediately meaningful to us. Part of the difficulty also resides in our incapacity fully to imagine an era before the disembodied music of radio and phonograph. Hanslick's theories, which offer oblique theoretical support to the gradual distillation of our musical experiences through these profound changes in the predominant musical venues of the European-based "classical" tradition, have become so entrenched that they have come to represent "common sense." For us in the twenty-first century, the orthodoxy of "absolute" music has isolated the musical work as a singular creation of its composer; performers act either as vessels through which audiences gain seemingly direct access to the composer, or assume the role of preemptive coauthors, exerting their own creative energies and thereby, to some extent, shutting off access to the composer, whose work is treated as the raw materials for something essentially new.

This dichotomous situation obscures a potential legitimacy for the performer, once taken for granted, as a genuine participant in a three-way transaction, in which composed work, performer, and audience have independently viable functions.[14] Indeed, in the enshrinement of "the music itself," the audience also fades in importance, reduced to reverent silence and passive contemplation. But the audience retains certain prerogatives, among them the privilege of evaluating the performance and providing its justification. The performer, in contrast, is servant to both composer and audience, and risks censure if s/he calls untoward attention to the performance as such. Although we routinely refer to the "interpretations" offered by specific performers, this is nearly always in reference to an independent conception of the "work," against which a particular performance is to be measured.[15]

More critical even than this public demotion of the performer is the loss of a private transaction between composer and performer. This has become particularly evident in recent decades, when performers routinely execute music of daunting difficulty without really interacting with the work as such, either because individual parts are so demanding that a focused attention to individual execution precludes an acute awareness of the larger effect, or because maintaining a lucid relationship between an individual performing part and the whole is rarely a high priority of the composer. If it is no wonder that performers (especially amateur performers) are generally not enthusiastic about performing new works, enthusiasm among professionals for performing the standard repertory is scarcely any higher. Typically, performances of concert music are tightly controlled by a conductor, who figuratively represents both the composer and the audience, and who is in fact the most privileged audience for the music; in this dual capacity, the conductor exercises preemptive authority over all aspects of performance, ranging from interpretation to evaluation. While orchestral performers can derive significant satisfaction from skillful execution and deserved approbation, and a fair degree of pleasure from contributing to a successful performance, this narrows considerably the spectrum of interactive and aesthetic possibilities latent in the performance of much composed music.

With the rise of the public concert, and reinforcing this estrangement of the individual performer, came an increased tendency to regard the orchestra as something analogous to a single instrument. Central to this development was Hector Berlioz, whose contributions included the first important treatise on orchestration, orchestral compositions that gave increasing emphasis to coloristic effects over more traditional thematic and contrapuntal elaboration, and a convincing practical demonstration of what an orchestra could do under the direction of a "virtuoso" conductor. Berlioz's *Grand traité d'instrumentation et d'orchestration modernes,* first published in its entirety in 1843, ironically signaled the demotion of the individual performer to a subordinate function within a more complex sound world even as it promoted with unprecedented sophistication the specific qualities and potentialities of each individual instrument. In more immediately practical terms, Berlioz, as a composer for the orchestra, profoundly influenced the future course of orchestral composition in favor of an increasingly imaginative use of individual instrumental color.

However exciting performers found these advances, their individual contributions, as musicians, were inevitably diminished, as they found themselves increasingly peripheral to the process of bringing music to life, forced to defer to a larger conception controlled by someone else and hierarchically beyond the reach of their individual contributions. Berlioz's career as a conductor, building on the achievements of Weber, Spohr, and Mendelssohn, proved that the then-modern conception of the orchestra as a single instrument responding to the will of a single virtuoso was indeed a viable one, providing the principal model for the hierarchical organization we now take for granted; marking this arrival is Berlioz's 1856 treatise on the new art, *Le chef d'orchestre: Théorie de son art.* To be sure, these developments stem as much from the growing complexities of orchestral scores during the nineteenth century as from Berlioz's various individual contributions. Nevertheless, his central role on all fronts has a singular significance, particularly given his veneration of Beethoven, and the continued use (even today) of Beethoven's symphonies as a critical standard for evaluating conductors. A deferential position toward Beethoven has from the beginning been basic to the institution of the concert hall—which, arguably, was developed in large part as a venue for his works.[16]

If we may find in the reception of Beethoven's orchestral music, from the beginning of the century onward, the central musical motivation for most of the developments I have traced here, we may find at the end of the century a culmination of sorts, with an ironic reception history of its own. The intricacies of Gustav Mahler's orchestral scores, even more than those of his contemporary Richard Strauss, derive from his experiences as a tightly controlling conductor, and manifest an orchestral conception of unprecedented suppleness and nuanced subtlety. At times, Mahler's orchestra threatens to fragment into a bewildering thicket of fussily individual gestures, were it not for the control exercised by the conductor, comprehending and managing the whole. The precarious and volatile nature of this situation, in which the musical thread is maintained by no single instrument or instrumental group, and the full available orchestral power is seldom deployed, has been likened, somewhat inappropriately, to the condition of chamber music.[17]

The irony of this mischaracterization is twofold. First, the utter dependence of Mahler's orchestra on a conductor, and the corresponding subordination of individual performers, contradict what has traditionally been understood as the essential nature of chamber music. And, second, by Mahler's day, the "chamber" of chamber music was largely a nostalgic idealization; starting with Beethoven, chamber music tended to borrow the dynamic and expressive manner (and sometimes the venue) of an orchestra, or risked not being taken seriously as art. In the process, orchestral and chamber styles were so conflated that, by the end of the century, the relative intimacy of Mahler's orchestration, especially when coupled with a deep sense of nostalgia, could be taken for the intimacy of chamber music, understood—especially in this context—also to betoken a valued subjective realm.

Standing close behind Beethoven's symphonies, which defined the prevailing sense of the symphonic for the nineteenth century and well into the twentieth, are the later symphonies of Haydn, in which symphonic thinking and a chamber-like intimacy coexist in a way seemingly analogous to Mahler's chamber/symphonic style. But the analogy is both misleading and, because of its very persuasiveness, poignant testimony to the magnitude of what had been lost in the interim. As I will argue in chapter 2, Haydn's "Military" Symphony—arguably among the most "symphonic" of his symphonies—plays almost as if it were chamber music, notwithstanding its larger forces, its enriched sound world, and its enhanced potential for creating and manipulating referential meaning. By contrast, the most intimately "chamber" of Mahler's symphonies, his Fourth, which I have discussed at some length elsewhere,[18] marks a later stage of arrival in the radical transformation of the chamber-music ideal during the century that separates the two symphonies, in terms of both its symbolic status and the realities of performance—and this despite the many close parallels between the two works (for example, in using differentiated instrumental textures to generate a strongly stated spatial dimension, within which an alien presence threatens an idyllic setting).

Yet, also standing close behind Beethoven's symphonies—and behind the many shifts in the understanding and practice of music across the nineteenth century—is a fundamental shift in the prevailing philosophical basis for music, especially and initially in the German lands.

INFINITE PERSPECTIVES: GERMAN IDEALISM, NATIONALISM, AND ABSOLUTE MUSIC

The basis for music's distillation in the nineteenth century, both in practical terms and according to aesthetic and philosophical theorizing, was German Idealism. German Idealism, based initially on Kant's writings of the 1780s, rose to sudden preeminence during the 1790s, a decade marked not only by a prolonged political crisis in Europe (defined above all in terms of the French Revolution and the death of Austria's Joseph II in 1790), but also by a musical crisis of sorts. It was during this decade that Haydn, after the deaths of both his own longtime employer, Prince Nikolaus Esterházy (1790), and Mozart (1791), found his most important audience in London; meanwhile, a then virtually unknown Beethoven reeducated and reinvented himself as a performer and composer in Vienna—mostly independent of Haydn, his ostensible teacher.

Notwithstanding this volatile musical environment and the rapid ascension of Kant and his followers, German Idealism's immediate and lasting impact on both the practice and theory of music seems remarkable. To be sure, Kant's impact on intellectual discourse in the German lands was quick, pervasive, and lasting; almost from the beginning, some form of German Idealism has served as a kind of commonsense foundation that allowed ready negotiation among the claims of science, religion, and aesthetics, and facilitated the formation of both personal and group identities (including nationalism) within shifting political and philosophical contexts. Yet, all this seems to relate only indirectly to music, often considered to be a realm unto itself. Arguably, however, the very forces that supported the rapid rise of German Idealism virtually assured its transformative influence on music, which acquired an exalted status among the arts precisely in step with the rise of German Idealism.[19]

Kant's most significant writing in the 1780s was *Critique of Pure Reason* (1781, with a second edition in 1787), a difficult text that became the basis for a philosophical movement a decade later only because of a supporting network of scholars and writers working at or near Weimar. Weimar, much more centrally located than Kant's Königsberg (in East Prussia), was the seat of an important if small Saxon duchy, Saxe-Weimar-Eisenach. Though neighboring the Catholic lands of Bavaria and Bohemia, Weimar, like most of Saxony, was predominantly Protestant. Under the reign of Grand Duke Charles Augustus (1758–1828), the court at Weimar became the most important intellectual center in greater Germany, and by the late eighteenth century the nearby University of Jena, known for its political radicalism, was reaching the peak of its influence. The network of intellectuals and artists that formed around Johann Wolfgang von Goethe, who arrived in Weimar in 1775, early on included Johann Gottfried von Herder, Christoph Martin Wieland, and Karl Leonhard Reinhold, and later accrued such luminaries as Friedrich Schiller (in 1787), Novalis (law student from 1790 and an occasional later visitor), Gottlieb Fichte (in 1794), Johann Christian Friedrich Hölderlin (in 1794), August Wilhelm von Schlegel (in 1796), Jean Paul Richter (in 1797), Friedrich von Schlegel (in 1798; Friedrich was August's brother), Friedrich Schelling (in 1798), Johann Ludwig Tieck (in 1799), Georg Hegel (in 1801), and Arthur Schopenhauer (in 1807, briefly, after a general dispersal of the circle just after the turn of the century). Notably, the extended group, with its membership shifting over time, included two main, interconnected subgroups: Kantian philosophers and literary figures, with considerable overlap of interests between and among poets, novelists, playwrights, aesthetic theorists, and philosophers. This mix is vitally important to the way that Kantian philosophy became, fairly quickly, as important for its aesthetics as for its capacity, seemingly, to weld science to a system of ethics that, although standing at a partial remove from religious belief, was comfortably similar to the central moral tenets of Christianity, especially Protestantism.

Part of what made Kant's philosophy congenial to Goethe and his growing circle was circumstantial. In 1769, when Goethe met Herder—one of Kant's students, though he would become prominent before his teacher—Herder had already developed and would soon begin to publish what would be his central contribution to German intellectual and political history: theories involving the ways that folk poetry affirms shared heritage, language, and other vestiges of collective identity (often encapsulated in Herder's term *Volksgeist*), which would become the foundation for various German nationalist theories and projects.[20] When Goethe began to build his intellectual network at Weimar, he early on secured a post for Herder (1776), and thus established a fairly direct link between Weimar and Kant, even before the appearance of *Critique of Pure Reason*.

Largely independent of this connection, Wieland and Reinhold forged their own connection between literary and philosophical interests, in the process creating the central conduit between Kant and mainstream Germanic thought. Wieland was an important poet whom Goethe had come to admire in the late 1760s (although Wieland would soon actively oppose the Sturm und Drang movement with which Goethe became identified). Shortly after Wieland's arrival in Weimar (1772), he established *Der teutscher Mercur* (1773), an innovative and influential journal devoted to poetry, literary reviews, and essays on a variety of literary, philosophical, and scientific topics. Reinhold, a Viennese Jesuit priest, came to Weimar in 1783 after his interest in freemasonry hopelessly undermined his connection to Catholicism. In Weimar, he converted to Protestantism, collaborated with Wieland on his journal, and became Wieland's son-in-law. Reinhold's interest in Kant led him to publish several "letters" on *Critique of Pure Reason* in Wieland's journal (1786–1887, published separately in 1790 and 1792), which led to his appointment at Jena University (1787) and created a context for his own major work, *Versuch einer neuen Theorie des menschlichen Vorstellungsvermögens* (1789), in which he sought both to explicate and "unify" Kant's thought, and to create his own synthesis.

But if Herder's presence at Weimar and, especially, Reinhold's popularizing elucidations were critical components of Kant's widening influence, the success of the project ultimately hinged on two other factors. The first is the cultural basis not only for Kant's wider reception, but also for this dual presentation of Kant's ideas, since neither Herder nor Reinhold were neutral filters. And, second, both Kant's own stature and the consequences for music depended on the specific ways that German Idealism developed in interaction with its larger cultural basis, especially as influenced by the literary figures and philosophers at Weimar-Jena. In the remainder of this section, I shall consider four interrelated facets of the first before sketching the sequence of historical events that defines the second.

The interest of Goethe and his literary circle in Kant's philosophical position was ultimately neither just circumstantial nor a matter of personal affinities. Rather, Kant's philosophy resonated powerfully with their aesthetic project (German romanticism) in four main ways, all deriving from a shared basis in intense subjectivity. First, many members of this group were engaged—much more than Kant himself—in an ongoing exploration of the inner life of the individual, what we might think of as the *realm* of subjectivity. We may see this not only in their literary output—Goethe's *The Sorrows of Young Werther* (1774) is the most famous exemplar of this interest—but also in Reinhold's emphasis on, and extension of, the subjective dimension of Kant's argument, and in the even more extreme subjectivism of Fichte, who succeeded Reinhold at Jena in 1794. Second, as creative artists, Goethe and his circle were especially preoccupied with the inner life of the *artist*, and with the specific role of subjectivity in creative acts. Here, the increasing degree to which Kant's followers (especially Fichte) were willing to consider subjectivity as the locus of origin for what is conventionally thought of as "real" (the "thing in itself") resonates particularly well with the experience of the creative literary artist, who routinely reinvents the world from the imagination.[21]

Third, and more complexly, subjectivity was understood by many in this group to provide the basis for collective identity. Herder's positioning of the folk as a repository of Germanness became an important basis for German nationalism (as noted), supported not only by his own folkloric research, but also by that of the next generation, which included especially *Des knaben Wunderhorn* (1805–1808), compiled by Achim von Arnim and Clemens Brentano, both of whom had important ties to Goethe and his circle. From a different perspective, Fichte explored the relationship between a person's subjectivity and other subjects, and in his political writings revealed himself a fervent nationalist, involving a complex set of concerns that included ongoing reforms of the university (also one of Kant's projects) so as to encourage a purer pursuit of knowledge in line with German Idealism. (In the political arena, notably, his more purely philosophical arguments often gave way to virulent railings against Jews and the French, anticipating two important touchstones for German nationalism as it developed across the nineteenth century and into the twentieth.) These positions, too, were natural fits for this generation of literary romantics, whose inclinations toward the subjective fused with an automatic German-centered orientation, based in language but embracing also *Kultur*, and drew strength from their sense of being part of a growing movement that combined nationalism (at least cultural nationalism), philosophy, and aesthetics.

The fourth and most subtle way in which Kant's philosophical position appeals to an aesthetic mindset—especially one already attracted by the enriched play of free subjectivity that it endorses—is Kant's mechanism for regulating such freedoms, the "categorical imperative." Kant placed the subjective individual at the center of his moral system, yet sought to regulate that system so that it would apply to all equally. Accordingly, neither individual impulse nor outside authority, be it human or divine, would serve his needs, nor even the authority of nature—the "thing in itself" that would be one of the main points of contention among Kant's followers. Kant found his requisite regulating mechanism within the reasoning individual's ability to weigh particular imperatives for consistency, stipulating that a *categorical* imperative must apply, without contradiction, to all. Moreover, once deciding that an imperative was indeed categorical, an individual had a moral duty to act in accordance with it. The great practical strength of this regulatory device was that its results accorded remarkably well with moral and legal systems already in place, and most especially with Protestant Christianity, which had already to some extent wrested moral authority away from the central institution of the Catholic Church and placed it within the individual. Moreover, it also accorded well with notions of right-based freedoms—a cornerstone of Enlightenment political thought—since individuals were free to act so long as they did their duty; this freedom in turn permitted a "division of labor" between science and religion, allowing science its place (on earth) while ascribing to God the role not of setting down laws but of sitting in judgment, and rewarding those who did their duty during their time on earth.

Kant's categorical imperative thus guaranteed the essential freedoms prized by the Weimar literary and philosophical figures, but—and this is both vital and easily overlooked—it also functioned in close parallel to a kind of "categorical imperative" that had begun to govern literary art, as well. Perhaps most apparently indicative of this trend was the growing suspicion of the deus ex machina as a dramatic ploy, by which an irretrievable plot situation is rescued at the expense of believability. (Oddly, in this regard, Kant's system essentially reduces God's ongoing function to that of a deus ex machina writ large—inevitably, this was another feature of his system that would remain contentious.) But there was a more subtle dimension at work, as well. As with Kant's categorical imperative, what mattered in drama and literature was a reasoned consistency; a character in a story could act in any way whatever, if consistent with her or his established character; moreover, as in Kant's system, a character's moral choices would matter more than the direct consequences of those choices. It was thus no coincidence that Shakespeare's plays enjoyed a German renaissance during this period, for they offered many stunning demonstrations of how effective character-driven dramatic action could be. (This renaissance was fueled by Wieland's often inadequate prose translations of twenty-two of them between 1762 and 1766—a few years before his move to Weimar—and by what would become the more standard translations begun by August von Schlegel in 1797.) Moreover, the real-world criteria—as opposed to internal consistency—were roughly the same for dramatic believability and applications of the categorical imperative. As Alasdair MacIntyre astutely points out, the categorical imperative, which requires that "a true moral precept [can be] consistently [universalized]," is not in itself particularly restrictive, since, "in fact, . . . with sufficient ingenuity almost every precept can be consistently universalized."[22] The categorical imperative, definitionally governed by reason alone, thus provides an elaborate basis for rationalizing whatever people already believe, and it was, initially at least, what people already believed that served as the crucial test of Kant's acceptability. Given that this situation is nearly identical to that of an author trying to achieve dramatic credibility, it is small wonder that so many poets in Goethe's extended circle took so easily to philosophizing.[23]

But if Kant's subjectivism was for many in the Weimar-Jena group deeply attractive, it was not as easy a sell to the larger intellectual community, newly energized by Friedrich Heinrich Jacobi's revivals of Spinoza and Hume to demand better metaphysical grounding of Kant's "thing in itself."[24] Jacobi was an early associate of Wieland (whom he helped in launching *Der teutscher Mercur*, before their falling out in 1777), who denounced Kant and advocated a faith-based metaphysics at the same time (1785–1787) that Reinhold was becoming Kant's principal advocate, thus placing himself as a conservative in relation to what he termed Kant's "nihilism" (a term he coined). Many of Jacobi's ploys backfired, however, probably due in part to his confrontational style. Thus, his reintroduction of Spinoza as a foil, nearly a century after his death, brought many new converts to Spinoza's pantheism and antagonized many others who might have been allies, whereas his insistence on a faith-based metaphysics overclouded his early demonstration that Kant's presentation of the "thing in itself" was profoundly self-contradictory, setting the stage for Fichte's more intense subjectivism. More fundamentally, his intense opposition to Kant, even before Kant became well known, did much to insure that Kant would be taken seriously, as one pole of a well-defined binary opposition. And, finally, Fichte's more radical form of German Idealism—to some extent precipitated by Jacobi's failure to provide a convincing, reason-based alternative to Kant's metaphysics—along with Kant's resulting rift with Fichte, moved Kant to a dominating middle-ground position by century's end.

The immediate success of Hegel's dialectically based synthesis of German Idealist thought, which followed soon after, has tended to obscure the fact that the initial appeal of German Idealism was largely aesthetic and political, in both cases because it freed the self from outside authority. Moreover, the specific conjunction of German Idealism and music—which came to seem entirely natural by the end of the nineteenth century because music seemed freer than the other arts, and more of the mind—had seemingly only a fragile foundation within the Weimar-Jena group, whose aesthetic basis was predominantly literary. But the nature of that foundation was, in some particulars, decisive for the long term. Kant himself, in *Critique of Judgment* (his principal text on aesthetics, 1790), while distrusting music's primary appeal to the senses (as opposed to the mind), nevertheless includes untexted music in his category of "free beauty" because of its apparent universality and its removal from representation, which also removed it from exterior motivation and rendered it more purely an object of contemplation. In 1794, the year that Fichte published the first version of his watershed work, *The Science of Knowledge,* Schiller displayed a similar ambivalence, finding many occasions in his *On the Aesthetic Education of Man in a Series of Letters* to place music in an inferior position relative to more literary arts, but also producing what could have been a draft for Walter Pater's famous maxim, "All art constantly aspires towards the condition of music" (from "The School of Giorgione," 1873). Thus, from Schiller's "On Matthison's Poems": "In short, we demand that every poetic composition, in addition to its expressed content, at the same time, through its form, be an imitation and expression of feelings and affect us as if it were music."[25]

Following quickly on Schiller's observations—which in the end still favor the traditional hierarchy—were a number of other younger figures more willing to overturn this hierarchy, such as Schiller's close friend Christian Gottfried Körner, who wrote of the idealizing potential of music ("On the Representation of Character in Music," 1795, published in Schiller's journal *Die Horen*);[26] Wilhelm Heinrich Wackenroder, who rhapsodized on music's idealistic power, asserting it to be the most "wondrous" of the arts (*Outpourings from the Heart of an Art-Loving Monk*, 1796); Friedrich Schlegel, who probed the affinity of music and philosophy (*Athenaeum Fragments* no. 444, 1798); and Ludwig Tieck, a longtime friend of Wackenroder, who elaborated further on music's essential separateness from known reality ("Symphony," 1799). The process seemed complete when Herder, reversing his earlier opinion that music should be ranked below the literary arts, declared music to be the highest art, alone capable of approaching the absolute (*Kalligone*, 1800)—just before Beethoven's major works seemed to take him up on that challenge and more than a decade before E. T. A. Hoffmann's famous review of the latter's Fifth Symphony, in which he declared "infinite longing" to be the essence of romanticism, and music to be the most romantic of the arts ("Beethoven's Instrumental Music," 1813).[27] (Hoffmann, historically the most famous of the romantics who argued for music's transcendent potential, was born in Königsberg five years before Kant's *Critique of Judgment*, and settled in Berlin in 1805, which had by then become the center of the philosophical/aesthetic movement.)

If idealist poets were thus the most eloquent advocates for music's ascension, with a few of them able to trade on a higher degree of musical expertise (e.g., Körner, Wackenroder, and Hoffmann), the real foundation for music's place atop the idealism-inspired aesthetic hierarchy was erected by philosophy more purely, which provided the key language and concepts for the developing argument. And in this process, Hegel was largely irrelevant; the key players were Kant, Fichte, Schelling, and—bypassing Hegel, his nemesis—Schopenhauer.[28] In order to resolve Kant's difficulty over the "thing in itself," Fichte posited an "absolute consciousness"—a notion that has been variously interpreted as an intensified subjectivism deriving from his concept of the "self-positing I," a version of pantheism, or a predecessor to Schopenhauer's universal Will (or, plausibly, all three). This concept, in which the individual is part of a larger consciousness that embraces all existence, then becomes, for Schelling, the basis of an "Aesthetic Idealism"—just as if German Idealism had not already and always been dominated by aesthetics. Once the aesthetic faculty became (more explicitly) elevated in this way, romantic art became the means for individuals to contemplate, celebrate, and otherwise experience the infinite, or absolute. While this is obviously sufficient foundation for E. T. A. Hoffmann's codification of romanticism as a longing for the infinite, and for the case to be made that music alone could hope to bridge the gap between the ego and the absolute, Schopenhauer's later contribution would nevertheless be crucial.

It was Schopenhauer's writings that, at midcentury, gradually prodded Wagner away from his "progressive" but actually rather conservative views of music, in which he derided "absolute" music as a "woman" trying to fertilize itself without the seed of the manly "poet."[29] Even in that scandalous formulation, which was merely a recast relic of eighteenth-century thought (reactionary even then), Wagner was partaking of Schopenhauer's bold importation of sexuality into philosophical speculation. Thus, Schopenhauer, in replacing Fichte's "absolute consciousness" with the "Will," based his speculations on sexual experience and its culmination, during which the "I" seems to merge into a kind of blind striving beyond consciousness. In this view, art becomes not so much a *celebration* of the absolute as a space in which to engage it; music, being nonrepresentational in a conventional sense, was the most directly connected to the Will, and so—as Schopenhauer elaborated at some length, if sometimes inexpertly—provides the most vital conduit.[30]

In an important sense, then, Idealism gave a kind of "content" to untexted music, making it about something, but defining that something out of known existence. Fortuitously, at each of the two main stages of this process, a German composer provided an extended practical demonstration of how music could fulfill the newly specified function. In its Fichtean version, that something was a universalized version of the self, and Beethoven provided just such an experience, creating musical "images" of the heroic that could seem to embrace, at the same time, his own story and the story of a larger collective (variously: Germany, mankind, humankind). Schopenhauer's more radical version of that something, the Will, added a strange, scary otherness to the absolute, and Wagner demonstrated—as I have discussed more fully elsewhere—how music, when deployed in staged drama based in myth, could seem both deeply subjective and representational of that blindly elemental, alternative world.[31] Then, coincident with Wagner's Schopenhauerian culmination, Hanslick produced a contrasting argument about music that seemed, naïvely, to wrest music away from intense idealist speculations, away from its pretensions to the sublime and back to the beautiful. But by then the battle against the tide of romantic excess was well lost, for Hanslick's formulation proves itself to be but a more conservative product of German Idealist thought, providing a welcome middle ground whose principal contribution was to suggest that the separateness of music could be demonstrated in quasi-technical ways, establishing the groundwork for music theorists to provide that demonstration more fully.

Yet, a strange irony accompanied music's heady rise in esteem, deriving directly from the basis of that rise in German Idealism, but also bearing some resemblance to other kinds of rags-to-riches stories. Especially in the wake of Beethoven, and beginning in the German lands, one of Kant's basic concepts began to assert itself, ever more strongly, and in the process to redefine the social context for music. As music's function as a conduit to something larger became paramount—and that something might extend from self-improvement to community to nation to religion to the infinite—musical engagement was increasingly channeled so as to maximize this function. *Listening* to music became the most privileged musical activity, the focal point for what music was deemed, in essence, to *be*. This was because listening to music provided the opportunity and the basis for *contemplation*, an activity—and it was increasingly regarded as activity, rather than passive immersion—directed both inward and outward, both to the soul and to the infinite. In this way, listening to music—the right kind of music—became a categorical imperative, a moral act of self-improvement. And so, as engagement with music was increasingly afflicted by its own upwardly mobile aspirations, listening to music became a *duty*.[32]

The burden music has carried as a result of being elevated to the status of a moral duty is hard to calculate. On this basis, in ways already noted, modes of musical engagement have been circumscribed so as to encourage thoughtful contemplation, especially within the most highly valued repertories (that is, what has at various historical points emerged as the "canon"). More to the immediate point, the collective value of whole categories of music has been, and remains today, habitually discounted. While we may track, however incompletely, what repertories and practices have flourished as a result of German Idealism, and to some extent also trace the ways in which various practices have accommodated successfully to its paradigms (often entailing a loss of some kind), we can do little more than speculate about those that did not flourish or were less successful in adapting (since there may well be other reasons for their failures), and it is nearly impossible to pin down those myriad activities that did not occur because of the prevailing musical environment. But as a starting point, we may at least recount some of the attitudes, strategies, and institutions that either emerged in response to German Idealism, or were encouraged by it, and from that standpoint assess the effect on repertories—such as much of Haydn—that conform only partly to the new paradigms (thus, "near misses"), and those other repertories that stand apart from or even opposed to German Idealism, including especially US American popular music traditions ("nemeses").

NEAR MISSES . . .

Before E. T. A. Hoffmann's "Beethoven's Instrumental Music" in 1813, whatever specific exemplars might have served to document music's ascension to the top of the hierarchy of the arts remained somewhat obscure, since most of the German Idealist writers did not specify particular pieces or even composers, and in the few instances when they did so, those specified do not conform to our latter-day expectations.[33] The dearth of actual examples is understandable, since the abstract theorizing that these writers engaged in required them to essentialize aesthetic experience; they were, after all, idealists, not empiricists. But their failure to identify specific works that are familiar to us today may also be understood in historical terms since, during the crucial half decade between 1795 and 1800 (as traced above), the composers now most familiar to us from this general period were not particularly "hot." The much-venerated Mozart was dead, Haydn was until late in the decade off in England catering to the tastes of his London audiences, and Beethoven was barely on the horizon. In any case, as I will argue more fully below, Mozart and Haydn were at a slight remove from the intellectual and artistic traditions that fostered German Idealism, mainly because they were Catholic and Austrian, but also because, in more broadly general terms, they accepted a societal basis governed by a strong central authority, an acceptance that left telling traces in their music. We may thus well understand why an emergent general view of an elevated music might be both disinclined, and somewhat at a loss, to point to particular examples in support of music's elevation.

Nevertheless, the sudden widespread popularity of purely instrumental music in the last decades of the eighteenth century, especially in its most elaborate form, the symphony, was widely observed and theorized by a range of cultural observers quite apart from the Weimar-Jena group, and increasingly seen as a particularly German phenomenon, at least in origin and by inclination.[34] As discourse grew around the symphony in particular, it intertwined with those discourses centered around German Idealism and German nationalism in many fruitful but potentially misleading ways. In the first decade or so of the nineteenth century, German composers (German in the wider cultural sense) were credited with creating both the genre and its most important repertory, and Haydn, Mozart, and Beethoven were routinely cited as its greatest masters. Moreover, performances of symphonies were often described, as Mark Evan Bonds has established, as "expressions of a collective voice,"[35] a mode of reception that shaded easily into the Fichtean strand of German Idealism on the one hand, and either nationalist or cosmopolitan ideologies on the other. But the connections between these various discourses varied in strength and over time. That between the symphony and either German Idealism or German nationalism was not as strong, early on, as the connection between the latter two. As a result, until Hoffmann's essay, Haydn and Mozart did not figure prominently in idealist/romantic discourse, and Hoffmann himself presents them as part of a clearly defined hierarchy, as precursors and supporting cast to Beethoven—positions they would not easily shake however often they were to be cited as German master composers.

Because of both idealist theorizing and political events of the period, however, German nationalist concerns quickly became intertwined with the development of German Idealism, including its aesthetic and, over time, specifically musical spheres. The most persuasive theorizing was by Schiller and Herder, whose ideas, when synthesized, would form the basis for the aesthetic wing of German nationalism, and would in that capacity provide a ready and serviceable model for other nationalisms. Schiller himself was not a nationalist in the developing political sense of the term, yet his theoretical realignment of the state with aesthetics in *On the Aesthetic Education of Man* (1794), considered along with his delineation of the role of the poet in *On Naïve and Sentimental Poetry* (1795–1796) and combined with Herder's *Volksgeist* and the emergence of music atop the aesthetic hierarchy, provide a particularly persuasive framework for assigning music a specific role within the newly forming nationalist enterprise.[36] The central political events relevant to German nationalism in this period included already mentioned uncertainties relating to governmental secession in Austria and France, shifting alignments within the German states north of Austria, the partial relocation of much German Idealist/romantic activity away from Weimar-Jena and mainly to Berlin (in large part as a result of tensions stemming from allegations of atheism made against Fichte and others), and—perhaps most decisively—the Napoleonic Wars and their specific effects on the German lands. Of these two kinds of forces, it is most important for us here to consider the former (idealist theorizing), since the latter, more concrete forces are much better known, and were more immediate in their impact.

Importantly, Schiller provides a metahistorical context for his conception of the role of the poet, who stands between the past and the future and is aware of both. This awareness for Schiller defines the teleological context for art and dictates its function; as will be seen, this framework is easily adapted to the goals of nationalism, be they cultural (as they tended to be early on) or political. Within the historical schema Schiller advances in *Naïve and Sentimental*, "we" in the urbanized present (that is, Schiller's urbanized present) stand in imperfect relation to a more ideal past—identified variously depending on one's situation and beliefs as "Arcadia," "Sicily," or "Eden"—a past in which the human and the natural were in much closer alignment than "now." Significant remnants or "echoes" of this lost past may be found among the folk of today's countryside (that is, the late-eighteenth-century countryside), traditionally the subject of the pastoral as a genre. From the vantage point of an imperfect present, we may look forward to a return to this alignment (Utopia, Elysium, or Heaven), and it is the poet who articulates our position and attitude. Satire, for example, critiques current reality; the idyll and the elegy look nostalgically to the past as a lost ideal; and the pastoral purports to represent vestiges of that past as they survive in today's countryside and country life. The supreme task of Schiller's poet is to create hope in the face of realist confirmation that hope is not justified, by projecting as real what can never be achieved; to this end, elements drawn from all of these approaches—satire, idyll, elegy, pastoral—may come into play, with the latter emerging as particularly important since it purports to correspond to at least a part of current reality.[37]

This structure, coupled with Herder's *Volksgeist* (the spirit of a people) and substituting the artist more generally for Schiller's poet, becomes a recipe for the nationalist artist: the idealized past, for the nationalist, is the past of a "people" who survive into the present (that is, in the *Volk* of the countryside), and the ideal future for which one strives is a "nation" in which that people is restored to its earlier oneness with the land of its past.[38] Moreover, in the emergent view of music as potentially transcendent, no art had greater potential than music for establishing a link between the individual and such an imagined larger spirit, especially given the nature of Herder's research and theorizing about folk song. Thus music, and more particularly the composer, soon acquired a central role in the nationalist agenda.

The most public genres—symphony, oratorio, concerto, and opera—were particularly well suited for this role, since they positioned the individual in relation to larger forces, whether on stage, as in the latter two (although successful and suitably German operas were until Wagner few in number), or by critical reception; symphonies, as noted, were seen to invoke a productive dynamic between the individual and affiliated others, bringing Fichtean idealism into easy alignment with nationalism in a single aesthetic experience. But chamber music also had its place, since chamber music, by extended analogy, provided a contemplative space for the individual at a remove from that larger collective. This at times had a literal basis; for Chopin, a fervent nationalist who found himself removed from his people and their claimed territory, the chamber (or salon) proved to be the only viable setting for expressions of nationalism that were at once intensely subjective in their appeal and disconnected from the redeeming collective or homeland.[39] (This kind of conflation of the chamber with the intensely subjective, encouraged especially by Beethoven's late works for either piano or string quartet, established the conditions for the apparent paradox discussed above, wherein Mahler's Fourth Symphony, though impractical to play in a chamber setting or without a conductor, may be after all taken for chamber music, as reconceived in terms of German Idealism.)

To some extent, German nationalist musical strategies were exportable, so that French grand opera, Chopin's mazurkas and polonaises, Verdi's operas, Russian operas and symphonies, Grieg's lyric pieces, Smetana's and/or Dvořák's orchestral works, and Sibelius's tone poems could all serve to advance nationalist causes on an international stage. Yet, many of the associated institutions and practices were understood—by Germans, at least—to be essentially German; these included not only the symphony as a genre (often the musical genre of choice for nationalism), but also the musical capacity that was required to evoke not peoples and places but an intense subjectivity. Sometimes theorized in terms of the North German climate (for example, by Jean Paul Richter, writing in 1804),[40] but eventually essentialized as a national trait, this capacity for aesthetic inwardness—*Innerlichkeit*—was especially prized, and had to be protected against exposure to music that did not flow from the German spirit.

Regarding the latter danger, specific perceived hazards were often a matter of proximity and relative susceptibility to irritation. Beethoven in his last years reportedly dismissed Rossini as suitable for "the frivolous and sensuous spirit of the time," and disparaged his productivity, noting that he needed "only as many weeks as the Germans do years to write an opera."[41] As Sanna Pederson has shown, music critics in Berlin and Leipzig during the generation after Beethoven's death reviled most Italian opera as potentially injurious to the greater depth of German music, and encouraged more frequent performances of Beethoven.[42] When foreign-born composers seemed exceptionally valuable according to emergent Germanic criteria, they were sometimes "adopted" or actively encouraged to move to Germany or Austria, where they would find a more appreciative public. Thus, for example, both Schumann and Franz Brendel—both partisans of German music, but most often at odds with each other—found Berlioz a worthy successor to Beethoven;[43] Brahms worked hard (but in vain, and against the tide of Viennese reception) to persuade Dvořák to move to Vienna;[44] and Mahler deliberately gave up his direct connection to Jewish musical traditions in order to work as a conductor and symphonist in the German tradition.[45]

In the quarter century before the German nationalist project reached fruition with the creation of the Prussian state in 1871, a variety of conflicts arose concerning what best represented German music, the artistic tradition that had increasingly come to be regarded as Germany's crowning artistic and cultural achievement. These conflicts were basically of two types, involving either direct oppositions—Wagner versus Brahms, Hanslick's theories versus advocacy of opera and programmatic music, center versus periphery—or a kind of boundary control, taking the form of either exclusionist maneuvers such as Wagner's diatribes against the French, Italians, and Jews, or inclusionist maneuvers such as Brendel's extension of his "New German" category to include the Hungarian Liszt and the French Berlioz.[46] But whatever their specific individual content, these conflicts and competing claims, in chorus, aggressively asserted "German music" and "serious music" to be one and the same thing, a claim that became a widely accepted truism (if not precisely true) in the process. With this extended moment of arrival, German music both claimed a kind of universality and consigned other nationalist musics—as Richard Taruskin has sagely observed—to a kind of self-imposed colonialism, celebrating their differences in terms of indigenous "flavors" but borrowing discursive modes, forms, and genres from the Germans to achieve a semblance of depth and substance.[47]

Already with the Italians, importing a Germanic sense of seriousness and enhancing the presence of the orchestra had converted opera from a thriving entertainment in the first decades of the nineteenth century to an effective vehicle for nationalist sentiment. Verdi's own name became an acronym for the Risorgimento and, in the end, Italy managed to complete its own nationalist unification even before the Germans (in 1870), and more completely than the Germans initially were able to accomplish—albeit aided significantly by the diversion of Prussia's successful wars with Austria in 1866 and France in 1870–1871.[48]

Similarly, in more direct imitation, French composers in the wake of the Franco-Prussian War resolved to create a French instrumental music that could rival the German tradition. This project's apparent success was, initially, deeply ironic; the Société Nationale de Musique, with its motto *Ars gallica*, effectively completed the German military victory, since the music of this generation derives most of all from German traditions.[49] It was only after this first effort that French composers—those most often labeled "Impressionist," if contentiously so—managed a more successful break from German models. Significantly, that break was supported by a radically different philosophical-aesthetic basis, based in objectivity and utility rather than subjectivity, and subverting as much as possible the tendency of the subjective to reshape the objective in the process of comprehending it.[50] While one may easily find distinctive traces of Wagner's harmonic and motivic procedures, and even direct allusion, in Debussy, those traces are "objectified"; they no longer betoken human urgings and teleologies, but simply *are*, presented by Debussy as if they were bits of unprocessed reality, analogous to the points of light in a Seurat painting or the splashes of color in Monet. But, in so rejecting subjectivity in favor of a detached objectivity, French composers of this generation also accepted, implicitly and as a philosophical given, the unassailable separation of "objective" outside from the "subjective" inside.[51]

As German Idealism became aligned with German nationalism across the first half of the nineteenth century, its most significant musical project was to reform and newly assess musical practices within Germanic culture. As noted, Beethoven became the cornerstone for music's newly defined status as a "serious" art form, and the traditional concert format (still widely in use today) celebrates his centrality by providing a reliable venue for the three most important public genres of untexted music in his oeuvre: overture, concerto, and symphony. But for the same reasons that early theorists of music's transcendent potential tended not to restrain their observations and conjectures to specific works, Beethoven could not stand alone. If one wants to claim credibly that either *music*—or *good music*, or *German music* (as opposed to *Beethoven's music*)—has by nature a certain power, one needs either no specific exemplars or a much longer list. To acquire such a list, the discipline that would eventually be known as musicology gradually took shape, with four main (and mainly implicit) tasks: to lay out the inner life of (German) composers through biography, to create a canon of great (German) musical works stretching back into the past, to explicate and promote those works, and to construct a master narrative of (German) music history.[52] Among those from the most recent past who would earn a place beside Beethoven were Bach, Mozart, and Haydn, who had each acquired an elevated reputation before Beethoven had fully secured his. But in the process of being recovered for an increasingly *idealist* musical environment, they—along with many others, over time—had to be "made over," each in a different way, to fit prevailing paradigms.

The beginning of the "Bach revival" in the nineteenth century is traditionally—and I believe correctly—linked to Mendelssohn's performance of Bach's *St. Matthew Passion* in 1829, on what was then believed to be the hundredth anniversary of its first performance and—which may be more to the point here—just over five years after the premier of Beethoven's Ninth Symphony along with movements from his *Missa solemnis*.[53] To be sure, the seeds of the Bach revival were well sown, by, among others, Gottfried van Swieten in Vienna, Carl Friedrich Zelter in

Berlin, and Johann Nikolaus Forkel's biography of 1802. The last, in a much-quoted passage, gave voice to the particular way in which the German musical heritage was both to be celebrated and accepted as a shared cultural duty (emphasis added): "And this man . . . was a German. Be proud of him, Fatherland, . . . but, *be worthy of him, too.*"[54]

Despite these antecedents, Mendelssohn's performance of this prodigiously difficult work stands as the central landmark of the Bach revival for two main reasons. It was, first of all, a great public success *in Berlin*, a city that was both a longtime repository of Bach's works and the new seat of German Idealism/romanticism. Moreover, Bach's *St. Matthew Passion* was performed by the Berlin Singakademie, which had long been both an important musical group with direct lineage from Bach (founded by C. P. E. Bach's pupil Carl Friedrich Fasch) and a vessel for German nationalism, especially under Carl Friedrich Zelter, who created a separate men's group to this end in 1808. And Bach's *Passion* was also particularly well suited to serve the aims of both German Idealism and German nationalism: not only did its elaborate instrumental and vocal forces satisfy the new paradigm of symphonic music as an expression of collective subjectivity, especially in the wake of Beethoven's Ninth, but it was also—given its combination of choral singing with the fervor of shared religious expression—ideal for building a sense of community (or nation) on a large scale. As Richard Taruskin has observed, large-scale performances of Handel's oratorios in London had long since proven the value of this kind of work for promoting national feeling.[55] With this great success of a dauntingly huge work securing Bach's reputation as a composer who could work with large forces and on a broad scale, his already well-known craft, without equal especially in the realm of counterpoint, became a renewed source of wonder. Bachian counterpoint became an emblem of German intellectual prowess and depth of soul, and even the relative obscurity of his career served as a lesson in Kantian duty, as he labored to uphold standards against the tide of fashion, and so forsook immediate reward in the service of God and the "holy German art" of music.[56]

To a comfortably large extent, the Bach reinvented by the German Bach revival in the nineteenth century was a good fit with the historical Bach, and despite the loss of significant amounts of his music during the intervening decades, there was ample material available to support his new role as a major pillar of German music, to stand alongside Beethoven.[57] But what the nineteenth century found in Bach was most importantly a reflection of its own ideals, and so there were inevitable distortions, manifest most obviously in repertory. Since those ideals had been most fully realized in Beethoven, it should not seem remarkable that Bach's own emergence as an Idealist composer ran in close parallel to Beethoven's career. As with Beethoven, Bach was best known early on for his keyboard music, and was known during Beethoven's lifetime primarily as a composer of instrumental music, a category represented mainly by the *Well-Tempered Clavier*, the *Art of Fugue*, the *Goldberg Variations*, and the accompanied violin sonatas. After the *St. Matthew Passion* established Bach as a master of the large as well as the small, other large-scale works also entered the repertory, including the *St. John Passion* and the Mass in B Minor. To these vocal works were added a sprinkling of cantatas, as well, but by midcentury, with the launching of the Bach Edition, enough of his music for larger instrumental ensembles had also become known so that the general assessment of Bach remained close to that of Beethoven: a master composer of instrumental music who on some important but fairly rare occasions created magnificent large-scale works by extending that idealist realm to include voices.

Also around midcentury, however, a crucial contradiction in this constellation of canon and ideology created the first significant rift among idealist/nationalist German romantics concerned with music. This rift, which would in turn have a significant impact on Bach reception (to which we will soon return), requires a separate discussion.

The idealist/nationalist conception of the symphony—prized for being multitudinous, untexted, and German—had no obvious place for the emergent roles of choral singing, useful not only for building a sense of German culture and community in the present but also for establishing a living heritage grounded in German culture, and for forging a link between present communities and that heritage. It was this contradiction that led Wagner to coin the phrase "absolute music" in order to disparage it, using Beethoven's Ninth as his principal exemplar; in his view, music unguided by a text was merely empty form, and barren. In terms of his development as a composer after midcentury, Wagner's codification both makes sense and entails a central contradiction of its own. Music, for Wagner, was too sensuous in nature to represent the reasoning mind effectively; thus, according to his infamously essentialist formulation, "music is a woman," and needs the masculine word to give it meaningful shape and fertility. But in (mostly) eliminating in his subsequent music the empty forms that music, on its own, tended to create, Wagner at the same time harnessed and exploited capacities that were themselves specifically musical, in order to suggest both depth and something beyond the safe confines of the discredited standard forms.

By eliminating those forms, as I have argued elsewhere,[58] the flow of Wagner's "formless" music merged the self directly into a deep sense of "the world," bypassing the phenomenal world and its meaningless structures ("civilization"), while borrowing from Schopenhauer the audacious suggestion that sexual culmination provides an important model for this kind of projected merger. In *Tristan und Isolde*, for example, the titular pairing is first achieved, during the extended love scene of act 2, as a unison melodic climax on the final word of the phrase, "Selbst dann bin ich die Welt" (Even then am I the world). Only music among the arts has the capacity for suggesting this kind of fluid simultaneity of self and world, a capacity that is grounded in neither the body nor the reasoning mind but rather in a kind of feeling that has, indeed, often been characterized as womanly. But this dimension of womanliness was more of the spirit than of the body, most often presented in German romantic writings (and in several Wagner operas) as offering a spiritualized, redemptive love. (To cite one of many relevant examples: Goethe concludes *Faust* with an image of "das Ewig-Weibliche" [the eternal feminine].) In conventionally essentialist terms prevalent in the nineteenth century, the contradiction between Wagner's dismissal of (essentialized) music and his actual musical practice relates directly to the perceived dual potential of women, to be either wholly sensual (of the body) or wholly spiritual (of the soul).

But quickly emerging alongside Wagner's attempt to impose directed meaning on music through adding text back into the mix, were three other prescriptive and receptive modes, all with roots in Beethoven and all potentially defensible according to German Idealist and nationalist aims. As noted above, this apparent fragmentation into a kind of factional warfare, while seeming to threaten the very foundations of German music—translating the oft-repeated question, "What is German?" into "What is German music?"—was precisely the kind of conflict that solidified an easily generalized position: that German music was the music that mattered, and identifying music's true nature meant, at bottom, identifying the true nature of German music.

Liszt, with Brendel's encouragement, proposed to move decisively in the direction of program music, presenting symphonic music (mostly) without vocal forces, but at the same time identifying particular referents for it; the practice, derived from Beethoven's Sixth Symphony and overtures, had in the intervening years been most significantly advanced by Berlioz. Hanslick, as noted, proposed to hold the category of "music" to its purest form, asserting that external referents, even to feelings, were musically irrelevant; from this perspective, vocal music, as music, followed a specifically musical logic and succeeded or failed on that basis to be "beautiful" (thus inspiring a long and often unfortunate tradition of analyzing vocal music without consideration for the words). Related to this, and following Brahms's early career (which seemed to many to substantiate Hanslick's claims), was Nietzsche's argument—taking Wagner's main exemplar head-on—that the words in Beethoven's Ninth Symphony were irrelevant, because what truly mattered was vocality.[59] While Nietzsche's emphasis was on the aesthetic effect of *hearing* a community of voices raised in song, his observations resonate well with the ways that community-based singing actually functioned across the nineteenth century in the German lands, providing opportunities, often for amateurs, to sing great music (or patriotic music) together, with the precise meaning of the sung texts often serving an important topical function, but in the end assuming a decidedly secondary role compared to the activity of group singing. And, after all, it was this performance environment that brought the matter to a head in the first place, not only securing both a symbolic and practical place for Bach's large-scale music, but also inspiring Mendelssohn, Schumann, Brahms, and others to contribute new works that could serve this dual need.[60]

Of the latter alternatives, Nietzsche's emphasis on the *sound* of voices raised in song, rather than the activity of singing, was most clearly in line with German Idealist understandings of music, which in the end created a crisis of sorts for the Bach revival. As the Bach Edition continued to produce volume after volume of Bach's more than two hundred surviving cantatas, it became increasingly necessary to reassess Bach's position as a composer primarily of instrumental music, and to develop new strategies for understanding his specifically musical achievements in the developing receptive environment. For a long time, that environment has dictated that all Bach's music should be understood as a specifically *musical* exploration, in many cases serving as a compendium of the possible (one thinks most immediately—but not only—of *The Well-Tempered Clavier, Art of Fugue, Goldberg Variations,* and *Musical Offering*).

Only in recent decades has some mainstream reception begun to understand Bach's music—instrumental as well as vocal—in terms of his Lutheran worldview and his heavily circumscribed life.[61] As this has happened, it has become increasingly apparent that Bach's music does not connect easily to German Idealist notions of the Infinite, being grounded in very specific texts, attitudes, religious beliefs, and expressive modes. Only by suppressing this knowledge, and so retaining notions of music's inherent separation from such considerations, might one continue to see Bach's music—as it is indeed still very widely understood—as a kind of realized perfection. Yet, demonstrably, the frictions that he deploys in his counterpoint, embodies within his arrangement of concerted forces, and expresses through his interactive engagement with a variety of traditions and texts, all correspond to palpable frictions that deeply affected his life as a musician and human being. We have been learning, in recent decades, to *unlearn* Bach as recovered by the nineteenth century, to hear past the vaunted perfection of his music to the wrenching pain and grief, and occasional laughter, that his mastery of musical craft allowed him to express more fully than anyone else.

Like Bach, Mozart has long served as an emblem of perfection, and it has in recent years seemed even harder to rescue him from that burden. Early on, however, Mozart was the more problematic fit for idealist/romantic/nationalist agendas, especially given that a good part of the mix of biography and myth that quickly engulfed his legacy was not to his credit as a man. That his music did not seem to "work" the way Beethoven's seemed to—it apparently had no place for the titanic, Kantian struggles that Beethoven's music simulated, beginning with the *Eroica* in 1803—was too easily reconciled with the paired myths that he composed quickly and without effort, and that his disposition was that of a child, with full measure of both childlike innocence and childish indulgences, the latter manifest in grotesque descents into profanity and scatological humor, and in extravagant spending beyond his means. Moreover, much of his copious musical legacy seemed too trivial in aspect and affect, or too fussily ornate, to match the growing aspirational demands placed on the newly elevated art of music. Even so, some aspects of the Mozart mythology seemed either ready-made or easily tailored for the new ideals, and the continued success of his music made it imperative both that it be inducted into service as part of the Germanic legacy, and understood in terms of the emerging aesthetic.

The reception of Mozart's mature operas points both to his importance to this and later generations, and to the problems that this prominence presented. *Die Entführung aus dem Serail* (*The Abduction from the Seraglio*), for example, made a considerable splash, and was very widely performed across the German lands in the few years after its 1782 premiere in Vienna. Although one might reasonably suppose that a successful opera in German as well wrought as this one would have been embraced as a national treasure by Goethe and his cohort, it was perceived at the time more as a kind of interference, its success blocking the way to what they considered a better solution to the problem of German opera. Emperor Joseph II's apocryphal dismissal of Mozart's *Singspiel*, as having "too many notes"—usually cited to discredit Joseph and to show how ill-appreciated Mozart was in Vienna (as in Peter Schaffer's *Amadeus*)—in fact reflected and to some extent anticipated a growing sense, especially among the Weimar group, that a truly German operatic form ought to be simpler and more "direct" in style, with more obvious ties to German folk music. In this regard, *Die Zauberflöte* (*The Magic Flute*, 1791) served much better, and even became a model of sorts for the next generation, because of its appeal to magic realms accessible only through music, its occasional decorous deployment of a folklike musical style, and its earnest presentation of manly virtue. Yet its indulgence in Italianate vocality (mainly in the Queen of the Night's arias) presented much the same problem as had *Entführung* (and, more generally, Italian opera), in too readily gratifying audience's tastes for vocal display.

The operas Mozart wrote with librettist Lorenzo da Ponte presented a different set of problems. Most successful for the romantics was *Don Giovanni* (Prague, 1787), with its titular hero defying society, death, and the underworld with equal panache (notwithstanding an occasional show of cowardice, as when he leaves his servant Leporello behind to answer for his crimes), all in the name of free love and personal liberty. Moreover, in the Commendatore's music Mozart created one of the most effective musical evocations of the sublime from the eighteenth century. Yet, the nineteenth century, in keeping *Don Giovanni* in the repertory (which was exceptional in itself), developed the curious habit of omitting the final celebratory chorus, after Giovanni descends into Hell, apparently in the belief that this conclusion betrayed the daring conception—as it was then widely understood—of an opera that otherwise celebrates unabashedly the misdeeds of a miscreant. Even after later practices restored Mozart's conclusion, however, it was seen as dramatically flawed; thus, the extensive major-mode peroration at the end can still seem to violate dramatic sense, especially if one imagines that the familiar title and locus of sympathy for the opera are one and the same.[62] To be sure, we may find explanations for Mozart's dramatic "miscalculation" within specific operatic conventions and a generalized sense of how music is presumed to "work": a specifically *musical* sense of balance, one may argue, imposes itself on and through Mozart's operatic sense.[63] Yet, it is naïve to assume that musical conventions have nothing to do with conceptions of either drama or real life;[64] in any case, it is fairly easy to relate most of those features of Mozart's music that seemed problematic to later generations—including this one—directly to Mozart's worldview, which was decidedly different from that of German Idealism.

To start, it is instructive to compare and contrast how Giovanni and *Figaro*'s Count Almaviva (in *Le nozze di Figaro*, 1786) are treated. Both are aristocrats bent on abusing their privileges through exercising sexual license, and they inhabit comic operas composed one year apart by the same set of collaborators. Moreover, the outward fates of both characters are similar: neither succeeds in his central sexual adventure, and each is repeatedly rebuked and ultimately punished (if only by embarrassment in *Figaro*). But Almaviva is no Giovanni, especially as he functions within the story; with his accoutrements of wife, household, and established legal authority, he provides not only an aristocratic foil for an oblique assertion of "natural" rights as they were being theorized in the eighteenth century, but also, through the "education" he undergoes during the opera, what might well be construed as a "sauce-for-the-goose" demonstration of how Kant's categorical imperative might operate to curb aristocratic excess within an enlightened monarchical system. But while the central plot of *Figaro* may thus seem fairly congenial to the politics of German Idealism, the opera has seemed—being essentially a comedy—of a lower order and thus less important than *Don Giovanni*, even if the latter is ostensibly also comedic (sharing with the other two da Ponte operas the designation *dramma giocoso*). There is no real hero in *Figaro* (unless it is Susanna, in the unlikely guise of a soubrette), whereas Giovanni is often understood to be precisely that: a hero who transcends and transforms his own comic environment in large part because he is utterly unsusceptible to the kinds of embarrassment that *Figaro*'s Count has to accept, both along the way and in the end. It is in Giovanni's refusing the embarrassment that must come with his proffered chances for redemption that the character becomes a hero and the opera itself, in reception, a tragedy.

The nineteenth century, post-Napoleon, was prone to forget why it had been important, in the late eighteenth century, that Giovanni was *Don* Giovanni. If, for the nineteenth century, Giovanni's aristocratic station mainly served to facilitate his elevation to the status of hero, it had more crucial importance for da Ponte, Mozart, and their first audiences, allowing them to savor both Giovanni's presumption and his consequent undoing in full measure—thus the full title for the opera, *Il dissoluto punito, ossia Il Don Giovanni* (*The Profligate Punished; or, Don Giovanni*). The opera's genius consists, in part, in its presentation of a genuinely tragic story *fully within* the confines of an ordered society, which is threatened and nearly overturned by Giovanni's disruptive conduct but in the end restored. In this pre-idealist eighteenth-century context, *not* to rejoice in the restoration of society or to celebrate the demise of its greatest threat would have signaled a tragedy on a larger scale than that of the errant Don, since his departure would then have left only desolation in its wake. To be sure, Mozart, as with the "too many notes" in the earlier *Entführung*, was aesthetically and politically behind the times; in performances in Vienna, after the Prague premiere, the finale was already being curtailed and, in references to the opera, "Don Giovanni" almost immediately displaced "The Profligate Punished."

Mozart's basic political conservatism, which places primary value on the preservation of society and its underpinnings, and *not* on those individuals who threaten its stability—however heroic, or sympathetically drawn, they may be—lies behind most of what the nineteenth century found problematic in his music. And, paradoxically, it is those problematic features that have, in many cases, seemingly triumphed in Mozart reception, reducing him—and "reducing" is indeed the operative verb—to an emblem of musical perfection on the one hand, and of aristocratic cultural complacency on the other (which is how his music has tended to function in films over the past few decades). But the paradox is only on the surface. Mozart's propensity to include "too many notes," in whatever specific form that takes, is by no means random or indiscriminate, but rather tends to reinforce stability in the large at the expense of interest in the moment or the particular. This creates a musical situation fully in line with political conservatism and nearly impossible to reconcile with German Idealist thought, which begins with the moment and the particular (in this sense), and insists that the "large" (whether the "thing in itself" or universal consciousness) may be grasped only through that lens.

Those in the nineteenth century who responded above all to the pathos of Mozart's individuated voices, whether in *Don Giovanni*, in the *Requiem*, or in the preponderance of his minor-mode instrumental works—especially the D-minor and C-minor Concertos (K. 466 and 491) and the second G-minor Symphony (no. 40, K. 550)—felt betrayed by his extended passages of "filler" material or other vestiges of "empty" formality. That a Mozart concerto begins, for example, with a long stable section for the orchestra alone, formally and harmonically self-sufficient (the formal version of "too many notes"), and that the soloist, later in the movement, routinely creates pedestals for the orchestra's return, bowing obsequiously with extended courtier-like perorations (the virtuosic version of "too many notes"), befuddled those who wanted to think that the concerto, intrinsically, was primarily about the soloist, conceived as a kind of musically embodied hero. But these features are surprisingly easy to read when one understands *both* Mozart's devotion to societal order and his sympathy for the individual perspective of exception-making genius, and grasps further that the former, for Mozart, must always prevail.[65]

It was Hanslick's version of absolute music, in which music answered, in the end, only to its own "internal" demands, that eventually allowed these and related features of Mozart's music to be rationalized within an idealist framework, a solution that demanded that his music (especially his instrumental music) be understood whenever possible apart from any particular real-world context. Some of the Mozart myths helped in this, in particular the conceit that he was a childlike (even child*ish*) vessel for divinely inspired music—thus, "Amadeus" ("Beloved of God")—whose essential naïveté protected his music from worldly taint.[66] The post-Hanslick construction of the absoluteness of Mozart's music does not really depend on the Mozart mythology, however, and has to some extent displaced it, particularly in being able to accommodate, with earlier nineteenth-century generations, a special affection for those moments in Mozart that seem overwhelmingly sympathetic to an imperiled, and occasionally heroic, individual perspective, so long as they are managed according to Hanslick's sense of the musically beautiful. Indeed, the affinity between Mozart's music and Hanslick's theoretical perspective finds ready corroboration in Mozart's own much-quoted statement about avoiding musical excess (in a letter to his father, September 1781): "Music, even in the most terrible situations, must never offend the ear, but must please the hearer, or in other words, must never cease to be *music*."[67]

This solution to the "Mozart problem," however, gives theoretical shelter to a resistance in Mozart reception to taking his "perfection" for what it actually was: a politically reactionary glorification of an established, aristocratically based societal order (notwithstanding that many filmmakers seem to take this implicit attitude for granted, as noted). This resistance is understandable though not excusable when thus stated, yet it derives as much from a mostly unacknowledged philosophical conflict as from a desire to remove Mozart's music from his politics into a realm of "pure" and "universal" art. On the one hand, Hanslick's protoformalist codification of the "beautiful" in music, aligning itself with German Idealism in its removal of music from the real world, became the basis for justifying, in terms of beautifully balanced forms, Mozart's seeming dramatic lapses and dependence on "filler." On the other hand, those beautifully balanced forms—particularly as they depend on "filler," empty flourishes, or complacently courtly formal procedures—stand at a far remove from German Idealism, not only in giving primacy to the musical equivalent of extant realities, but also in giving that replication a reactionary political face. For Mozart (and his music), the "thing in itself" that mattered—taking precedence over any and all subjective positions—was a hierarchically structured society, presumably a version of the "enlightened monarchy" simulated in *Zauberflöte* (a political ideal, it should be noted, that was and continued to be favored by many, if only as an alternative to revolution and a hedge against empowering those who lacked education and sensibility).

But even aside from the specific politics involved, the "perfection" of Mozart's music cannot actually be understood as such without also taking some measure, even if only subliminally, of the fact that there actually is a *something*, very much tied to Mozart's realities, that is being given perfect form. Moreover, that unacknowledged something is being served even (and perhaps all the more so) when it is being ignored in deference to its quality of perfection, and particularly so when that quality transmutes into a presumed (and clearly specious) universality—a maneuver that has unfortunately become a cliché with regard to Mozart. Ironically, the "unacknowledged something" most relevant to Mozart's music is in fact directly opposed to German Idealism, especially as it becomes more intertwined with political nationalism across the nineteenth century: Mozart's music routinely, and as if inevitably (as a matter of how form and beauty in music must work), controls and manages the subjective position by reinforcing hierarchical societal order, in this way siding, across the board, with *Zivilisation* rather than *Kultur*.

Despite such lapses of logic, claims of perfection and universality have, with Mozart as with Bach, provided a rationale for erasing their music's specific content, not because such content has been understood as irrelevant to the aesthetic experience of music, but, according to Hanslick's theorizing, because content in this sense does not actually exist within the category of music as rightly understood. On this basis alone, Hanslick significantly reinforced the place these composers held within a German Idealist framework and its developing canon. To be sure, the difference between Bach's and Mozart's specific modes of perfection is significant, since Bach's music typically elaborates a single (albeit often complex) musical idea, and may thus more readily be understood within the German Idealist paradigm that Mark Evan Bonds terms "music as thought" (see above). But it is the category of perfection itself that matters most in this case, because it has guaranteed Bach and Mozart a secure place in the canon—whatever aspects of their work get left behind in the process—that has mainly been denied to Haydn, whose music has not been understood in such terms.

Indeed, the category that has most threatened to swallow up Haydn's music is that of "entertainment," which has rarely if ever been linked to either "perfection" or the contemplative mode of engagement demanded by the new aesthetic. That so much of Haydn's music *is* entertaining, often hilariously so, has tended to make him a suspicious commodity from the perspective of German Idealism—that is, not only suspicious but also a *commodity*, as opposed to *art* according to an Idealist aesthetic.[68] What, after all, does entertainment have to do with the infinite, or hilarity with art in this elevated sense? Perhaps the real surprise in Haydn reception is not the gradually declining interest in him across the nineteenth century but rather the persistence of such interest, which did not merely lapse but instead found him a place in the Beethovenian concert hall (although he would eventually fade to little more than a dependable but dispensable "extra"), and has periodically led to periods of significant cultivation outside the concert hall.[69]

There are many reasons for this persistence. Perhaps fundamental is the human capacity to find value in whatever sustains interest, so that lasting entertainment value, however rationalized, is what ultimately matters not only for Mozart, whose operas held the stage independent of German Idealism, but also for Bach and Beethoven, whose most revered works were also those that entertain best. But even aside from this convenient correlation, Haydn had much to offer from the standpoint of German Idealism. In the realm of instrumental music, he set the standard for not only the symphony, a central genre of the new aesthetic, but also the string quartet; indeed, both Mozart and Beethoven had more difficulty approaching Haydn's success with the latter than with the symphony.[70] The developmental rigor of Beethoven was based directly on Haydn's methods, as Charles Rosen demonstrates, crediting Haydn for making the musical language of his generation "coherent."[71] Haydn's *Creation* offered a large-scale choral work to match Handel's, taking its place among those works of Bach, Beethoven, and Mendelssohn that combined the symphonic and the choral. Perhaps as important as this public function, however, is *The Creation*'s evocation of the sublime at the very outset, with the breakthrough moment from chaos to the creation of light becoming a central model for not only Beethoven but also, and as extended by Beethoven, for one of the nineteenth century's favorite musical tropes, "from darkness into light."

There were built-in problems with all of these features, however, deriving from the fact that Haydn's context and aesthetic were far from those of German Idealism. His religious sense was much too cheerful (in both his late oratorios and his masses) to offer a convincing suggestion of the infinite, especially as the nineteenth century wore on and Schopenhauer's "Will" replaced Fichte's "absolute consciousness."[72] Even the "Representation of Chaos" at the beginning of *The Creation* seems politely civilized alongside the descents into dissonant disorder offered up by Beethoven's *Eroica* only five years later. And this kind of awkward comparison with Beethoven operates across the board; in each instance where Haydn may be credited with advancing in a direction congenial to German Idealism, it is always Beethoven who actually "arrives," be it with regard to evocations of the sublime or in creating Kantian developmental procedures.[73] If this seemed to later generations to be a failure of Haydn's genius (or a sign that he lacked true genius, as suggested in Count Waldstein's famous and prescient inscription to Beethoven just before his departure to Vienna and Haydn's London trips),[74] it might be better understood as a product of two circumstances. First, Beethoven—unlike any of his predecessors—actually *sought* to compose within the new aesthetic, finding the models he needed in both Haydn and Mozart (and Charles Rosen has, again, provided the best explication for how he did this),[75] but turning their means to decidedly different ends. Second, Haydn's frame of reference was the social rather than the subjective, except in rare works such as *Seven Last Words* (which he confessed to have had extraordinary difficulty writing). While Mozart's frequent focus on the subjective *within* a social frame allowed him an entrée into the new aesthetic, Haydn's individuation is rarely fraught with the pathos of alienation, which is frequently suggested in Mozart and would become a central trope of musical romanticism.

It is instructive in this regard to contrast the idealist perspective on Haydn with how his music was experienced and rationalized by English audiences and critics. There—within a generation that was still translating Aristotle while Kant was taking over the German philosophical landscape—rationalizing the experience of a Haydn symphony did not depend on understanding the orchestra as a "collective voice." Rather, as David Schroeder has demonstrated, it depended on detailing Haydn's ability to instill Aristotelian virtues, such as tolerance, through his symphonies—an ability based directly on first of all engaging an audience through entertaining them.[76] In this environment, entertainment was no barrier to aesthetic value, but was instead entirely to the point, since engaging an audience was itself a demonstration of virtue, creating the social conditions necessary for civilized discourse. When Haydn was compared to Shakespeare—as indeed he was in England, but could never have been by the German Idealists and romantics, who had their own idea of what Shakespeare was about—it was because Shakespeare was first of all a superb entertainer, who used the platform of an engaged audience in order to elevate the thought and sensibilities of that audience.

While Haydn's London reception is instructive in helping us grasp what of Haydn has been lost by his forced marriage to a German Idealist aesthetic, it is only part of the backdrop for the lapsing of that marriage into a kind of thwarted coexistence, without passion or mirth. The basis for that marriage in the first place, as with Mozart and Bach, was a process of reconciliation of philosophical and aesthetic viewpoints that were to some extent discordant. While it might be taken for granted that the process was—especially for Haydn—more one of rationalization than of reconciliation, the fact that some such process was necessary also meant that it had to be convincing. And this is the persistent awkwardness that has most undermined Haydn's position in the canon, for the idea that Haydn's entertainment value was actually secondary to his pioneering exploration of incipient German Idealism (instead of the reverse) is simply—and I use the word advisedly—laughable. It is one thing, for example, to resort to a musical depiction of a fart (late in the slow movement of Symphony no. 93), and quite another to construct an entire movement so as both to lead inexorably to that fart and to make that moment of release both surprising and satisfying, *aesthetically*. While, either way, the event itself may be regarded as simply crude, the skill and effectiveness of Haydn's elaboration belie any notion that the joke is incidental to the proto-idealist procedures that set it up.[77]

Haydn's situation in relation to German nationalism was also complicated in a way that highlights the close connection between German nationalism and German Idealism. Early in Haydn's career, as his fame grew and he was allowed by his prince to accept commissions, he strove to write quite specifically for his designated audience. In this, he was perhaps not different in kind from Mozart, or even Bach, in writing for the singing and instrumental skills available on the one hand, and writing to the projected tastes and sensibilities of his audience on the other. Yet this mode of accommodation is decidedly different from how Beethoven operated, often at odds with his performers and acknowledging near the end of his life (with regard to the late quartets) that he was not writing for the moment but for posterity.[78] Beethoven's attitude is well in line with the subjectively oriented aesthetic of German Idealism, to which accommodation of the sort practiced routinely in the preceding decades quickly became suspect. It is from this perspective that Bach's relative obscurity and Mozart's mythologized neglect in Vienna came to be regarded as signs of artistic virtue, whereas Haydn's local and international acclaim augured for an eventually declining reputation.

Even Beethoven had to be remade in various ways to fit developing paradigms, and so may in this somewhat limited sense also be regarded as a "near miss." For a very long time, his ties to what later became known as the "classical era"—the era of Haydn and Mozart—were downplayed as secondary to the vaunted revolutionary aspect of his works. As the man who "set music free,"[79] Beethoven, along with his music, had to be detached from inconvenient baggage, such as a clear allegiance to the balanced forms of his immediate predecessors. Moreover, Beethoven's musical ties to a fading era find an analogue in his seemingly incongruous habit of trading on his presumed nobility;[80] both betoken a reactionary strain in

Beethoven that has been hard to reconcile with his popular image as an iconoclast and liberator. Even if strong arguments were advanced in the second half of the twentieth century for the continuity between Beethoven and his immediate predecessors, most influentially by Friedrich Blume and Charles Rosen,[81] the nineteenth-century makeover of Beethoven has largely survived such efforts.

The substance of that nineteenth-century makeover consists largely in increasingly ritualized performance traditions, and, within those traditions, in significant accommodations to Wagnerian formal and orchestral practices.[82] These two dimensions were actually at odds, if obliquely, although both undermined the connection between Beethoven and Kantian Idealism. Thus, the former tended to efface the revolutionary emphasis on subjectivity in Beethoven's music, shifting initially toward a collective experience of a shared subjective position (an analogue of Fichtean absolute consciousness, as suggested earlier), and gradually tending from that to something like familiar religious rituals, whose meanings entail not the revolutionary as such but rather the safe familiarity of an enshrined, mythologized revolution. While this gradual demotion, in terms of immediacy, was perhaps inevitable for such a revered figure, the Wagnerian makeover offered some compensation by recasting Beethoven's orchestra into blended choirs and reimagining his architecturally controlled forms as flows of ideas, both by employing systematic tempo fluctuations and by eschewing many formal repetitions, especially within sonata forms.

. . . AND NEMESES

Alongside the "near misses" of Bach, Mozart, Haydn, and even Beethoven, and in reaction to the growing seriousness of music as it increasingly came under the sway of German Idealism, alternative musical practices developed that made little pretense to deeper meanings, although often enough and over time they merged into a general project of aesthetic elevation (which William Weber terms "musical idealism"),[83] especially through the mediation of an evolving middle-class culture. But by that time an increasingly polarized divide between emergent popular modes of musicking and the trappings and substance of high art had solidified, in part because popular music habitually made the latter the object of parodic mockery, a foil that was often merged with moral, political, cultural, or religious authority to form a generalized target for ridicule. While this kind of divide between elite and popular musical cultures was not itself new, but rather a recurring and arguably cyclic phenomenon,[84] the intensity and perseverance of the divide in the late nineteenth century and throughout the twentieth were unprecedented, creating a cultural split that has become a definitive feature of European-based musical culture, especially in the United States. The split was reinforced on either side, by the growth of music-based commerce on the popular side, and by the development of musical paradigms based in German Idealism into the "difficult" music of musical modernism on the elite side.

On the continent, the earliest and most persistent site of resistance to German Idealism and its associated musical practices and attitudes in the nineteenth century was in Paris, whose *operette*, emerging around midcentury as a distinctive type, became the basis for similar entertainments in most large cities, but especially in London, Vienna, and New York. France had long stood in an ambivalent relationship to foreign music, characteristically welcoming to a wide variety of entertainments and appreciative of the exotic, but just as often uneasy about specific foreign influences, especially German and Italian. Thus, Beethoven had (according to some accounts) been a hard sell in Paris, early on, and Wagnerian reception there was a kind of roller coaster, moving from early rejection to fashionable fascination in the immediate aftermath of the Franco-Prussian War, and then, even before the turn of the century (and certainly after), to intensified rejection, the latter accompanied by a more deliberate shift from subjective to objectifying musical modes, as noted.

England, too, responded enthusiastically to the increased availability of musical entertainments as the century wore on. Already in the early decades, the continued appeal of symphonies of all stripes was grounded first of all in their entertainment value, if only because the success of public concerts in London was and continued to be primarily a matter of commerce and only secondarily of aesthetic ideals.[85] Alongside its entertainment-based concert tradition, beginning around midcentury (in step with Parisian *operette*), London also supported a thriving music-hall tradition, with roots in saloon and pub entertainments. And, soon after, London also welcomed distinctive popular types from France and the United States, with both *operette* and minstrelsy building and maintaining sizeable audiences there—the former in translation before being largely displaced by local products, most importantly by Gilbert and Sullivan's string of successful operettas.

Indeed, through the latter collaborations, the two imported types briefly came together when, in their penultimate operetta (*Utopia Limited; or, The Flowers of Progress*, 1893), Gilbert and Sullivan based a musical number directly on minstrelsy as it was then being performed at London's St. James's Hall by Christy's Minstrels ("It Really Is Surprising").[86] The ironies of this reference to minstrelsy run deep and are probably not all intentional; these include, above all, the context for the number, which is performed by an upwardly mobile South Seas "native" who adopts a minstrel performance style under the supposedly "civilizing" instruction of his British exploiters. But, typical for Gilbert and Sullivan, the satirical point of view is hard to pin down, especially since the two were themselves self-consciously upwardly mobile in their collaborations, early on insisting on a decorous respectability as an alternative to the risqué situations common to Parisian *operette*, and later indulging their aesthetic ambitions at the expense of the continued commercial success of their partnership. (Significantly, the aspirations of Sullivan, who was trained in Leipzig and aspired to compose more "serious" dramatic works, were particularly undermining to their joint ventures.)

Notwithstanding its success with the public, entertainment music in Paris and London was not generally seen as a fundamental threat to the more "serious" music of the concert hall, salon, or opera house, even if there were, as always, scaremongers to decry the corrosive influence of such music, and although the case of Sullivan offered a cautionary tale of sorts. For many in the United States, however, in the period after the Civil War, entertainment music seemed to constitute a formidable obstacle to the reemergent nation's larger cultural aspirations. Despite strenuous, continuous, and even largely successful efforts to establish and sustain European musical traditions in the United States, those traditions have continually required subsidization by subscription, charity, or public monies.[87] (While these modes of support hold true for Europe, as well, there is less political support for them in the United States, which has always tended to look askance at European traditions of artistic patronage, perhaps owing to their origins in aristocratic privilege.) More central to musical life in the United States, at least as measured by commercial success, were a wide variety of popular musical genres. Many of these had either roots or analogues in European types, especially such genres as variety, vaudeville, extravaganza, and burlesque, all closely related to English music hall and operetta.[88] But while these developed into distinctively New World types—in the first decades of the twentieth century becoming American operetta and the American musical, alongside continuing revue-based traditions—the most distinctive musical contributions to popular musical traditions from the United States derived from the interaction of African American and European American musics.

The various musical types associated with either African Americans or white imitators in blackface (or both) were all to a large extent musical crossbreeds, as a fairly direct consequence of the enforced separateness of the social and cultural worlds each group occupied, and of the severely unbalanced power relationships between those worlds.[89] Jumping Jim Crow—a distant precursor to tap dance but more immediately a direct antecedent of the blackface minstrel tradition in the United States, which took root in the two decades before the Civil War—was a purported imitation of black dance styles, presented without apparent recognition that what was being imitated, like the later cakewalk, was probably itself a black parody of whites dancing, and derived in any case from then-current Irish styles of dancing. Spirituals, which alone of such crossbreeds seemed conducive to assimilation within European-based concert traditions, at least in the nineteenth century (most influentially in Dvořák's Symphony "From the New World," 1893; see below), derive from blacks making European and US American hymnic practices their own. The cakewalk initially developed as a vehicle for mockery through imitation, aimed in both directions across the racial divide. Ragtime developed into a classicized (thus, Europeanized) version of how African American rhythmic tendencies were being performed at the quintessential nineteenth-century European instrument—the piano—employing European tonal practices as if by default. Blues and jazz, too, found their roots, and later much of their sustaining energy, in cross-racial imitation. With all such hybrids (especially in the development of jazz and excepting the spiritual), the imitative attitude ranged fully from mocking parody, through playful affection, to deep respect, with no clear monitoring of the borders between and among these perspectives.

That these processes of back-and-forth influence remained to a surprising extent invisible to most observers at the time had much to do with the interlocking theoretical frameworks, involving philosophy, aesthetics, and politics, that developed with and alongside German Idealism in the nineteenth century. As noted, the essentializing component of nationalist thought ceded crucial authenticating agency to folk music, as a vestige of a people's valuable past, and as a means through which individuals could find resonance with a nation-based collective. Within this context and in order partially to counter (but not deny) US American racial attitudes, the specific basis for spirituals in white hymnody, for example, while hard to ignore completely, had to be put aside in favor of qualities that could be identified as more exclusively the property of blacks, who might thereby be understood to constitute a genuine, essentially unified *people*. Moreover, there was a lot at stake in this mode of understanding, since spiritual singing—soon after emancipation and extending well into the civil rights era—became an important means for persuading skeptical whites that blacks were fully human, with a capacity for deep religious feeling. In spirituals, this capacity was manifest on several levels, but especially in their combination of reverence with the beauty of harmoniously blended voices, which betokened the individual's relationship both to the larger group and, through shared expression, to something well beyond that group.

Dvořák's use of actual and invented spirituals in his "New World" Symphony thus presented a problem for European Americans. His introduction of this already blended idiom within a symphonic fabric that also drew extensively on Indianist tropes, mainstream European forms, and Russian orchestral and "magic" harmonic practices, advanced an incipient Americanist melting-pot ideology more strenuously than most European Americans were then ready to accept.[90] Moreover, the point of the blend was made fairly explicit by Dvořák in interviews and other public statements during his visit, although many felt his comments to be much more naïve than they actually were about musical cultures in the United States and their potential for this kind of blending.[91]

Dvořák's appearance of naïveté probably had three main supporting causes. First, he was a foreigner; while respected as a musician of the first rank, he was in sociocultural terms an immigrant from Eastern Europe. Second, as an outsider from an aspirational nation (Czech) under the dominion of a foreign power (Vienna), his perspective on the United States was attitudinally different from that of the more established European Americans, foregrounding more vividly the conflicted legacy of the United States, with its ideology of human equality clashing terribly with its treatment of indigenous peoples, blacks, and immigrants of strongly marked racial or ethnic difference. Third and most critical, however, was the manner in which US Americans aspiring to a more elevated culture framed the specific question of musical aspiration, to which Dvořák's perspective remained mostly oblivious. Specifically, those in this generation who wished to raise musical sensibilities in the United States mainly strove to establish and support "New World" venues for European traditions, and so had already rejected the evocative musical strains that captivated Dvořák with what he saw as their potential for nationally meaningful symphonic development, as either inadequate or fundamentally inappropriate.

Over time, US Americans embraced the "New World" Symphony as a great symphony generously offered as a kind of gift *to* the United States, but not necessarily expressive *of* it (thus in effect discounting Dvořák's own prepositional construction, "*From* the New World"). This qualified acceptance sprang doubly from a sense that spirituals could not carry the burden of representing the United States as a nation, and from a complex kind of denial concerning the symphony's obvious use of that idiom, a denial grounded in German Idealism and its associated ideologies of nationalism and absolute music.[92] Within this receptive context—the very context in which US Americans' belief in the uplifting potential of European concert music was rooted—spirituals simply could not "signify" as part of the symphony's content. The doctrine of absolute music doubly effaces their presence, first because that very presence could be so easily doubted out of consideration (until fairly recently), and second because this kind of content could be categorically disregarded as "extramusical." Moreover, notions of nationalist authentication kept spirituals, even if one acknowledged their presence in the symphony, from carrying national "content," simply because Dvořák was neither black nor US American. By the same token, rather, the symphony's authenticity and ultimate value were seen to stem directly from the distinctiveness of Dvořák's "voice" as a symphonist, so that the symphony was understood first of all as a *Czech* symphony with—perhaps—borrowed "New World" content. Only in this way could Dvořák be rescued from seeming either presumptuous or inauthentic, in addition to being naïve.

The careful fence US Americans built around the "New World" Symphony's idiomatic sources underscores how much more of a problem vernacular content apparently posed for this generation in the United States than in Europe, although from a longer view (as Richard Taruskin has argued; see above), any such materials, when offered as nationalist content within musical genres and forms integral to German traditions, enacted a form of cultural colonialism regardless of what (non-German) "nation" might be involved. In that sense, however, many US Americans were then more than willing to be colonized, musically, as an alternative to the encroachment of vernacular musics whose aims and attitudes were either devoid of the moral uplift promised by the German Idealist aesthetic or actually hostile to it. There was, to be sure, an ugly racial component to some US Americans' willingness to be colonized, manifest in their strong desire to cleave to a European heritage as a bulwark against the onslaught of infectious (and infectant) musics associated with "inferior" races. As expressed without this racial dimension (but surely stemming from it), the moral uplift promised by nineteenth-century European musical traditions, especially those grounded in German Idealism, was felt by many to be jeopardized by the frivolity, frequent mockery, and wanton dance basis of many nascent popular idioms (including, for example, Gilbert and Sullivan operettas imported from England), which were more immediately appealing and left little room for reverence and contemplation.

Translated to the New World, the nationalist component of German Idealism thus began to unravel, in its musical dimension, under strain from what would soon become its most potent nemesis, popular music. According to the German Idealist-nationalist alliance as it took shape in Europe, folk-based material offered both a potential bond uniting a people and, through a parallel fostering of elemental simplicity, a source of aesthetic strength. But this would not do for culturally conscious US Americans, who tried to harness the larger European-based aesthetic in order expressly to *combat* the insidious spread of popular music, which was seen both to undermine morality and to be altogether devoid of aesthetic value. And, again, the "New World" Symphony highlighted the contradiction inherent in the US American project of self-imposed colonization, by harnessing the elemental simplicity of Indianist and spiritual-based materials, which in combination with a similarly conceived Russian dimension contributed to a strong sense of a primitive natural landscape tinged with ancient magic. Arguably, the only real problem with this musical tableau concerned the peoples (that is, the indigenous peoples) who might be understood to inhabit that landscape. What eventually displaced Dvořák's musical image of the US American landscape, some four decades later, in a form suitable for the concert stage and answering to mainstream national myths, was the "empty" soundscape introduced by Aaron Copland, who, once freed of his infatuations with overt jazz idioms in the 1920s, developed his "open plains" idiom in the 1930s and 1940s, and proceeded to "people" it with a variety of European-derived communities in the process of nation building (thus, Shakers, cowboys, and the like).[93]

But neither Copland nor Dvořák—nor any of an array of other "serious" US American composers (including Charles Ives or even the later crossover figure of Leonard Bernstein)—engaged fully with the rich variety of popular musicking that developed in the United States during the late nineteenth century and across the twentieth, often directly antagonistic to European concert and operatic traditions, which seemed to many US Americans either an increasingly quaint if culturally valuable concert tradition (functioning in the manner of a museum, and set apart from day-to-day life) or, in its modernist phase, utterly uncongenial for most audiences to either contemplation or pleasure. The alternative was, indeed, stark. Composers who did work comfortably within popular idioms or genres—such as George Gershwin and his cohort writing for Broadway and Hollywood, and occasionally for the concert or operatic stage—have been routinely discounted as less important than their more "serious" counterparts, most often in the academy but also outside it, among self-appointed guardians of high culture. It is largely this ongoing prejudice that prompts me to undertake in the second half of this book to lay out more clearly how and why popular music engaged antagonistically with the aesthetic agenda of German Idealism, and in the process managed to reclaim, at the price of prestige (if often compensated by commercial success), a quintessentially human function for music.

PART II | HAYDN'S DIFFERENCE

2 | ENTERTAINING POSSIBILITIES IN HAYDN'S SYMPHONIES

The special appeal of Haydn's ensemble chamber works (which will be the object of greater scrutiny in the following chapter) derives from a constellation of pleasures they provide to both performers and listeners. For his performers, Haydn provides an enhanced level of meaningful participation, an often witty engagement with various musical conventions (both formal and syntactical), and an interactive dimension that involves not only highly nuanced interplay with the other performers but also a heightened difference in perspective between the performers and any listeners who might be present. Listeners may readily partake of all of these pleasures, as well, in roughly increasing levels of immediacy; moreover, even if their perspective is necessarily outside the inner space occupied by the performers, they may also share with the performers an appreciation for the twists and turns the music takes as it manipulates convention and expectation, so that shared appreciation, among performers and listeners, may also be counted among the music's proffered pleasures. In all these ways, Haydn's chamber music "entertains" more according to the word's historical derivation ("to hold mutually") than according to modern usage ("to engage").[1]

These musical pleasures, which are also present to varying degrees in Haydn's more elaborate instrumental works, relate to what I term a "dynamic of accommodation," a persistent feature of Haydn's musical sensibility. This dynamic, often rendered in comic terms, involves highly individuated musical elements seemingly at odds with established modes of musical order, but which nevertheless demonstrate their musical competence without having to deny whatever quality originally sets them apart. To put this in a variety of other ways, we might say:

1. that eccentricity generally flourishes in the musical worlds that Haydn creates;
2. that when we encounter the unusual in Haydn, we do not react by thinking, "This can't be right" or "This can't work" but rather by speculating "How is he going to make this work?" or simply waiting to see how he does it;
3. that convention, for Haydn, is configured in terms broad enough that it can allow the eccentric element sufficient room both to define an identity and to prove its musical viability; or,
4. that the eccentrically individual in Haydn is nearly always *presumed* to be musically competent, even if it does not initially appear to be so.

These pleasures, this dynamic, and other elements that combine to make Haydn a "fun" composer do not relate easily to German Idealist aesthetics. Any engagement in the here-and-now of music making—which always plays some part in Haydn's "fun," and which he often virtually insists on—will detract from music's ability to evoke the absolute or to convey to the contemplative listener a sense of connection to the infinite. Fun is a problem for the idealist listener first of all because it interferes on an immediate level with the potential for contemplative engagement. Idealist listeners must either create barriers against this element or listen "past" it for deeper meanings; the only alternative within an idealist context is to give in to the fun and consign Haydn to a lesser position in musical hierarchies. If the first two of these strategies represent the most common approaches of Haydn's musicological defenders, the third alternative points to the inevitable outcome when what passes for a considered defense of Haydn falsifies the "evidence" (that is, his music) through misplaced emphasis.

Consider the "Representation of Chaos" that opens Haydn's *Creation*. In its later stages, including after the entrance of the chorus, it beautifully sets up the sublime moment of Creation itself ("And there was . . . LIGHT"), yet it seems oddly off target for much of its duration in two related respects. First, its "chaos" is too intelligible; too often, we recognize its musical bits and half-formed gestures as broken pieces of something familiar, creating an effect more postapocalypse than precreation.[2] Second, the resultant "constructed" feeling of the piece gives the strong impression of rationality *playing at* being irrational; this dimension of rationalist play in the piece then becomes almost laughable (or perhaps merely more outrageously playful) when, just after the first words that mark the Act of Creation, we "hear" the stage machinery of creation itself, as the single separate stroke of the pizzicato strings suggests the divine equivalent of striking a match or (for later audiences) throwing a switch.[3] **<AE2.1>** From an idealist perspective, there are two main ways of understanding the piece's odd profile: either Haydn is not fully up to the challenge of the occasion, or he is deliberately drawing attention to the artifice of *his own* creation, opting to entertain us—making light, perhaps, of *fiat lux*—rather than allowing a more effective evocation of the void to engulf us with its scary sublimity. Although Waldstein's condescending words to Beethoven about Haydn (see note 74 in chapter 1) predate both *The Creation* and the full emergence of an idealist musical aesthetic, they seem oddly prophetic with regard to this celebrated—yet, for later audiences, disquietingly tame—prelude to Haydn's greatest work, with his perceived lack of "true genius" traceable to his inability to move beyond his own propensity to entertain.

These two features of Haydn's symphonic works—his accommodation of eccentricity and what has often seemed an overly comic tone—are at the crux of what he offered audiences of his time but what would soon be understood as too lightweight for the new paradigms that arose with German Idealism. Of these, the most problematic is tone, which creates, for the idealist listener, the impression that Haydn is either unwilling to give serious topics their due or, perhaps, just a bit too ready to make light of them.

NARRATIVE AND TONE

Many of Haydn's symphonies deploy familiar topics or other evocative musical gestures so as to create a kind of narrative, although the details of such narratives often prove elusive or open to multiple interpretations. At the same time, typically, his arrangement of performed musical events will also suggest a different kind of narrative, perhaps better described as an argument, based more concretely on how the music and its performers engage with a variety of musical conventions. These narrative modes—which we may call "dramatic" and "musical," respectively—interact with each other, with varying levels of mutual accommodation; sometimes they will support, inform, inflect, or adapt to each other, while at other times one will displace or preempt the other. While these two narrative modes must be mutually accountable (since they occupy the same temporal and musical space), they satisfy different imperatives and create different kinds of meanings. However often they may be in at least approximate alignment, there is always potential for opening up a space between them, a kind of expressive disjuncture that must ultimately be managed through the prevailing conventions of genre and through something akin to rhetoric (the latter to be taken up later). In this way, the intersection and possible interaction of the dramatic and musical narrative modes, where they are both palpably present, create much of what we might describe as the *tone* of a symphonic movement, where "tone" may more generally be understood to be the manner in which movements treat their themes, affects, or referential narratives.

It is in this respect that Haydn's flexible treatment of sonata form (as it was later identified) becomes especially significant. In Mozart and Beethoven, whose forms became the basis for the codification of sonata form in the nineteenth century, the imperatives of the form often seem to align with other large-scale imperatives—society, fate, and the like—especially when something individuated seems to be at stake. To this end, the regular features they employ, in conforming to a developing set of conventions, will tend to reinforce such alignments. These regular features are particularly telling in the recapitulation, which most often in Mozart and Beethoven becomes a full-scale *ca*pitulation, as it rehearses in full the progress of themes from the exposition, in their original order but now fully conforming to the sway of the tonic. In minor-key movements, material originally heard in the major will generally return in the minor (though not always), further reinforcing the conformance (seemingly) dictated by the form. Indeed, many apparent exceptions to the latter tendency may be understood, from a longer perspective, merely to capitulate differently to the same imperative. In the first movement of Beethoven's Fifth Symphony, for example, the breakthrough to the major in the recapitulation is tempered through instrumentation (with bassoon substituting for the exposition's dramatic horn call), and the major mode is subsequently rescinded by an extended minor-mode coda.

Haydn's recapitulations are, in contrast, more often thoroughly recomposed versions of his expositions. Most explanations for this practice, which is at odds with many nineteenth-century descriptions of the form (but not eighteenth-century practice), center on his tendency to launch his second group with a transposed, sometimes altered version of the main theme, with a result often described—usually inaccurately—as monothematic.[4] This thematic repetition in the exposition often (but not always) means that the two statements will be collapsed together in some way in the recapitulation so as to avoid redundancy and perhaps monotony. But Haydn's recapitulations have other features that seem unusual according to nineteenth-century codifications of sonata form, as well; for example, he is more apt than Mozart or Beethoven to retain the major mode for a second-group theme in a minor-mode movement, and to incorporate renewed development of his material. No doubt, the standard explanation for the latter has some validity in a "monothematic" sonata form; thus, Haydn's addition of further development serves to balance the durational weight of the exposition in a recapitulation absent one of the exposition's thematic sections. Yet the frequency with which Haydn's recapitulations are substantially shorter than his expositions, combined with other nonnormative features of his forms (such as his "false recapitulations" or occasional early returns to the tonic), point, for modern audiences unfamiliar with late eighteenth-century practices beyond the established canon, to a highly individualized treatment of the form, much more flexible than Mozart's and Beethoven's.[5] While larger forces do impose their will in a Haydn sonata form—for example, he always resolves important material into the tonic, and concludes securely with a cadence to the tonic—the road to that final cadence is by no means predestined, so that his sonata-form movements are necessarily as much about narrative as about balanced thematic groupings and processes, or predetermined outcomes.

Some Haydn sonata-form movements invite dramatic narrative readings more insistently than others. If those less inviting of this mode of engagement scarcely lack for a distinctive tone, there are nevertheless important reasons to focus first, as I will do here, on a symphony that evokes a dramatic narrative with particular force. Such narratives heighten our awareness of tone, which shapes our engagement with both dramatic and musical narratives. Moreover, strongly evocative material in a Haydn symphony has tended to increase the likelihood that the symphony would be "adopted" by early audiences (often acquiring a pet name in the process) and thereafter retain some canonic repertory status.[6] I will thus here first consider at some length a symphony with a strongly marked referential narrative, in which dramatic narrative and tone seem on occasion markedly at odds with each other. In order to highlight this differential, I will in my discussion first consider the dramatic narrative, mostly absent a consideration of tone. Then, in considering how this dramatic narrative comes across to listeners, we will be able to gauge in fuller measure the importance of tone.

NB: In the following and later sections, I interweave somewhat technical discussions of the musical argument with considerations of the suggested dramatic narrative, in order to bring out the alliances and partial disconnects between the two narrative modes. I have provided musically notated examples of some key passages to support this discussion, and included other supporting material on the book's website; see explanatory note at the front of the book.

Symphony No. 100 in G, the "Military"

The "Military" Symphony <TE2.2> earned its nickname primarily from the sudden and surprising intrusion of Janissary instrumentation after the innocent, somewhat naïve musical environment Haydn creates in the first fifty-five bars of the second movement.[7] Yet, if this moment is extremely jarring, it is scarcely unprepared. Almost from the beginning, the symphony engages in unusual and topically related instrumental practices.

Thus, a similar if less extreme intrusion occurs already in the introduction to the first movement, where, as in the second movement, a naïve tone is displaced by the minor mode just at the point of arrival (m. 14), in this case coincident with a dramatic crescendo and the addition of horns and trumpets. The disquieting effect of this *ombra* intrusion colors the remainder of the introduction,[8] with repeated alternations in mm. 19–20 of the same enhanced instrumentation and a ***sf*** clash in the outer voices between C♯ and D, to which a melodic inner voice adds a cross-relating C♮, briefly creating a virtual tone cluster. <AE2.3>

Equally disruptive is the two-bar rest that launches the development in mm. 125f, which sets up an excursion to the ♭VI. Here, the intrusive effect is actually heightened by the reversal in dynamics, as the affirmative arrival on D that concludes the exposition, reinforced by horns and trumpets, is quietly put aside after the hiatus by a new beginning in B♭ major, at first using only lower-register strings, with pizzicato cellos and basses. <AE2.4>

The biggest surprise in the first movement, however, is probably the opening of the exposition proper in m. 24 (see ex. 2.1), where, after a *fortissimo* fermata on the dominant concludes the introduction, three solo winds (one flute and two oboes) playing *piano* in the upper register establish the new *allegro* tempo. **<AE2.5>** This unusual departure from the normal dominance of the strings in symphonies of this time, especially in an opening *allegro*, may be explained in various ways.

First, it provides a significant if oblique preparation for the Janissary outburst in the second movement in its imitation of the military fife, since both invoke the "military" topic reflected in the acquired title of the symphony. This evocation is significantly enhanced by the shift in dynamics and the absence of bass support, which helps to create the momentary impression of distance, as if the fife is heard outdoors and across an open expanse, such as a parade field. The effect of distance, in turn, allows the "fife" music to serve as a spatially removed background for the response in the strings, which is foregrounded not only by virtue of the upper strings' placement in front of the winds in conventional orchestra seatings (both then and ever since), but also by its more conventional sound as a four-voice string choir playing in a comfortable middle range, even if still *piano* and not fully "grounded," lacking basses and the deeper notes of the cellos.

Second, the opening provides, in its broader outlines, a simple expansion on what was for Haydn a familiar strategy: proceeding from a dramatic slow introduction to a quiet *allegro* theme, setting up a *forte* orchestral *tutti* that elides with that theme's concluding cadence.[9] Here, the quiet opening proceeds in two stages as noted, setting up the *tutti* in m. 39 as an arrival within a spatial realm in addition to its more generic formal function, as it collapses foreground into background and brings the "distant" wind sound into suddenly close proximity.

Third, the three-voice wind group functions as a *concertante* element within the first movement, recalling to Haydn's London audience the *Symphonie concertante* they had heard near the end of his previous visit, in March 1792,[10] but also offering a harbinger of the concerted dynamic that will take over the second movement. And, fourth, the increased importance of the winds within the orchestra—especially when treated as an independent group, as here—represents an important trend in symphonic writing, traceable also in the symphonies and concertos of Mozart and Beethoven, and, in this case, understandable in part as a response to the

Ex. 2.1: Haydn, "Military" Symphony, mvt. 1, mm. 24–39

performance capacities of his London musicians, and to their audience's taste for a larger scale and more varied orchestral palette.[11]

The opening of the exposition of the first movement thus prepares the later introduction of Janissary instruments in specific ways. Not only does it contribute to a "military" topic, but it also takes up the dynamic of assimilated intrusion that was established in the introduction, now presented in *concertante* terms. Indeed, this dynamic, especially involving a concerted or *concertante* dimension, connects the most unusual features of the symphony, and on a level more abstractly musical than the *ombra* topic, simulated fife music, and the use of "Janissary" instrumentation. Much of what happens in the first movement, for example, may be well understood in terms of concerted trajectories of intrusion and assimilation, which govern the deployment of the conventional formal patterns of introduction, sonata-form exposition, and so forth.

In the introduction, the intrusion in m. 14 is thus "assimilated" within the exchanges in mm. 19–20, and grounded within the reinforced half cadence of the final bars. Later intrusions in the first movement—in particular those involving the "fife" instruments—lack the feeling of genuine threat present in the introduction, due to a prevailing cheerful tone reinforced throughout by the major mode and faster tempo. Yet they are handled as carefully as if they were every bit as dire as the intrusion in the introduction, and we do well, from a musico-narrative standpoint, to regard the intrusions as serious business, notwithstanding the lighthearted tone (an apparent disjuncture of narrative and tone to which I will return).

In the exposition, the opening "fife" music, initially echoed in the strings and dissipated in the culminating *tutti* of m. 39, returns undeterred to mark the arrival in the dominant in m. 73. At this point, the process of assimilation begins in earnest, as the fife theme, even before concluding its first phrase, provokes a challenge from the strings, who now play in the same register (m. 81). After this initial challenge, a conversational exchange begins between the foregrounded strings and intruding winds—more a negotiation than a conversation, really, but then there is always something being negotiated in Haydn's "conversations." Although the exchange is brief, and even polite, there is apparently much at stake, as both sides are augmented—backed up by basses and bassoons, respectively—and their interchange made to feel more urgent due to an acceleration of the units of exchange from two bars to one. Then, just as the winds attempt to continue the fife theme, they are cut off by an assertion of authority, as the *tutti* beginning in m. 87, dominated by strings and notably lacking the distinctive timbre of the flute, takes up the fife theme, destabilizes it harmonically, and carries us directly into the restored normality of a new theme introduced to launch the closing thematic group (m. 93). **<AE2.6>** At this point, "assimilation" is complete: as a characteristic low-string accompaniment launches the new theme, the winds are consigned to a subordinate role wholly in keeping with established symphonic practice.

In brief, then, the conventional events of a sonata-form exposition are remapped according to a trajectory of intrusion and assimilation, as follows:

first group: intruding fife theme in upper winds, answered by midrange strings
bridge: *tutti* arrival, forcing an alliance between intrusion and foreground
second group: returning fife theme, engaged more urgently by the strings / *tutti* liquidation of fife theme ("purple patch")[12]
closing group: new theme with more conventional orchestral setting

The development extends this kind of mapping of narrative onto convention. Most of the development is based on the closing group, and moves, broadly, within a tight chromatic compass, from ♭VI/V (B♭), through V/v (A), to V/vi (B), the latter being a conventional destination for the development of a major-mode movement. After an emphatic half cadence in vi (that is, to B as V/e; m. 196), the retransition begins, based initially on the fife theme in the middle range. Two-bar alternations between winds and strings briefly reestablish and then dissemble the original fife instrumentation; thus, we first hear four-voice winds in the middle range, then the original instrumentation and register, then oboes echoed by bassoons. At the same time, the fife theme becomes increasingly fragmented, until it reduces to the figure shared by both it and the theme from the closing group (beginning with the oboe/bassoon alternation in m. 177). These processes complete, the winds return to a subordinate position within a *tutti* dominant preparation for the return (mm. 183–199). **<AE2.7>**

Haydn's procedure here, of reintroducing less stable versions of the exchanges and thematic material from the second group and closing group, which defined the final assimilation of the fife theme in the exposition, might reasonably have been employed as a means to return to the opening condition, in order to set up a recapitulation in parallel to the exposition. Such a strategy would have been eminently logical in musical

Ex. 2.2: Haydn, "Military" Symphony, mvt. 1, mm. 195–203

terms, but would have to a large extent denied reality to the dramatic narrative of assimilation, in effect behaving (narratively speaking) as if nothing had happened. On this basis alone we may well understand Haydn following his more usual procedure for "monothematic" sonata forms of conflating the first and second groups in the recapitulation. But these broad strategies are less immediately relevant here than musical detail, which simply does not allow us to lose awareness of the movement's narrative progress. In the final stages of the interplay during the retransition, as the fife instruments answer to the strings in the foreground, the sense of the exchange is redefined within the context of assimilation. The result is a kind of double image at the point of recapitulation: while the formal downbeat in m. 202 is unmistakable, it occurs almost in midstride, before the fife instruments have completed their response to the strings seven bars earlier (see ex. 2.2):

Plausibly, the fife theme might be heard at this point as an extended, augmented version of the lower-neighbor-note figure that opens the closing-group theme. Even in the original thematic ordering, in the exposition, the latter figure derives audibly from the fife theme, but that derivation matters less than the effect of newness at that point. Now, however, it stands fully revealed, and the apparent hierarchical order of derivation is reversed. The lower-neighbor-note figure is much worried over throughout the retransition, until it eventually converts to an oscillation between upper and lower neighbors for the passage shown in ex. 2.2, at which point it provides a smaller-scale preecho of the fife theme.

Far from reestablishing the opening condition, then, the retransition effectively grounds the returning fife theme within the normalized textures and the principal thematic material of the closing group. In this way, the intruder has been thoroughly domesticated by the time it launches the recapitulation, and is easily brought into check by the ensuing *tutti* (beginning m. 210), which moves quickly from its original show of force to a brief rehearsal of the previous cycle of assimilation. **‹AE2.8›**

Accordingly, the recapitulation first reinforces the response to the fife theme with lower winds, brass, timpani, and lower strings in the ensuing dialogue passages (mm. 216–225), then proceeds directly into the complacency of the closing group, substituting a coda-like excursion in m. 239 for the *tutti* that had concluded the exposition. Just before this excursion, Haydn indulges a brief, seemingly symbolic reversal of roles, as the fife instruments (reinforced by bassoon) follow the strings in a brief echo of the closing theme (beginning m. 233). Yet even with this echo, the 101-bar trajectory of the exposition reduces to a mere thirty-seven bars of recapitulation, so that it will fall to the excursion/coda to give a balancing durational weight to the reprise, by reviewing, extending, and resolving the harmonic digressions of the development—thus beginning in E♭ (♭VI/G) and continuing and extending the theme of the closing group. However central the intrusion of the fife music is to the basic dramatic trajectory of the movement, it plays no part in the coda, which, at fifty-one bars, is considerably longer than the recapitulation proper.

At first consideration, narrative and tone in the first movement seem in reasonable alignment. The assimilation of the fife element into textures and formal procedures that are, for Haydn, fairly normative, provides a trajectory that in itself enforces alignment between the two narrative modes. Yet we may well wonder why a referential narrative concerning military fifes, after an introduction of significantly dire portent, is so exceedingly cheerful, and proceeds so readily toward assimilation. In this sense, the musical effect of light, even birdlike wind instruments playing in an upper register and in the major mode seems to render the referent threat of an approaching military force entirely irrelevant, lacking even a ceremonial or parade-based connection to war, unless, perhaps, we imagine the military presence to be a completely benign one, as with a local militia on parade. Nevertheless, we have been fairly warned in the introduction of something much more dire, and will soon get confirmation (in the second movement) that the threat is more serious than the first movement's overall tone lets on, against which the local militia (if that's what the first movement's military presence is) will prove no match.

The second movement, which introduces Janissary instruments (cymbals, bass drum, and triangle, supported by timpani and trumpets) as an intruding element, is transcribed directly from the central movement of Haydn's Third Concerto for Two Lire Organizzate, composed in 1786–1787 on a commission from the King of Naples; the symphony movement follows the concerto movement precisely until the end of the earlier version, after which, in m. 152, a trumpet fanfare launches a coda that has no referent in the earlier version. Given the fife element in the first movement and the return of the Janissary instruments in the finale, it seems probable that the symphony was planned around this adaptation of the earlier movement, and that the first movement, in particular, was composed with this continuation in mind. In the concerto movement, both the naïve tone of the opening and the minor-mode intrusion are reinforced by the primitive, hurdy-gurdy-like solo instruments, which combine (either together or separately) a bowed string sound and wind pipes, at their most strident sounding somewhat like bagpipes, at their mildest as bowed upper strings without vibrato. Although there are no indications in the original version for switching between these sound options, there is ample opportunity for doing so both before the minor-mode episode and before the retransition, so that something like the Janissary effect in the symphonic version was probably planned for the original as well.[13]

Haydn's good-humored response to the commission to compose these concertos, for which his patient tolerance of Prince Esterházy's devotion to the baryton undoubtedly helped condition him, apparently led him in some cases to downplay the incongruous profile the paired lire organizzate present against a more refined sound world, and in others (such as in this movement) to exploit it. In the former case, the lira organizzata might appear as a charming emblem of rusticity, in the latter as a Bottom-like buffoon unaware that its low-culture aping of high culture could seem humorously out of place. Indeed, in an earlier symphonic borrowing from these concerti (in the second and fourth movements of Symphony no. 89 in F, adapted in 1787 from the Fourth Concerto in the same key), Haydn preserves both elements.

Something of this dual effect is reproduced in the second movement of the "Military" Symphony, as well, but Haydn ups the ante considerably by confronting us with militant Turks instead of country bumpkins. Already at the outset of the movement, Haydn sets us up for a fall, deriving the complacent, naïve tone of the opening from the smugness of the previous movement's ending. The movement opens comfortably in the subdominant of the previous movement (C)—a common enough choice for the slow movement in a symphony—taking up, in its leading motive, the turn figure that marked the first attempt to assimilate the fife music in the exposition of the first movement (see ex. 2.3).[14] <AE2.9> Haydn's manipulation of this figure across the second movement will help shape the dynamic between naïveté and outside threat; thus, for example, retrograde-inversion later refashions this figure into an uneasy major-mode response to the initial entrance of the Janissary instruments (mm. 61f), and thence, with the return of the Janissary instruments and the minor mode in m. 70, so as to mock this response with a menacing sneer. <AE2.10> At the opening of the movement, however, the figure is entirely complacent, and the extended binary form of the opening theme affords ample opportunity for Haydn to settle even further into this complacent idiom, as the pastoral tone of the winds, led by the oboes, is increasingly allowed to dominate in repetitions (mm. 9–15 and 37–56), representing not only the generic pastoral but also the domesticated fife from the first movement, its threat now—seemingly—fully dissipated.

Significantly, Haydn adds a pair of clarinets for this movement (and only for this movement), most obviously in order to enhance the pastoral tone of the opening, but also to add muscle to the less benign wind presence that will reemerge later in the movement, a potential that their early alignment with the pastoral does much to disguise. But it is the flutes who have the central role in the transmutation of the winds' representational significance from the rustic to the martial. The flutes add their tone to that of the strings early on to enhance the *semplice* tone of the opening, and

Ex. 2.3: Haydn, "Military" Symphony, mvt. 1, mm. 38–39, and mvt. 2, mm. 1–2

to allow the independent wind band—which, without the flutes, consists entirely of reed instruments (oboes, clarinets, and bassoons)—to project more effectively a tone of rustic simplicity, perhaps evoking the original lira organizzata setting of the movement. Later in the movement, the flutes will reunite with the oboes within the new order that will soon be imposed by the Janissary instruments, and it is within this environment that the clarinet presence provides an additional source of power not available in the first movement.

Once complacency is shattered with the entrance of the Janissary instruments in m. 57, the interplay of established normalcy and disruptive intruder becomes the central preoccupation of the movement, with shifting instrumental alignments playing a central role. The initial appearance of the Janissary instruments, with full *tutti* and an abrupt turn to the minor mode, lasts less than four bars; the immediate aftermath is a temporary escape to the relative major (m. 61), with an anxious conversational exchange between winds and strings reaching a temporary stability in which the reunited "fife" instruments (flute and oboes) remain suspended above growling bass oscillations (m. 65). This moment of uneasy equilibrium is abruptly shattered, however, when the Janissary instruments reassert themselves in a four-bar arpeggiation of V/c (m. 70; see ex. 1 in Appendix A), after which they continue to play quietly, as if to supervise the acquiescent march of the strings to a C-minor close in m. 80; in this supervisory role, they are joined by the winds, who preside over the strings' retreat with repetitions of the turn motive. That the retreat is, indeed, a reluctant one is confirmed by the implied protest of the ascending violin line and the final outcry of an anguished diminished sonority in m. 78, just before the quiet cadence. This passage, from the Janissary bluster on V/c (m. 70) to the docile string cadence in C minor, is then repeated with slight changes to close the middle section, confirming that the Janissary intruder has, in effect, imposed a coup d'etat, in which the strings, representing normalcy, have been subdued, while the fife instruments (flute with oboes, now with the addition of the clarinets), have regrouped and, once again, become a dominating presence. **<AE2.11>**

The details of Haydn's instrumentation are, at times, apparently inconsistent with this scenario. The "normal" strings, for example, are also a part of the *tutti* that supports the loud entrances of the Janissary instruments, an instance (fairly common in orchestral music) of some instruments or combinations of instruments having to play multiple dramatic roles, or, as in this case, doubling as a member of a crowd. Clearly, however, it is the *tutti*, not its individual components, that is meant to register here as the relevant dramatic presence, an inference borne out by the fact that every *tutti* passage in this movement involves Janissary instruments. Possibly more problematic are the violas' doubling of one of the oboes during the winds' motivic reiterations in mm. 74–78 and 85–89, at the same time that the other oboe is doubling the acquiescent violin line. In this apparent crossing of enemy lines, as with the strings' role in the Janissary *tutti*, sonority is the issue; on the one hand, the oboe needs the weight of the viola for balance in its exchanges with the flute and clarinet, while, on the other, the oboe provides a plaintive edge to the lamenting violin line. The oboe is thus called upon at various moments in this movement to represent rusticity (with the lower reeds), military fife (with the flute), and lamentation (with the strings); according to these manipulations of the oboe's varied topical personae, the fastest change of costume is about to occur, as the movement reverts immediately after the cadence in m. 91 to its rustic guise, coincident with the return to the major and the opening folklike theme.

As with the recapitulation in the first movement, this return only masquerades as a restoration of the opening condition. Although the return initially presents itself as a reprise of the reed version of the tune, this time with the strings offering *pizzicato* support, this presentation of the theme systematically keeps the strings in a subordinate position throughout, even though the fife instrumentation is withheld until the late stages. Initially, the displacement of the strings to a lower order of importance is reinforced by an enhanced horn presence, in mm. 92–99, expanding a distinctive horn figure introduced briefly near the end of the first version of the theme (mm. 49–50). The second phrase of the theme (beginning in m. 100) offers a subtle reworking of the opening texture, in which the flute had doubled the strings; here, the flute tone dominates, with clarinet support and with the violins doubling in a lower octave in token of their lower position within the new order. **<AE2.12>**

Only with the return to the opening phrase in mm. 112f, however, do we get full confirmation that this is no simple return within a ternary arrangement but, rather, a continuation of the coup narrative. In a move perhaps more dramatically shocking than the original appearance of the Janissary instruments (if, however, even more reasonable from a musical perspective), Haydn at this point brings them back to endorse this triumphant version of the main tune, now played by flute, oboe, and horn—the favored instruments in the new order—with the violins playing in a purely accompanimental role. Like the final phrase of the middle section, this culminating phrase is repeated; before this repeat, within a bridge passage played out over a tonic pedal, the fife instruments re-create the defining oscillating textures of the fife from the first movement (mm. 123–125;

Ex. 2.4: Haydn, "Military" Symphony, mvt. 2, mm. 120–128

see ex. 2.4), followed by negotiating exchanges that seem directly transplanted from the first movement, now with the clarinets substituting for the strings (beginning in m. 125). <AE2.13>

Yet, the narrative does not simply conclude, as did the first movement, by confirming the new order. It *seems* to conclude in this manner, coming to a full close in m. 152 in precisely the way that the original concerto movement did, but Haydn seizes this opportunity to provide another stunning coup de théâtre that is also, once again, referentially a military coup; after a half-measure pause, the trumpets enter with a fanfare that can be understood only as representing a new presence, unprepared except, perhaps, by the overly complacent tone of the preceding passage. While it is not entirely clear with whom the trumpets are aligned, they are clearly *not* aligned with the Janissary instruments,[15] who have just seen their coup to an apparent conclusion; rather, they facilitate a stunning reemergence of the strings, whose electrifying arpeggiation of the ♭VI (A♭) allows them a presence in the *tutti* response to the trumpet fanfare (beginning m. 161) at least equal to that of the Janissary instruments, which have dominated every previous *tutti* in the movement. This sudden appearance of A♭ in itself recalls the first movement, in which similar excursions to the ♭VI marked each ascension of the "normal" string-dominated textures (thus, immediately following the exposition and recapitulation). **‹AE2.14›**

The culminating *tutti* passages for the two sets of exchanges that conclude the movement, each led by the strings but completed by the upper winds, vividly recall the world of opera buffa, suggesting, specifically, a tableau of opposing parties in a two-act drama staring each other down as the curtain falls on the first act. Arguably, this impression of a buffa atmosphere may itself be deliberately referential, since the scenario traced above closely resembles the plot of what has long been celebrated as the apex of this tradition: the second-act finale in Mozart's *Le nozze di Figaro* (the midpoint of the four-act opera), an opera Haydn had hoped to stage at Eszterháza a few years earlier.[16] In Mozart's finale, as in the first two movements of Haydn's "Military" Symphony, conventional authority initially maintains the upper hand against a perceived threat, until the addition of reinforcements brings about a temporary reversal of power; ultimately, an unprepared intrusion leaves the outcome in doubt by challenging the usurper and restoring substantial power to conventional authority. The deployment of the key players for these parallel plot developments is summarized in table 2.1.

Quite apart from this parallel, which encompasses both tone and narrative structure (but not narrative content), there is a broad correspondence between the events of this movement and the military events that established the political dominance of the Habsburg Dynasty over a large swath of central Europe, a little over a century before Haydn's symphony. The Habsburgs, centered in Vienna, had maintained dominion over much of this territory since the early sixteenth century, following the partitioning of Hungary after its defeat by the Ottoman Empire's Suleiman the Magnificent in the Battle of Mohács (1526) and the Turks' unsuccessful siege of Vienna in 1529. Continued conflicts with the Ottoman Empire over the next century and a half came to a head in 1683, when for two

Table 2.1: Deployment of Key Players in *Le nozze di Figaro* and "Military" Symphony

	LE NOZZE DI FIGARO	"MILITARY" SYMPHONY
Conventional authority	Count	string-dominated textures
Perceived threat, initially defeated	Countess	fife instruments
Reinforcements, effecting reversal	Susanna	Janissary instruments
Unprepared usurpers	Bartolo, Marcellina, and Basilio, allied with the Count against Susanna, the Countess, and Figaro	trumpet fanfare, inciting the strings against the Janissary-fife alliance

months the Turks again besieged Vienna, before the city and its remaining residents and troops were rescued—literally at the last hour—by the arrival of an international force led by King Sobieski of Poland. The Battle of Vienna proved decisive, and soon led to the expulsion of the Turks from Europe.[17]

The late eighteenth-century popularity of the "Turkish," or "Janissary" musical topic, which forms the basis for this movement's intrusions, sprang directly from these events. In Haydn's generation of Austrian-based composers, the central repertory work to employ the topic extensively—*Die Entführung aus dem Serail* (*The Abduction from the Seraglio*, 1782)—anticipated the centenary of the Battle of Vienna by one year, and participated in a fetishizing of things Turkish (or, as in opera and music more generally, merely "Turkish") that had been ongoing since well before the Battle of Vienna itself. Haydn himself employed the topic in two of his operas, in association with a comic disguise in *Lo speziale* (*The Apothecary*, 1768), and more extensively in *L'incontro improvviso* (*The Unexpected Encounter*, 1775). As even this small sampling indicates, musical practices ranged widely, from purely comic engagements with the topic to attempts to represent Turks more directly, through an Orientalist idiom that could be taken for Turkish mostly because of its style (either military or primitive, or both) and a crude approximation of the instrumentarium of the Janissary band: bass drum, cymbals, triangle, and shawmlike double-reed instruments, with the frequent addition of piccolo to enhance the effect of shrillness.[18]

The second movement of the "Military," especially in conjunction with the first movement's "fife" music, thus raises a number of issues relating to narrative and tone, evoking in the same musical space the buffa style and a specific narrative of quite serious import—remembering that, for Vienna and the other European powers who fought against the Turks a century earlier, the latter represented a barbarous threat to the very core of not only existing political power but also Christianity, the Renaissance, and European civilization itself. The Battle of Vienna, in expunging this threat, was seen by many in Haydn's generation as the direct antecedent to the Enlightenment. And even on a personal level, the buffa tone seems incongruous, since Haydn's paternal great-grandparents were victims of the Turks' massacre of civilians in Hainburg, and his grandparents on both sides saw firsthand the devastation the Turks brought as they burned this and other towns to the ground just prior to their siege of Vienna in 1683.[19] Thus, the second movement seems to trivialize through tone what ought not to be trivialized, to make light of what is by any measure deadly serious. The remaining movements of the symphony, at first reckoning, do little to resolve this apparent disjuncture between narrative and tone.

The third movement, for the most part, resembles a fully typical minuet-trio. Although a *tutti* interjection intrudes briefly on the otherwise quiet trio, and although the minuet's tread is often a bit heavy, the movement is in line with Haydn's usual practice, since he often indulges a touch of incongruity or otherwise undermines the characteristic elegance of the minuet as a type.[20] Even with only these minor departures from the norm, however, Haydn extends the ongoing narrative thread, supported by an overt motivic reference to earlier movements. The opening turn figure of the minuet—which becomes its principal motive—derives from the main theme of the second movement (itself derived from the first movement, as noted), asserting an immediate connection to what has come before. Then, more subtly, Haydn alters the repetition of the first phrase of the minuet, which is given first as a *tutti* (*forte*, with trumpets and timpani reinforcement), by placing it within a more delicately etched texture (*piano*, with reduced instrumentation), so as to provide something like a refined echo of the gruff opening. **<AE2.15>** While the heavy-footedness of the first iteration of this phrase might suggest the *Ländler*, as in other Haydn minuets—for example, those of Haydn's final three London symphonies, nos. 102–104—the effect here is more that of unwitting parody, as if the unrefined were aping the refined—or, given the order of presentation, that the latter were correcting the former by example. This effect would seem to be the specific point of the repeated juxtapositions, which, because they are written out, must be performed in full even when other structural repeats are not taken.[21]

One senses here a vexed scenario of assimilation, an attempt to "teach" refinement to those who cannot appreciate it, with the long chromatic "sigh" just before the return of the opening phrase (mm. 35–42) acknowledging the inherent frustrations of the task. **‹AE2.16›** It is perhaps ambiguous who precisely these lowbrows are: that they are not Austrian, falling into *Ländler* rhythms, would perhaps not matter much to Haydn's London audience, who could as easily take them to be working class, town folk, or rough-edged foreigners. But the trio clarifies this ambiguity. In the trio overall, delicacy leads the way, with a *semplice* theme of lightly tripping dotted rhythms, establishing a style that holds throughout except for a rude interjection just before the return (mm. 68–71). The interjection takes over the dotted rhythm for four bars of a brutish, *forte tutti* (thus, again with trumpets and timpani), transforming the delicate rhythm into a rough military tattoo, tinged with a Turkish overlay through the imposition of the minor mode and the melodic use of the harmonic minor scale, whose distinctive augmented second had long served Western European composers as a marker for the "East." **‹AE2.17›** After this clarification, heard twice as part of the trio's binary structure, the returning minuet acquires a more precisely understood dynamic between refinement and its Other—a dynamic that is, as in the second movement, neither resolved well nor treated with the gravity one might expect regarding the projected invasion by a barbarous military force.

In broad terms, the finale pushes the discrepancy between narrative and tone to an even greater extreme. It partakes freely of the blustery bustle and comic misdirection that typically characterizes the second half of an opera buffa, refers frequently (if briefly) to the conflicts of the earlier movements, and at the end brings back the Janissary instruments, thereby inviting comparison to the last-minute, comic defeat of the Count in *Figaro*, following the parallel noted above. Given the reversed dynamic outlined above, however, in which the Turks assume the sympathetic plot position of Susanna, Figaro, and the Countess, the symphony would seem to end, surprisingly, with a rousing celebration of their victory. If we are to take the ongoing narrative seriously, which in its earlier stages parallels the culminating events of the barbarous Ottoman military adventure in Europe, this ending is on the face of it quite distressing and by eighteenth-century standards even immoral, all the more so since the tone is overwhelmingly comic. And yet, it has never been taken that way, even by those early audiences who reacted with something like terror to the initial introduction of the Janissary instruments in the second movement.[22] How do we explain this?

We might begin by revisiting the minuet to ask (if only rhetorically): When—other than in a Haydn symphony—would one find nearly vanquished citizens teaching their barbaric would-be conquerors how to dance?[23] Yet, the logic of the projected situation is unassailable: with dance standing in (from a European perspective) for civilized behavior more broadly, such is precisely the gesture most appropriate to Europe's Enlightenment project, and directly parallel to the missionary impulse. The gesture is at once optimistic according to notions of "progress," and complacently, unconsciously Orientalist. If we were to understand the symphony's dramatic development as straightforward narrative, we might reasonably understand the minuet as an attempt to resolve, through civil processes of interaction, the standoff at the end of the second movement. But this politico-philosophical grounding seems somewhat beside the point. While it was surely important, for both Haydn and his audiences, for the symphony's narrative to line up with Enlightenment values (if not so well to historical fact), such an alignment is asserted first of all and unassailably by the music's tone. Turks on a musical stage, whether in London, Vienna, or Eszterháza, were after all just Western Europeans in colorful costumes and elaborate makeup—and that description not only serves as an apt metaphor for the more tolerant of Enlightenment beliefs but also applies equally well, if still figuratively, to most deployments of traditional Turkish musical topics.

Thus, the simplest explanation is probably the best. The comic tone of the minuet and finale—indeed, of all four movements—does not permit us to hear the ending as a victory for the Turks, which would in eighteenth-century terms have been a tragedy understandable only as part of a catastrophic alternative history of Europe. The finale presents a striking demonstration that tone cannot be separated from narrative as easily as might be supposed; rather, the one directly imposes on the other. In this case, the tone of the ending, well supported by the instrumentation, which joins rather than opposes its Janissary component, tells us that *both* Turks and Europeans celebrate *together.* <AE2.18> There is no triumph of one over the other, but instead a mutual triumph. The question then becomes: How did we move, and so quickly, from a narrative of narrowly averted conquest to one of apparent assimilation and joyous coexistence?

We didn't, of course; in the context of musical comedy—a context established, in a symphony, by tone—these narratives merge seamlessly. But if we are to understand tone as having this kind of narrative consequence, we must make two initial adjustments to the dramatic narrative basis I've advanced here for the first two movements of the symphony. The first adjustment is to assume that *there is no disparity between tone and dramatic narrative*; this adjustment occasions the second, which is a drastically revised narrative account of the symphony, reoriented around the prevailing comic tone.

There are really only two places in the symphony where a darker tone might be heard to reinforce a serious narrative regarding the conquest, or the potential conquest, of a benign populace by a brutish invader: the early appearance of the foreboding *ombra* topic in the first movement, and the reenactment of the invasion itself in the second. The latter is indeed a fairly long narrative stretch unto itself, and for most listeners will represent the most memorable sequence in the symphony. Moreover, the early, introductory portent cannot be *simply* put aside, given that what it portends does eventually happen. Yet, the portent and its realization fail to achieve any kind of tragic synergy. While we might imagine, abstractly, that the Janissary intrusions in the second movement vindicate anyone who has taken the forebodings of the introduction to the first movement seriously, it is hard to imagine that many listeners would even remember those portents, viscerally, given the ebullience of the intervening *allegro* and the shock of the Janissary intrusion itself, which is in any case very different in kind from the *ombra* intrusion at the outset. Each of these is in its turn firmly put aside, largely through tone.

In the case of the second movement, where brutality emerges most palpably, and for a time triumphantly, the presentation of violence (or threatened violence) is secondary to a kind of musical engagement that is basic to how tone operates in Haydn's symphonies: Haydn is first of all playing to an audience of musicians and concertgoers. This circumstance both motivates and regulates his easily observed tendencies to gratify his musicians and audiences and, more specifically, to engage them through logical deception, that is, through dramatic surprises that might be absorbed into an ongoing musical argument and which, while calculated to surprise, may even be anticipated by those who understand the game well.

And what is that game? For an audience, it is to recognize and respond appropriately to a narrative mode based in exaggeration, with each exaggerated state tending to be a set up for its opposite. Thus, (exaggerated) complacency yields to the (exaggerated) shattering of complacency. Quiet passages set up massive *tutti* effects, and the reverse. In the case of this symphony, the dark foreboding at the beginning yields to a cheerful *allegro* in which a potential militaristic threat transmutes into a birdlike deployment of fifelike instruments, textures, and musical material. And the complacency of the second movement's opening pastoral virtually begs to be shattered. From this perspective, the movement's Janissary intrusions have much more in common with the "Surprise" Symphony's famous *ff* than with the Janissary passage in Beethoven's Ninth Symphony or even the *alla Turca* finale of Mozart's A-major Piano Sonata, K. 331. It is not the reference to Turks that matters *first of all*, but what they facilitate in terms of elaborately staged contrasts, a principle that applies equally well to both the operatic stage and this symphony. But the reference to Turks does matter *in the end*, for the game also entails an eventual rationalization of those contrasts, whether abstractly (say, within a theme-and-variation structure as in the "Surprise" Symphony) or in terms of dramatic narrative, as here and on the operatic stage.

In the "Military" Symphony, the Turks are introduced in part as a quasi-plausible consequence of the *ombra* introduction and simulated fife music of the first movement, but mainly as an exaggerated, contrasting reaction to the complacent pastoral opening of the second movement. Once introduced, they must be rationalized, which happens initially within the topsy-turvy plotting of the second movement. But in the final movements, they become a comically exaggerated version of out-of-town guests from the provinces, who may not know the dance steps but are more than willing to try. As such, they are at first indulged with a whiff of exasperation, but through their "disarming" enthusiasm eventually win over their more sophisticated hosts. Importantly, they win out, not through military conquest, but through their colorful musical costumes and their basic humanity, reminding the audience, on whatever level they need reassurance, that the Turks are just like them underneath.[24]

Within Haydn's symphonic milieu, the relationship between tone and narrative must in the end resolve in favor of tone. Both parts of this equation matter: there must be a resolution, and it must remain faithful to a well-established overall tone, which—in Haydn's mature comic style—will usually entail a widely appreciated dynamic of contrast and exaggeration, as noted. Tone thus functions as part of genre, determining what kinds of dramatic narrative may be effectively presented, and dictating how we are to experience and understand those dramatic narratives as they unfold. Within a dynamic akin to that of high camp, which will emerge on the other side of the German Idealism divide as a parallel means for permitting the comic presentation of serious topics (see part 3, especially chapters 4 and 6), it is this tone of comic exaggeration, which is most pronounced in Haydn's most cherished works, that places him decidedly at odds with the musical values that evolved in tandem with German Idealism across the nineteenth century.[25]

HAYDN AS PHILOSOPHICAL "OTHER"

Haydn's tone of comic exaggeration is critical to the "dynamic of accommodation" I refer to at the opening of this chapter. Exaggeration, as a strategy, tends to broaden the range of what can be assimilated into (or rationalized within) musical discourse, the latter standing in for ordered society (among other possible metaphorical referents). Thus, the "Military" Symphony and many other Haydn symphonies that maintain a similar tone and dynamic provide vivid examples of what David Schroeder has argued for Haydn's symphonic music more generally: that they argue for tolerance, while presenting themselves as entertainments.[26] In fundamental ways, both the musical argument for tolerance and the mode of presentation are significantly at odds with the agenda that German Idealism sets for music.

Music's supreme task, for the idealist, is to collapse the distance between subjectivity and the infinite; accordingly, in contemplating music, we merge with something larger, or at least are given a taste of what such a merger might be like. If something stands between the subjectivity of the individual and the infinite, it is largely irrelevant to that larger project except as it may be perceived to interfere with it, or can be enlisted in support of it. While an idealist must in some way account for and accommodate human societal relations and the phenomenal world, such concerns stand outside what counts musically, from an idealist perspective, for several reasons.

In broad terms, society matters to the idealist either because it might be seen to mirror subjectivity in some sense, or because it provides a placeholder for the infinite, taking the specific nearer forms, for example, of collective consciousness, or nation. Within such understandings, however, it is not society's *order* that matters, but rather the fact that society comprises humans who share something fundamental. This is the basis for the German distinction, used as a weapon against the French, between *Kultur* and *Zivilisation*.[27] Moreover, eccentricities, seen as departures from actual or idealized norms, interfere with rather than support the alignment of subjectivity with whatever larger projection is seen to matter at a given time and from a given perspective. Indeed, it is specifically because that larger projection is, indeed, always a *projection* (rather than something observed directly), based ultimately on the model of subjectivity (hence, potentially in alignment with subjectivity) and governed by the categorical imperative (hence, specifically *not* eccentric), that German Idealism has tended more toward intolerance than tolerance, despite the grounding Christianity has provided for the latter.

In musical terms, German Idealism charts a course away from top-down organization (that is, maintaining clearly balanced formal control, as in poetry) toward bottom-up organization (favoring motivic development and musical argument, as in prose). This evolution may be traced, with vivid precision, by observing the striking differences in musical language and organization between and among Mozart ("poetic" form), Beethoven (prose-based poetic form), and Wagner (musical prose).[28] As I have argued elsewhere, this line of development is directly in line with the demotion of societal order in favor of the subjective and its larger projections.[29] But entertainment, along with societal order, is also demoted in the process, first of all because entertainment tends to serve the interests of existing societal norms, even when it critiques them. More basically, entertainment engages through surfaces rather than through the newly prized potential for finding deeper meanings in music, accessible through individual contemplation (rather than laughter, shared visceral excitement, and other social pleasures). Music that entertains will thus always seem opposed to the specific way that music could provide the gateway to both the infinite and a deeper sense of self.

Haydn, by contrast, privileges eccentricity, which we experience neither as "us" (except by a mental process of abstraction) nor as "something larger" but rather as something irrevocably separate from us and confined to a human scale (perhaps, from the perspective of German Idealism, "all too human"). While the dynamic that accommodates such eccentricity may reassure us that our own oddities and shortcomings may be similarly tolerated, we are never overtly invited to identify strongly with the eccentric—quite the opposite, since its eccentricity is perceptible as such only from a presumed external, normalized perspective.

In a stretch, we might argue that Mark Evan Bonds's "Music as Thought" paradigm (see chapter 1) accommodates many of the procedures and musical experiences that contribute to this dimension of Haydn's music. Thus, certainly, Haydn's music follows a coherent "argument," as the basis for both his sometimes oppositional engagement with convention, and his ability to inspire our trust in his musical stewardship; in this he is most powerfully Beethoven's antecedent. Moreover, it is this aspect of Haydn's musical discourse that has consistently secured for him at least some share in the prestige accorded the German "masters," and has helped his music maintain at least some repertorial and musicological presence over the past two centuries. As I argue in the previous chapter, however, to valorize this proto-idealist dimension of Haydn's music at the expense of its more immediately appealing features is to shortchange both his music and the basis for his most devoted musical following.

But if not German Idealism, then what philosophical perspective grounds Haydn's music?

As David Schroeder has shown, Haydn's reception in London, documented in contemporary writings, provides a rich resource to help us identify Haydn's philosophical and aesthetic basis. Because the English were particularly vexed by the question of how music, especially Haydn's music, might be understood as valuable in a moral sense, we have a good public record of how their positive response was rationalized at the time in moral terms. And, since among Haydn's London friends and devotees were scholars steeped in Aristotle—such as, for example, Charles Burney's friend Thomas Twining, who had recently completed his translation of Arisototle's *Poetics* (1789)—that basis for the English was often couched in Aristotelian terms. Specifically, as already noted, Haydn's music was seen to engage its audience, through entertainment, in order to advance established virtues, such as tolerance.

Indeed, Haydn's music may be understood as Aristotelian in a number of respects, most immediately as a specific agent operating within a generalized account of morality based on a hierarchically arranged set of virtues. In *After Virtue*, Alasdair MacIntyre considers a number of such systems, which he argues constitute a tradition of which Aristotle was the key figure (a construction Aristotle himself would have rejected, however).[30] Within this "classical" tradition, a relatively few basic virtues preside over a more comprehensive list of virtues, each of which is understood to contribute to or otherwise support some concept of human flourishing. This basic structure supports not only Aristotelian morality but also, in MacIntyre's analysis, Thomas Aquinas's Catholicism, Benjamin Franklin's morality (rooted in utility), and Jane Austen's socially based moral sense—even if each system differs importantly from the others both conceptually and in the specific virtues it places in the foreground. Standing against this tradition, MacIntyre traces a modern development that he terms "emotivist," which may be understood as a mode of moral relativism with important roots in (1) David Hume's arguments concerning the relationship of morality to the passions, (2) the inadequacy of Kant's attempt to found morality in reason through applications of the categorical imperative, and, more broadly, (3) the subjectivism of Kant and Fichte (and eventually Nietzsche), among many others.

Thomas Twining, in considering the potential for music (in particular Haydn's music) to be considered of moral consequence, argued that some Aristotelian virtues, such as wisdom, courage, and eloquence, were particularly well suited to musical expression.[31] While his claims are surely valid, it is equally valid to claim that Haydn's connection to Aristotelian morality goes much deeper than that, extending importantly to both discursive mode and structure, and to the very practice of performing symphonic music in a public venue, or at least within a socialized venue. Haydn's music may be thought of as Aristotelian not only in light of the specific virtues it may be seen to advance (accessible through engaging its implied arguments and narratives) but also through its very organization, the socially based discourse it participates in and enables, and the ways that it affirms, parallels, and perhaps even exemplifies a basic structure of Aristotelian systems of morality, in which virtues are understood as always modulated by circumstance and judgment, rather than absolute.

We have seen, in the account given here of the "Military" Symphony, how some of this comes into play. Within the symphony's narratives, virtues are demonstrated both along the way and overall, including humor, peacefulness, perseverance, prudence, loyalty, courage, cunning, sympathy, hospitality, flexibility, generosity, tolerance, benevolence, and wisdom, among others. Some virtues are advanced within more purely musical (or composerly) realms as well, including humor, cunning, imagination, reason, and inventiveness.

Less obviously, Haydn's music, in combining seamlessly the modes of narrative and argument—which we tend today to separate into the somewhat artificial categories of "extramusical" and "musical logic"—runs parallel to a feature fundamental to classical philosophical argument: the couching of moral argument in the form of stories.[32] As a strategy, this tends to establish and maintain two interacting perspectives: to make human existence (flourishing) the context and standard for morality, while displacing that orientation to a certain objective distance, away from the subjectively experienced self. As a structure, this becomes something quite different around the turn of the nineteenth century, when such stories (for example, those collected by the Grimms) are viewed as a folk-based repository supporting ideas of nation on the one hand, and nascent *Bildung* narratives on the other, with a resultant emphasis displaced either outward to something beyond the immediately social, or inward to the developing self, in the process losing essential grounding in objective argument and the social dimension. This development, too, has important consequences for how narrative functions in music after Haydn, traceable early on in Beethoven's struggle to explain the programmatic dimension of his "Pastoral" Symphony, and later manifest in the intense subjectivism of Berlioz's symphonic narratives and Wagner's operatic fusions of myth and subjectivity.[33] But what matters most here is how closely Haydn's balance between these modes approximates classical argument, both as a method and in the resultant orientation around human society. And more specifically, as the next section of this chapter explores, it provides an important basis for a specific rhetorical orientation.

On another level, Haydn's symphonies participated centrally in furthering a still-emergent culture of concertgoing, which may be understood as a *practice*, a term MacIntyre uses to refer to social institutions that act as repositories of human flourishing, developing specialized hierarchies of virtues appropriate to each practice.[34] In Mitchell Morris's application of this set of ideas to musicology—which he rightly considers a practice in dire need of reform[35]—he touches on related aspects of musical practices more generally, practices that might be easily related as well to Christopher Small's concept of *musicking*.[36] But there are important differences between musicology and other musical practices. Musicology has evolved almost entirely within the ambit of German Idealism and its derivative nationalist discourses; indeed, until relatively recently, it has been mainly either a direct or an indirect consequence of German Idealist thought.[37] Thus, a virtues-based version of musicology as a practice must to some extent be imagined. With concertgoing, however, as with the balance between musical argument and narrative just described, we may usefully trace a transformation of the practice in step with German Idealist thought.

Especially in the decades after Beethoven's death, and encouraged by much scolding in the musical press and elsewhere,[38] contemplation became the preferred mode of listening to music in the German lands, an attitude that persists today regarding "Western" concert music. To support this mode, concertgoing acquired the trappings of churchgoing, with obvious (if not pervasive) parallels in dress, decorum, and ritual-based behavior. In Haydn's day, however, these trappings, to the extent they were present, were gestures of respect directed toward the aristocratic hosts (if the occasion were private), toward the perhaps upwardly mobile sociability of the occasion, and toward the performers (generally including the composer), in part so as to encourage the most pleasurable performance possible. And, of course, these trappings were often not present, at least to the degree that would become standard in the wake of German Idealism. But the relative looseness of concert decorum at this earlier stage was owing not only to a kind of adolescent phase in the maturation of the practice of mounting and attending public concerts but also to a different sense of what mattered to the practice. Specifically, its purposes and associated virtues were somewhat different early on, and those differences speak directly to why Haydn's music, which was unsurpassed in that setting (for which it was after all designed), would gradually fall to a second rank within the new order.

Haydn's audiences expected, as suggested by the provocative title of Melanie Lowe's *Pleasure and Meaning in the Classical Symphony*, to be entertained first and enlightened second by Haydn's symphonies. Audiences quite reasonably anticipated that Haydn would gratify them in a wide variety of ways, by acknowledging within his music their capacity to appreciate all of the virtues that his music advanced. Accordingly, he might be expected to challenge them, but also to reward their efforts to engage intelligently with a full slate of enjoyable musical effects. Among their expected pleasures were that they would hear well-crafted, beautiful, and exciting music played well by expert musicians, which would include episodes of good humor setting more serious music in relief (or vice versa), and which might include engaging "twists" on a variety of conventions (instances of Haydn's celebrated wit). And they could reasonably expect *not* to be driven too often inward to their own thoughts, or to be bored by extended periods of relative musical inaction. Above all, they could expect to enjoy and to appreciate the music and its performance, and to take pleasure in sharing those experiences with others. If they anticipated that at least some of Haydn's music might make them think, or direct them toward a contemplative mood, that was not the main reason they were there in the first place, although stimulation in these directions might figure prominently in what they took away from the experience.

The virtues advanced by these expectations and their gratification were copious, enriching all concerned, including composer, entrepreneurial management, performers, and audience, with the latter contributing a significant amount of sophisticated engagement that would spill over into the press and private correspondence, as noted. In flourishing, the practice well reflected and partially embodied a larger sense of human flourishing. Yet, while many features of this practice would continue with German Idealism, the hierarchy of virtues involved would shift so precipitously that new kinds of concertgoing had to be invented to accommodate those who preferred the older, less formal atmosphere, oriented more toward social pleasures than individual contemplation. Arguably, this realignment of "serious" concertgoing, so as to conform better to the sensibilities of German Idealism, is the single most important cause of the quickly growing rift between serious and popular modes of musicking. This rift was manifest early on in successful strategies to provide alternative, "lighter" fare in less formal surroundings (developing from the "promenade" concerts of the early nineteenth century to the "pops" concerts of the late nineteenth and twentieth centuries), and through the inclusion of such fare in more overtly popular venues during the second half of the nineteenth century, such as the music hall and variety.

Among the more extended consequences of this rift and its various border wars have been the prolonged tradition of a separate "popular" music, especially in the United States, and the entrenching of an aspirational mode of musical engagement that would come to be derided as "middlebrow." While Haydn has no truly congenial place within the new hierarchies, he has come to fit most comfortably into the latter cultural stratum, along with operetta and other "entertainment" genres with marked "serious" content. The gradual process of Haydn settling into this cultural niche, which could have more-or-less permanently demoted him from the pantheon of German masters, has been complicated by at least four factors: Haydn's evident mastery of his craft, the now-habitual veneration accorded him as an important predecessor to Beethoven (itself a kind of demotion, as "Papa" Haydn), his small corpus of fully "serious" works, and the growing need, verging at times on hysteria, for "classical" venues and institutions to appeal to aging and occasionally more youthful audiences through more readily entertaining musical programming.

Finally, Haydn's music may be understood as Aristotelian through the ways he manages potentially antagonistic elements through regulation and, at times, a kind of negotiation, within what I have termed his "dynamic of accommodation." While this aspect of his music relates to a number of specific virtues, such as moderation, balance, reasonableness, and tolerance, it also has a more fundamental role to play. Aristotle argued that virtues must be understood within a dynamic in which particular virtues, when carried to extremes, would no longer contribute to human flourishing, and thus would no longer constitute virtues. For example, courage might verge into foolhardiness, or acceptance into cowardice, and no longer serve as virtues but rather as their opposites. Aristotle explained this need for modulating virtues in terms of a golden mean, in mathematical terms a precise measurement, but which in this usage indicates the optimum degree of a particular quality within a given context, along a continuum. Within this dynamic account of the virtues, Haydn's music provides a similarly dynamic demonstration of how such a golden mean might be determined, specifically through the space created between dramatic narrative and musical argument, and by means of granting individualized elements a chance to prove themselves musically worthy, however unworthy they might appear at first, within a dynamic of accommodation.

While specific virtues might be invoked in the process, and while such strategies fall easily within the symphonic practice advanced by Haydn, whose celebrated wit could reliably resolve the eccentric and incongruous into the musically competent, there is a specific contextual orientation for understanding these negotiations, as well. Within these negotiations, Haydn provocatively merges the most subtle of his Aristotelian bases: the rhetorical potential of his blend of narrative and argument, and a dynamic account of diverse virtues conceptualized in terms of the golden mean. I now turn to a fuller consideration of this contextual orientation, which I call Haydn's "rhetoric of individuation."

HAYDN'S RHETORIC OF INDIVIDUATION

The presumption of musical competence for the eccentric in Haydn has two dimensions that may usefully concern us here. First, this presumption sets Haydn's music well apart from that of his most famous contemporary, Mozart; and, second, it is—often if not always—specifically through the rhetorical dimension of musical discourse that the eccentric in Haydn both establishes itself and proves its competence. These two dimensions go a long way toward explaining why rhetoric might seem a more central dimension to explore in Haydn than in Mozart,[39] and why Haydn's music often seems so much more congenial than, if not quite so beautiful as, Mozart's. More central to my present purposes, focusing on these two dimensions will both place Haydn's practice in historical relief and help us to understand that practice in more musically concrete terms. Moreover, Haydn's core dependence on rhetoric, whose project and success is based on a dynamic of *persuasion*, gives special emphasis to the implicit social contract between performers and audiences, as managed by the composer. From this perspective, music, as such—that is, music as it would be essentialized according to German Idealism—plays a secondary role to the discourse it supports, although it is crucially determinant of the nature and success of that discourse.

Generally speaking in Mozart, the highly individual, the aberrant, or simply the out-of-place, is supremely vulnerable to some kind of corrective action. Mozart routinely censures individuals (or their musical referents) who do not conform to existing realities or expected behavior, enforcing an aesthetic sensibility that esteems formal order above all else. Perhaps the most obvious instance may be found in *Don Giovanni* (discussed already in chapter 1), where the demise of the defiant Don occasions a community celebration of disquieting enthusiasm and duration. Another example, eloquently discussed by Susan McClary, is the slow movement of the G-major Piano Concerto, K. 453, in which the affectively dissonant soloist is resignedly brought to heel in the denouement.[40] Indeed, the latter is but one instance from this particularly rich literature; without exception, Mozart's solo keyboard concertos elaborate a strictly controlling environment for their most individuated element, the piano solo, enforced from the beginning by a massive *tutti* section that, like the ending to *Don Giovanni*, has seemed to later audiences an excessive gesture, even dramatically ineffective (see chapter 1). Also problematic for many later audiences is the trajectory of *Così fan tutte*. However the ending is staged, there is no getting around the fact that Mozart and da Ponte, while making their neatly plotted game tokens heartbreakingly human, have nevertheless stripped them in the end of any claim to individuality or difference, which they might have achieved either through their adhering steadfastly to a sworn love, or through their exhibiting a freely celebrated maturation into a more genuine or powerful love. The lovers in *Così fan tutte* are not elevated through their enlightenment but reduced, humiliated, and chastised, and with them the totality of human aspiration to break free of abject conformance to a singularly unexalted account of human nature.

Or, we might consider the more obviously relevant *Ein musikalischer Spass* (*A Musical Joke*), which is routinely cited as Mozart's closest approach to Haydnesque wit. But it is actually as far from being that as it could be. From beginning to end, there is no expectation that the musically eccentric will prove competent, for the eccentric is marked on all levels as inherently *in*competent. Despite its opposite tack to Haydn, however, *Ein musikalischer Spass* does help shed light on a particular feature of Haydn's comic style that is particularly relevant here. Mozart systematically ridicules two main sites of incompetence—inept composition and inept performance—and it is noteworthy that we become most keenly aware of musical individuation in the latter case, especially when he displaces ensemble playing with more soloistic textures. In Haydn, too, the eccentric can quite often be heard as composerly, as when the eccentric element is given ensemble articulation, but it is, again, when an individual voice breaks free from the rest that the eccentric element is most vividly individuated, and the way most obviously cleared for a rhetorically based denouement. Put another way, when the eccentric element is embodied by a smaller contingent within the full ensemble, the result is a dramatic enactment of individuation within the work, rather than an individuation that is effectively coextensive with the work itself. We may also note that this kind of individuation, in both *Ein musikalischer Spass* and in Haydn, puts conventional order at risk in two ways, by threatening both formal order and the integrity of the larger group.

The capacity to project an individuated rhetoric is, I believe, rooted in Haydn's chamber style, but its most intriguing manifestations occur in his symphonies, at moments when the chamber style, and particularly this facet of the chamber style, assumes a prominent role in the symphonic discourse. Within an orchestral setting, *tutti* sections can represent a responsive audience for the chamber-based sections they introduce or follow, and so may delimit more clearly the dynamic dimension of rhetoric. To be sure, the core elements of musical rhetoric may well be presented without such an embodied response, through a close working of material, a coherently traced argument, rhetorical grace and eloquence, or an effective use of figures and topics—indeed, the very ability to stay on topic, which is inevitably called into question whenever something we are apt to call eccentric is introduced. But the traditional rationale and proof of rhetorical effectiveness lies in the ability to persuade, as confirmed by specific changes in the attitude or conduct of an audience. For eccentricities that may be taken as composerly, that audience exists primarily within the larger arena of performance, in which music is being both performed and listened to: the performers, as agents of the composer, attempt to persuade the listeners (including those performers who assume an active listening role). But for more individuated eccentricities, it is the larger performing group that embodies the responding perspective within the communicative dynamic of rhetorical exchange. Indeed, the very fact of a changed course, of a *tutti* that manifestly acts differently because of what it seems to respond to, can often be enough to suggest a rhetorical dimension, with or without the mechanics of rhetoric being fully elaborated.

These symphonic instances of dramatically enacted rhetoric, which pit the highly individuated against an authority represented jointly by the orchestral *tutti* and traditional formal designs, create the possibility for a Beethoven-like engagement between the individuated and opposed larger forces, which might be construed, alternatively, as human or societal authority, as nature, as the supernatural, or as some combination of these or other forces. While it is fairly rare for Haydn to push the confrontational possibilities of such situations, it will be useful here to consider instances in which he does just that, with resulting symphonic works that rank among Haydn's most eccentric: the "Military" (briefly considered anew from this perspective), *Il Distratto*, and the "Farewell."

In considering these musical situations, however, it will be important to avoid the often-unacknowledged tendency to see Haydn primarily as a predecessor to Beethoven (a fate he has shared with Mozart). This tendency is strongly entrenched within historical narratives of this period. Because Beethoven's extension of the classical style stands distractingly between us and his two principal models, his powerful projection of a heroic impulse that threatens to overbalance an established order prismatically distorts our perception of his predecessors, emblematically reducing the Mozartian to a fetishized formal perfection, and the Haydnesque to a preoccupation with triviality that sometimes borders on camp. (Which is not to say that formal balance is not central to Mozart's aesthetic, nor—especially considering the larger argument of this book—that camp has nothing to contribute to our understandings of Haydn.)

As in the worldview projected through Mozart's music, Haydn's more accommodating approach also pits individuation against the dual authority of larger group and musical form, but with such a high degree of invested sympathy that form and ensemble must redefine themselves accordingly. Superficially, this formulation would indeed seem to place Haydn as a trivialized precursor to Beethoven's heroism, which also invests its sympathy with the individuated perspective. But Haydn's world and Beethoven's are philosophically incompatible; Haydn's Aristotelian outlook directs us toward tolerance, the golden mean as applied to any particular virtue, and the sympathetically human, rather than toward the kind of Kantian self-actualization and the pushing to extremes typical of Beethoven. Lacking in Haydn are the markers for idealist morality we take for granted in Beethoven: an earnest sense of duty and the embodied notion that only through struggle may good be achieved. Instead, we find an Aristotelian celebration of human flourishing however and whenever it may be encountered or furthered. Thus, we may hear in Haydn's eccentric individuations an appealingly human but stubbornly unaccommodating "other," which first engages an audience's sympathy for the eccentric, and then, in flourishing, supports a liberal view of the proper balance between authority and freedom.[41]

It is also important to acknowledge that the use of chamber textures in Haydn's symphonies has many precedents; indeed, such textures seem

Table 2.2: Instrumentation for the First Theme (mm. 1–56) in the Slow Movements of Haydn, "Military" Symphony and the Concerto in G for Two Lire Organizzate (Hob. vii h:3)

NB: In the "Military" Symphony, **T**=strings & flute; **S**=reed choir (2 ob, 2 cl, 2 bn)

	A/8 bars	**A**	**B**/12 bars	**A**	**B**	**A**
Symphony:	**T** (*tutti*)	**S** (*soli*)	**T**		**S**	
Concerto:	**T** (*tutti*)	**S** (*soli*)	**T**/4b – **S**/8b	**S**	**T** – **S**	**S**

almost to be a given feature of the eighteenth-century orchestra, appearing as a natural outgrowth of the desire for timbral variety that fed the growing popularity of the medium. If there would thus seem to be nothing inherently individuating about their use, a case may nevertheless be made that such was indeed the point of such textures, routinely and with due intent on the part of the composer. In fact, the second movement of the "Military" Symphony makes this case, implicitly, all on its own. Haydn's transformation of this movement from the middle movement of his Concerto for Two Lire Organizzate was neither rote nor especially complicated; in general, he maintained the concerto dynamic by adding reed instruments and separating them off, as a group, from the rest of the orchestra. As shown in table 2.2, he gave the concerto dynamic even greater formal clarity in the symphony by keeping the sections more integral, as *tutti* and reed choir alternate with more equality and regularity than in the original.

Notably, this material is not especially eccentric, except perhaps in the extreme complacency of the pastoral idyll projected by the shawmlike reed choir. Thus, Haydn demonstrates that individuation does not always have to involve the highly eccentric, although issues of competence and authority are set in higher relief when it does. But this instance also demonstrates with particular clarity the deliberateness of Haydn's approach, as he adopts a concerto-like procedure, within a symphony, to set apart a smaller grouping within the larger group, establishing a perspective within the music itself to be threatened and bullied by the military passages to come. That his model was quite literally a concerto movement with a similar (if less extreme) dramatic trajectory lends substantial credence to our attempts to find similarly constructed perspectives in others of his symphonies.

Symphony No. 60 in C, *Il Distratto*

Il Distratto, as a symphony, ‹**TE2.19**› manifests its eccentricities early on primarily through moments of distraction within a quieter, chamber-like texture, in each case subsequently brought to heel by the larger group.[42] The affect of distraction, already in the first movement, suggests an individual whose mind wanders or loses context, even if the distracted perspective is not consistently embodied by a single instrument. Individuation is manifest in this case through consistency of affect and contrast with the larger group, which embodies the authority to impose corrective order. As indicated in table 2.3, within the exposition in the first movement there are two such episodes of distraction and correction. In the first, at the beginning of the *allegro* (after a 2/4 *adagio* introduction), we hear a clearly stated fast triple meter (3/8, notated within 3/4), which the *tutti* corrects to a broader metrical basis (3/4) in two increasingly emphatic stages. ‹**AE2.20**› Later in the exposition, after the rhythmic impulse of the first theme has accommodated to the broader meter, the isolated strings seem confused by a premature return to the original tonic, hovering uncertainly until an increasingly impatient-sounding *tutti* gives the needed shove toward the cadence.[43] ‹**AE2.21**›

After the symphony stumbles through an outwardly straightforward rehearsal of a traditional symphonic shape, albeit eccentrically rendered, we arrive at what seems to be a minor-mode *presto* finale (movement iv), a *tutti*, played *furioso*, through which impatient authority calls the distracted individual to a final reckoning.[44] ‹**AE2.22**› Quintessentially, this might be the wrath of the Furies, but what confronts them is, seemingly, no Orpheus; after the first extended barrage (which is repeated in toto), we hear only befuddled mutterings by a unison string choir, which serve merely to ratchet up the rage of the larger group. Befuddlement turns out to be an oddly effective rhetorical device, however, since it inspires rage in the larger force, which finally unbalances it, infecting it with the very disease it seeks to root out: distraction. ‹**AE2.23**› Thus, the *tutti* fails to complete its discourse with the requisite recapitulation, and a celebratory coda takes the movement to a bizarre and premature conclusion. ‹**AE2.24**› Befuddlement, eccentricity's principal embodiment in this movement, persuades specifically (if unwittingly) through its manifestation of the uniquely human, and through its befuddlement the chamber presence drives the larger force to reveal its own similarly human face, equally susceptible to distraction.

Table 2.3: "Synopsis" of Haydn, *Il Distratto* Symphony

	Movement	Section	Content
i.	**Adagio** (C Major, 2/4)	Introduction:	Grandiose *tutti* | chamber song
	Allegro di molto (C Major, 3/4)	Exposition:	1st group: chamber in 3/8 → corrective *tutti* in 3/4
			2nd group: "distracted" chamber → cadential *tutti*
		Development:	chamber in 3/8 → "Sturm und Drang" *tutti* in 3/4
			Retransition: "distracted" chamber →
		Recapitulation:	chamber in 3/8 → *tutti* in 3/4
			"distracted" chamber → cadential *tutti*
ii.	**Andante** (G Major, 3/4; gesturally fragmented, with rhythmic irregularities)		
iii.	**Menuetto** (C Major, 3/4; oddly contrapuntal second phrase and "distracted" C-Minor Trio)		
iv.	**Presto** (C Minor, 2/4)		"*Furioso*" *tutti* exposition (C Minor → E♭ Major)
			"Befuddled" chamber response → developmental *tutti* rant
			(no Recapitulation)
			Unprepared C-Major Coda (with horns, trumpets, & timpani)
v.	**Adagio di Lamentatione** (F Major, 2/4; "Orpheus" song with impatient *tutti* interjections)		
vi.	**Finale: Prestissimo** (C Major, 2/4; Celebratory *tutti* accommodating eccentric chamber)		

The consequences of this *tutti*-based distraction are mainly two, and nested: the fourth movement, which begins in "finale" mode but trips up on the *tutti*'s excesses, fails to provide a balanced conclusion for the symphony despite the bravado of the C-major coda, and so engenders an extension of the symphonic cycle to include an additional two movements, the first featuring a surprisingly compelling "Orpheus" quelling the "Furies" through instrumental song, followed by a short movement—the actual finale—that maintains an equilibrium between the blatantly eccentric and the celebratory larger group.

Without the misfired finale of the fourth movement, there would be no space for the song that follows, either formally or gesturally. Continuation is mandated by the failure of the larger group to regulate its reactive gestures adequately; moreover, that continuation must first be advanced through reduced forces, since it is specifically the *tutti* that has failed in its role. Indeed, the ongoing success of the "Orpheus" song is itself dependent on the temporary disempowerment of the *tutti*. **‹AE2.25›** As the movement proceeds, it is the *tutti* midway through the movement that seems distracted, with its premature and gesturally inappropriate celebration of the arrival of C, and it is the reentering chamber group that restores balance. <AE2.26> And, although at the end of the movement the *tutti* reasserts its authority, it is once again undermined by its own impatience.[45] Rushing through its concluding affirmation of the chamber song, with a fast, loud version of the chamber group's quietly assured concluding phrase of the song, the reasserted authority of the *tutti* rings false, betrayed by its affective disconnect with the song it ostensibly echoes. <AE2.27>

While the "Orpheus"-like movement is the most obviously rhetorical within this sequence, since it models both eloquence and a persuaded (if impatient) subject for that eloquence, the crucial rhetorical exchange remains that of the fourth movement. The unbalancing of the *tutti* in that movement, maintained through its abstractedly impatient responses to the lamentations of the smaller group in the fifth movement, provides the basis for the celebrated retuning joke near the beginning of the finale. <AE2.28> Thus, the finale's opening *tutti* extends the impatience shown by the *tutti* sections of the previous movement by, ostensibly, launching the movement before the violins have retuned, so that they must stop to do so before continuing. The joke is especially well conceived in harmonic terms, since it serves, implicitly, to balance the premature celebration of C major midway through the previous movement: as the tuning violins bring their lowest note, a *scordiatura* F, up to the required G, they in the process also elaborate an extended cadential progression in C major that redefines F (the tonic of the previous movement) as subdominant to the dominant G.[46]

Symphony No. 45 in F♯ Minor, the "Farewell"

In the first movement of *Il Distratto*, at the height of authority's growing impatience with the persistent 3/8 distractions of the smaller group in the first part of the development, Haydn draws upon a Sturm und Drang texture to evoke a suitably stormy *tutti* response (m. 109), which is in fact a straightforward recollection of the first movement of the "Farewell" Symphony.[47] <AE2.29> <AE2.30> One plausible way to hear that opening (that is, of the "Farewell" Symphony) is as an embodiment of the discontent of the musicians who, as the "program" for the work famously has it, are impatient to leave for a needed holiday. <TE2.31> But Haydn's recollection of the passage as an authoritative *tutti* in *Il Distratto* suggests a different dynamic, which may be confirmed later in the first movement of the

"Farewell" Symphony when, with no obvious musical motivation, Haydn introduces a pastoral dancelike passage in D major—a kind of "trio"—which advances within its chamber textures a perspective that may be much more readily attached to that of a beleaguered, overworked band of musicians dreaming of respite.[48] This notoriously eccentric passage, which appears late in the development after several minutes of unremitting Sturm und Drang, is set in the hopeful, subjunctively inflected key of the ♭VI, and concludes uncertainly, with an imploring, single-voiced ascending line arpeggiating a diminished-seventh chord.[49] **<AE2.32>**

The dynamic of authority that frames this passage seems clear: the ensuing *tutti* abruptly denies the sanguinities of the dancelike alternative, spurning both its major-mode setting and its supplicating conclusion. Within the first movement, we might say, the rhetorical competence of the eccentric is thereby denied—the *tutti* seems rather unconvinced—but later events will show it to be far from put aside. The case will be put again in the finale, once again by abruptly switching to a dancelike idiom in a related major key.

As in the "Military" Symphony, an important point of reference here is the concerto, with its built-in mechanisms for individuation; thus, in the finale of the "Farewell," the chamber texture appears suddenly as an interruption of the concluding cadence, almost in the manner of a cadenza. **<AE2.33>** The task of this ensemble "cadenza" will be to deflect the authority of the *tutti* through a compelling rhetorical demonstration of chamber-based competence, thereby accomplishing the larger task of focusing attention fully and solely on the individuated perspective. Haydn's method for accomplishing this task is twofold: giving specific expressive and functional tasks to individual instruments and, through each subsequent instrumental exit, drawing the focus ever inward, to the more intimate level of the individual within the larger group. Thus, for example, before their exits, the solo horns sound individual farewells, the oboes add a layer of lamenting pathos, and the double bass carries us securely back to the tonic, leaving a diminishing string choir, increasingly without lower-register support, to carry the movement to a formally balanced conclusion—or, figuratively, to labor on long after the time for leave-taking. **<AE2.34>**

Haydn's rhetoric of individuation, as a practice, arguably provides the best context for understanding the extraordinary trajectory of the "Farewell" Symphony, which begins with Haydn's most ferocious *tutti*, but ends with a chamber group charged with a particular task of rhetorical persuasion. But who exactly is to model the received effect of this rhetoric, if the *tutti* has evaporated by the end? With the full transformation of orchestra to chamber ensemble, and as the remaining performers become one with the rhetorical position they argue, the resident authority naturally shifts from stage to audience. Thus, the target of the chamber group's rhetoric undergoes a shift across the finale, turning from the *tutti* orchestra to the princely audience, who occupies the receptive vacuum created by the departing players, and whose response will determine the success of their rhetorical ploy. We may in this context usefully recall the situation presented in *Hamlet*, and may well conclude that, next to Haydn's "Farewell" Symphony, Shakespeare's device of catching the conscience of the king through a staged play comes across as a comparatively primitive device. How much more deliciously sophisticated it is to enlist the prince himself as a player in the drama, so that his very applause, substituting for the absent orchestra's *tutti*, implicitly concedes a rhetorical victory to the players.

TRIUMPHS OF ECCENTRICITY—AND OF NORMALITY

At the very heart of Haydn's concern for musical rhetoric we find a generosity of spirit that celebrated the eccentric, that privileged the individual voice of the most individually human. Paradoxically, however, while it may seem fitting, as I have done here, to explore Haydn's engagement with the eccentric within three of his most eccentric symphonies, it may also seem an inadequate representation of his practice as a whole. In the end we must ask: Do these examples represent compelling evidence of a general stylistic disposition in a composer celebrated for composing an extraordinary number of symphonies that dependably deliver a full range of *familiar* gestures, within formal environments that satisfy through their equal familiarity? Just how effectively can we expect the eccentric to represent the normal?

This question is potentially vexing, but it may be usefully recast by asking whether these symphonies *depart* from Haydn's more usual practice in the ways they engage eccentricity and employ an individuating rhetoric, or whether they merely *exaggerate* practices that may be found, distinctively, throughout Haydn's symphonies. If they represent radical departures, then they may not stand as exemplars but only as interesting case studies. If, however, they are exaggerations, then they may serve as particularly apt examples, since they display these practices more vividly than usual. Thankfully, it proves easy enough to argue in this way that these three symphonies are, in fact, of a piece with Haydn's work in general.

First, each of them shares material with other works by Haydn, either from symphonies or from a related genre, as already noted. The "Military" borrows nearly an entire movement from a concerto, whereas *Il Distratto*, even beyond its theatrical origins, borrows from the "Farewell"—and not its most eccentric music, either, but its most stereotypically Sturm und Drang material. To be sure, these borrowings might be more reassuring to skeptics if they were examples of eccentric works borrowing from normal works, rather than of the eccentric borrowing from the eccentric. But even given that, they should offer considerable reassurance. The "Military" does not become truly eccentric until the borrowed material has already unfolded at some length; it is doubtful that the symphony would have seemed all that unusual to listeners right up to the actual entrance of the Janissary instruments, well into the second movement. And *Il Distratto* displaces its borrowing from the main theme of the "Farewell" to a more "normal" formal position for such angst-ridden material, by relocating it to the development.

Moreover, *Il Distratto* is not alone among Haydn's symphonies in quoting the opening of the "Farewell." No. 85 in B♭ ("La Reine"), among the most "normal" of Haydn's Paris Symphonies (nos. 82–87, composed 1785–1786), also quotes this passage in the development of the first movement, albeit with different preparation and to a somewhat different end. **<TE2.35>** Reportedly receiving its nickname because it was a favorite of the queen (Marie Antoinette, a fellow Austrian), the symphony opens in an approximation of "French overture" style, with prominent dotted rhythms and dramatic flourishes suitable to its acquired royal appellation. But the real interest of the movement comes just after the introduction, for the argument of the *vivace* that follows is fraught in a particularly Haydnesque way.

The exposition (beginning m. 12) opens simply with a descending bass pattern and a sustained tonic in the treble. This unassuming thematic profile presents an ambiguity familiar to Haydn, as it becomes clear only well into the first statement of the theme that the sustained treble and not the staccato descending line is the true melody.[50] Nor is the matter that easily settled, for it seems to come under renewed dispute in the *tutti* that marks the final cadence of the theme (m. 23 following), when the flourishes from the introduction combine with an arpeggiated version of the descending line, driving resolutely to the cadence and eventually pulling the sustained treble tonic (in the winds) along with it. If at this point the staccato figure has reasserted its dominance, it once again assumes a secondary role when the main theme returns immediately thereafter (m. 31), at which point it is actually demoted, being now consigned to an inner voice. With the ensuing *tutti* (m. 42), however, the two melodic strands become fused yet again, this time over a violently syncopated texture redolent of Sturm und Drang, although still in the major mode. With this setup, characteristically, we might expect a quietly stated theme to launch the second group, in parallel to the beginning of the exposition, and possibly deriving from the main theme. Instead, as the local culmination of this process, we hear a *tutti*, minor-mode version of a descending arpeggio figure to mark the arrival on the dominant (m. 62). This new version of the figure extends into a full thematic statement by alternating every two bars with its mirror image, in the process deferring the expected quiet beginning to the second group to m. 78, when we do indeed hear a recast version of the main theme. **<AE2.36>** Finally, the development completes the transformation of the theme into a thematic allusion to the opening of the "Farewell," by adding Sturm und Drang syncopations to the arpeggiated version of the thematic complex, initially in the major mode (m. 114), but traversing the minor, as well (m. 124).[51] **<AE2.37>**

In this way, a rather mild-mannered descending scale, initially cheated of its presumptive melodic role, gradually reasserts itself across the exposition before taking a leading role in the development (but not in the recapitulation, which systematically short-circuits these processes). The full process may be summarized as follows:

Measure		
12	Main theme:	descending staccato scale yields melodic interest to the treble line
23	1st *tutti*:	conversion of descending figure to an assertive arpeggio
42	2nd *tutti* bridge:	adding syncopated textures (still in the major mode)
62	2nd group:	*tutti*, minor-mode version of arpeggio figure, falling and rising

114 Development: *tutti*, major-mode version of arpeggio figure, falling and rising, with Sturm und Drang textures, including syncopations, moving through minor mode (m. 124)

That this elaborate procedure occurs in so "normal-sounding" a movement should remind us how commonplace it was for Haydn to indulge the idiosyncratic demands of his material, however unassuming that material may seem at first. In most cases, as here, and as with the first movement of the "Military," Haydn assimilates his unusual thematic processes within "normal" formal procedures (normal for him, that is, reflecting his propensity to repeat or vary the main theme to launch the second group, and to completely rework the recapitulation).

But not always. Without in other ways seeming to verge into the unusual, and without even drawing particular attention to the fact, Haydn sometimes will allow processes such as these to recast the form radically (as with the String Quartet, op. 64, no. 3, to be considered in the next chapter). That such instances can seem so very normal—and thus might seem in that sense worlds apart from the central examples considered in this chapter—indicates, correctly, that they all lie comfortably within Haydn's general procedures.

And what are those general procedures? Clearly, they both reflect general practices of his time and, more particular to him, include a strong tendency to allow compulsions internal to his material to determine his forms. In some cases his procedures may respond to obvious tokens of eccentricity, but in others, as in the first movement of "La Reine," the eccentric element emerges from within a more "normal" thematic array. If this description seems oddly in line with German Idealism—in particular, with the assertion of Richard Strauss that content must dictate form—it is most assuredly not, for there is in Haydn no overturning of what comes across as a normalizing reasonableness along the way.

Nevertheless, the best argument for accepting the symphonies discussed in this chapter as exemplary, if exaggerated, examples of Haydn's "business as usual" may be found in the historical record. An extraordinary number of his symphonies were given nicknames by his audiences, and nearly always in response to an aspect of their narrative or argument that especially intrigued his audiences. While Mozart's nicknamed symphonies carry such acquired titles as "Paris," "Prague," or "Jupiter,"[52]

Haydn's carry names, sometimes originating with him, that are directly referential to their character, such as "Morning" (no. 6, replete with sunrise and imitations of farm animals), the "Philosopher," the "Bear," the "Surprise," and so on. Whatever the generic pleasures Haydn's symphonies provide, as befits their role both in court and in the emergent concert culture, they also exhibit an astounding degree of individuated diversity, betokened by so many of them being "named" in reception, most often in response to what is individual about them. The true validation of Haydn's musical politics of assimilation lies in how eagerly his most eccentric works were themselves assimilated into the repertory, in direct parallel to his own composerly practice.

3 | HAYDN, THE STRING QUARTET, AND THE (D)EVOLUTION OF THE CHAMBER IDEAL

Along with the symphony, the string quartet has been the most enduring of Haydn's contributions to the musical traditions fostered by the new paradigms of German Idealism. Indeed, the symphony and the quartet were also the central genres of his public and published success during his lifetime. For both genres, publications across the nineteenth and early twentieth centuries attempted to winnow Haydn's staggering output to manageable collections; understandably, these tended to lead off with Haydn's most famous and familiar works, and rarely extended beyond these.[1] As a result of this practice, Haydn's ability to compose to the pleasures of his audiences has been continuously reemphasized, which has led to his being "typecast" as a composer who courted popularity, concerned more with entertaining an audience than with providing, in accordance with German Idealist precepts, the basis for contemplation and serious engagement.

Haydn did indeed "court popularity," but that phrase suggests to modern sensibilities a situation quite different from Haydn's actual relationships with his various publics, especially his performers and audiences.[2] One of the reasons for our changed attitudes is the full ascendency of mass musical culture, an environment we now take for granted but which had only begun to manifest itself during Haydn's career. As William Weber argues, a crucial element of mass culture is the need to sell directly to an unknown public in a transaction that is impersonal and distinctively commodity-based: "In the musical field the term "mass culture" can be defined . . . as performance or dissemination of music which does not rest upon personal relationships between musicians and the public and for which obtaining—indeed, manipulating—a wide public is a primary goal. This is not just a matter of brute numbers of people buying music or going to concerts. What has characterized musical mass culture primarily has been rather the impersonality of relationships between listeners and performers and the active exploitation of a broad public by the music business."[3] Although Haydn published more widely than most other composers of the time, his publications, as with all new musical publications and many concert ventures, were promoted through subscription, rather than through the more speculative environment we now think of as the "marketplace."[4] This meant that publication was arranged within a growing but circumscribed circle of known individuals, not for the more impersonal mass market that would eventually predominate. Even Haydn's later works, some of which were published with wider audiences in mind (e.g., *The Creation*, the first musical work to be published with textual underlay in two languages), were originally written for specific venues and audiences that Haydn knew well. Because of its basis in personal connections among those involved—composer, performers, audiences, patrons, commissioners, publishers, and subscribers—Haydn's music tends to be more *social* than music that came before these kinds of networks came into full blossom, or after such networks yielded to increasingly impersonal mass marketing. Moreover, the social dimension of Haydn's music often found direct musical expression, since he was remarkably good—as were many of his contemporaries, such as Luigi Boccherini, Franz Asplmayr, Johann Vanhal, Ignace Pleyel, Mozart, and Carl Ditters von Dittersdorf—at playing to that dynamic within his compositions. Before Haydn's generation, although music may have had an important social function, it was not *in itself* as social as Haydn and his cohort would make it.

The string quartet was but one of several chamber genres particularly well suited to expressing sociality, and in some respects it was not even the one most naturally expressive of this dynamic attribute, arguably inferior to accompanied sonatas, keyboard trios, and the like, with their greater diversity of instrumentation combining effectively with the greater intimacy of a smaller ensemble. Yet, despite Haydn's success in these other genres, his quartets were especially prized in part for their demonstration that the quartet's "conversation among equals" could be just as effective in this regard, and often and in some respects even more so, offering partial compensation for the potential problem of generating sufficient timbral variety and interest within an ensemble of instruments belonging to a single, remarkably integral family.[5] So important was this demonstration by Haydn and his cohort (for which Haydn, deservedly or not, would take most of the credit), that a composer's ability to meet this particular challenge would become, as with the symphony, an important composerly credential for later generations, especially as the quartet, like the symphony, came increasingly under the sway of German Idealism.[6]

Because my subject is Haydn, and in particular the afterlife of his chamber music in the emergent context of German Idealism, my primary focus here will be Haydn's string quartets. This is not to say that a wider study is not warranted; clearly, it is, even if Haydn's quartets may be understood to stand in for not only his own chamber works more generally but also the chamber music of those contemporaries whose work has not sustained active repertory status. But in focusing on Haydn's quartets, I position myself also to consider how later quartet music—the symbolic standard-bearer of chamber music meanings and ideals in the following generations—offered a subtly altered dynamic of presentation and involvement even when advancing some mode of sociality. Accordingly, I probe in the main part of this chapter both the social dynamic embedded within Haydn's quartets and the subtle alteration of this dynamic that began to appear in quartet writing soon after. In particular, I will consider key movements from Haydn's six op. 64 quartets (1790, published 1791), written just before his London trips and capping a line of development from his breakthrough op. 33 set of nine years earlier,[7] before more briefly considering important contributions of later composers.[8]

There was in many respects a smoother path from Haydn to German Idealism in the chamber realm, as compared with the symphony and other public genres. Core to what made the quartet different from the symphony in this regard is its dynamic between "inside" and "outside," but this dynamic, too, underwent an idealist-based transformation after Haydn, albeit more subtly rendered than that of the symphony. To understand this dynamic better, and before turning to specific examples, I begin by exploring the inside-outside dynamic of the string quartet in broad terms. In reflection of my subject, I couch my discussion as a kind of four-way conversation between myself and three other writers. (Of necessity, I lead the discussion—for once, despite being in practice an unabashed "second violinist," I willingly accept the duties of the first violinist.)

LISTENING IN

Audiences today listen to string quartet music differently than they listen to almost any other music, even other chamber music. While this is probably true even with regard to recordings of this music, what I have in mind is a condition that existed long before there were recordings, namely, that the string quartet, at least in its early history, was essentially private music that an audience, if any, was privileged to overhear. This is a condition, originally not unique to the genre, that quartets especially have tended to preserve, and that audiences (that is, not mere auditors) continue to relish.

Two caveats must accompany this claim. First, string quartet music, like all chamber music, has for a long time served as public music with varying degrees of success. Second, as noted, the condition I refer to is shared to some extent by other forms of chamber music. Nevertheless, string quartets have sustained this quality—of private musical utterances that an audience overhears—to a greater degree than other genres, despite both the paradigm shifts brought about by German Idealism and their gradually augmented "public" side, the latter engendering an increasing deployment of more broadly symphonic effects.[9] The reason for this may be partly abstract, stemming from the ability of the medium to project this quality through its four more-or-less equal voices.[10] But it also has to do with the historical genesis of the string quartet. In general terms, the genre, like most chamber music, was cultivated within an Enlightenment-based intellectual climate that valued sociability differently than it was valued before and after. But more specifically, this quality derives from its cultivation by Haydn, who—for future generations that placed Haydn above his contemporaries in this regard—set the standard as to the shared, conversational dimension of string quartet discourse. Through developing this capacity, and early enough in the genre's history to help establish the genre's "ground rules," Haydn proved capable of embedding sociability within the very fabric of quartet writing, in a way that could be especially manifest in performance.

So what is the special quality of quartet music that we so cherish? Why do we—that is, those of us who have discovered this pleasure—listen to string quartet music with singular relish, especially in live performances? Although individual answers will vary considerably, most of us would not immediately think to point out the great musical thought that string quartets sometimes present—which tends to get very specific very quickly—but would refer instead to more general qualities, such as its sound, or its ability to move from very intimate interactions to more broadly scaled gestures, or its quality of conversation, or the manner in which it engages the listener. As we actually listen to a particular string quartet, there is of course a lot more to what the experience offers than these things. To rehearse a few familiar characterizations: there is a great deal of humor, if it is Haydn; of grace and charm, if it is Mozart; of complex musical thought, if it is Beethoven (and even more conspicuously complex if it is Brahms); of sentiment, if it is Schubert; of a challenging blend of folklike themes, irregular rhythms, and crunching dissonances, if it is Bartók; and so on. Indeed, these are things we might point to if we are asked about a particular composer's string quartet music; more generally, however, we would try to identify things that are to some extent shared by all, or at least by those quartets we especially like.

One common observation—that string quartets often seem to engage in something like musical conversation, a kind of interactive discourse in musical terms—might seem to be a promising starting point for our inquiry.[11] But the quality I refer to does not actually depend on our ability to understand string quartets as a kind of conversation; in fact, the metaphor of conversation tends to get in the way a bit, for I am particularly interested in the *musical* interaction of the four players, which, as we listen, we hear from both the inside and the outside, observing the interaction itself as we appreciate the musical results.

In identifying this quality, I do not claim it as something a work must have to "qualify" as a genuine string quartet. Nor do I claim that this is the only quality that may serve to distinguish the quartet from other genres. However, one of the challenges that composers have most consistently met in writing successfully for this medium has been that of preserving this quality in particular, despite changes in cultural settings, performance venues, and, perhaps most problematic, composers' personalities. Moreover, I *do* claim this quality to be categorically central, if on no other basis than the frequency with which it, or something very like it, is described in writings about string quartets. It is with three such writings that I wish to converse here, in order to "place" this quality, as I understand it, in relation to similarly described aspects of string quartet discourse.

Robert Martin, in discussing the performance of Beethoven's string quartets,[12] provocatively describes the ways in which the members of a string quartet accommodate to each other and to the demands of the music they play, primarily in terms of the decisions, both implicit and explicit, that must be made in preparation for a performance. His discussion is fascinating enough on its own terms, but becomes particularly germane here when we consider two aspects of the situation somewhat exterior to his concerns.

First, the circumstances he describes are absolutely dependent on the quartet's position between the often impenetrable inside—the composer's intentions for the work or, more abstractly, the work itself and all the problematic issues that arise with such characterizations—and the projected outside, the performance or, perhaps, documentation of the work before an audience.

Second, this position is somewhat artificial, given the profound differences between the conditions for which much quartet music was written and the conditions of modern performance. But that is almost beside the point. The position of the players in a modern string quartet between composer and audience, and the particular ways in which a string quartet has to manage that position, serve to heighten the polarization, from a listener's perspective, between "inside" and "outside." This quality of inside/outside has thus been preserved and intensified as a byproduct of the conditions of modern performance, which tend to emphasize the "public" side of chamber music, transferred in performance to an intense preoccupation with the musical work that can in itself so fascinate audience members that they are drawn into the music even as their position "outside" the musical discourse is reinforced.

In the same volume as Martin's discussion, Joseph Kerman writes about the intended audience for Beethoven's quartets, tracing a three-stage trajectory for that audience from the performers (after the classical model), to the public (that is, in a concert setting), to Beethoven himself. Kerman closes with the following summation:

> Because in his last period Beethoven often gives the impression of shutting out an audience, listeners ever since have had to get used to a situation in which they are suddenly made privy to a singular colloquy, now hushed, now strident, but always self-absorbed. The conversation of the classical string quartet [Kerman's first stage] is obviously de-

> signed to be heard and, within a discreet circle, overheard. The discourse of the professional quartet [stage two] is meant to be broadcast. Listening to certain movements in the late Beethoven quartets, one feels sure that neither of these situations holds. The music is sounding only for the composer and for one other audience, an awestruck eavesdropper: you.[13]

This is a convincing, and rather tidy, explanation for the difficulties that Beethoven's late quartets have given audiences, but it is horrifying in the pathos of the image it projects, of a composer writing his most demanding and personal music for the only audience that could not hear it performed, at least in the literal sense. The pathos of this image strikes a deeper chord, for the late quartets can seem to be, in a sense, *about* Beethoven's isolation from music making, from the literal existence of music in sound. But they are also about his isolation from the transaction between those who make music and those who listen—and here the image of him abstractedly turning pages at the conclusion of the first public performance of his Ninth Symphony, oblivious to the response of his audience, comes vividly to mind. But as Beethoven's deafness removes him from this transaction, so also does it focus his attention on it, and I think we can see a more knowing manipulation of his listeners' "outside" perspective in the late quartets than Kerman seems to suggest, as I argue below.

Kerman's notion of the audience "overhearing" the "conversation" of Beethoven's early quartets, or "eavesdropping" on the private utterances of his late quartets, is seemingly close to my own formulation. Kerman, however, is making a distinction between the two, claiming that we "overhear" the string quartet players in the early quartets, but, in the late quartets, "eavesdrop" on Beethoven himself. For Kerman, the string quartet players in Beethoven's late quartets become essentially invisible—perhaps even inaudible, as they were for Beethoven—which does not, I think, correspond very well to our experience of these works in performance. Quite the reverse, in fact, if I may judge from my own experience, for I have never been as aware of performers and their interactions as when I have been privileged to witness successfully subtle navigations of the intricacies of these singular creations. Moreover, I suspect that this is due to the same circumstances that make Beethoven especially suited for Martin's exploration of a quartet's performance preparation, since there is perhaps no other music for which the performers' intense involvement both in the music and with each other is on such full display.

I suggest, as a modification to Kerman's view, that Beethoven is *staging* a self-absorbed discourse, deliberately difficult to follow, if at times tantalizingly direct in its declamation. We may wish to understand what he is doing, metaphorically, as representing the painful difficulties of musical discourse for a deaf composer. Or, more simply, we may wish to understand these quartets *as* the painfully difficult musical discourse of a deaf composer, confirming that the frequent dismissal of these works in the nineteenth century on this basis was after all not completely out of line. But, however we choose to interpret the music or the larger situation, we should not leave out the "intermediaries"—the quartet players—who are impelled to project what we take to be the self-absorption of the composer as a necessary condition for performing such difficult music. Nor should we discount Beethoven's awareness of his "outer" audience, whom he is so skillfully manipulating, if less directly, through his more "inner" manipulation of his players.

My third interlocutor is Gretchen Wheelock, who also seeks to involve the audience in the quartet's conversation. In *Haydn's Ingenious Jesting with Art*, she takes up the "metaphor of conversation," finding it

> obviously attractive in characterizing the voices of the string quartet as listening and responding to one another—agreeing, contending, even changing the subject. Understood in these terms, the conversation of a quartet is heard by its players, whose intimate exchange may or may not be "overheard" by others. . . .
>
> But why not extend the metaphor precisely to bring the audience into the conversation? Here the model of discourse may be more inclusive: even if the most immediate conversation is that between the players, themselves primary and requisite listeners, the audience of contingently present listeners is also engaged in dialogic interaction with the work in progress. . . . The more broadly inclusive concept of conversation suggested here makes room for listening that is more than eavesdropping, for quartets that address listeners in the overt manner of a performance.[14]

In this view, the composer acknowledges the audience, challenging auditors to understand and appreciate—and thus, in some sense, to "participate" in—his play with the conventions of musical discourse. This model, however, leaves stubbornly elusive the very quality I am seeking to locate. As with the performance issues discussed by Martin, the interactive basis identified by Wheelock acts to draw us into the music, but her model, like Kerman's, tends to bypass the performers as such, introducing a "conversation" between the composer (or, perhaps, the work in progress) and the audience.

I propose an alternative model, distinct from these others but illuminated by them. Wheelock's and Kerman's models point out the possibility that the composer may seem to communicate directly with the audience, and, in their examples, they demonstrate that the resulting communicative act is most provocative when it is oblique, skewed expressively or humorously from the "normal" (whatever that may be). For the audience, however, the performers are more concretely present than the composer, whose presence they project through their absorption in the music and their closer knowledge of what is "actually" going on in these oblique communicative acts. Indeed, the performers are in a privileged position, serving not only as audiences for the composer's acts of communication (as in Wheelock's model), but also as representatives of the composer to the audience.

But there is a vital distinction between performers and audience, however often we may read or hear of how string quartet performances seem to blur this boundary, as, for example, in early nineteenth-century accounts of a spectator who felt that he was "playing along" with the performers—we should bear in mind that the spectator in this case was the composer Zelter addressing Goethe[15]—or in the frequent assertion, correct as far as it goes, that the players are the first audience for quartet music. The distinction is, fundamentally, a literal one, for however actively we listen to music, we do not thereby alter its production from without. This is a fairly trivial observation in itself, but it speaks to the aspect of control that is at the heart of the matter.

We may try to isolate this distinction by observing that the players know what will happen while the audience does not. But the distinction extends beyond the performers being "in the know" about the music they are playing just because they can see, to take a typical Haydnesque example, that the music doesn't really end when it pretends to (as in the finale of the "Joke" Quartet, op. 33, no. 2, or the opening movement of op. 50, no. 3). This kind of knowledge is only part of a larger area of control, for it is the performers who make the false ending "work" in each case, and give it its particular flavor of spontaneous jest. My point here should be quickly acknowledged by anyone who has played the music they are hearing performed by another quartet, or by listeners who have heard the work before and are thus "in the know," because an effective performance will inevitably inflect our experience of the work with a fresh perspective, firmly establishing our position "outside" the music despite our inside knowledge. If our knowing the punch line does not spoil the joke in cases like this, it is because players and audience have accepted their quite different roles, in bringing the joke to life on the one hand, and appreciating it afresh on the other.

The players in a string quartet do not bring the joke to life by joining the audience; rather, they must establish a distance between them and the audience, to some extent maintaining the fiction that there is no audience. If they themselves laugh at the joke, it is among themselves and, perhaps, a little at the audience they have fooled, but they ought not to laugh *with* the audience. To acknowledge their audience in this way is to risk depriving them of the delicious feeling of "overhearing" the performance.

The distinction between "inside" and "outside" in performance is in many ways automatically established and maintained, yet it is constantly tinkered with in the course of a work. The composer who consciously manipulates these areas will tease the audience by making access to the inside seem both attractive and possible. One technique is to withhold important information; here, the metaphor of an overheard conversation is particularly useful, since, as with the eavesdropper, the string quartet audience has to reconstruct some aspects of the larger context in order to understand what is being "said." Haydn is particularly adept at withholding vital information about the larger context, usually through misdirection, so that the listener must at some point reconsider her or his first impressions. We may consider the openings of several of Haydn's op. 64 quartets as exemplars of this strategy, since fully half of the quartets in this set begin "falsely," necessitating a startling correction of an opening assertion regarding key, meter, or thematic hierarchy.

Haydn's Op. 64 Quartets, Nos. 2, 3, and 5

Op. 64, no. 2 begins with a solo melody in the first violin, by default (but inconclusively) in the major mode, beginning on the apparent tonic, D (ex. 3.1). <TE3.1> With the entrance of the lower instruments, however, we are suddenly plunged into the actual tonic, B minor, whereupon the phrase is repeated twice for clarification, at first echoing the beginning but fully harmonized in B minor, and then, more forcefully, moved down to its "correct" melodic level, beginning on B. **<AE3.2>**

As Charles Rosen points out, this opening pointedly recalls the opening to op. 33, no. 1, in the same key;[16] **<AE3.3>** moreover, the dramatic profile shared by these two quartets—suggesting major but then turning emphatically to the minor—also anticipates the openings of Beethoven's Fifth and Ninth Symphonies.[17] Although the opening to op. 64, no. 2 may be taken as a bit of comic misdirection (as may its op. 33 correlative), the latter associations underscore an underlying seriousness inherent in the device, reminding us that no good Haydn joke is *merely* a joke, an observation that might return us, if we choose, to the previous chapter's discussion of tone. But in this case there is at work something more basic to the genre itself than the device's potential for making the initial emergence of the minor mode more dramatic.

Haydn's beginning, with its quirky, nervously repetitive, unharmonized melody, sounds disembodied. Even if we accept the violin's scrap of a tune as major mode, we wait for clarification, an effect directly parallel to his earlier experiment with this device in op. 33. Haydn's creating a need for clarification, and making us wait for it, even briefly, has the double function of establishing our position outside and fostering our desire for inside information. Moreover, as the quartet continues to "mull over" the harmonic ambiguity as part of its shared, quasi-conversational discourse, the players' attention seems poised between audience and the music, pointing *inward* (resembling a shared thought process) at the same time that they seem to seek and together arrive at an outer consensus to resolve the ambiguity.

Resolving the opening harmonic ambiguity is, in the first movements of both quartets, the most important work of the first thematic group, whereupon each movement then moves on to the originally suggested key of D major, fulfilling a convention of sonata-form movements in the minor mode. Both opening movements thus effectively frame the minor-mode tonic within its relative major across the exposition as a whole. And, in both cases, the repeated exposition does not simply repeat this opening, but *reconsiders* it, since the opening appears no longer as misdirection but rather as a retransition to B minor from the D-major conclusion of the exposition. Although this situation again anticipates Beethoven's Fifth Symphony, the effect is quite different. Whereas in Beethoven, the return

Ex. 3.1: Haydn, String Quartet, op. 64, no. 2, mvt. 1, mm. 1–10

to minor bears significant dramatic freight, representing the inexorable reimposition of fate from without,[18] in Haydn's quartet movement, the gaze remains inward; even this harmonic containment serves as a directional marker, pointing toward an internal minor mode from a major-mode exterior.

The opening of op. 64, no. 5 presents a somewhat less dramatic profile, whose misdirection might easily be missed or passed over. **<TE3.4>** Haydn begins in this case with a conversational exchange among the three lower instruments (ex. 3.2). As with op. 64, no. 2, there is something missing, since the first violin is left out of the exchange—a fact that is even more obvious to us if we are "overwatching" instead of merely "overhearing." More subtly, the exchange is a trifle too bland, too pat, for it to serve as an opening idea for a Haydn quartet; if we don't know what comes next—which is in fact the famous melody that inspired the quartet's nickname, the "Lark"—we are either disappointed in Haydn or ready to wait him out, to see what he is up to. (We may note, with some satisfaction, that for once "conversation" serves in the continuation as a satisfactory background for music, rather than the reverse.) **<AE3.5>**

The famous "lark" melody itself fills in directly many of the chordal gaps in the conversational interchange that serves as its background. Within the first phrase, for example, the opening A sounds against D-F# (across mm. 8–9), and the upward leap to F# descends to a D-C# resolution within a V_7 that originally appeared without the third (m. 11; cf. m. 3), before concluding the first phrase with a voice exchange with the viola (C#-D-E, mm. 11–12). While all this may result from a "back construction," since Haydn probably first wrote the lower parts as support for the "lark" melody before isolating them for the quartet's opening, the effect this device imparts to the violin's entrance is one of deft assurance backed by inevitability, as counterweight for the sheer, lovely surprise of the soaring melody itself. But for the other players, the effect of the device is even more critical, as we remain much more aware of their rather nonchalant interplay throughout the "lark" melody than we ever would have been without the opening seven bars, converting what might have been a rather conventional presentation of melody accompaniment into something extraordinary, and charging every subsequent texture in the movement with its aura (and there is, indeed, a startling variety of diverse textures in this movement), as well as helping to keep the melody itself fresh across seven extended repetitions.

Ex. 3.2: Haydn, String Quartet, op. 64, no. 5, mvt. 1, mm. 1–12

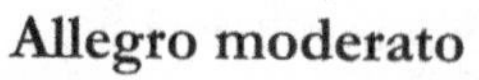

Refreshing as this opening is, and however extended its effects, Haydn's most startling and far-reaching bit of opening misdirection (and not just in this set of quartets) occurs in op. 64, no. 3, <TE3.6> which begins with an apparently straightforward tune involving all four instruments, with nothing obviously "left out," heard to be in a fast triple meter, perhaps 3/8 or 6/8 (ex. 3.3). <AE3.7> There are a few aural clues that Haydn is up to something, for example, when the violins regroup to produce a hemiola effect (m. 4), or when the cello drops out just after the phrase cycles back to the opening lick. But this time we seem to have all we need to understand the "conversation"—until suddenly, that conversation breaks off. What follows the break shows us that we have not understood at all, for the meter is really a *slower* triple meter (3/4, as suggested by the "hemiola" in m. 4), with a correspondingly broader thematic character. The difference is dramatically clarified when the opening melodic gesture returns a few bars later, in m. 17, at which point we cannot help but hear it in 3/4.[19] <AE3.8>

The first movement of op. 64, no. 3 is in other ways a highly unusual movement. The recapitulation is quite short, even for Haydn, and even though it does not follow one of Haydn's "monothematic" sonata designs. Specifically, the recapitulation cuts twenty-four bars from the exposition's sixty-nine, in part by displacing the recapitulation of the main secondary theme to the middle of the development, where it appears (all eight bars of it) in the tonic minor.[20] These and other unusual features of the movement are all traceable to the quirky rhythmic profile of the opening, and the elaborate ways Haydn addresses that profile across the exposition (given in its entirety in ex. 2 in Appendix A). As bits of the opening theme continue to resurface, each recurring element serves either to reorient a salient part of that theme toward 3/4, or to bring out a somewhat different potential of the 3/4 meter itself. This process is systematic enough to warrant an enumeration of its steps:

1. (mm. 8–17) After the lower instruments rhythmically reconfigure the opening neighbor-note motive so as to lay down a clear pulse in 3/4, the first violin takes up the new figure (m. 10) and elaborates it in the following bar so as to replay in specific terms the three instances when sixteenth notes appear in the opening theme (two of which had already been emphasized there through doubling). Thus, the turn figure at the head of m. 2 also heads m. 10, and the figure is immediately

Ex. 3.3: Haydn, String Quartet, op. 64, no. 3, mvt. 1, mm. 1–10

repeated so as to articulate the new pulse; similarly, the concluding scalar figures from mm. 4 and 6 complete the bar. As these figures are reintroduced, their specific placement within the bar (repeated in full as m. 15) directly parallels their placement in the opening theme, forming part of a targeted "retraining" regarding how we are to "hear" the opening theme, within the actual meter of 3/4 instead of the originally implied 3/8 or 6/8.

2. (mm. 17–32) At the conclusion of this phrase, the opening returns, recast through figuration, dissonance, and accent so as emphasize the newly established downbeat. This treatment addresses a specific misdirection in the opening presentation, which encouraged quite different metrical understandings (that is, 3/8, or 6/8 beginning either with a full bar or half bar), and grows ever more insistent in its emphasis on the downbeat. This passage also serves as a harmonic bridge, pausing on V/V to set up the second group.
3. (mm. 33–42) This highly profiled lyrical theme at the head of the second group should (by textbook accounts of sonata form) be featured centrally in the recapitulation, but it does not appear there at all. Rather, Haydn exploits its brief turn to the minor (a traditional device for shaping and stabilizing the second thematic group in a sonata-form exposition) by expanding it into a full-scale presentation in the tonic minor during the development (mm. 87–96). Although couched entirely in the minor, this displaced recapitulatory gesture adds significant thematic weight to the tonic, offsetting the shortness of the recapitulation, even though it represents within the development a kind of double parenthesis—or, perhaps, *because* it is so bracketed. Specifically, the passage appears sandwiched between thematic iterations of A♭ (based mm. 8f); A♭, in its turn, functions as a parenthetical digression from C minor, which frames the entire episode and serves as the main structural key of the development. **<AE3.9>** Within the metrical "reorientation" of the exposition toward 3/4, the theme establishes a lilting 3-1 rhythmic pattern, borrowing the sixteenth-note scalar figure as part of its emphasis on the third beat (in m. 35), and supported by a striding 1-2 rhythmic figure in the cello.
4. (mm. 42–47) This brief section, which serves as a second dominant preparation within the second group, presents the head motive in close

canon, thereby emphasizing the quarter-note pulse and, more particularly, providing new emphasis to the second beat. While this material is part of what will be left out of the recapitulation, its canonic treatment of the head motive reappears in a more compressed form during the retransition (mm. 122–123), which prepares the relative minor but substitutes the tonic at the point of arrival at the recapitulation.[21] **<AE3.10>**

5. (mm. 48–65) With its separate dominant preparation and closed shape, this section will stand in the recapitulation for the second group as a whole—albeit significantly elided with the previous dominant preparation, so that mm. 32–51 of the exposition do not return in the recapitulation. Three things mark this passage as a culmination:

   First, it traces a full-circle shift in thematic hierarchy, with the opening sixteenth-note figure becoming background to the impulse figure in the lower instruments (mm. 48–49), which, when transferred to the first violin and sustained (mm. 50–51), takes over the melodic interest until m. 56, whereupon the first violin extends the phrase so as to restore the sixteenth-note figure to melodic prominence.[22]

   Second, the complex gesture of a quickened pace (the sixteenth-note melodic basis) yielding to the much broader gesture of one melodic note to a bar, itself expanding upward and becoming syncopated in acceleration, has the effect of broadening the rhythmic scale. Specifically, the passage expands what has been the metrical focus of the exposition up to this point, from a preoccupation with the configuration within the bar, to establish a discourse that takes the bar itself as a building block. Even within the sixteenth-note figuration, there is an expansion of the concluding scalar descent to two beats, converting the sixteenth-note patterning of m. 11 (turn, turn, descending scale) to make the concluding gesture of the measure more expansive (ascending arpeggio, two-beat descending scale).

   Third, this complex metrical expansion doubles the melodic ambit of the overall gesture, setting up the elaborate ascents and descents that define the dramatic trajectory of the emergent first-violin melody. The cadential extension (mm. 58–65) then brings the focus back to the stress-configuration within the bar, resolving the metrical conflict between melody and accompaniment that began in m. 52 (third- and second-beat emphases, respectively), eventually, through the cadential trills, reaffirming the second-beat emphasis.

6. (mm. 65–69) This concluding return to the opening motive is completely normalized within 3/4 before being abruptly, if briefly, "reset" at the very end, providing a disorienting hiccup just before the double bar. Depending on how well the listener has attended to the exposition's metrical clarifications, s/he either will be newly thrust into the 3/8–6/8 metrical sphere with the repeat of the exposition, or will hear the opening quite differently, in 3/4. The disorienting stumble that concludes the exposition thus seems calculated to challenge the attentive listener and befuddle anew those who will need the repeated exposition to fully assimilate to 3/4, which will not be effectively undermined again in the movement, even during the recapitulation.

The elaborate means by which the first movement of op. 64, no. 3 builds an entire movement on its opening misdirection are extreme. But this extremity lies mainly in the formal peculiarities that result, and will not for most listeners register in the way the quartet "feels," nor disrupt the sense that everything flows, in natural consequence, from an opening set of gestures. In this sense, an opening misdirection functions much like the establishment of "tone" does in a Haydn symphony, as discussed in the previous chapter, determining how everything that follows will be understood. But there is a critical difference in effect, stemming from the difference in perspective between the players and audience of the work, both of which will be able to trace the effects of these opening conditions but cannot abandon their respective positions within the performance hierarchy.

I have described the opening gestures for these quartets in mostly traditional ways, in terms of Haydn playing with his audience, drawing us into the music through our need for clarification of an opening misdirection. But this does not correspond entirely with our experience of the music in performance. In writing these quartets, Haydn was serving two sets of clients, first of all his players, and more secondarily his eavesdroppers. Our enjoyment of the jest as listeners, in op. 64, nos. 3 and 5 (especially the former), is nothing compared to the pleasure of the quartet players who set us up for it and deliver it, then play the remainder of the movement under its sway. In an important sense, Haydn himself is no longer there but only the performance situation he has created, in which relative "inside" and "outside" positions are established and exploited, each with its own advantages.

This is the duality that defines the quality of the string quartet I have been trying to identify, a quality pioneered and developed if not actually invented by Haydn, who may in this sense be the true inventor of the string quartet, despite a multitude of forerunners and contemporary practitioners. Haydn found a way of building into the genre a style of discourse that affords different but equally enjoyable roles to performers and auditors, establishing a standard that later composers learned to meet in their own ways. Haydn's way generally involved a witty play with musical conventions, in which the more knowing "inside" players could entice and manipulate those "outside," listening their way in. I will return to "Haydn's way" in the final section of this chapter, in order to consider other dimensions and consequences, after I consider more briefly what later composers did with this particular inheritance.

Listening In, After Haydn

Beethoven devised his own application of "Haydn's way" early in his career, but also developed, alongside his imitation of Haydn, a more individual way that would ultimately provide a more attractive model for later composers. In the final member of his first set of quartets (op. 18, no. 6), Beethoven offers a scherzo whose rhythmic perversities make it virtually impossible to "overhear" correctly, so that the clarifying points of arrival, which should orient us, instead tend to sound confused and unsynchronized until he repeats them often enough for us to "switch gears" (see ex. 3.4). **<TE3.11>** After the contrasting trio, which is disarmingly simple in its metrical orientation, Beethoven gives us a second chance to "get" the metrical orientation of the opening; this time, if we are clever enough, we may listen past the violins to the lower instruments, which articulate the actual metrical structure with little ambiguity. **<AE3.12>**

Beethoven seems here to be engaging in a fairly extreme bit of Haydnesque play, although the tenacity of his challenge takes him well beyond the playful benevolence of his models. But he is also adding another factor that enhances the separation of performer from auditor. The disjointed character of this music makes it extremely difficult to play as an ensemble, forcing the directed focus of the players further "inward." Practically speaking, they have little opportunity to enjoy the effect on the audience of Beethoven's jest, if that is what it is, for they are too busy making sure they aren't taken in along with their audience. In a sense, Beethoven does not let his players assume their privileged position as a matter of course, but instead makes them fight their way "inside."

Ex. 3.4: Beethoven, String Quartet, op. 18, no. 6, mvt. 3, mm. 1–8

In this example, Beethoven turns technical difficulties to his advantage in establishing and exploiting the "inside" and "outside" of the performance situation. But the device eventually has a wider application for him, as virtually any problem, even a fairly abstract one, will serve this end. In op. 95, the second of the two quartets "in between" his middle and late quartets, which he labels "Quartetto serioso," <TE3.13> Beethoven provides a "serious" scherzo (marked "Vivace ma serioso") that pushes to the extreme the misdirection of Haydn's openings. Here, Beethoven enacts a fearful struggle for the quartet to establish thematic and harmonic stability after the concluding phrase of the slow movement is left hanging on a diminished-seventh chord, a struggle that will be re-created twice more in the course of the movement (see ex. 3.5).

Technically, Beethoven's device is fairly simple: he merely leaves out the opening phrase or section of the traditional form (that is, that part preceding the first double bar, traditionally repeated), beginning each time, literally, with the middle. But few performers and fewer listeners will realize or concern themselves with the simplicity of the means when faced with the violence of the resulting formal rupture. In this case, Beethoven requires his players to perform an act of musical mutilation, alarming and, in a way, wounding his listeners in the process. **<AE3.14>**

In Beethoven's enigmatic late style, which Kerman (as quoted above) takes as essentially private utterances, the difficulties are no less violent, but typically much less forbidding than in his disturbing "Quartetto serioso." Another scherzo movement, this time from op. 131, provides convenient illustration. **<TE3.15>** Here, tunes emerge and disappear with disconcerting suddenness, "discourse" is interrupted without warning, and we begin to feel a bit like a tennis ball might: no sooner do we start to enjoy a particular flight of Beethoven's fancy, when we are suddenly whacked in a new direction. The "difficulties" are on many levels, but they all conspire to turn the focus inward. Performers must either work hard to coordinate the disparate gestures of this music, to provide a continuity in performance that can absorb and carry through the disjunctions of the music's surface, or work just as hard to deal moment by moment with the difficulties that will accrue from choosing *not* to aim for such a continuity. Listeners, observing the concentration of the players, will strain to hear a broader coherence, some kind of wider context in which the bits of broken discourse they "overhear" can be comprehended. The disparity between the sometimes trivial tunes and the complex ramblings of the greater discourse pull us inward, but never all that far "inside." In this sense, Kerman is undoubtedly correct, for the only true "insider" for this music died nearly two hundred years ago. **<AE3.16>**

Composers in the nineteenth century had difficulty extending the line of development indicated by Beethoven in his final period, with the string quartet no less than with the symphony and piano sonata. All of these genres became, to some extent, "sacred" genres, extremely problematic, yet automatically assumed to carry the most profound utterances of those composers brave enough to attempt them; this assumption was very seldom justified. Brahms provides both a paradigm and, in some respects,

Ex. 3.5: Beethoven, String Quartet, op. 95, mvt. 2, mm. 186–end, and mvt. 3, mm. 1–11

an interesting exception. His early sonatas announced his bold intention to compete head to head with Beethoven, but did little to demonstrate that he could do so effectively, and are, in fact, most interesting when they are least like Beethoven; in any case, he did not return to the genre. His early string quartets were suppressed and reportedly discarded. He failed to complete his first attempt at a symphony as such, and put aside his second attempt for over a decade. Then, in his forties, he turned to both string quartet and symphony, completing symphonies that were immediately and lastingly regarded as worthy successors to Beethoven, and string quartets that have been somewhat less successful in this, despite his by that time well-established reputation as a composer of chamber music.

Brahms's seriousness in approaching the task of writing quartets has a lot to do with the resistance they have encountered. He was an admirer of both Beethoven and Haydn—he owned not only their complete works for string quartet but also the autograph of Haydn's op. 20 quartets—yet nevertheless seemed to recognize primarily the serious side of the models they provided. That Haydn's op. 20 quartets held a privileged position for Brahms was surely no accident, for these are the works that most obviously mark Haydn's resolve, early on, to write in a serious manner for the medium—with their fugues and relatively frequent use of the minor mode, these quartets are usually regarded as part of the "prehistory" of the mature Haydn quartet, with the next set, op. 33, marking his "arrival."

Brahms signaled his seriousness rather broadly by publishing, as his first set of quartets, two quartets in the minor mode, the first (like the First Symphony), in the Beethovenian key of C minor. Perhaps even the opus number for the set (op. 51) is relevant here, since it reproduces that of Haydn's most seriously toned string quartet, the chamber version of *The Seven Last Words of Our Savior on the Cross*, discussed below. In the finale to the second of the quartets from this set, in A minor, ‹TE3.17› Brahms uses his characteristic cross-rhythms as the basis for a heated "argument" among the players, in a "serious" extension of the "conversational" aspect of the medium (see ex. 3.6). Thus, the first violin seems to be playing most of the time in a slower triple meter than the other three instruments, with each side of the "argument" holding to its rhythm at the outset.

As the "argument" continues, the viola takes up the melody, and the second time around seems to "win over" the other players, who switch to its rhythm in m. 19 after first trying yet a third rhythmic pattern, derived from the second half of the melody. The victory is a convincing one partly

Ex. 3.6: Brahms, String Quartet, op. 51, no. 2, mvt. 4, mm. 1–10

because the viola is the deepest voice at this point, with the cello temporarily silent. With the reentry of the cello, the four combatants achieve a hard-won accord, which they endorse with appropriate ferocity. ‹AE3.18›

As we listen to this argument and its temporary resolution, the inside/outside dynamic is apparent, in both the senses I have indicated here. Most immediately, the audience is clearly not part of the argument, nor are the players in a suitably "objective" position to be true auditors. A discerning audience observes not only the conflict but also the complex rhythmic patterns produced by the conflict, taking in the inner cause and the outer effect while contemplating the relationship between them. To a large extent, the elaboration of this kind of inside/outside dynamic depends on the medium, which places us in close proximity to a small group of performers of relatively equal status.

We return to the argument at several points in the movement, most interestingly when a brief but intense canonic passage introduces a new mode of contention (mm. 161–172), which is then applied to the opening melody (mm. 186–193). In the first of these canonic passages, each instrument begins on a different repeated pitch in a rising sequence, intensifying the conflict and making it a four-way dispute, heating up as it goes. But in the second, the canonic treatment of the opening melody produces a constant, regular stream of faster notes, so that a larger sense of order seems this time to displace the more local dispute, an effect reinforced by a temporary drop in volume. **<AE3.19>** Brahms confirms this larger sense of order with the final appearance of the opening melody (mm. 293–300), just before the elaborate slowdown for the concluding *stretto*; here, the dynamic level is even lower, the tempo somewhat slower, and the canon more precise. **<AE3.20>** There is thus in this movement a progression of sorts from inside to outside, from close encounters to a more distant consideration, as an opening rhythmic contention evolves into a more cooperative, evenly measured flow of notes, forcing the listeners' perspective to widen so as to take it all in.

In the twentieth century, the string quartet was revitalized as a medium of intense personal expression, largely due to the contributions of Bartók, who more than any composer before him found ways to use the less conventional models Beethoven provided in his late quartets. Bartók's specific models were not particularly congenial to the dramatic, teleological formal procedures preferred through most of the nineteenth century, but proved to be quite compatible with the quality of string quartet music I have been concerned with here. Thus, arresting local effects, gestures that refuse to connect easily with their neighbors, are commonplace in Bartók's quartets. So, too, is the larger shaping that Beethoven implemented in two of his late quartets (opp. 132 and 131), based more on large-scale symmetries than on dynamism; in these models, as in most of Bartók's quartets, the work as a whole, consisting in an odd number of movements, is constructed around a broadly scaled central movement, providing a temporally arranged basis for the act of "listening in."

In his second quartet, Bartók uses a three-movement symmetrical plan, in which the second movement functions as a disruptive scherzo along Beethovenian lines, set off by its lyrical, sometimes ethereal neighbors. **<TE3.21>** Bartók's inspirations here, as is so often the case, are the challenging rhythms he derived from folk music, but his procedures recall

Beethoven in a number of ways. Thus, the opening of the movement (ex. 3 in Appendix A) presents an immediate problem for listeners, demanding their full concentration in order to make sense of its initial complexities. There is no clear downbeat until well into the movement despite the violent, driven impulse of the music, so that, with the disruptive patterns of off-beat accents we are given instead, we are likely to "overhear" the beginnings of each gesture as downbeats. Even when we do start hearing genuine downbeats on a regular basis, we don't immediately hear them as such. Coupled with this rhythmic manipulation is an intense application of motivic development, typical for Bartók, through which even the harmonic language of the movement derives. **<AE3.22>**

As with Haydn's op. 64, no. 3, the disruptive opening is essential preparation for the larger formal treatment (although configured much differently, of necessity). In a movement of this turbulence, we may reasonably expect a central relaxation, a contrasting "trio" section. And, indeed, we are given such a relaxation, but only in the sense that slower, more lyrical gestures do appear midway through. These gestures appear, however, as disruptive interruptions of continuously driving motivic developments and so provide no true relaxations but rather a strangely unsettling formal tension, such that Bartók cannot simply return to his opening material to round out the form. Instead, he "modulates" from duple meter to triple meter as he returns to a faster tempo, creating yet another source of tension that is not resolved until the very end of the movement. **<AE3.23>**

Throughout these continuously evolving processes, the pull on the audience is twofold: drawn into the inner workings of the music in order to grasp its basic rhythmic coherence, and, at the same time, directed to reconsider the larger formal context as expectations are acknowledged, challenged, and put aside for the sake of a more individually conceived logic. All in all, this is a lot to demand of an audience, and it is somewhat gratifying to observe that he is asking a good deal more than that of his performers. As in late Beethoven, audiences observe a group of players intensely involved in executing dangerously difficult music, challenging them to follow and accept the tortuous path of its logic.

§

The self-absorption of the players in modern performances of string quartet music is visually apparent; most typically, they face inward toward each other, rather than outward toward the audience, their very posture serving as an emblem of the relationship between performers and their audience in this medium. Whether or not the composer has established a respective "inside" and "outside" in the music itself—through "conversational" give and take, humorous or expressive misdirection, sheer technical difficulty, complex patterns of shifting moods and styles, or some other means—the procedures through which the performers prepare and perform the works that they have, in a sense, co-opted from the composer, ensure that this quality will inflect even the smallest details of their performance. We expect a professional string quartet to "own" the works they perform, so that we overhear, necessarily as outsiders, a seamless merging of the abstract "work" and the performers' more tangible performance of that work. The final paragraphs in Robert Martin's discussion of decision making within a string quartet confirm the reasonableness of this expectation:

> The best performers . . . take pains to convince themselves that they are doing what the composer would have wished, even when, after years of studying and performing a work, [they] feel they have made that work their own, [and have thereby] obtained some of the rights of joint ownership. . . .
>
> When it comes time for a performance, there is often a conscious attempt to cover up the hard work of decision making, to give the performance a feeling of spontaneity. A fine performance has a quality of inevitability about it, as though there had been no decisions to be made.[23]

Needless to say, all of this separates the performers from their audience as decisively as anything the composer may write into the music, institutionalizing in our day the inward gaze of the performers. Symbolically, this "inward gaze" is a common strand linking the time when there would have been no "outside" beyond the performers themselves, passing through the age that produced such quaint curios as string quartet tables, and preserved—for our privileged and rapt attention—in the best of modern performances.

SALON VERSUS CHAMBER

While there is a fairly continuous line of development from Haydn to Bartók that preserves, with ever-renewing emphasis, the inside-outside dynamic of the string quartet performing situation, there is also, just as clearly, a remarkable transformation of that dynamic over the same span.

This transformation is in many respects incremental, as indicated by my brief sketch of its history. But those incremental steps by which Haydn becomes Bartók are set in motion by a more radical reconsideration that only seems incremental: that by which Haydn becomes Beethoven.

Beethoven, like Mozart, struggled to respond to the challenge posed by Haydn's string quartets; indeed, their struggles contributed crucially to the growing mystique of the genre itself (not to mention the eclipsing of other composers of quartets in Haydn's generation). Mozart's notorious difficulties in responding to Haydn's op. 33—which resulted, however, in the superb set of six quartets that he dedicated to Haydn—were echoed in Beethoven's struggles with his entrée into the genre, op. 18, another set of six.[24] Each composer found occasion in the final quartet of his set to express an enigmatic angst that seems plausibly to reflect those difficulties, rendered through intense expressivity and unusual formal procedures. Regarding Mozart's "Dissonance" Quartet (K. 465), even Haydn—as nearly everyone—was hard-pressed to explain the opening, with its infamous cross-relations.[25] The intensely dramatic slow movement of Beethoven's first quartet from op. 18, set in the characteristic "dark" key of D minor, moves in a direction often cited as central to Beethoven's quartet style, toward a dramatic mode of presentation that borders on the symphonic. Indeed, this movement's presentational profile is entirely in line with Beethoven's own reported explanation for this movement, that it was based in the tomb scene from *Romeo and Juliet*.[26] But the final movement of op. 18, no. 6 (a quartet discussed earlier with reference to its scherzo) articulates a critically different line of development.

The finale to op. 18, no. 6 is highly idiosyncratic, in that its dramatic introduction seems irreconcilable with the brief, dance-like sonata-form movement that follows, both proportionately and affectively. Beethoven overtly acknowledges this incongruity in the movement's coda, where both elements are placed, as it were, side by side, making their recalcitrant differences in sensibility even more palpable. Perhaps as partial explanation, as well, Beethoven takes the unusual step of giving the movement a title, "La Malinconia"—which has, however, more underscored the enigma than explained it.[27] Yet in the present context it matters less what exactly Beethoven meant by "melancholy"—or, for that matter, what specifically prompted his writing such a movement as a culmination to this set of quartets—as the fact that Beethoven's title points inward, to a *mental* state. Whereas the dissonances at the beginning of Mozart's "Dissonance"

Quartet are presented as clashes among members of a group engaged in a presumptively socialized discourse, Beethoven's "La Malinconia" explicitly represents an individual sensibility or state of mind. Indeed, this representation and its directive energy inward is presented in terms of both register and dynamics, with frequent descents in both realms evoking a sense of a deep, only partially accessible interior life.

This constitutes a shift, well encapsulated by the title of Mark Evan Bonds's book *Music as Thought* (see chapter 1), that directly parallels the increasing influence of German Idealism on conceptions of music and its representational possibilities. Put succinctly: although Beethoven maintains the inside-outside dynamic he inherited from Haydn, as described above, he reconfigures the "inside" as a mental space rather than a social space. Granted, there was already then a substantial history of representing mental states in music, perhaps most relevantly in opera. The "Juliet at the tomb" scene, as Beethoven purportedly set it in the slow movement of op. 18, no. 1, is as operatic as it is symphonic, at times almost histrionic in its dramatic expression of grief. Moreover, opera is only one of many vocal genres, spanning the history of notated music, in which the intense expression of mental states is common. As Bonds notes, however, there is a distinction that may be drawn between rhetoric and "truth" that began to matter anew during this period.[28] As a quasi-operatic "scene," the slow movement of op. 18, no. 1 elaborates on well-established rhetorical gestures for dramatic presentation, and more particularly for the portrayal of anguished grief; while this deployment of traditional rhetoric does not make the movement less "truthful," or less moving for audiences, it does make it more conventional in some sense. Yet it is fairly *un*conventional in advancing the conceit that the string quartet is an appropriate medium for dramatic scenes of this kind. Although the movement is operatic in its rhetoric, it is much more abstract than opera, even if we know its "program," since what we see and hear is not a grieving woman at a tomb but rather four string players. Thus, "her" voice becomes theirs, at once more personal and less specific, moving decisively toward a more collective, generalizable mode of expression.

Even here we may find precedent in Haydn. In the original performance of *The Seven Last Words of Our Savior on the Cross* (1786), the individual movements served as orchestral elaborations of (or meditations on) Christ's final utterances, as read out from the scriptures by the officiating priest at the Cathedral of Cádiz, which had commissioned the work. Although Haydn thus did not conceive the piece as a string quartet, his authoring (or authorizing)[29] the quartet arrangement in the following year represents an important step in reconfiguring the genre's relationship to its audience, by presenting an expressive statement, delivered by a unified ensemble, that at no time becomes "conversational" in the manner characteristic of Haydn's quartet writing. As would Beethoven in the slow movement of op. 18, no. 1, Haydn unites his players within a coordinated rhetoric, so that the quartet "speaks as one." While there is inwardness and dramatic presentation, and an intense collaboration among the players—all markers of the inside-outside dynamic discussed earlier—there is no playful interaction among them, no sense of conspiratorial fun. It is not surprising, then, that Haydn also approved an arrangement of the piece for keyboard, where this rhetorical mode was for him more typical.

We might usefully contrast this kind of rhetoric-based drama, borrowed from the public spheres of church, opera, and concert hall, with the intimacy of the *Lieder* tradition. Especially as cultivated during the first generation after Haydn's death, the *Lied* maintained a space where (poetic) truth trumped rhetoric, and where interactions between singer and pianist, while not generally playful, were always intimate and in some way part of the point of each individual song. Because of this intimacy of performance dynamic, the *Lied*, like the string quartet already in the previous generation, was essentially *overheard* by its first audiences even when presented to them in a formal setting—although this seems less true of performances today, which tend to take the form of a vocal recital, more overtly directing the performance outward to the audience. But in the *Lied* during the first decades of the nineteenth century, as increasingly with many of Beethoven's quartets, the inwardness associated with the genre and with the performing space began to shift in a way that aligns easily with the distinction often made, if only implicitly, between "salon music" and "chamber music," with such transient institutions as the *Schubertiad*, which might include *Lieder*, solo piano works, and small ensembles, in this figurative sense occupying a place in between the salon and the chamber.

Indeed, the now standard distinction made between chamber music and salon music—the one much respected, the other generally sneered at (typically with an implied "mere" preceding "salon music")—seems particularly useful in understanding the shift of sensibilities between

Haydn and Beethoven regarding the string quartet. Salon culture in the late eighteenth century, as Elisabeth Le Guin has demonstrated, is perfectly in tune with the aesthetic of Haydn's chamber music.[30] And it is a world that had not (yet) come under the sway of German Idealism, with its dual focus on the infinite and the subjective. Thus, in her paraphrased translation of M. de Buffon, as recounted by Mme Necker, "In the salon we remain among the concerns of ordinary men and women. Here, we are more likely to feel indifference toward a very ingenious work; our taste will be for a simple but useful reading. What is the reason for this? In the one, the author speaks to me of myself, and in the other he speaks to me only of himself."[31]

But by the early nineteenth century that same culture seemed increasingly to lack seriousness, especially from the perspective of an idealism-fueled German *Kultur*, from which prospect salons were not only French—a cornerstone of their disparaged *Zivilization*—but also increasingly suspect because they were hosted and managed by women. These alignments were confirmed in several relatively high-profile instances. Chopin, for example, once stigmatized with the "salon" label—an association seemingly reinforced by his purported effeminacy—achieved a partial rescue in the early twentieth century when Heinrich Schenker proclaimed him an honorary *German* composer.[32] Schenker was both following Franz Brendel in using "German" in this regard to indicate the only musical tradition that could be understood as serious, and subscribing fully to the German Idealist offshoots that found musical seriousness within a mystical fusion between musical process and basic truths, with such Schenkerian concepts as the *Urgrund, Ursatz,* and *Urlinie* standing in for the infinite (or absolute) and its imputed connection to basic musical structures. Likewise, Fanny Mendelssohn's status as a *salonnière,* however extraordinary her success in that realm, was the highest she could aspire to as a respectable woman, since she was denied the life of a professional musician, first and most famously by her father.[33] Perhaps respectability was even more of an issue for Fanny Mendelssohn because of her Jewish heritage; in any event, she (mainly) kept to her assigned place, composing and performing for the *salon* while her famous brother Felix—when he wasn't writing for larger forces or helping to establish the standards for serious German musical endeavors through his positions as *Kapellmeister* in Berlin and Director of the Leipzig Conservatory of Music—wrote and performed *chamber music.*[34]

But if the chamber, in this sense, came to represent the aspirationally *thought*-driven, consummately subjective dimension of music, and if the string quartet increasingly represented the most intense manifestation of that line of musical development,[35] the more socially directed aspects of domestic music making did not simply disappear. Haydn's string quartets, along with Mozart's quartets and quintets, continued to—and still continue to—enact the spirit of the salon even within the "chamber" realm. Moreover, the quartet and other forms of salon-styled chamber music continued to be cultivated as well, in France and elsewhere, in forms and styles more evocative of the social than of Beethoven's and later composers' intensified inwardness.

As the nineteenth century wore on, however, a more drastic rejection of the intensified inwardness of music under the sway of German Idealism was taking place in the New World, in very different venues, and for very different kinds of audiences.

PART III | NEW WORLD DUALITIES

4 | POPULAR MUSIC CONTRA GERMAN IDEALISM

Anglo-American Rebellions from Minstrelsy to Camp

Blackface minstrelsy and camp are seemingly worlds apart. Certainly, their trajectories have been different: minstrelsy enjoyed huge success in the second half of the nineteenth century and well into the twentieth before its overt racism made it an object of outrage and collective shame, whereas camp came to general attention only in the aftermath of Susan Sontag's "Notes on Camp" (1964),[1] having spent decades in clandestine obscurity. Moreover, minstrelsy's distinctive look and predictable routines make it (or allusions to it) instantly recognizable, whereas camp's ready attachment to other, more mainstream practices has allowed it to elude easy identification; indeed, camp's capacity to pass unrecognized has been critically important to the closeted male homosexuals with whom it has been most closely associated. To put it perhaps too neatly: minstrelsy is a practice that entails a set of sensibilities, whereas camp is a sensibility that informs a set of practices. And, although both minstrelsy and camp may be understood as theatrical cultures connected to groups historically shunned by mainstream (that is, presumptively white and heterosexual) society, there is a huge gulf between them, with one now hopelessly mired in an uncomfortable past and the other, at times, fashionably au courant. Minstrelsy's fall has been precipitous, from being a celebrated cultural export to being regarded as the irretrievably tainted legacy of institutionalized slavery and entrenched racism. Camp, conversely, has emerged from its closet to become a much-discussed and, within academia and some other circles, much-celebrated aspect of twentieth-century cultural life.[2]

Despite these differences, I propose here to consider minstrelsy and camp in tandem, as closely related phenomena. What unites them, in this context, is not their shared theatrical basis or their association with marginalized groups, however important these parallels will turn out to be at a later stage of my argument. Indeed, their association with marginalized groups—for many the most important features of camp and minstrelsy—must initially be put aside if we are to see clearly what links minstrelsy and camp at a more basic level: a shared spirit of rebellion against the seriousness of art and, more specifically from the late nineteenth century on, of music as redefined in the wake of German Idealism.

Minstrelsy's foundation in blackface implicitly asserts, with appalling casualness, that African Americans do not actually matter as people, that they are in fact less than fully human, and that their appearance of humanity is no more than a simulation. In its use of blackface, minstrelsy both parodies that simulation and uses it as a mask, but rarely (at least for the main span of minstrelsy's popularity) allows its white audiences to dwell on the actual experiences of black human beings in the United States.[3] This situation became increasingly more complicated when African Americans began performing more widely in blackface after the Civil War, which added a new layer to the parody and caused the emergently multiple masks to slip a bit. But in an important sense, these complications were distractions that generically had to be ignored even as they were being exploited by performers, since, despite how it may appear to latter-day sensitivities, race was not minstrelsy's primary concern. While minstrelsy may have found it essential, over time, to keep blacks "in their place," it was not racism as such that drove that necessity but rather the desire to maintain the entertainment value of minstrelsy as an institution.[4]

Thus, notwithstanding the central role of race in US American culture, and despite minstrelsy's racialized basis, minstrelsy in its heyday was not primarily "about" race. That such a flagrantly racist institution should be primarily about something else, something for which its racism was only ancillary (though also indispensable), is in itself outrageous. And, perhaps, it may seem outrageous even to make this claim, since minstrelsy's most indelible impact has been its development and perpetuation of racial stereotypes. But we must remember that minstrelsy, while invested in keeping blacks in their place, did not put them there in the first place and could never have accomplished or sustained the subjection of African Americans on its own. Indeed, minstrelsy, though an instrument of black oppression, also became an important vehicle, however oddly configured, for their gradual emergence into the mainstream. But that particular story is not the one that most concerns me here.[5] Rather, I wish to consider, in relation to German Idealism's transformative effect on musical practices, *how* minstrelsy entertained, what needs it spoke to, and what its cultural agenda was, by first looking beyond its racial basis and impact.

Camp, for its part, has likewise seemed to be "about" the group with which it has been most closely associated: homosexual men. Through Sontag's essay and in its long afterlife, camp has been generally "outed" as this group's special, even exclusive domain.[6] Indeed, before Stonewall and the gay liberation movement it helped invigorate,[7] camp had for decades provided a covert means for building community among gay theatergoers, who might through shared camp tastes recognize each other within mixed populations that included both closeted gay men and straights, two groups who would typically respond either differently, or similarly but from different perspectives, to the same theatrical performance or film. The basis for this particular community builder is a shared sensibility, a shared predilection to appreciate, nurture, and otherwise value certain theatrical elements that might be overlooked or shunned by the mainstream. Yet, even without specifying what those elements might be, one may well question how exclusively their appreciation has been confined to gay men, since sensibility and sexual orientation are not, in fact, coextensive, and never have been. Not only will there always be gay men who do not appreciate or even "get" camp, but there are also many others, among women and straight men, who appreciate camp. Moreover, camp's capacity to "pass," in parallel to the (closeted) gay population served by that capacity, meant that it had at least to overlap with other tastes that had a broader, more mainstream (read: heterosexual) base of appeal. Even though there are social mechanisms that have helped align camp performance and reception with gay theatrical communities—a mix of social networking, "packaging" of identities, and a corresponding fear of stigma among straight men, whose responses might make them appear gay if they weren't watchful—camp sensibilities inevitably leaked into mainstream reception.

But might not the direction of that flow been the reverse, early on? Any historical account of camp must make some plausible case for its origins within existing practices and tastes, which may have been tweaked and repurposed, but only to an extent that would continue to indulge more mainstream tastes, as well. I propose to make such a case here, and to argue that camp sensibilities, at least in the United States, originated from the same spirit of rebellion that manifested itself through minstrelsy. I propose further to explore—and it is necessary to do so at some length—the development and latter-day coexistence of somewhat disparate camp sensibilities, wherein a gay-centered camp appreciation and a straight-centered camp appreciation might overlap and intermingle, and to show how both forms relate easily to a mainstreamed, New World rejection of the musical archetypes imposed by German Idealism.[8]

In exploring the shared basis of late nineteenth-century minstrelsy and camp in a US American rejection of German Idealism's essentialized redefinition of music, I argue more broadly for this being a sustained, if partial basis for the enduring "popular" side of the New World split between "classical" and "popular" music, which became entrenched as a central feature of music over the course of the twentieth century. The "classical" side of that split in the United States resulted from the importation and fostering of "serious" European traditions under the sway of German Idealism, which history has been a mainstay of traditional musicological accounts of music in the New World.[9] The music I consider in this chapter is, conversely, deliberately *un*serious for the most part, and quite often playfully tweaking seriousness—not, however, in the manner of Haydn, who predates German Idealism, but rather in clear reaction to the attitudinal changes brought about by what William Weber has termed "musical idealism."[10]

In Weber's understanding of these changes, which deeply affected musical practices in Europe during the first half of the nineteenth century (and, later, in America, largely in emulation of Europe), they were "born from a utopian vision of music-making rooted in Romantic thinking that made claim to a kind of artistic truth," positing "a higher musical experience . . . rooted in individual contemplation," which gave rise to a new seriousness in programming and a higher general musical literacy, among other distinguishing features, such as a "serious demeanor during musical performance," a "hierarchical ordering of genres and tastes" and the "expectation that listeners learn about great works to understand them appropriately."[11] Musical idealism was obviously informed by the new paradigms for music that came into play at precisely the same time through German Idealism, through which, as discussed in chapter one, music came to be seen as a conduit, activated through contemplation, between individual subjectivity and something much larger, variously defined as God, absolute consciousness, infinity (or eternity), the Will, or some other profoundly sensed but immaterial force or construct. Yet, although musical idealism rested, philosophically, on this new regard for music's capacity, as Weber argues it became a culture onto itself: what we now call "classical" music, a set of practices that can usefully be (and in practice, usually are) differentiated from their philosophical underpinnings, and that, in aggregate, insisted to an unprecedented extent on taking the art of music seriously.

Late nineteenth-century minstrelsy and camp—as well as other, related types of musicking, such as ragtime, early jazz, burlesque, satire, and musical comedy—tend to regard musical idealism as pretentious, and with a great deal of suspicion, while at the same time taking some measure of what its repertories and institutions had to offer as entertainment, through imitation, parody, or something in between. I will consider, in the chapter following this one, more ambitious attempts to crossbreed popular music with sincerity and serious intent, such as later jazz, serious blues, some varieties of rock and folk, some dimensions of operetta and operatic musicals, and gospel-based pop, engaging as well with the cult of authenticity that informs many (but not all) of these types and is itself a derivative of German Idealism. But as a starting point, I focus here on some important consequences of the impulse toward rebellion as specifically manifest in minstrelsy, camp, and associated musical practices.

PUTTING ON

The phrase "putting on" encapsulates much of what minstrelsy and camp offered in response to the new and continued seriousness of European-derived concert and operatic music, which in the twentieth century became known as classical music. The phrase suggests many related things: insincerity or feigned sincerity ("you're putting me on . . ."),[12] attempting to persuade through the simulation of alternatives to existing realities ("putting on a show," "putting on an act"), or pretentious overreaching ("putting on airs," "Puttin' On the Ritz"). Indeed, the latter example has particular relevance here, since the original lyric for the Irving Berlin song of this title (before he rewrote it for *Blue Skies* just after World War II) is explicitly about African Americans pretending to a sophistication they could never achieve, following a familiar minstrelsy trope based on Zip

Coon.[13] "Putting on" thus indicates the performance of a false reality, often but not always accompanied by a knowing wink (or its equivalent) to acknowledge that it is all an act.

"Putting on" overlaps significantly with what is called, often disparagingly, *theatrical*, a category that also takes in other things that may be easily "put on," such as costumes, a well-defined mode of acting (as of a stock role or stereotype; a *shtick*), or a mask, whether literal or figurative. Masks, in particular, are tricky to decipher (and often usefully so), since hiding the face obscures the extent to which the performer may or may not identify with the part being played. Donning costumes, applying makeup, and performing stereotypical characters can also do this readily, as they all enforce a separation between the acted persona and the actor who performs that role. To be sure, acting in the conventional sense often does this, as well, but just as often—and usually by design—gives the impression that there is in effect no act, that the character and actor have become one (if only for the duration of the performance), so as to facilitate the audience's belief in the "dramatic truth" of what they are seeing and hearing.

More consistently than any other acting mode, performing a stage song can create and sustain a sharply defined ambiguity regarding the split or unity between character and actor. Moreover, there is more to this sustained double image than what is entailed in the act of singing itself, which activates what Scott McMillin terms the "crackle of difference" between dramatic speech and song.[14] Stage song is almost always accompanied by instrumentalists, who create an ongoing musical stream that suspends the performed role in time and within its rhythmic flow. This situation is blatantly artificial, especially within dramatic scenes, but it is also naturalizing in its effect, since it creates a habitat of sorts for the performed role—which habitat may, however, function in its turn as no more than another kind of costume or mask.

The naturalizing capacity of music, as just described, functions much differently within the musical paradigm offered by German Idealism, where it serves to reinforce the idea that music provides access to a noumenal world, a world beyond what we can perceive directly through our senses. For this paradigm to be convincing, performance as such has to disappear, generally to be replaced by "interpretation," a mode of musical delivery that aims to bring out as effectively as possible the "true" meaning of a musical work, in order to enhance its capacity to conjure the world beyond, to bring that world into close proximity so that listeners might, through contemplation, immerse themselves in it.[15] If there is a theatrical side to musical interpretation, it lies in how the performing musician models the immersion of the self into the flow of music. But interpretation must not *seem* theatrical; to be effective, this modeling cannot come across as something "put on," but must instead seem deeply felt by the performer.[16]

Minstrelsy and camp, on the other hand, reject this paradigm outright, along with the belief structure that supports it. Indeed, their embrace of theatricality argues implicitly, through insinuation, that "interpretation" is itself just another pose, something "put on" even though it may pretend to be (or even genuinely feel) otherwise. In a classic articulation of this general skepticism, Mrs. Cheveley, near the beginning of Oscar Wilde's *An Ideal Husband* (1895), first dismisses optimism and pessimism as "merely poses," then declares that being natural is itself just another pose:

> SIR ROBERT CHILTERN: You prefer to be natural?
> MRS. CHEVELEY: Sometimes. But it is such a very difficult pose to keep up.[17]

Moreover, like Haydn's string quartets, minstrelsy and some modes of camp are decidedly *social* in their appeal, acknowledging their audience through entertaining role play (and through a sense of play more generally), and demonstrating the capacity of musical performance to enact—or, perhaps better, to *stage*—a social world within its textures and through the interactions of its performers.

Because minstrelsy and camp so often do these things in different ways, however, I must now subdivide the argument into two broad sections, in order to do more justice to each type. The need for this subdivision, as well as the disparity of length between the resulting sections, testifies to important differences between minstrelsy and camp, stemming in part from their different historical trajectories. Most central to the presentation of my argument, there is a vastly different level of credibility regarding the paired notions that minstrelsy and camp arose from a similar spirit of rebellion, and that among the targets of that rebellion—regarding music, and at least during the late nineteenth century—was the new paradigm for music as an elevated art according to the emergent, imported European culture of musical idealism, underwritten by German Idealism. While minstrelsy's rebellion was much broader than this, and arose before the transformations of musical practices wrought by German Idealism took root in the United States, most will find it already plausible that it might later have included this new paradigm of serious music within the wide compass of its scattershot cultural critique. But camp, because of its latter-day, often essentialized attachment to gay subcultures, seems removed from this kind of generalized critique. It is thus necessary here to place camp more securely in history, specifically tracing its evolution from the late nineteenth century to the mid-twentieth-century camp tastes that have provided the basis for its identification in more recent decades. In the event, the covered historical span will be similar for each section, arching from the generation of Gilbert and Sullivan to the practices of the first two decades of synchronized sound films in Hollywood.

MINSTRELSY: FROM REBELLION TO NOSTALGIA

One of the most distinctive features of the nineteenth-century minstrel show was the "lineup," which probably originated with Edwin Christy and the first of many groups bearing his name, the 1846 edition of Christy's Minstrels. In the traditional minstrel show lineup, the blackface musicians, including two percussionists (playing tambourine and either bones or another type of handheld clicking instrument), and at least two melodic/harmonic instrumentalists (traditionally playing fiddle and banjo) stand in a curved line facing the audience, with the percussionists—"Mr. Bones" and "Mr. Tambo"—at either end, all awaiting "Mr. Interlocutor," who takes the center position and commences the sequence with the instruction, "Gentlemen, be seated." From this formation, the musicians then performed musical numbers interspersed with humorous verbal byplay between the interlocutor and the "end men," who interacted much as a comic-and-straight-man team would in later vaudeville or burlesque. Indeed, the latter would often recycle the same repertory of jokes, which in minstrelsy were generally at the expense of the stiffly formal interlocutor, and calculated either to distract him from his ostensible function of presiding over the musical proceedings, or otherwise to undercut his authority.

Beyond the lineup, as I have argued elsewhere:

> Minstrelsy . . . gave its audience an appealing perspective on upper-class entertainments—especially those imported from Europe, whether operatic or instrumental—staking an implicit claim to at least some of the

> attractions of the "high style" without falling prey to its pretentiousness. In so doing, it honored and validated its audience, flattering their sensibilities and suggesting that their perspective, as lower-to-middle-class white Americans, was after all the most privileged. In a broad sense, this dimension of minstrel shows allowed them to function as the "endmen" of society, undermining from its fringes the high-cultural pretensions of an imagined upper-class "interlocutor," through deft musical mimicry and crude verbal wit; thus, a blackface burlesque given in 1845 New York by the Ethiopian Opera Company (including Edwin Christy) was given the title *Som-am-bull-ole,* alluding at once to Bellini's popular opera *La sonnambula* and [violinist] Ole Bull, two favorite subjects for blackface burlesque.[18]

As suggested, the kind of undermining banter that occurred during the lineup sequences, in which the end men relentlessly sabotaged Mr. Interlocutor's authority as master of ceremonies, also informed the comedic dimension of minstrelsy on a larger scale. Much of the rest of a minstrel show and some of the lineup's presentations would typically comprise parodies and spoofs, including as their targets (beyond those already mentioned) respected operatic works such as Donizetti's *Lucia di Lammermoor* and Rossini's *Semiramide*; celebrated performing musicians such as soprano Jenny Lind and violinist Henri Vieuxtemps; nonmusical cultural and societal authority figures such as preachers, public lecturers, Shakespearean actors, and politicians; and, more generally, the ideals of gentility and the institutions of respectability (such as marriage), usually through parodic courtship songs and dramatic skits that might include drag performances in what were known as "wench" roles.[19] Moreover, the two best-known stereotypes of minstrelsy beyond the lineup, Jim Crow and Zip Coon, carried the dynamic of undermining pretension and authority into the other segments of a minstrel show. Seen from this perspective, Jim Crow's penchant for sly, passive-aggressive resistance and braggadocio echoed the end men's more active engagements with authority, while Zip Coon's dandyism lampooned upper-class pretensions. Both types figured prominently in skits and, as William Mahar's survey of minstrel song types demonstrates, also animated a wide swath of the repertory (mostly excepting the more nostalgic or sentimental types).[20]

All of this traded in a fundamental ambiguity about who exactly was the butt of the joke, the institution or figure being mocked through parody, or the blackface stereotypical character who ventured to simulate his betters and their (presumably out of reach) sensibilities. Moreover, that ambiguity was amplified by the operative cultural and societal hierarchies, since all potential targets—high culture, African Americans, and women—were "Other" to the white working-class men who made up the core audience for minstrel shows. The various masks of minstrelsy used this ambiguity to advantage, officially (but not really) deflecting satiric barbs from the more powerful groups and institutions being imitated (cultural and societal leaders, more expensive and "high-class" entertainments, and respectability more generally) to the least powerful group (the African American personae), in case offense were ever to be taken by those being ridiculed. Just as important to the carnivalesque dynamic that provided the foundation for minstrelsy (before the Civil War, at least, and in many venues thereafter) was the fact that the performers were, like their audiences, predominantly white males, which was often explicitly demonstrated through staging a number or two without blackface. The spirit of carnival, with its characteristic reversal of societal hierarchies (as theorized by Mikhail Bakhtin), thus reigned throughout a minstrel show, extending to include both performers and audience within its raucous embrace.[21]

Notwithstanding the pervasiveness of minstrelsy's spirit of carnival, however, its rebellion against musical idealism came into a particularly sharp focus during the lineup sequences themselves. As the primary setup for performing nondramatic musical numbers, the lineup explicitly replaced the presentational structure and style that might be expected at a formal concert. Thus, Mr. Interlocutor's genial persona reminded audiences of that discarded formality but was undermined in performance through exaggeration and the incommensurability of the setting, and more pointedly rejected through his irreverent treatment by the end men, who would enlist the audience, through their laughter and applause, as collaborators in deflating Mr. Interlocutor's earnest decorum. Moreover, the lineup's mix of comedy and music brought the end men's clownish behavior into the music itself in various ways. First, it placed their professional performances into sharp relief, through the incongruity of a primitive buffoon being capable of virtuosic musical performance (an incongruity well in line, however, with already formed cultural stereotypes regarding African Americans' innate musicality and rhythmic sense).[22] More subtly, and in consequence of the greater attention thus drawn to the end men's contributions, the ensemble numbers that followed episodes of verbal sparring implicitly overturned the conventional hierarchies of ensemble performance, in which the lead singer or instrumentalist is the main focus of attention. Instead, percussion and the rhythmic element more generally became at least as important, often even paramount, an elevation that accrued additional carnivalesque overtones because it was both motivated and inflected by the impertinent personae of the percussionists themselves. As Steven Baur describes the end men's importance to both minstrelsy's music and its role in critiquing society:

> The predominance of rhythm and percussion and the indispensability of dancing to music making are among the primary elements that set minstrel songs apart from other popular song traditions of the period and they are the primary elements through which minstrelsy accomplished much of its cultural work. Not coincidentally, it was the percussion wielding, dancing endmen—"the most unruly of the lot"—who performed the bulk of the social criticism in the early minstrel show. From their position at the margins of the stage they leveled their attacks, pranks, and ridicule—backed with a percussive beating—against the pretentious, authoritative interlocutor occupying center stage. For those at the margins of society, the endmen in the minstrel show would have been empowering figures.[23]

How minstrel show lineups functioned in this regard was obscured over time by a variety of causes. By far the most important of these was the shift within the minstrel tradition itself, which transformed from

1. a lively show enacting the spirit of carnival for working-to-middle-class white men out for a boisterous good time (across the nineteenth century and well into the twentieth), which came to include, after 1850, a more sentimentalized component whose repertory overlapped considerably with Stephen Foster's parlor songs; to
2. something presented more formally to a broader audience whose idea of a good time was somewhat more inhibited (or merely more vicarious), as in the case of "slumming" in urban centers such as New York, or as with Londoners across the later nineteenth century relishing the refined vulgarities of an American import; to
3. a variety of acts within other entertainment venues, such as early twentieth-century vaudeville and burlesque (where the lineup, as such, tended to disappear); to

4. something performed thereafter, often in highly stylized form, as an appeal to nostalgia for the performance mode itself.

It was the latter step, largely because of its documentation in mainstream Hollywood films, and notwithstanding the persistence in some areas of earlier minstrel traditions, that had the biggest impact over time, underscoring the minstrel show's racism and making that racism central to perceptions of minstrelsy generally and of blackface in particular. Two steps in the transition of minstrelsy from carnival to object of nostalgia—specifically, the long London run and nostalgia-driven Hollywood films featuring blackface—are especially worth revisiting here, because they have produced interesting artifacts that are in different ways at odds with minstrelsy's initial impulse toward rebellion.

As Ann Douglas argues, the multiple and layered masks of minstrelsy—for example, of post–Civil War blacks playing whites imitating (plantation) blacks who probably had been imitating whites in the first place—were part of the entertainment dynamic of American minstrelsy.[24] Yet, the same could not be said for minstrelsy as exported to England, or at least not in the same way or to the same degree, simply because reading layered masks requires an immediate familiarity with behavioral nuance, without which the mask will generally be read more simply and the performance accepted more readily as ethnographically authentic, at least by intention. Despite this, and even partly because of it, a comparable level of subtlety does enter the mix when the minstrel show lineup is invoked in the parodic context of Gilbert and Sullivan's penultimate collaboration, the moderately successful (though seldom revived) operetta *Utopia Limited; or, The Flowers of Progress* (1893). **<TE4.1>**

London audiences had responded well to minstrelsy ever since Thomas Dartmouth Rice first "jumped Jim Crow" there in 1836.[25] English tours of minstrel troupes from the United States continued to be successful through the 1840s and beyond, including appearances of the Virginia Minstrels in 1843 and of the Ethiopian Serenaders in 1846–1847, but an extended Christy's Minstrels tour in the late 1850s soon turned this taste into an institution. Among many similarly named groups spawned by Christy's Minstrels was one that played from 1862 until 1904 in St. James's Hall (a favorite concert venue especially for "light classical" music and similar fare), and it is this group that served as a point of reference for Gilbert and Sullivan. Near the beginning of act 2, *Utopia Limited* simulates a minstrel show lineup in order to parody English courtly behavior, ostensibly as part of an ongoing effort to "Anglicize" the tropical island paradise Utopia, which effort provides the operetta's central conceit. The number in question, "Society Has Quite Forsaken," includes a typical Gilbert patter ("It really is surprising") set to a closely harmonized melody borrowed directly from minstrelsy.[26] <TE4.2> To prepare the number, six Englishmen (the "Flowers of Progress" in the operetta's subtitle), led by Lord Dramaleigh (who, as "Lord High Chamberlain," is running the show), set up a "cabinet meeting" with Utopia's King Paramount so as to resemble a minstrel lineup, arranging themselves, replete with "plantation" instruments,[27] to either side of the king, who is thus made unwittingly to play the part of Mr. Interlocutor (fig. 4.1). <IE4.3> <AE4.4> Although the King senses something amiss—"You are not making fun of us? This is in accordance with the practice of the Court of St. James's?"—he is partly reassured by Lord Dramaleigh: "Well, it is in accordance with the practice at the Court of St. James's Hall."[28]

The six English "Cabinet Ministers" are all clearly in on the joke, functioning together as end men to undermine the king's authority, since the musical number, like the operetta itself, is framed by King Paramount's status as a primitive who naïvely imitates customs he does not understand. So described, this situation corresponds roughly to how an actual minstrel show lineup might have then seemed to Londoners: savvy end men undermining an already dubious authority figure, combined with the spectacle of "primitives" who are inadequate to the social roles they imitate but who perform music superbly. But the layers for the number are more complex than this, and much more specific, even if they could never come close to the nuanced behavioral interplay enjoyed by late nineteenth-century minstrel audiences in the United States—except perhaps in early performances of the operetta for London audiences well attuned to topical nuance and political allusion.

To begin with, "Society Has Quite Forsaken" presents King Paramount not merely as a primitive but also as a king with a cabinet, so that the number directly parodies the organization—and, perhaps, to some astute observers, the personages—of the English Court of St. James itself, which is referred to in the setup to the number, as noted. Indeed, there were claims that Edward VII, then Prince of Wales, was sufficiently offended by the show that he never again visited the Savoy Theatre, although he had previously arranged a command performance of *The Gondoliers*—the

Fig. 4.1: Caricature of minstrel lineup in *Utopia Limited.* Lower segment of "Scenes from a performance of Gilbert and Sullivan's 'Utopia Limited' at the Broadway Theatre in New York City." Publication unknown; probably *Harper's Weekly*, 1894. Thure de Thulstrup, artist. Reproduction courtesy of Schlesinger Library, Radcliffe Institute, Harvard University; used with permission.

immediate predecessor to *Utopia Limited,* which also satirizes royalty—at Windsor Castle for Queen Victoria.[29] Several details in the act I finale, which introduces the Flowers of Progress, indirectly confirm this specific political context for the parody, and help explain how the show might have seemed more offensive to Britain's royals than *The Gondoliers.* The most prominently pointed musical element in the finale, apart from a brief instrumental quotation from "Rule, Britannia," stems from the inclusion, among the Flowers of Progress, of Captain Corcoran (now Captain Sir Edward Corcoran, KCB) from Gilbert and Sullivan's *H.M.S. Pinafore,* a show that openly ridiculed the real-life appointment of William H. Smith (a bookseller) to the position of First Lord of the Admiralty, so obviously targeted that he was thereafter frequently referred to as "Pinafore Smith." After Captain Corcoran is introduced, in a brief recollection of the "Captain's Song" from *H.M.S. Pinafore,* he claims "hardly ever" to have "run a ship ashore." Earlier in the same sequence, a more oblique reference implies that England's military power is virtually nonexistent, by implicitly placing it on a par with the nonexistent "Troops" of the Town of Titipu in *The Mikado*; thus, Britain's army "in serried ranks assembles," a verbal reference whose accompanying trumpet calls confirm its connection to Nanki Poo's "A Wandering Minstrel, I." But the knockout blow is saved for last: the act ends with an extended and direct satirical attack on England's system of limited liability, which King Paramount agrees to adopt after admitting that "at first sight it strikes us as dishonest."[30] **<AE4.5>**

During the minstrel number itself, moreover, the king's verses report, in parallel to the superior musicianship characteristic of minstrelsy's "savages," the "surprising" success of the imported English customs, laws, and institutions. Specifically, the song details that Utopia (unlike England herself) has through Anglicizing eliminated crime, divorce, unearned privilege, urban blight, poverty, hunger, pandering, and commercialism. If the Cabinet Ministers' responses to the king resemble the undercutting interjections of minstrelsy's end men, it is to inverse effect—something audiences would have come to expect from Gilbert, given his fondness for topsy-turvydom. Thus, they allude with interjections in each verse to England's relative *lack* of success in eradicating these societal ills, reiterate at the end of each verse that "this happy country has been Anglicized completely" (repeating the final word twice for ironic emphasis), and note in the "banjo" chorus's patter that Utopia "is England—with improvements." **<AE4.6>**

Underwriting these particular barbs targeting England's institutions and pretensions is an implicit anti-imperialist scenario, which argues that Utopia is in fact ill served by its quest to Anglicize—a scenario that reads critically in both directions, since it is the islanders' absurd naïveté that leads them foolishly to imitate England in the first place. As I suggest elsewhere, this dimension of *Utopia Limited*'s minstrel sequence, like the operetta more broadly, was probably aimed most particularly at the United States, as reflected in Utopia's "naïve Anglicizing tendencies and its combination of sometimes laughable innocence and corrupting commerce."[31]

In the cut and thrust of *Utopia Limited*'s parody of the minstrel show lineup, masks are switched and superimposed willy-nilly, so that the satire may conveniently slip from one object to another, offering deniability regarding any specific satirical target. In the process, the pointedness of minstrelsy's often-subtle engagement with black-white relations in the United States is mostly lost. In effect, *Utopia Limited* substitutes one kind of "cut and thrust" for another, since by that time US American minstrelsy was no longer *merely* racist but also covertly undermining its racist framework at every turn, with its lineup continuing to provide the main societal referent for minstrelsy's spirit of rebellion. In *Utopia Limited*, all this is replaced with a satirical yet sentimentalized consideration of England's relationship to the native populations of its remote imperial holdings, involving a kind of vaguely defined "yellowface" based in part on Anna Leonowens's sensationalist tales of Siam (*The English Governess at the Siamese Court*, 1870; and *Romance of the Harem*, 1873), which would together become the basis for *Anna and the King of Siam* and *The King and I*. These tales, in parallel to *Utopia Limited*, depict the heroine, an English educator, as a kind of "Flower of Progress" bringing "enlightenment" to a primitive King in a remote kingdom, at the same time as they indulge feelings of nostalgia for a fading era (or, in the case of the later treatments of her tales, for a lost era).[32]

For quite different reasons, "minstrelsy as nostalgia" in Hollywood films also effaces minstrelsy's rebellious engagement with black-white race relations. Ironically, the process of muting the more contentious racial interplay of a previous century's minstrelsy, in favor of a more benign take on the history of black-white race relations in the United States, makes the overt racism of the institution appear all the more disturbing, especially when we today view the resulting nostalgic renderings of blackface, several decades later.[33] The impulse toward an idealizing nostalgia disencumbered these latter-day representations of minstrelsy from the subtle manipulation of masks that had given increased agency to minstrelsy's black stereotyped personae, thereby leaving the institution's native racism with nothing to fight against it. This increasingly placid presentation of minstrelsy's blatantly racist basis, more nakedly exposed, has left later audiences appalled and mystified, especially when it is combined, as it often is, with sentimentalized histories of both minstrelsy and US American racial politics more generally.

Nostalgia has always played a major part in minstrelsy, since the plantation life it ostensibly reproduced as part of the show was, from the beginning, constructed as a kind of pastoral. Moreover, the nostalgic pastoral of nineteenth-century minstrelsy worked on two levels at once, idealizing not only plantation life—a dimension that came into even sharper focus after the Civil War, evoking a kind of "Paradise Lost"—but also the primitive as such.[34] Even if minstrelsy has seemed designed to keep blacks in their place, then, that place is to some extent an idealized one, with the gaze of nostalgia serving ends similar to Orientalism.[35] It is in this regard that the innate musicality and natural sense of rhythm, which minstrelsy projected onto its stereotyped African American personae, come to the fore. As well, this dimension of minstrelsy's nostalgia reinforced working-class audiences' identification, even early on, with the perspective and musical presence of the end men, who, being closer to nature, were instinctually savvier than the authority figures they mocked. Even the upper-class Englishmen in *Utopia Limited* find this mix irresistible (as did, by extension, the Londoners who attended the decades-long run at St. James's Hall), and so enthusiastically assume the role of end men in the operetta's simulated minstrel show lineup, supporting and undermining King Paramount in turn, and relishing, along with their audience, each vocal rendering of the banjo chorus, with its rapidly unfolding harmonies redolent (for later generations) of barbershop quartets.

Hollywood film presentations of blackface during the early synchronized sound era, however, owing partly to their generational position, added a third level of nostalgia that largely displaced the other two, namely, nostalgia for the performance mode itself.[36] This is not so much the case with films rooted in the 1920s and earlier, such as *The Jazz Singer* (1927), based on a successful play from 1925, or *Show Boat* (1936), based on an even more successful musical from 1927. In the former, the rebellious basis of blackface performance provides an important background, though not the sensibility, for the protagonist Jack Robin (né Jakie Rabinowitz) as he negotiates, within a newly emergent racially blended culture that Ann Douglas terms "mongrel Manhattan," between Jewish cantorial traditions and "jazz singing" (which means, in this context, singing in blackface). Similarly "mongrel," *Show Boat* (Jerome Kern and Oscar Hammerstein II, based on the 1926 novel by Edna Ferber) daringly mixes blacks and whites not only on stage but also within the dramatic action. To be sure, the dramatic contours of these mixes are themselves broadly traditional (which is to say, racist), for example, featuring a "tragic mulatta" figure, Julie, married to a white man (they later divorce), who twice sacrifices her own career for that of the white heroine, Magnolia. Moreover, the 1936 film version of *Show Boat* also mixes in a fair dose of nostalgia for blackface, albeit tempered with the naïveté of the young Magnolia (played by Irene Dunne), who performs "Gallivantin' Around" in blackface as part of her stage debut. In Dunne's performance of this number—newly written for the film—the masks become especially tricky to decipher, since her exaggerated performance (based on the "Topsy" persona described below in connection to "Abraham" in *Holiday Inn*) seems designed to distance Dunne herself from both Magnolia and the blackface role she is playing. The result has proven as discomfiting for later audiences as her earlier "shimmy" dance with the black chorus during "Can't Help Lovin' Dat Man," even for those attuned to these scenes' camp appeal. **<VE4.7>**

As was becoming a hallmark of blackface performance in film, before the number itself Dunne is seen applying the transforming burnt cork makeup, ostensibly to make it clear to audiences that the blackface stage performer they are about to see is indeed Dunne (thus functioning in parallel to nonblackface numbers in older minstrel shows), but also, and as importantly, to lend nostalgic emphasis to the blackface tradition qua tradition, through displaying its rituals (see fig. 4.2). When actual burnt cork is used in such sequences, as here, these scenes more specifically evoke a variety of religious rituals involving candles, burnt offerings, or incense.

Other blackface numbers, such as Fred Astaire's "Bojangles of Harlem" (in *Swing Time*, 1936; by Jerome Kern and Dorothy Fields) or Bing Crosby's "Abraham" (*Holiday Inn*, 1942; by Irving Berlin), not only involve this ritual of watching the performers apply the blackface but also incorporate additional "rituals" drawn from a set of conventions that habitually (if not always ritualistically) frame many of Hollywood's blackface numbers. Both of these numbers, for example, pay tribute to figures thought to be especially venerated by African Americans—Bill "Bojangles" Robinson and Abraham Lincoln—although each was also somewhat problematic in this regard.

In "Bojangles," for example, Astaire's character ostensibly honors Robinson as the most famous of black tap dancers, leaving aside the circumstances that many other blacks saw Robinson as an "Uncle Tom" figure (that is, too obsequious toward whites), that other dancers (including Astaire himself) were openly critical of his dancing style, or that other black dancers (e.g., the Nicholas Brothers) found still other reasons to dislike him.[37] That the number's gesture toward Robinson is more ritualistic than substantive is borne out not only by its racist imagery and its having no real musical tie to Robinson,[38] but also, and more importantly, by its having nothing to do with Robinson's dancing style, and everything to do with Astaire's characteristically clever play with the potentials of cinematic presentation of dance. In this case, this play involves, first, the projection of a giant—and particularly offensive—facial caricature that is then revealed to be a pair of giant black shoes, and second, the projection of three giant shadows of his dancing figure, whom he then "defeats" in a dance-off reminiscent of a blackface tradition of dance contests that predates Christy's Minstrels.[39] **<VE4.8>**

Similarly, "Abraham," like most cinematic tributes to Lincoln projected onto the perspective of blacks by whites in Hollywood (cf. "You're a Grand Old Flag" in the nearly contemporaneous *Yankee Doodle Dandy*), offends both through its patronizing approach, especially in retrospect, and through its many minstrelisms (beyond the blackface itself), involving exaggerated declamation, dialect, and costume, and by the insertion of a verse that isolates a black "Mammy" figure (Louise Beavers) holding two "pickanin-

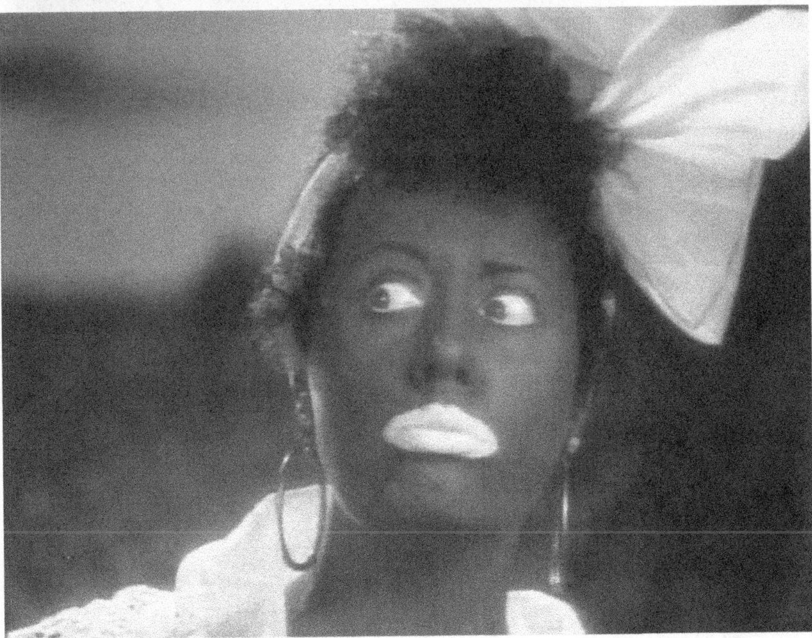

Fig. 4.2: Irene Dunne's Magnolia burning cork over a candle flame on the dressing room table while blacking up (*top*), and then performing "Gallivantin' Around" (*bottom*) in *Show Boat* (1936).

nies" in her lap, passing on to them the legacy of gratitude toward the (white) man "who set the darky free" (lower image of fig. 4.3). The insertion itself seems oddly produced, since there is no visual connection between the scene for this verse and the staged musical number. While it thus feels "tacked on" as a somewhat awkward gesture toward racial inclusion (giving actual blacks, without blackface makeup, a place in the number), it was nevertheless, according to Todd Decker, positioned carefully so as to prevent its being excised for distribution in the South, where it was still very much an issue to include blacks and whites in the same musical frame—even during the war years, which brought special efforts in Hollywood to "welcome" blacks to the war effort.[40] Also odd in this number is Crosby's appearance: in blackface and long white sideburns, he looks almost like a photographic negative of Lincoln, producing an odd blend of dignity and caricature well in line with the problematics of Hollywood's nostalgic minstrelsy. As Todd Decker explains, however, his persona and Marjorie Reynolds's (described just below) are drawn from a slightly different, overlapping tradition from the nineteenth century, of theatrical productions of *Uncle Tom's Cabin* (familiarly called "Tom Shows"); thus, Crosby's Jim appears as Uncle Tom and Marjorie Reynolds's Linda as Topsy (upper image of fig. 4.3).[41] **<VE4.9>**

As with Astaire's "Bojangles" number, the manipulation of blackface in "Abraham" provides an additional "excuse" for blacking up in the first place, while at the same time redirecting it through a presiding persona somewhat foreign to the tradition. Moreover, the number also justifies its use of blackface within the movie's plot, where it serves as a means to allow Linda (Jim's girlfriend/fiancée) to escape detection, a ruse that also justifies making her caricatured appearance even more grotesque.[42] The "disguise" ruse was another of blackface's many cinematic rituals, a popular device that was frequently employed, for example, by Eddie Cantor, who often combined it with "accidental" blackface, as when he pops out of an oven in *Whoopee!* (1930), his face blackened.[43] The "disguise" device shows up even in Hitchcock's *Young and Innocent* (1937), where the real murderer is finally discovered hiding in plain sight as the drummer in a blackface jazz band. And in an early Judy Garland film, *Everybody Sing* (1938), she auditions in blackface ("Swing Low") as an attempt to escape detection, since she has supposedly been shipped off to Europe by her parents to keep her from pursuing a performing career.

Fig. 4.3: *Top:* Bing Crosby's Jim (as "Tom"), Marjory Reynolds's Linda (as "Topsy"), and *bottom:* Louise Beavers's Mamie, performing "Abraham" in *Holiday Inn* (1942).

Garland would appear twice more in blackface on film, each time as "Mr. Tambo" teamed with Mickey Rooney's "Mr. Bones" within elaborately stylized re-creations of the minstrel show lineup. Together, these two extended medleys, which form the musical climaxes of *Babes in Arms* (Busby Berkeley, 1939) and *Babes on Broadway* (Busby Berkeley, 1941), are among the most purely nostalgic of Hollywood's many blackface sequences. In both films, the culminating minstrel sequences represent attempts by a younger generation to reclaim the tradition of the "old-fashioned minstrel show," a phrase used in the introductory songs for both films' minstrel sequences. In *Babes in Arms*, the turn to minstrelsy stems directly from the lead characters' parents having performed in a now-defunct vaudeville; whereas in the second, the homage is part of a more general gesture of respect for older theatrical traditions, set up by the earlier "Ghost Theater" sequence (of which, more below). But in general terms, the relationship between the two films is as haphazard as that between the 1939 film and the original Rodgers and Hart Broadway musical from 1937 that it was ostensibly based on, which was quite different from the film, and whose song list provided the latter with only a handful of its many songs.

While *Babes on Broadway*, as "sequel" to *Babes in Arms*, uses different situations and characters, it also maintains significant parallels to the earlier film. Both stories involve youthful ambitions to perform on Broadway, give Mickey Rooney the primary functions of author, producer, director, and star in the resulting extravaganza, and require Garland to play the almost-but-in-the-end-not-thrown-over ingénue and love interest for Rooney's character. More to the point here, the final minstrel show for *Babes on Broadway* re-creates the lineup personae from *Babes in Arms* and seems in many ways intended to complete the minstrel show from the earlier film, which was cut short by the sudden onslaught of a hurricane (which conveniently washes away some of Mickey Rooney's makeup, just in case audiences had lost track of him under the makeup and with all the confusion).

In each film, the stars are shown applying blackface makeup, in the first while the "Dixie Minstrels" march in to Stephen Foster's "De Camptown Races" after Garland's introductory "My Daddy Was a Minstrel Man" (by Roger Edens), **<VE4.10>** and, in *Babes on Broadway*, as part of the "business" in "Blackout over Broadway," an introductory number that was reportedly reshot to include the blacking-up sequence after preview audiences failed to recognize the stars beneath their makeup (fig. 4.4).[44]

Fig. 4.4: *Top*: Mickey Rooney and Judy Garland, as Tommy Williams and Penny Morris, blacking up while performing "Blackout over Broadway" in *Babes on Broadway* (1941), and *bottom*, as Mickey Moran and Patsy Barton, performing "Oh! Susanna" as Mr. Bones and Mr. Tambo in *Babes in Arms* (1939), framing (in the background) Douglas McPhail's Don Brice as Mr. Interlocutor.

<VE4.11> Each film backs up the lineup itself with a large ensemble; both were, after all, directed by Busby Berkeley, although even Berkeley makes some allowance for the fact that the minstrel show in *Babes in Arms* is supposedly an amateur performance in an outdoor theater, whereas that in *Babes on Broadway* is a professional production in a large Broadway theater. In both cases, the distinctive intimacy of the nineteenth-century lineup is lost, and is scarcely recaptured by the elaborately mounted, sung interchanges between the end men and Mr. Interlocutor (Douglas McPhail in *Babes in Arms*, Richard Quine in *Babes on Broadway*, each dressed in a white tuxedo, without blackface).[45] Both lineups are initiated by the interlocutor's "Gentlemen, be seated," leading to an elaborate single exchange with each of the end men in turn, and then proceeding to other musical numbers. In *Babes in Arms*, the exchanges are based on the most familiar, clichéd minstrel jokes available ("That was no lady, that was my wife," and "Why did the chicken cross the street?"), spun out so as to fill in the verse structure. **<VE4.12>** In *Babes on Broadway*, the exchanges are also old chestnuts from minstrelsy, though perhaps not as familiar to vaudeville, based like many such exchanges on horrible puns ("I feel just like a stovepipe . . . sooty," and "I feel just like a fireplace . . . grate").[46] **<VE4.13>**

In most respects, the numbers that follow these interchanges produce little if any of the flavor I describe above, wherein the end men's interchanges inform their music making, simply because Rooney's Mr. Bones and Garland's Mr. Tambo are not actually percussionists. For this reason (among others), we remain intensely aware, throughout, that it is Mickey Rooney and Judy Garland *playing* these characters, a circumstance acknowledged when they take the lead in nearly all subsequent musical numbers in the sequence.[47] After an introduction that takes them into the lineup proper, both shows follow much the same pattern, albeit slightly reordered between the two stars (thus confirming that the show in *Babes in Arms* was basically complete, even if the hurricane interruption allows for a different concluding number for the movie itself). In both films, Rooney performs a double number as Mr. Bones: a song-and-dance number in *Babes in Arms* and a virtuoso banjo solo in *Babes on Broadway* (the latter featuring train effects, with Rooney's banjo dubbed by Eddie Peabody).[48] Garland performs one number as Mr. Tambo in *Babes on Broadway*, and in both films disappears as Mr. Tambo so as to reappear in feminine garb and lighter blackface ("brownface") to perform the final number in the sequence, joined midway through by Rooney, still in full blackface but now in more formal costume.[49] It is because the minstrel show in each case morphs into a vehicle for Rooney and Garland that it so rarely moves beyond a straightforwardly nostalgic evocation.

The performances that adhere to the end men characters offer partial exceptions, especially those in *Babes on Broadway*. Rooney's puckish performance on banjo, for example, does capture the blend of performance and performer's persona I describe in general terms above, probably all the more so because it is so unabashedly dubbed (even as it is also better synced than most virtuosic instrumental numbers filmed to playback in Hollywood movies). Particularly striking in this regard is the segue into the second of the two banjo numbers, which originates in a dissonant arrival chord at the end of the first number (sounding at first like a mistake), which launches the accelerating train effect and thereby brings the percussive potential of the banjo to the fore. **<VE4.14>** Likewise, Garland's rhythmic strut in "Franklin D. Roosevelt Jones," heard just before, keeps Mr. Tambo's persona, and "his" identity as a percussionist, engaged even though the vocal belting is pure Garland, and even though the song ends with a Busby Berkeley crane shot that fully eclipses any such subtlety (upper panel in fig. 4.6). **<VE4.15>** But it is actually to the point that these persona-based performances be blunted through being so thoroughly absorbed into spectacle. Thus, Rooney's banjo solo devolves into a banjo choir, suddenly appearing next to him as the "traveling" camera widens focus and pans, revealing the larger stage panorama just as the pit band produces "full-speed" train whistle effects (lower panel in fig. 4.6). Berkeley's sense of spectacle, in each case, creates the sense of distance required by nostalgia, and imposes it against the grain of minstrelsy's characteristic engagement between persona and performance, just when Rooney's and Garland's performances reach their liveliest evocation of that mode of engagement.

In these and other ways the transformations and fragmentation that minstrelsy underwent in the late nineteenth and early twentieth centuries dispelled the immediacy with which, earlier in the nineteenth century, its end men imposed their will on the fabric of musical performance, enforcing the primacy of rhythm and percussion and making that point as impudently as possible. While traces of that dynamic—what we may term "rhythm with attitude"—remain in latter-day evocations of the minstrel show lineup, finding those traces requires sensitivity and deft reading of a tradition coarsened by its own inherent racism and softened by nostalgia, producing a situation that is a far cry from the in-your-face hooliganism of earlier end men and their musical renderings. Yet, the broader musical transformation effected by that dynamic was much more lasting, evolving through both minstrelsy's wider musical practices and the more authentically African American traditions of tap dance, ragtime, jazz, rhythm and blues, and hip hop, to form some of the core developments in US American popular music. And, in a distant echo of the role of end men in minstrelsy, percussionists, whether in nightclubs or on live television shows, do double duty, performing with the band while also offering punctuating support for verbal comedy. Even the fundamental impulse toward dance, driven historically by popular music's emphasis on insouciant rhythms at every turn, partakes, at its root, of minstrelsy's sense of rebellion.[50] While, arguably, it was dance that ultimately fueled the most explosive potential of popular music, it was minstrelsy's impulse toward rebellion that lit the fuse and, facing in the other direction, constituted the welcoming committee for musical idealism whenever and wherever it threatened to take root in the United States, with a figurative Bronx cheer at the ready.

CAMP'S AMBIVALENT REBELLIONS

While film has not been a friend to minstrelsy's latter-day reception, for camp sensibilities it has been the gift that keeps on giving. Hollywood films, especially genre films, and most especially musicals, have been a major repository for both intentional and unintentional camp.[51] Unintentional camp emerges most often with older films that inadvertently document the peculiarities of now-outmoded presentational styles, regarding dress or personal appearance (such as hairdos), stylized dramatic situations, settings and furnishings, distinctive acting modalities such as mannered or idiosyncratic gestural or verbal expression, or extravagance regarding any of these or other aspects of the cinematic arts. Most susceptible to camp tastes among the latter are those filmic techniques that often serve as intensifiers, such as close-ups (whether of faces or objects), camera movement and montage, color saturation, or the use of music, especially when employed excessively or when following well-worn (and perhaps now-outmoded) expressive tropes. All of these elements are devalued by mainstream receptive habits as matters more of *style* (or, perhaps, "production values") than of *substance*, secondary to what really matters in a film, and considered from that perspective more as potential threats to a film's artistic value than as enhancements or as the basis for its long-term appeal.

Although much that will seem unintentionally campy in older films may have been *deliberately* exaggerated or stylized, intentional camp as a category applies more comfortably to situations in which the filmmakers consistently, and thus probably consciously, play to camp tastes. Often enough, anecdotal evidence will also substantiate claims of intentionality, although anecdotes and reminiscences can be (and often are) shaded to suggest that observed phenomena were intended. The question of intentionality, in general, is a somewhat trickier question in film than in live performance, since in the latter a performer has an immediate sense of an audience's reactions and can more obviously either ignore those reactions or accommodate them. And, further, the question of intentionality across all media changed dramatically in the wake of Susan Sontag's "Notes on Camp," since widespread and even mainstreamed awareness of camp (that is, beyond the well-worn category of spoof) has facilitated the success of intentional camp. There is some irony in this, since Sontag herself argues against intentional camp, asserting that "Camp which knows itself to be Camp ('camping') is usually less satisfying," and that "Probably, intending to be campy is always harmful."[52]

In paying special attention to intentional as well as unintentional camp, I am—with a multitude of others, if sometimes only implicitly—taking exception to this aspect of Sontag's remarkably cogent analysis. More broadly problematic, she asserts earlier on, with some caveats, that some arts (e.g., "contentless" concert music, Wagner, jazz) are resistant to camp, whereas others are "saturated" with it.[53] Yet, given that camp is vested more definitively in sensibility than in the camp objects or events themselves, it seems absurd (to paraphrase Algernon Moncrieff in *The Importance of Being Earnest*) to have a hard-and-fast rule about what is and is not camp, especially since more than half of camp culture—with its rapacious tendency to read camp into everything—depends on the ability to appreciate camp elements that others may have overlooked. Sontag is, of course, speaking to a particular historical moment, for example noting the recent annexation of popular music. More importantly, she is speaking to what her particular (New York–based) sensibilities in that historical moment respond to as camp.

As Sontag's situation makes clear in retrospect, camp, as with any broadly defined taste, will accommodate many variations. In my own case, for example, while I consider myself reasonably open to a variety of camp appreciations, I also find myself resistant to some strains and particularly gratified by others. Among the latter are those instances in which serious situations mix with camp so as to heighten emotional involvement. In such cases of what is often termed "high camp" (and which I have sometimes been tempted to refer to as "Earnest Goes to Camp"), the predilection of camp tastes to displace emphasis from the important to the trivial, often through exaggerated intensification, first carries a camp appreciation to a laughable intensity involving elements of "style," and then lays bare the more serious "substance," at this point pitched at a more intense level and without the emotional insulation that the earlier indulgence in camp tastes had provided. To be thus brought to simultaneous laughter and tears strikes me as one of camp's great possibilities, especially when laughter in the end intensifies rather than diminishes pathos. In camp's play between surface and substance, between illusion and reality, abides a particularly powerful expressive force, all the more so for being deniable. As Richard Dyer describes this dynamic (in relation to *The Pirate,* which I discuss below), "It is in the recognition of illusion that camp finds reality."[54]

Since unintentional camp reduces mainly to a receptive sensibility, it lives always in the present tense, as an adjunct of nostalgia that views art, along with elements of design and fashion, with the affectionate condescension of a more sophisticated taste or sensibility. The receptive dimension of intentional camp can also seem bound to the present tense, even considering that, with anything other than what is added by live performance, it colludes with the sensibilities that fashioned the artifacts being read as camp, sensibilities that are manifestly grounded in the past. These circumstances, coupled with the fact that much of the discourse on camp has been centered on determining not only *what* camp is but also *whose* it is, have anchored camp firmly in the "now," however broadly viewed, and discouraged the pursuit of historical questions except as they relate to the specific objects and events that have supported camp readings in the present and near past. Moreover, this circumstance has in turn conspired with the sheer variety of specific camp tastes (and distastes) to make camp seem always, in this sense, a *local* phenomenon.

Yet, that very diversity of camp tastes speaks to a mostly hidden history of camp, a history consisting of more than the sense (and occasional assertion) that similar responses to art and fashion have operated at earlier times—which even if supported by a multiple delineation of such moments would not constitute a history, absent some kind of narrative to connect them. Moreover, the current predilection to theorize camp tastes in essentialist terms—a problematic tendency that besets theorizing more generally—also tends to shut down historical inquiry. Given this situation, and given the specifics of current understandings of camp, it seems reasonable to ask, "From what and how did camp tastes evolve?" and to further inquire how and when, and the degree to which, camp became embedded in modern gay culture—since, as I've already argued, it cannot have always been so embedded.

To ask these questions is important in any case, but more particularly so because I am here interested in connecting camp to the spirit of rebellion that resisted idealist musical practices in the United States in favor of music that cultivated, through pleasurable and otherwise engaging surfaces, a shared social space. This shared social space is conceptually different from that fostered by minstrelsy, where it is unavoidable, being fundamental to the carnivalesque nature of the form. With camp, rather, there is a choice. For those who wish to engage on this level, it is the *now*ness of surfaces—that very *now*ness that inhibits asking historical questions—that creates that social space for those who wish to enter it, while at the same time resisting, if only temporarily, the timeless depth that German Idealism seeks in music and other arts that aspire to "higher" sensibilities. In this sense, the initial impulse toward camp, like the impulse toward minstrelsy, is against earnestness, providing a means to neutralize more serious freight through displaced or redirected emphasis.

As a way to establish and give historical grounding to this role for camp—and so address, if not fully answer, the questions just posed—it will be useful here to explore at some length two distinct camp traditions. One tradition accrues to the persona and aesthetic predilections of Oscar Wilde and leads fairly directly to the gay-centered camp culture now occupying the mainstream of what for most people today constitutes camp as a category. The other is based on theatrical (and musical) depictions of piracy as they evolved across the late nineteenth century and into our own time, for the most part readily understood within heterosexual contexts. Because these two traditions are each rooted in the late nineteenth century, are each advanced through operetta and related artifacts, and intertwine with each other within the first two decades or so of Hollywood film musicals, it seems reasonable to frame them within two separate discussions, with the second addressing some aspects of their eventual and occasional merger.

Camping in the Wilde

"It is perfectly phrased! And quite as true as any observation in civilised life should be."

—ALGERNON MONCRIEFF, *The Importance of Being Earnest*, act 1

Oscar Wilde—the lodestone and patron saint of modern camp tastes—both defines camp's rebellion against earnestness through countless witticisms (often excerpted as epigrams), and demonstrates camp's often-disguised concern for the more serious substance that camp tastes ostensibly put aside in favor of style. While it may not always be obvious—and notwithstanding camp's originary impulse against earnestness—camp tastes, like minstrelsy, do take "substance" into account, if often within an inverted hierarchy, as an adjunct to style. Moreover, camp—especially intentional camp—does so for basically the same reasons as minstrelsy. Because substance is part of the sincerity that typically serves as camp's (and minstrelsy's) foil, it must at the very least and as a starting point be invoked. Additionally, regarding camp, engaging the widespread appeal and resonance of particular themes and topics can offer yet an additional element of play, and/or heighten the effect of the camp element. Such engagements may also serve as a cover for indulging other appreciations lurking within audiences mostly (or outwardly) attuned to more straightforward readings. And, finally, within the kind of high camp offered up by Wilde, a scrupulously tended substance will help ensure that the highly polished surfaces retain their luster over time, across repeated engagements from a variety of perspectives.

The title of Wilde's best-known play, *The Importance of Being Earnest* (1895), is in this respect both overtly ironic and covertly *un*ironic, as is reinforced by its seldom-used subtitle: *A Trivial Comedy for Serious People.* **<TE4.16>** The epigraph that heads this section provides a particularly useful exemplar for how this works. Algernon—the character who seems most often to function as Wilde's stand-in—here protests his friend's dismissal of a proffered epigram for being (merely) clever, and defends it on the basis of both its form and its substance. As I will demonstrate, these claims are not idle, for his epigram is indeed perfectly phrased, and its substance—properly understood, and to whatever degree it may be "true"—is entirely relevant to the dramatic situation. Here is the full exchange, which comes immediately after "a pause":

> JACK: You don't think there is any chance of Gwendolen becoming like her mother in about a hundred and fifty years, do you, Algy?
>
> ALGERNON: All women become like their mothers. That is their tragedy. No man does. That's his.
>
> JACK: Is that clever?
>
> ALGERNON: It is perfectly phrased! And quite as true as any observation in civilised life should be.[55]

Algernon's "perfect phrasing" is immediately evident when the four sentences of his bon mot are arranged on separate lines, revealing how adeptly the parallel structure (A B / A' B') defines a telescoping meter. Thus, the nine syllables in the first sentence reduce in the second to six, and thence to three and two, while the accented syllables reduce from three to two to one. Coordinated with this progressive contraction, the plural nouns and possessive pronouns of the first two sentences give way to the singular "man" and "his" of the final two, while the metrical feet transform, as shown, from the relatively complex amphibrach to the simple iamb:

All **wo**men / be**come** like / their **mo**thers.	three amphibrachs
That is their / **trag**edy.	two dactyls in an iambic metameter
No **man** does.	one amphibrach
That's **his.**	one iamb

The specific contraction of "That is" in the second sentence to "That's" in the fourth indicates how meticulously Wilde manages the epigram's rhythm and flow, in this case ensuring that the meter of the final sentence reproduces the metameter of the second, which assonance is reinforced by the more elaborate elision that reduces "their tragedy" to "his."

Wilde's phrasing also supports the epigram's substance and sentiment in subtle ways. "Feminine" cadences give way in the end to a stark "masculine" one, isolating the bereft situational tragedy of "man" as the ontologically inevitable consequence of replacing "All women" with "No man." Even more subtly, the elisions in the second half alternately intensify and eclipse the pain of a man's necessary separation from his mother. Thus, in the third sentence, "man" is denied even the expression of what he is forbidden, as "does" replaces the indicated parallel, "becomes like his mother." In the final sentence, on the other hand, the omission of the word "tragedy" makes man's ownership of his fate more important than its inevitability or anguish. Indeed, each half of the epigram uses a different mode for expressing inescapable fate, as the flowing regular rhythms of the first half irresistibly convey daughters to their inevitable resemblances to their mothers, whereas the broken, abrupt endings of the second, with similar surety, deny this to the son.

Finally, the epigram is characteristically witty, finding tragedy in two outcomes that would usually be considered "natural" and to be desired, and asserting those tragic outcomes to be universal: that women should become like their mothers and that a man should not. The parallel structure underscores the generative wit of extending the observation to include men in the first place—they are not, after all, the concern of Jack's question—leading to the payoff assertion that man's avoiding the tragic fate of women is itself a tragedy. The resulting tidy structure, presented as a paradox, thus apportions tragedy equally and symmetrically between the sexes.

But the epigram's appearance of universality is misleading. In practical terms, it excludes orphans, those men and women whose actual mothers have not been present in their lives, so making any resemblances to them unprovable and beside the point. Not coincidentally, this is precisely Jack's condition and the crux of the play's two romantic plots, since the fact that both Jack and his ward Cecily are orphans directly impedes their proposed betrothals to Gwendolen and Algernon. Even if *The Importance of Being Earnest* appears to assume the frothy frills of light romantic comedy, filled with unlikely coincidence, its basic "substance," to which it returns repeatedly, is the wrenching psychological turmoil of the adult orphan who craves knowledge of his birth family. Jack, a foundling who just before the quoted exchange converses with Algernon about his absent relations (in dialogue that was cut for the familiar 1952 film version), and who later seems willing to believe he has never been christened, must legitimate his own origins before he can join with another.

Lady Bracknell's objections to his proposed marriage to Gwendolen, however absurdly presented, thus speak to the heart of the matter. Many orphans, as adults, tend like Jack to feel unsettled and tentative in their lives. In *Earnest*, this feeling is brought into relief by contrasting Jack with Algernon: the latter is perpetually in debt but exudes confidence (as Lady

Bracknell puts it, "He has nothing, but he looks everything"), whereas the outwardly more solvent and responsible Jack is perpetually uncertain except in his devotion to Gwendolen. Indeed, Jack's assumption of the name Ernest directly reflects his demeanor; as Algernon tells him, "You look as if your name was Ernest. You are the most earnest-looking person I ever saw in my life."[56] To be sure, with all his high moral tone, Jack has admitted to a brazen lie, having invented a financially profligate and dissolute younger brother as an excuse to escape the country and go into town. But creating an imaginary brother who needs him is, after all, wholly consistent with his foundational craving for family, and should be taken as yet another expression of that yearning—despite Algernon's apparent belief that Jack's fictions cloak more clandestine activities, as is the case with his own fabricated invalid friend. Moreover, Jack has in fact invented nothing, as we will learn, but only assumed a name that was his by birth and correctly imagined his actual family situation, since the financially profligate Algernon—as we learn by play's end—is indeed his younger brother.

In a more oblique way, too, the epigram's substance bears directly on the play's situation, regarding its implied subplot of homosexual (or homosocial) youth resolving into a heteronormative adult marriage. By the time we hear the epigram, we know not only of Jack's being an orphan but also that Algernon goes often to the country under false pretenses, which visits, given his "incomparable expression" for this activity—he is a devoted "Bunburyist"—must surely involve homosexual trysts (a rather different mode of "camping in the wild" than what I explore in this section). Indeed, the playfully crude pun entailed in Algernon's calling his imaginary invalid friend "Bunbury" seems to acknowledge this, perhaps even by way of an allusion to Gilbert and Sullivan's *Patience; or, Bunthorne's Bride* (1881), whose pain-in-the-ass poet (thus, "bun-thorn") has been widely understood to be an aggregate parody of Oscar Wilde and Algernon Charles Swinburne (among others), and who is in the end left without a bride despite the assurances of the operetta's subtitle. It is in this regard that the full significance of Algernon's caveat about the truth of his "perfectly phrased" epigram may best be assessed, for men who *do* become too much like their mothers will thereby bring their own sexual proclivities into question by "civilised society." Under these circumstances, how could Algernon *not* complete his epigram by considering the parallel case with men, since for him the operative subject was not women but becoming like one's mother, a subject tinged with a wistful sense of tragedy for a man who is soon to foreswear Bunburyism. In retrospect, and notwithstanding nineteenth-century England's tendency to read effeminate men as oversexualized heterosexuals (see below), Wilde was skating perilously near the edge with *Earnest*'s thinly veiled allusions to homosexuality; it would be during the play's initial run that his conflict with the Marquess of Queensberry, regarding Wilde's dalliances with the Marquess's son, Lord Alfred Douglas, would come before the courts, with disastrous consequences for Wilde.

Operating from a much different cultural position, Gilbert and Sullivan also did much, through their operettas, to encourage theatrically based camp sensibilities, and they are largely responsible for securing a place for camp on the musical stage in a form that could be adapted and sustained in the United States (that is, in Broadway and film musicals). Basing their operettas on the French *operette*, they chose turf that was already prime for camp, since it was a foreign genre given to operatic parodies and sexual suggestiveness, but which they steered toward respectability in expression of their own strong hankerings to be taken seriously as artists. Their ambivalence made their joint venture an even more potent mix for camp, which readily bore fruit even if their later collaborations would rein in the element of camp to some extent. Within five years of the international success of *H.M.S. Pinafore* in 1878, with its campy version of the British navy and admiralty, Gilbert and Sullivan camped pirates and police in *The Pirates of Penzance* (1879), modern poets in *Patience* (1881), and the British peerage in *Iolanthe* (1882). Of particular interest here will be *The Pirates of Penzance*, with its inauguration of what I term "pirate camp" (not to mention its preoccupations with paradox and orphans), and *Patience*, with its parody of Wilde and his poetic cohort, more specifically reinforced as a parody of Wilde himself when Carte sponsored Wilde's 1882 lecture tour of the United States in tandem with the operetta's New World tour.[57]

Notably, Gilbert and Sullivan do not occupy the same camp domain as Wilde, neither by serving as a touchstone for later camp tastes nor by investing themselves in projecting so purely a camp sensibility. Their stock-in-trade was parody and satire, whether political or cultural, presented in such a way that it could be read both forward and backward. Gilbert's penchant for paradoxically saying both one thing and its apparent opposite was an adjunct to unlikely situations, improbable plots, and implausibly happy endings, all based on coincidences, puns, sophisms, and paradoxical reversals. To be sure, the coincidences that allow *The Importance of Being Earnest* to end happily are on a par with the Captain and Ralph having been switched at birth in *Pinafore*, or with the pirates in *Penzance* turning out in the end to be "noblemen who have gone wrong." But these convenient resolutions, though outwardly similar, play quite differently. Despite the improbability of *Earnest*'s resolution, it is so well grounded in the action of the play that it functions not as a reversal but rather as an explanation, and on multiple levels. While something similar might be said about *Pinafore*'s resolution, as well, given earlier musical numbers by the Captain and Ralph that suggest, stylistically, their actual birth stations,[58] the conceit of babies switched at birth runs blatantly counter to many of the operetta's operative realities, beginning with the apparent relative ages of the two men. And, concerning the deft resolution of the plot in *Penzance*, Ruth—long since proven even more incompetent and untrustworthy than Buttercup, her counterpart in *Pinafore*—is, like Buttercup, the sole authority for the assertion of birthright that resolves the plot to everyone's satisfaction.

But even apart from these telling differences, Gilbert and Sullivan's relationship to camp will seem to most people today to be fundamentally different from Wilde's, and this probably has to do mainly with later developments that have affected their respective receptions over the long term. Most important of these have been the circumstances of Wilde's trial, coupled with the subsequent and lasting association of his tastes and affectations with homosexuality (and so with camp tastes generally),[59] which have in turn cast Gilbert and Sullivan's unsympathetic portrayal of these in *Patience*, as both phony and worthy of ridicule, in a different light. ‹TE4.17› On the one hand, *Patience* provides an opportunity to indulge, through camp, the very thing it seeks to ridicule. But on the other hand, its treatment of Bunthorne exemplifies the mean-spirited cruelty—usually directed toward women—that runs throughout Gilbert's work, which, though often presented campishly, leaves an acrid aftertaste of genuine scorn that runs counter to the affectionate spirit more typical of camp indulgence. For better or worse, and notwithstanding whatever historical facts might impinge on the matter, Gilbert and Sullivan have come to represent a decidedly straight—and straightlaced—opposition to Wilde's protocamp. But, crucially, their operettas don't generally play that way. Indeed, it has been convenient to camp readings of their operettas (in both performance and reception) that their Victorian respectability seems beyond reproach, for this offers an ideal cloak for the wealth of material in them that can play to either gay or camp sensibilities (if these can easily be distinguished from each other in this context).[60]

Camp in Gilbert and Sullivan may stem from many sources, but it seems heavily dependent on live performance, as attested by the dearth of successful film versions of their operettas.[61] This may be partly explained by the ways in which a number of their conventions support camp readings, and as well by the persistence of many of those conventions—which thrive best in a live theatrical setting—in mainstream and "Golden Age" Broadway musicals. These conventions include their cleverly tidy plots (generally in two acts, in which the first finale sets up the second either by parallel or by inversion [or both]); the visual displays offered by sets, costumes, and (initially) unisex choruses arrayed across the stage; the often highly idiosyncratic and/or stereotypical characters whose stories unfold within those plots and against the backdrop of those displays; and the tendency for song less to prolong or elaborate the dramatic moment (as in opera or "integrated" musicals) than to distract from it, albeit often with at least a thin pretext toward contributing to the dramatic action.[62] The performer's role in such situations comes, in a sense, prelabeled as artificial, and so is readymade for camp. But it is worth noting that even with more "integrated" songs—and there are a great many of these in Gilbert and Sullivan's operettas, as well—the highly stylized mode of acting required to sustain the dramatic energy of a song will also generally accommodate camp tastes.[63]

Even in general terms, the calculated artifice of theatrical display and performance as practiced by musical theater of all kinds (yes, even Wagnerian opera, despite Sontag's caveat) is highly conducive to camp reception, if typically muted in the case of more serious opera. In lighter, more comic forms (operetta and musicals), camp will often depend on some kind of flow between performers and audience, but this generally intentional, perhaps even collaborative form of camp indulgence can intermingle with other kinds of camp, some of which may be unintentional. These general features, coupled with more specific elements typical of English operetta, are reinforced by Gilbert and Sullivan's penchant to satirize operatic conventions such as recitative, as well as by their reliance on a stock company of performers—with a resultant recycling of character types that are strongly defined within the genre—so as to provide a particularly potent basis for camp performance.

This is nowhere more evident than with the character of Bunthorne in *Patience*, who provides a convenient locus for observing how the combination of elements tends to work. Bunthorne has two set pieces early in act 1: a recitation of a comically overwritten poem, "Hollow, Hollow, Hollow," and his recitative and aria combination, "Am I Alone, and Unobserved?" / "If You're Anxious for to Shine." But perhaps his signature moment comes during his subsequent exit lines, after Patience refuses his offer of marriage and asks him to leave her in peace. His acquiescence includes an "impromptu" poetic outburst, a kind of epigram that he recites and then verbally "signs":

BUNTHORNE: Certainly. Broken-hearted and desolate, I go.
(Goes up-stage, suddenly turns and recites)
"Oh, to be wafted away
From this black Aceldama of sorrow,
Where the dust of an earthy today
Is the earth of a dusty tomorrow!"
It is a little thing of my own. I call it "Heart Foam."
I shall not publish it.
Farewell! Patience, Patience, farewell![64]

Performed as much to the audience as to Patience (recalling the spirit of his recent sung soliloquy), the speech will typically be interrupted by laughter and even applause at several junctures, rewarding and encouraging the performer's exaggerated presentation style, so that, for example, "It is a little thing of my own" will seem almost to be an aside to the audience, in acknowledgment of their response to his epigrammatic poem.

Like Algernon in *Earnest*, Bunthorne provides a gloss for his epigram, but it is not about its form or correctness, dwelling instead on its emotional impact (on him, of course). Despite his recent confession to Patience that he dislikes poetry, he nevertheless seems overwhelmed by his own poetic creation, which he finds so affectingly personal that he cannot bear to see it published. And yet not only is it grotesquely titled (an extravagantly precious gesture for an unpublished epigram), but it is equally grotesque in following, within its short span, the melodramatic expression of inner torment ("Oh, to be wafted away") with a seemingly inappropriate biblical reference ("Aceldama") and a not-quite-sensible verbal paradox that cloaks another biblical reference (from "dust" to "dusty"). Moreover, the supposed heartfelt—or, perhaps, "heart-foamed"—sentiment of Bunthorne's epigram is undercut by its strict adherence to a simple singsong rhythm, typical of Gilbert's poetry and lyrics in general. Each half mechanically alternates accented syllables with two unaccented syllables, ending with a "feminine" cadence. There is but one subtle touch within this simple arrangement: switching from dactyls in the first half to anapests in the second leaves the opening anguished "Oh"—which can and should be made much of in performance—as the sole instance of beginning a line with an accented syllable. Yet the tradeoff for this expressive detail is to make the verbal paradox in the second half seem all the more supercilious.

Bunthorne's epigram is clearly a parody and not to be taken seriously. At the same time, however, it resonates closely with the later action of the play—even if any such relevance is occluded by the epigram's referential obscurity, poetic clumsiness, and overly theatrical presentation.

"Aceldama" ("Field of Blood") refers to the field just outside first-century Jerusalem that was purchased with the thirty pieces of silver Judas Iscariot received for betraying Jesus, and which was later used as a burial place for non-Jews. For those who may not recognize this reference, the otherwise redundant "black" and "sorrow" allow it to work anyway. But those who do recognize it will find the first of these modifiers misapplied, and may also be troubled by other aspects of the reference. Since the field in question was known for its red clay (hence, "potter's field"), "black" is inaccurate, even if it describes Bunthorne's mood and produces a telling assonance with the first syllable of Aceldama. More troubling is Bunthorne's seeming presumption in relating his own plight with the fate of Jesus; as if to compound this bit of blasphemy, the epigram leaves it frustratingly unclear whether he is identifying with Jesus or with Judas, something that the verbal paradox of the second half of the epigram only makes worse, not least because these lines are in themselves doubly confusing. First, they allude to *both* the finality of death (dust to dust) and the possibility of resurrection in a "dusty tomorrow." Second, notwithstanding the adroit contrast between "earthy today" and "dusty tomorrow," the actual content of the verbal paradox remains elusive. How, exactly, does today's dust become tomorrow's earth, and what is represented by those substances and that transmutation? If sense is to be made of these lines, they must refer to an embodied resurrection of some kind. But we must then also assume that this resurrection takes place *in Aceldama*, which once again conflates Judas with Jesus, in this case by relocating Jesus's promise of resurrection to the very location that constitutes the legacy of his betrayal by Judas (and where the latter committed suicide). To be sure, it is possible to read an implied "to" at the head of the penultimate line (thus, "To where the dust . . . ," elided, presumably, for the sake of rhythm). But even were this indeed the intended meaning, the actual grammatical construction ties everything in the final two lines to Aceldama itself. In either case, the epigram seems to voice the despair of Judas as he contemplates suicide, but who then—as if he were the one betrayed and not the betrayer—proceeds to imagine his resurrection à la Jesus.

In the end, the whole thing works best if one does *not* know (or conveniently forgets) what "Aceldama" means, just as the effect of Bunthorne's earlier "Hollow, Hollow, Hollow" depends on his listeners not really knowing what "amaranthine," "asphodel," and "colocynth" mean, even if the logic of the poem will be easier to parse for those who do know.[65] It is like an in-joke that is staged wholly for the benefit of those who are excluded from the in-group—and this impression is reinforced by the exaggerated, theatrical mode of presentation, in both cases, which renders the gesture of theatrical delivery decisively more important than the content. Bunthorne's parting epigram seems, indeed, to follow the strategy he himself had recently laid out in song (at the conclusion of the first strophe of "If You're Anxious for to Shine"):

> You must lie upon the daisies and discourse in novel phrases
> of your complicated state of mind,
> The meaning doesn't matter if it's only idle chatter
> of a transcendental kind.[66]

Yet the meaning *does* matter, since the content of Bunthorne's epigram, even including its confusions, is entirely relevant to the subsequent action of the play. Not long after his exit, he reappears festooned and marching in procession with the women's chorus, which so alarms the dragoons that they speculate (in song) that he is being prepared either for ritual sacrifice or execution. If all of this reinforces the parallel to Jesus in evoking the crown of thorns and the Via Dolorosa, the actual cause of his bizarre appearance aligns him more with Judas. As we soon learn, he has, "By the advice of his solicitor, . . . put himself up to be raffled for,"[67] agreeing to wed whatever maiden draws the lucky ticket. While this sordid monetary transaction is not exactly on a par with Judas's betrayal for money, it is perhaps as close a parallel as musical comedy would allow. Indeed, if Bunthorne is somehow imagined to be *both* Jesus and Judas, we might further imagine that the latter's betrayal of the former reduces precisely to Bunthorne's selling *himself* for money, as a kind of hypertheatricality in which he insists on playing all the parts, in the manner of Wagner "performing" his operas for his friends. Since both Jesus and Judas were in the end shunned by their closest companions, even Bunthorne's eventual brideless fate leaves it unclear which of the two he is meant to resemble, especially since his acknowledgment of his fate in the finale seems rather too cheerful, all things considered:

> In that case unprecedented,
> Single I must live and die—
> I shall have to be contented
> With a tulip or lily![68]

Although the epigram's literal content thus turns out to matter (if only obliquely and indecisively), the content that Bunthorne himself sets store in—the epigram's *emotional* content, its capacity to move—does not. Patience herself is unmoved ("What on earth does it all mean?").[69] We in the audience can only laugh at the discrepancy between his feigned despair and the trite poetic meter in which he expresses it, made even more laughable by the disparity between the severity of his obscure reference and the tidy verbal paradox with which he concludes. As with Algernon in *Earnest*, appearance (in this case, theatricality) is made to seem everything, yet Bunthorne is not only inept at creating those all-important surfaces but also too obvious in his emotional investment, which ultimately betrays him. This is in sharp contrast to Algernon, whose personal stake is, from beginning to end, carefully hidden, even if it is at the same time plainly visible to those capable of seeing it (since it is communicated above all by his mannered sensibilities and impeccable personal style). Because of this seamless joining of performance mode with dramatic content in *Earnest*, our laughter and admiration line up across the board; we appreciate in equal measure Wilde himself, the character Algernon, and (one hopes) the actor who plays him. *Earnest* is high camp. But in *Patience*, while we appreciate author and actor, we are made to laugh *at* the character Bunthorne; however much we may wish his pose to work (or not), we know it cannot. His is the camp of abject failure, of aspiring to a style he cannot hope to achieve, and because he is an unscrupulous fraud, we cannot love him for it (no more than can Patience, who finds him repulsive). While the level of Gilbert's wit may be high, the camp itself is thus rather low; or, perhaps—if the actor is up to it—a high-camp performance encases a low-camp core, so that the character Bunthorne, as designed by Gilbert, represents unintentional camp within a theatrical setting that encourages the performer toward intentional camp.

If Bunthorne is, as a dramatic character, essentially Gilbert's creation, it is Sullivan's music that shapes his character most particularly in performance. Enduring tropes of operetta and musicals make music the medium both for a character's *performance* of self (often more projected than real) and for *revealing* the true self. For an aspirational character, these two might merge, so that a character's vision becomes a reality through musical performance, reinforced by the notion that s/he could not convincingly perform music that was not somehow "true" to character. In Bunthorne's first musical number, these complementary tropes appear in quick succession, as he "performs" theatricality in the recitative leading up to his "revelation" of his true self in "If You're Anxious for to Shine"; in both cases, as often in operetta and musicals, the music demands a style of bodily movement that produces the extended number's central dramatic effects. **<TE4.18>**

The recitative comprises two main sections, each based on clichés of musical accompaniment to melodrama. And, as often in Sullivan's parodic use of recitative, the presentation is more dramatic than the situation or the following aria or song warrants. First, diminished-seventh chords introduced with snarling trills and harsh snaps give way to Sturm und Drang passages (chromatic, minor-mode, and syncopated), not only preparing the scene but also rendering laughably absurd the conventions of soliloquy as a theatrical device, as Bunthorne sings, in recitative style,

> Am I alone,
> And unobserved? I am!
> Then let me own
> I'm an aesthetic sham![70]

This opening sets up a mostly intoned, syllabically unmeasured "confession" that concludes with two more carefully measured phrases that give "mediaevalism" its full six syllables:

Let me confess!

A languid love for lilies does *not* blight me!
Lank limbs and haggard cheeks do *not* delight me!

. . .

[measured:]
In short, my me-di-ae-val-is-m's affectation,
Born of a morbid love of admiration!

While staging for the number may be quite varied from production to production, it will probably involve some "Mickey Mousing" activity to correspond with the dramatic musical gestures of the first part, and struck poses (aesthetic "voguing") for much of the second, all exaggerated so as to match the overly dramatic musical gestures from the orchestra. **‹AE4.19›**

All this changes for the song proper, which unfolds as a kind of mincing march, adopting the sensibility of a slightly effeminate burgher on promenade—a sensibility we must take to be that of Bunthorne's "true self." Sullivan deftly manages the transition from *misterioso* melodrama to public promenade by shifting a quick three-note rising figure from a strong "masculine" position within the meter (double sixteenth-note pickup to downbeat within a 2/4 meter, *allegretto grazioso*) to a slightly fussier, "feminine" position (beginning on the downbeat; see ex. 4.1). Harmonically, this transition starts on the same dissonant chord as the recitative ends (the augmented-sixth chord of the dominant), arriving on the tonic D major precisely as the new articulation begins, with both resolutions achieved at the top of a rising octave scale over a dominant harmony. The play between sixteenth notes and eighth notes in this passage is especially effective, as Sullivan uses a staccato, augmented form of the new rhythmic impulse (thus, three eighth notes) to mark the final introductory cadence, and continues to use this new rhythmic figure as the basis for the accompaniment in the first half of the song, before switching to staccato sixteenths for the remainder. His careful management of the accompaniment's rhythmic profile, deriving one type of motion from the other, supports the vocal line's more flexible alternation between sixteenths and eighths, which comes across as both fussy and playful, but never out of step with the accompaniment.

The song unfolds as a leisurely patter song in three strophes, each strophe first confiding a particular strategy of self-presentation before

Ex. 4.1: Gilbert and Sullivan, *Patience*, "Am I Alone?," transition from recitative to song

concluding with a refrain detailing how the recommended behavior will "play" to others:

> And everyone will say,
> As you walk your mystic way . . . [71]

Words and music alike dictate not only a "walking" performance for the refrain but also a particular style for that walk, combining a feigned aestheticism with a kind of swishing bourgeois stroll, as if aspiring to an eighteenth-century version of the courtly aristocrat. Indeed, in this regard Sullivan's music closely follows Gilbert, whose lyric neatly frames the eighteenth century by referring to "the reign of good Queen Anne" as "Culture's palmiest day," and averring that "Art stopped short in the cultivated court of the Empress Josephine."[72] Reinforcing this connection to the previous century, the final sung syllables of each verse coincide with a dainty cadential trill in the orchestra, in the best *galant* style, reminding us also of the very different trill with which the musical number set up its introductory recitative.[73] **<AE4.20>**

Bunthorne's is not the only parody of aestheticism in *Patience*. A trio drawn from the most prominent of the dragoons also gives it a try, offering a particularly awkward version of aesthetic poses "both angular and flat" during and after their musical number "It's Clear That Mediaeval Art."[74] **<TE4.21>** Once again, and even more exaggeratedly, Sullivan gives "mediaevalism" its full six syllables, setting the song to a precisely regulated staccato dotted rhythm governing both vocals and accompaniment, an articulation that confirms in musical terms that the military has joined forces with the aesthetic movement. And once again, Sullivan's music suggests a particular style of movement. Its austere regularity, in this case, indicates something bordering on the robotic, that is, both precise (as befits the dragoons' military training) and exceedingly awkward and jerky (as befits their status as neophyte aesthetes). **<AE4.22>**

But having made their point—they have become aesthetes only in order to win back the affections of the ladies, who are suitably gratified by their efforts—the dragoons quickly give it up, and celebrate their reversion to normalcy in a merry 6/8 dance, "If Saphir I Choose to Marry." This song explores, in Gilbert's typically lawyerly fashion, the awkward mathematics that will govern the final outcome: as a quintet consisting of three men and two women, the musical number leaves one man without a partner. **<TE4.23>** **<AE4.24>** Shortly thereafter, both Bunthorne and his rival Grosvenor also happily adapt to more congenial burgher rhythms in "When I Go Out of Door," as each resorts to his "natural" status as an "Everyday young man."[75] **<TE4.25>** Their song, too, is set in 6/8, although somewhat faster than "If Saphir," so as to suggest either a gigue or a comfortably bourgeois rider. **<AE4.26>** Both songs are soon reprised, in reverse order, "When I Go Out of Door" as the women's chorus also reverts to more normal dress and behavior, and "If Saphir" as the finale, where it is Bunthorne who is left without a bride (see lyric quoted above). In these ways, a relatively quick 6/8 serves as an "everyday" rhythm to set the operetta's various stages of resolution. Indeed, this use of 6/8 marks a kind of rhythmic reprise, since it reproduces the meter and approximate tempo for the introductory songs of the only relatively "normal" people at the beginning of the operetta: Patience's "I Cannot Tell What This Love May Be" and the dragoons' "If You Want a Receipt," the list song that concludes, "The soldiers of our Queen." **<TE4.27>** **<AE4.28>** **<TE4.29>** **<AE4.30>** Because this meter has not been heard in an upbeat tempo since then, these late numbers seem especially restorative, completing a musical frame of sorts for the operetta as a whole.[76]

The camp dimension of *Patience* has been enhanced by historical distance, partly because the operetta is not as well known as several others by Gilbert and Sullivan, and partly because it offers a gratifying mix of aspects and attitudes, some of which will seem quaint and outmoded, whereas others will seem particularly modern, highlighting one aspect of the operetta's camp appeal. Among the modern elements are a great many references that will be taken by most latter-day audiences to point toward homosexuality (especially if so emphasized in performance), seemingly reinforcing this dimension of modern camp tastes. In addition to the aspects of Bunthorne's characterization already detailed, there is also his swoon into the Colonel's arms after his first spoken line, and the fact that he ends up without a bride at the end. The latter is especially significant, since it reflects Gilbert's hierarchy of scorn, according to which Bunthorne, as an effeminate man, ranks even lower in the marriage stakes than Jane, Gilbert's quintessential unattractive and unmarriageable woman, who at the last minute overthrows Bunthorne in order to marry the Duke. Among other telling details, there is the following exchange with Grosvenor, during their dialogue just before "When I Go Out of Doors":

BUNTHORNE: Suppose—I won't go so far as to say that I will do it—but suppose for one moment I were to curse you! *(Grosvenor quails)* Ah! Very well. Take care.

GROSVENOR: But surely you would never do that? *(in great alarm)*

BUNTHORNE: I don't know. It would be an extreme measure, no doubt. Still—

GROSVENOR: *(wildly)* But you would not do it—I am sure you would not. *(throwing himself at Bunthorne's knees, and clinging to him)* Oh, reflect, reflect! You had a mother once.

BUNTHORNE: Never!

GROSVENOR: Then you had an aunt! *(Bunthorne is affected.)* Ah! I see you had! By the memory of that aunt, I implore you to pause ere you resort to this last fearful expedient. Oh, Mr. Bunthorne, reflect, reflect! *(weeping)*

BUNTHORNE: *(aside, after a struggle with himself)* I must not allow myself to be unmanned! *(aloud)* It is useless. Consent at once, or may a nephew's curse—

Besides Bunthorne's apparent orphanhood—a state he apparently shares with both Patience (whose only familial connection is to a great aunt) and Jack in *The Importance of Being Earnest*, not to mention the entire pirate crew in *The Pirates of Penzance*—the emotionality of both men, Grosvenor's posture before Bunthorne, even the potential pun of "reflect" (from one narcissist to another), and especially Bunthorne's privately uttered fear of being "unmanned" would all play to this dimension today.

But in 1881, and for some time thereafter, they would not have played that way. Effeminacy in men was at that time scorned (in England, at least) not because it betokened a sexual interest in other men but because it was believed, among those in respectable society, to indicate an unhealthy degree of interest in *women*, and seemed a disreputable strategy for associating with them more easily. As Alan Sinfield has argued persuasively, it was not until Oscar Wilde's trial and conviction that most people put any store in the accusations against him, and only subsequently that effeminacy and other affectations associated with Wilde would be understood by most observers as indicators of homosexual tendencies.[77] The earlier, pretrial understanding of effeminate male behavior precisely explains how the dragoons in *Patience* respond to Bunthorne: they regard him as a specifically heterosexual threat, and eventually adopt his strategies in order to compete with him. Even if the character of Bunthorne has often been played in recent decades as if he were gay (or latently so), and even if his conduct will read to modern audiences as a mode of closeted gay behavior however he is played, he is, as written, a heterosexual who deliberately acts effeminate in order to attract women. As *Patience* thus clearly indicates, incipient camp tastes could, as late as 1881, be conceived entirely from a heterosexual perspective, even when camping Wilde, and even if, among men sensitized to read them that way, such tastes could in other circumstances also covertly send a strong signal of same-sex attraction.

Moreover, it seems entirely plausible that *Patience* itself provided the springboard for the development of a Wilde-based notion of how homosexuals were expected to act. As previously noted, *Patience* was mounted just as Wilde was coming into prominence, and Carte's adroit use of Wilde's new status, as a marketing tool for *Patience*, also encouraged Wilde to appear as a recognizable version of Bunthorne, a mode of personal performance he apparently found entirely congenial (especially since it was already based in part on him) and proceeded to refine into the persona he would famously enact over the next decade and a half. And, certainly, he had every expectation that such modeling would generally be read by the general public as heterosexual, as it had then been understood for Bunthorne himself. Probably, the popular notion that Bunthorne is modeled after Wilde thus has it precisely backward. And if indeed Wilde camped Bunthorne as a means to create his own public persona, it might reasonably be said that the first person truly to enjoy "camping in the Wilde," as a mode of role-playing, was Wilde himself.

Pirate Camp

One of the most persistently successful domains for heterosexual indulgence in camp tastes, also deriving from this era but surviving as such into the present, is the theatrical portrayal of pirates, in what I term "pirate camp."[78] Gilbert and Sullivan's *The Pirates of Penzance*, in particular, gave the portrayal of piracy a major boost in that direction, two years before *Patience* and one year after *H.M.S. Pinafore* had presented a camped-up British navy to international audiences. <TE4.31> Pirates, as a subject, were by then ripe for this kind of treatment. As Peter Broadwell has shown, pirates had enjoyed a certain vogue as a subject for English musical theater since the seventeenth century,[79] overlapping the late eighteenth century's resurgence of "Turquerie," when—especially on the continent—the kind of exaggerated representations of Turks that informed Haydn's "Military" Symphony (see chapter 2) often provided opportunities to indulge in a more camplike appreciation of similar elements. Arguably, Gilbert and Sullivan completed a transmutation already under way, through which a taste for things Turkish was displaced in the later nineteenth century and since by a similar taste for things piratical. Pirates, like Turks as they were represented in western Europe during the eighteenth century, were ruthless, exotic, extravagantly beweaponed marauders given to pillage, devastation, murder, and rape, and who also—and just as importantly for theatrical camp exploitation—provided opportunities for colorful male costumes including earrings and turbans (or turban-like bandannas), and elaborate makeup including magnificent mustaches. Moreover, like Turks in such operatic productions as Mozart's *The Abduction from the Seraglio*, they could manifest a noble spirit—after all, pirates in real life had with some regularity been treated as national heroes—and so could (sometimes) serve as protagonists entitled to happy endings.

The topsy-turvydom of actual pirate histories, in which villains could be reclaimed as heroes, made piracy an ideal subject for Gilbert and Sullivan, and *The Pirates of Penzance* exploits those histories through camp, activated through the combination of two main components, one dramatic and the other musical. In dramatic terms, the operetta softens the real-life brutality of piracy through its broadly comic treatment of a band of rather ineffectual pirates, who sportingly do not attack parties weaker than they, who are well known for unquestioningly releasing any captive claiming to be an orphan, who threaten General Stanley's daughters not with rape but with marriage, and who in the end surrender to the police they have just bested in combat when charged to "yield in Queen Victoria's name."[80] Coupled with this broadly comic treatment is a captivating rendering of the rollicking, swaggering 6/8 meter, replete with dotted rhythms, that had already become a staple of the swashbuckling "soundtrack," deriving from rhythmic tropes associated with drinking and hunting songs, spirited dances such as the tarantella, ceremonial marches, and the musical simulation of a horse at full gallop.[81]

Probably the best-known symphonic use of this rhythmic configuration is in the first movement of Beethoven's Seventh Symphony (1812), where the prominent use of horns and an undergirding "gallop" rhythm evoke a rider-based heroism suggestive of battle. **<AE4.32>** A touchstone for the transfer of this idiom to the "outlaw" realm is Hector Berlioz's "Chanson de Brigands" (Song of the Brigands) from *Lélio* (1831–1832), which at times sounds as if it were modeled on Beethoven's Seventh Symphony, and elsewhere directly presages Sullivan's setting of "Oh, better Far to Live and Die" in *The Pirates of Penzance*. **<AE4.33>** Berlioz's "Chanson" begins, after an orchestral introduction (where the resemblance to Beethoven's Seventh is particularly strong), with the captain of the brigands extolling the life of brigandry as preferable to respectability:

J'aurais cent ans à vivre encore,
Cent ans et plus, riche et content,
J'aimerais mieux être brigand
Que pape ou roi que l'on adore.

Had I a century yet to live,
A century and more, rich and happy,
I'd prefer to be a brigand
Than worshipped as a pope or king.[82]

To which the opening of "Oh Better Far" offers a direct parallel:

PIRATE KING: Oh, better far to live and die
Under the brave black flag I fly,
Than play a sanctimonious part,
With a pirate head and a pirate heart.[83]

As well, the pirate band in the refrain of "Oh, Better Far," like the band of brigands in Berlioz's "Chanson de Brigands," responds with hearty affirmation to its leader's prompts: **<TE4.34>** **<AE4.35>**

PIRATE KING: For I am a Pirate King!
CHORUS: You are! Hurrah for our Pirate King![84]

Sullivan's settings of both "Oh, Better Far" (better known as "The Pirate King") and the opening number, "Pour, O Pour the Pirate Sherry," are exemplary of the 6/8 piratical idiom. **<TE4.36>** **<AE4.37>** But as Broadwell details, this idiom coexists with another type based in duple meter, following the hornpipe rhythms associated with British sailors. Indeed, by using the 6/8 idiom for the first two numbers that feature the pirate chorus in *Penzance*, Sullivan departs from the hornpipe rhythms he favored in *H.M.S. Pinafore*, while at the same time establishing a musically expressed sensibility from which the pirates can be heard to revert to their status as noblemen, who, having "gone wrong," are in the end willing to do right by the police and General Stanley's daughters. Probably decisive in this metrical distinction, both in *Penzance* and elsewhere, is the drinking song derivation of the 6/8 nautical rhythm (evoked directly in "Pour, O Pour"), which carries with it a distinct air of the disreputable that would have been unbecoming on board the HMS *Pinafore*.

Sullivan manages the effacement of the 6/8 pirate rhythms in *Penzance* in strategic stages. The first important competition to this rhythm is the waltz impulse of "Poor Wandering One!," which, as a type, offers a feminine, couple-dance rhythmic basis as a replacement for the masculine, group-dance basis of the 6/8 pirate rhythms. This waltz, which will return in the operetta's finale,[85] also prevails, more locally, against the duple meter initially favored by General Stanley's daughters, in two stages. After they introduce themselves in 2/4 ("Climbing Over Rocky Mountain"), the slow 3/4 of Frederic's plaintive ballad ("Oh, Is There Not One Maiden Breast") quickens to waltz tempo for Mabel's affirmative response ("Poor Wandering One!"). Then, as Mabel's sisters distract themselves by talking about the weather in their characteristic 2/4 ("How Beautifully Blue the Sky"), Frederic accepts Mabel's offer of a "couple dance" by joining her in a waltz duet ("Did Ever Maiden Wake"). During this number, the opening 2/4 is twice displaced by the couple's waltz rhythm until, third time around, the two rhythmic bases finish together in layered superimposition (ex. 4.2). <TE4.38> <AE4.39> In this way, 2/4 is made to support 3/4 both literally and figuratively, since, after all, Mabel's sisters actually do support her musical coupling with Frederic, not only allowing it to progress while they pretend to look the other way, but also taking vicarious pleasure in it and, implicitly, projecting a "subjunctive" version of their own betrothals, which will be accomplished only at the end of the operetta, when "Poor Wandering One!" returns as a full-cast reprise, completing the operetta's conversion of outlaws into in-laws.

Until then, the 6/8 pirate idiom is kept in play even though the pirates themselves do not use it again in straightforward celebration of their calling. In act 1, the Pirate King's lieutenant twice launches spontaneous brief reprises of "The Pirate King" to salute Mabel's father, the Major General; implicitly, the Major General is himself thereby likened to a pirate King. In the second of these brief reprises, the returning pirate rhythms yield to a "traveling" 6/8 rhythm so that the larger group might celebrate the couple's coming nuptials ("Oh, Happy Day, with Joyous Glee"). <TE4.40> <AE4.41> In act 2, the 6/8 pirate idiom largely goes undercover. Mabel's sisters layer a version of it onto the repeated "Tarantara" rhythms of the policemen's "When the Foeman Bares His Steel" ("Go Ye Heroes, Go to Glory!" and "Go and Do Your Best Endeavor"), perversely urging the constabulary on to almost certain death. <TE4.42> <AE4.43> Then, after Ruth and the Pirate King reenlist Frederic, from whom they learn of the Major General's duplicity (he is, it turns out, no orphan), they express their rage in a more *passionato* version of the idiom, recast within a 9/8 meter ("Away, Away! My Heart's on Fire").[86] <TE4.44> <AE4.45> The pirate band then takes up the original 6/8 version one last time ("A Rollicking Band of Pirates We"), but they do so only offstage and (mostly) *a cappella*, as a lead-in to the onstage numbers that displace piracy with duple-meter "burglaree" ("With Cat-like Tread, Upon Our Prey We Steal" and "Come, friends, Who Plough the Sea"). <TE4.46> <AE4.47>

More important for the present argument than Sullivan's deft structural management of rhythm is the way in which his employment of the piratical musical idiom establishes a camp-based situation in which audiences are encouraged to relish the accoutrement of the very thing being

Ex. 4.2: Gilbert and Sullivan, *The Pirates of Penzance*, culmination of combination song in "How Beautifully Blue the Sky"

lampooned. This, precisely, is the basis of pirate camp, which critiques or lampoons piracy—or, as in *Penzance*, uses a lampooned piracy as the basis for a broader satire—while also demanding that its characters, well, *act like pirates*, with all the extravagant theatricality that that entails. Indeed, camp prevails even in dramatized stories of "heroic" piracy. During the late nineteenth century and extending through Hays Code–era Hollywood, such stories had not only to disapprove of piracy itself and allow for some kind of moral uplift but also to provide opportunities for enthusiastic performance of piracy by sympathetic characters, a combination that opens a wide space for camp.[87] Camp thus became the default mode for any and all stories involving piracy, especially as they transferred to film.

The ability of pirates in many stories to assume or revert to different, more respectable identities (or vice versa) underwrites much of the capacity for pirate stories to play as camp on stage or screen, simply because the performance of piracy itself thus becomes a kind of mask, providing the means for piracy to be overtly theatricalized *within* the story's frame. In *Penzance*, the pirates are actually nobles, and Frederic himself is apprenticed to them through a miscommunication; similar devices inform such latter-day projects as *The Pirate Movie* (Ken Annakin, 1982), *Stardust* (Matthew Vaughn, 2007), and the still-unfolding *Pirates of the Caribbean* series (Gore Verbinski, 2003, 2006, 2007; Rob Marshall, 2011). Of particular interest regarding this dimension of theatrical piracy are musicals from three very different traditions: the operetta *Naughty Marietta* (Victor Herbert, 1910), the film musical *The Pirate* (Vincente Minnelli, 1948, with songs by Cole Porter), and the stage musical *The Scarlet Pimpernel* (Frank Wildhorn and Nan Knighton, 1997)—the latter of which, though not involving pirates, skirts the edges of pirate camp in interesting ways. **<TE4.48> <TE4.49>**

In a subplot of *Naughty Marietta* that did not make it into Ernst Lubitsch's 1935 film version of the operetta, Étienne, the effeminate son of the Lieutenant Governor of New Orleans, keeps a quadroon slave as a mistress (Adah) while secretly moonlighting as the notorious pirate Bras Piqué ("tattooed arm"). This subplot establishes an important basis not only for the theatrical romanticism that helped the original operetta achieve its lasting success but also for much of its extensive capacity for camp. Supporting the former are Adah's "ethnic" solo, "'Neath the Southern Moon," and the rousing quartet "Live for Today," which serves as the show's eleven o'clock number and provides the immediate dramatic basis for Captain Dick's decision to allow Étienne to escape capture. But the sympathy won through this number would not have been enough to warrant sparing Étienne were it not for the suggestion of ennobling motivation behind their piratical activities and—perhaps more important for the audience—the camp element that "secret identities" are wont to introduce, since they establish a sympathetic connection between performer and audience based on both the fun of the performance itself and the fact that the performance plays as a prolonged aside to the audience, who are being let in on a secret being kept from others in the drama.

The trope of a secretly heroic man adopting an effeminate disguise in "real life" had by 1910 already been established as an especially potent formula for camp, a new wrinkle to the campy Bunthorne pose that appeared in the wake of the Wilde trials. Most influentially, this trope provided the basis for *The Scarlet Pimpernel* (play by Emmuska Orczy, 1903/1905; published as a novel in 1905) and its many spin-offs. Not coincidentally, one of the most effective recent theatrical uses of the 6/8 pirate musical idiom comes from Frank Wildhorn's score to the 1997 musical version of Baroness Orczy's story (specifically, "Into the Fire"), a show whose extensive fan base thrived on the deft pairing of romantic sensibility and camped effeminacy that Douglas Sills brought to the role of Percy/Pimpernel,[88] reminiscent of Étienne/Bras Piqué in *Naughty Marietta.* **<AE4.50>**

Naughty Marietta may in some sense be seen as a missed opportunity to combine camp modes. While it indulges the camp possibilities of gendered role playing, regarding both Étienne's affected effeminacy and Marietta's disguise as a gypsy boy, it fails to make much of its opportunity for pirate camp, since piracy as such is given no musical or dramatic presence despite its importance to the storyline. To be sure, mixing modes of camp can be a risky undertaking, for several reasons. One particular danger—demonstrated to unfortunate effect by *The Pirate Movie*—is that the mix may so confuse the presentation as to undermine the effectiveness of the separate camp modes. In the case of *The Pirate Movie,* its imposition of 1980s-styled homosexual flirting on the pirate camp of *Pirates of Penzance* (from a century earlier) compounds the film's already muddled perspective, catastrophically ravaged in any case by the indiscriminate mixing of 1980s pop styles with the music of *Penzance.* It's not that an eclectic mixing of camp modes cannot work; *The Pirates of the Caribbean* and *Stardust* are as eclectic, and more so, yet also much more effective, since their guiding perspectives are more apparent and the sense of the fantasy worlds they inhabit is much clearer. The latter is to a large extent a matter of scoring: the main piratical themes in both *Stardust* and the *Pirates of the Caribbean* films, used to score most of their "swashbuckling" sequences, are based on the piratical 6/8 rhythmic idiom, as is the pirate song sung by Elizabeth and, later, Jack, in the first of the latter series.[89]

Yet the dangers of mixing camp modes do not manifest themselves only through ineptitude. Even as assured a film as *The Pirate,* which handles nearly all its camp modes adroitly, foundered with the public, who seemed unsure what to make of it.[90] *The Pirate* was based on *Der Seeräuber,* a 1911 play by Ludwig Fulda (one year after *Naughty Marietta*), which had been adapted by S. N. Behrman for Alfred Lunt and

Lynn Fontanne in 1942, and then developed into a musical for the Freed unit at MGM. <TE4.51> The resulting film exploits every opportunity for campish excess, yet, though the filming itself was beset with difficulties, *The Pirate* avoids the clashes in style and sensibility that would later capsize *The Pirate Movie*. Its diverse panoply of exploited camp opportunities includes

1. two interwoven dual-identity subplots, recalling plot devices familiar from *The Scarlet Pimpernel* and *Naughty Marietta*, linking a notorious pirate (Macoco, aka "Mack the Black") with a circus performer/actor on the one hand (Gene Kelly as Serafin), and the rich, portly mayor on the other (Walter Slezak as Don Pedro Vargas);
2. a fantasy-based obsession with piracy from the perspective of a young woman (Judy Garland as the orphan Manuela Alva);
3. five songs by Cole Porter that camp both his celebrated verbal wit and, in combination with Conrad Salinger's arrangements and scoring, contemporary "Latin" musical styles, including the mambo and the bolero, along with a variety of other film-music conventions;
4. showy dancing both acrobatic and clownish by Gene Kelly and the Nicholas Brothers (dance direction by Robert Alton and Gene Kelly);
5. an elaborately costumed circus troupe, including a dwarf and jugglers;
6. an extravagantly dressed entourage of characters who include Manuela's imperious Aunt Inez (Gladys Cooper) and her hilariously inconsequential (but no-less-extravagantly-turned-out) husband, Uncle Capucho (Lester Allen); and
7. the stunning visual style characteristic of the film's director, Vincente Minnelli.

Of the film's musical offerings, "Mack the Black" especially abounds in campish excess, in at least three separate realms in addition to the number's overt spectacle, its governing conceit that Manuela performs it spontaneously while under hypnosis, and its persistent preoccupation with the pronunciation of "Caribbean" (of which, more below). In the first verse of the song proper, the baby Mack is imagined to have had "a bottle, but a bottle of rum"; in the chorus, the men sing octave arpeggiations of "Yo-ho-ho-ho" to introduce each of Manuela's lines, then slow to "Yo-ho-ho" and overlap her final line to create the composite "Yo-ho-ho [and] a bottle of rum" in the precise rhythm nearly always given to the famous refrain from the "Dead Man's Chest" chant in *Treasure Island*:[91] <VE4.52>

MANUELA: For when feeding time would come,
Mack'd have a bottle, but a bottle of rum.

CHORUS: Yo ho ho ho!
MANUELA: Mack the Black! Mack'd have a bottle . . .

CHORUS: Yo . . . ho . . . ho . . . and a bottle of rum.
MANUELA: Mack'd have a bottle, but a bottle of rum.

Among other campy details in the song, for the final verse, the arrangement slows and we move in for an extended close-up of Garland that recalls some of the more intimate numbers in *Meet Me in St. Louis* (Minnelli, 1944), as Manuela prays to the "evening star" (fig. 4.5). While this moment belongs above all to Minnelli, who framed and lit Garland's face like no other could, it also allows Garland to linger over one of Porter's shining moments of lyrical virtuosity, sparkling in the midst of this seemingly throwaway lyric built around a singularly silly gimmick. Within the space of a dozen words, Porter's lyric refers to three separate tropes involving stars and their importance to both poetry and seafaring navigation (evening, wandering, guiding):

"Evening star, if you see Mack,
"Stop his wandering and guide him back."

Twice in the later stages of the film, the implicit sexual energy that fuels both Manuela's fascination with Macoco and her "awakening" under hypnosis ("Mack the Black") is turned to camp ends, in both cases releasing into songs that partake of the meaning of Serafin's name (Spanish for "Angel") and adopt a worshipful pose toward him that plays on some level as mockery. In "You Can Do No Wrong," Manuela—having just discovered that Serafin is not the real Macoco—becomes sexually provocative and engages in exaggerated, insincere praise of Serafin while cradling his head, à la Salome. <IE4.53> This campish framing of the song links it to the scene just before, providing a visual extension to her ironically rendered catalog of Serafin's body parts—"that sinister brow, the hawklike glance in your eyes, those savage shoulders, the ferocious nape of that neck"—a catalog that does not, however, descend to the stunning thighs and buttocks so evident in her earlier fantasy of him as Macoco, danced by Kelly in black piratical hot pants, waving a huge scimitar against a surreal orange-flame

Fig. 4.5: Judy Garland lit and framed in *Meet Me in St. Louis* (*top*: "The Trolley Song") and in *The Pirate* (*bottom*: "Evening Star" verse of "Mack the Black").

background. <IE4.54> In “Love of My Life,” again sung to Serafin (this time while she feigns being hypnotized), campish exaggeration of her devotion to Serafin taunts her affianced Don Pedro (the real Macoco) into revealing his identity. Both songs are better than their received reputation would indicate. In particular, the exquisitely rendered chromatic lines of “Love of My Life” remind us of the film’s proximity to *Kiss Me, Kate*, recalling especially “So in Love” in the fading chromatic lines at the end. Both songs show off Garland’s signature emotive singing style, and the camp dimension ratchets up the level of emotional expressivity, which probably contributed to the songs’ reputations as lesser Porter, since her delivery effectively overpowers the songs themselves. <VE4.55>

The film’s impish fascination with names and their pronunciations extends an element already present in the original play that is intensified through Porter’s contributions. Many of the characters’ names are coded; thus, for example, “Estramudo” (the pirate’s name in Behrman’s play) breaks down to “estra mudo,” which is Spanish for “strategic silence,”[92] “Serafin” means angel, as noted, and “Capucho,” capuchin (a small New World monkey often kept as a pet). “Macoco”—a hilarious name none of the characters in the film seems to realize is funny, although Garland and Kelly themselves seem to—was apparently a late substitution, giving Porter the “Mack” he needed for “Mack the Black” (which predates by several years the popularity of “Mack the Knife”), and playing on the nickname “Black” by suggesting both mocha and cocoa.[93] But even when—or *especially* when—delivered repeatedly with a straight face, the name “Macoco” sounds increasingly silly, evoking “cuckoo” and “macaw,” as well as the monkey genus “Macaca” (or “Macaque”), and registering as childish even though, in context, it is meant to provoke terror and romantic fascination. And the song “Mack the Black” thrives on a similar fusion of the passionate with the ridiculous, with the latter sufficiently evident in the verses and campy details quoted above, but even more so in the chorus (emphasis as indicated by the musical setting): <VE4.56>

Mack the Black—
’ROUND the CAR-ib-BE-an—
Mack the Black—
Or Ca-RIB-bean SEA.
Mack the Black—
’ROUND the CAR-ib-BE-an,
’ROUND the CAR-ib-BE-an or Ca-RIB-bean SEA.

This way of focusing on a seemingly trivial detail (yet who hasn't been perplexed by this quandary of pronunciation?) is a basic strategy of camp, echoed throughout the film in its meticulous attention to style and complementary lack of (apparent) concern for plausibility or deeper meanings. The song's adroit manipulation of textual accentuation is a familiar trope of musical comedy, calling overt attention to the composerly wit involved and sharpening the focus of the song's basic camp device of presenting the trivial as extravagantly as possible.

The film's fascination with names and their Spanish inflection is given early expression in "Niña," Serafin's "establishing" number based on the conceit (which is to say, based on *his* conceit, in both senses) that, since women are interchangeable, he might just as well simplify his dealings with them by using the same name for all, "Niña." Among other things, the song is a setup for his being rebuffed when he asks Manuela for *her* name in the scene following the song. But, more locally, the song affords Porter the opportunity for elaborately campy rhymes (gardenia, neurasthenia, schizophrenia), and Kelly the opportunity to establish the style of acrobatic dancing, exuding macho bravado, that he will use throughout the film, avoiding his usual combination of tap and ballet in favor of styles that will work with both his circus performer persona and his piratical pretensions. In line with all this are many bits of "business" in the extended dance that follows the song (e.g., his tonguing a lit cigarette back into his mouth for a quick kiss). As Richard Dyer has observed, the number also establishes Serafin as the object of the female gaze,[94] inverting both the usual dynamic in film musicals and the specific point of the song lyric. This dimension of the film, which receives much play throughout, may account in part for the film's lack of success, but it is entirely thematic, and of a piece with the film's wanton engagement with any and all modes of camp, many of which relate directly to Serafin's narcissism. To cite one detail among many, Serafin sports an earring, which may be easily understood as typical of both circus performers and pirates, but which also places him more pronouncedly as an object of display.

Key to the number's gender reversal of "the gaze" is the way the supporting dance idiom shifts as the number moves from song into dance, mostly abandoning the suavely seductive mambo rhythms of the song's accompaniment in favor of a bolero idiom.[95] The bolero extension of "Niña," in its early use of snare drum with alto flute and its frequent use of "Spanish" flourishes, directly evokes the famous *Bolero* by Maurice

Ravel—an erotic ballet piece featuring a solo female dancer—as if to draw further attention to the fact that here a man dances to seduce women rather than the reverse. **<VE4.57>** The shift is doubly campy, not only setting up a campy dancing situation for Kelly but also calling attention to itself through musical allusion.

Allusions are standard fare in film scores, and for that very reason they are readily appreciated as unintentional camp. In the camp-saturated environment of *The Pirate*, however, such allusions are clearly intentional, such as Conrad Salinger's contribution to the film's multifaceted camp extravaganza. To enumerate a few other instances of campy excess or allusion in the film's scoring:[96]

1. The musical cue for Don Pedro's two arrivals by carriage is a "portly" version of the piratical 6/8 idiom, featuring the bassoon in comic mode. **<VE4.58>** This theme appears a third time in the lower strings, when Serafin recognizes him as Macoco.
2. A familiar circus theme (from *Entrance of the Gladiators*, by Julius Fučík) serves as the basis for a leitmotif for Serafin, which also appears during many of the circus sequences, including the dance segment of "Be a Clown."
3. The cue for Manuela's first experience of the Caribbean Sea evokes Debussy's *La Mer*, framed by comedic allusions to Mendelssohn's *Die Hebriden* at the appearance of Serafin. **<VE4.59>** The allusion to *La Mer* later reduces to literalist association, for example, just as Serafin recovers Manuela's wide-brimmed sun hat, which had blown from her head and is now soaked in "*La Mer*." **<VE4.60>** The music seems hilariously oblivious to the fact that Manuela's enraptured mood, which provoked the allusion in the first place, has long since been shattered by Serafin's persistent presence, a shift in mood reinforced by his *Die Hebriden* motive shading into his circus leitmotif as the scene progresses.
4. The music that accompanies Manuela's flight after her circus performance of "Mack the Black" evokes Nikolai Rimsky-Korsakov's *Flight of the Bumblebee*. This sequence involves two other campy references unrelated to the scoring, both thematic. Prior to the cue, Serafin awakens Manuela from her hypnotic trance with a kiss, à la Sleeping Beauty or Cinderella, archly underscoring the fairytale dimension of the plotting. More subtle is an apparent allusion to Garland's most famous

role. As Manuela arrives back at her hotel suite, she cries, "Aunt Inez, Aunt Inez, wake up, I want to go home, I want to go home"; because of the assonance between "Aunt Inez" and "Auntie Em," and enhanced by Garland's characteristically tremulous delivery, the allusion draws attention to the situational parallel between Manuela and Dorothy (*The Wizard of Oz*, 1939), since both try to escape the fantasy realities their earlier fervent desires have conjured up.[97] **<VE4.61>**

5. The repeated horn whoops in the "Pirate Ballet" sequence allude to the opening prelude of Richard Strauss's *Der Rosenkavalier*, known as one of the most "graphic" representations of sex in the orchestral literature, and which uses horns as a symbol of cuckoldry. In *The Pirate*, these whoops inaugurate the ballet's "abduction" scenario. Toward the end of this part of the ballet, Serafin (as Macoco) seizes, embraces, and then abandons a female captive, as the music devolves into a generalized "Ballet Russes" sound, evoking a mix of Debussy, Ravel, early Igor Stravinsky, and even George Gershwin, with the last lick of the sequence being a jazz-piano version of the sequence's main melodic motive. **<VE4.62>**
6. "Mack the Black" is used extensively, even excessively, in the film's underscore, generally in connection with Manuela, in the manner of a leitmotif. Naturally enough, "Mack the Black" is the main thematic source of the "Pirate Ballet"—it is, after all, *her* fantasy of Serafin as Macoco. Two other instances stand out. Even before Manuela sings the song, we hear an "impressionist" version of the tune during her first encounter with Serafin, at his mention of daydreams as a substitute for real romance (this striking, quasi-Orientalist passage then functions as a specific pointer to that scene when she later lingers, while unpacking, over the hat that had blown off her head during that first encounter with Serafin). But the most elaborate transformation of the tune is the funereal version, replete with tolling church bells, that accompanies Manuela in her slow march to accommodate Serafin's summons, having prepared herself to make the "ultimate sacrifice" to save her town. As Serafin appears on the balcony, heroic trumpets interrupt the funeral march with a flourish, but that flourish is based on his circus motive, making its descending chromatic lines come across as a theatricalized sneer. Here, as in many of the other cited instances, it is the literalness of the leitmotif, along with its incongruity, that makes the cue campy. **<VE4.63>**

If there is a camp dimension that holds the diffuse camp modes of *The Pirate* together, it lies in Minnelli's direction, particularly in the visual realm.[98] Two aspects in particular stand out: the use of color and the careful framing of each sequence, the latter often coordinated with lighting.[99] Beyond examples already cited, we may note that, just as the careful framing that governs *Meet Me in St. Louis* is set up by the picture-postcard dissolves that demarcate the changes of holiday seasons across the film, so also is the no-less-meticulous framing in *The Pirate* set up through the elaborately bordered decorative map of the Caribbean that appears behind the opening credits, and the "picture book" introduction to the exploits of "The Black Macoco." **<IE4.64>** But whereas in *Meet Me in St. Louis* this framing and its careful lighting dimension serves mainly to draw our attention to Judy Garland (as it does often enough in *The Pirate*, as noted; see fig. 4.5), *The Pirate* also frames Kelly in this way, especially during the "Pirate Ballet" sequence. **<IE4.65>** Particularly vivid visual moments in the displacement of this framing technique from Garland to Kelly are the musical cues that demarcate the first extended "*La Mer*" moment, each briefly alluding to *Die Hebriden*, as noted. During the first of these, Serafin is revealed just behind Manuela as she moves toward the sea, so that it is suddenly he rather than she who fills the screen; **<IE4.66>** in the second, his presence suddenly imposes on the scene, breaking her enraptured mood as she stands braced by the sight, sound, and scent of the sea. **<IE4.67>**

This technique of framing, and its capacity to govern our sense of the world that a film has placed us in (including its camp dimension) is already evident in Minnelli's first directorial assignment in a Hollywood musical, the "Ghost Theater" sequence in *Babes on Broadway* (Busby Berkeley, 1941), a film I discuss earlier in terms of its extended minstrel sequence. Two things about "Ghost Theater" are especially relevant to *The Pirate*: the way in which the sequence at key moments displaces the film's focus on Mickey Rooney as its governing actorly sensibility with a focus on Judy Garland, and the way in which this sequence, through framing, lighting, and camera movement, creates a world (and a camp environment) distinctly different from, and even at odds with, the rest of the film, even while maintaining thematic and performative ties to it.

The sequence begins with a darkened shot of the grotesque face of a warrior figure in the long-abandoned Duchess Theatre, which Tommy and Penny (played by Mickey Rooney and Judy Garland) hope to reclaim as a venue for their show. The music cue establishes a mysterious and uneasy atmosphere, drawing on leitmotifs redolent of the turn of the twentieth century—the same period the sequence will attempt to re-create—evoking Richard Strauss in particular, and Claude Debussy and Maurice Ravel more generally. **<VE4.68>** As the camera pans to Tommy and Penny entering the theater from the back, the cue recedes into generic background music as they look around and as Tommy then expounds on the ghosts that haunt all theaters. The individual numbers that follow are based directly on faded theatrical posters—the most overt "framing" device in the sequence—using elaborate costuming and makeup to evoke the original performer in each role, as detailed in table 4.1[100]

In line with the film's engagement with the ongoing war in Europe, this sequence draws on a theatrical "melting pot" representative of the United States and its (future) allies. Each of its reproduced performances is strongly stamped with a national or ethnic identity, understood as integral to Broadway's theatrical heritage; these include numbers whose authors or performers are French (1 and 5), Irish American (2, 4, and 6), Scottish (3), and English (1). More specifically, the outer pairs of numbers (1 and 2, 5 and 6) both move from "heroic French" to "plucky American," with each number grounded in the personality of the reproducing performer. Most notably, Rooney's puckish Cyrano (French author and English actor) and Garland's passionate "Eaglet" (French author and actor) set the tone, implicitly, for US American participation in Europe's resistance to tyranny. In pursuing an inclusive yet partisan diversity, the sequence may also be seen to complement other "American" types included in the film ("Anything Can Happen in New York," "Hoe Down," and—despite its racist basis—the minstrel sequence discussed earlier in this chapter), as well as the other "imports": "Chin Up, Cheerio, Carry on," "Bombshell from Brazil," and "Mamãe Eu Quero." Adding to this ethnic, national, and racial mixing is an occasional bit of gender-bending, both in this sequence and elsewhere in the film, with Garland's "pants" role (number 5 above) matched by Rooney's drag version of Carmen Miranda in "Mamãe Eu Quero" and Garland's turn as Mr. Tambo during the minstrel sequence. And, as with the minstrel sequence, "Ghost Theater" is structured so as mainly to alternate turns by the film's two stars. Reinforcing these thematic and performative tie-ins to the rest of the film, the cleanup/rehearsal montage that follows immediately on "Yankee Doodle Boy" begins with

Table. 4.1: Numbers in the "Ghost Theater" sequence of *Babes on Broadway*

RELEVANT POSTER TEXT	HISTORICAL BASIS	RE-CREATED PERFORMANCE
1. Richard Mansfield; *Cyrano de Bergerac*; Duchess Theatre	Richard Mansfield originated the role of Cyrano on Broadway at the Garden Theatre, 1898	Tommy recites and pantomimes the "Duel in Rhyme"
2. Duchess Theatre; Fay Templeton; *Forty-Five Minutes from Broadway*	Fay Templeton originated the role of Mary Jane Jenkins at the New Amsterdam Theatre, 1906	Penny sings and dances "Mary Is a Grand Old Name"
3. *Sir Harry Lauder*	Harry Lauder's self-titled retrospective vaudeville show opened at Jolson's 59th Street Theatre, 1930	Tommy sings and dances "She Is Ma Daisy" (1904)
4. Blanche Ring singing "Rings on My Fingers and Bells on My Toes"; *Yankee Girl*; Duchess Theatre	Blanche Ring originated the role of Jessie Gordon at the Herald Square Theatre, 1910, interpolating "Rings on My Fingers" from *The Midnight Sons* (1909)	Penny sings and dances "Rings on My Fingers and Bells on My Toes"
5. Duchess Theatre; Mme. Sarah Bernhardt [pictured in the role of Napoleon II (Napoleon's son) in *L'Aiglon* (*The Eaglet*)]	Sarah Bernhardt originated the title role, which Edmond Rostand wrote for her, in Paris, 1900; Maude Adams originated the role on Broadway at the Knickerbocker Theatre, 1900	Penny performs a speech from the play, in French
6. "Yankee Doodle Boy"; *Little Johnny Jones*; Duchess Theatre	George M. Cohan originated the title role at the Liberty Theatre, 1904; "Yankee Doodle Boy" is a solo number for Johnny	Tommy sings and dances "Yankee Doodle Boy," joined by Penny

the same grotesque warrior figure with which the "Ghost Theater" sequence began.

Seemingly, then, everything that *could* be done to integrate the sequence into the film *was* done—except that it nevertheless stands stubbornly apart from the rest of the film. It looks different, is shaped differently, moves differently, and, on aggregate, feels almost entirely different from the rest of the film, creating its own world and belonging only to it. To be sure, its ghost theme suggests that the sequence *should* seem to belong to a different world; one might even conjecture on this basis that its differences were intentional. But even if those differences work to the film's advantage on some level, little else in the film shows a level of sophistication that might indicate a deliberate strategy at work, especially since the basis for this sequence's problematic divergence—its specific camp sensibility—would probably have eluded the film's principal makers, although perhaps not Minnelli's.

Berkeley's camp sensibility is that of exuberant excess, most often expressed through the breaking of frames. During the minstrel sequence of *Babes on Broadway*, for example, Garland's "Franklin D. Roosevelt Jones" ends with her singing to an ascending, then descending crane shot in the number's most blatant and extended departure from naturalistic theatrical presentation, and Rooney's banjo number in the later stages suddenly reveals, in typical Berkeley fashion, an enormous line of banjo players in a space that moments before had been empty stage, shot from a point of view that assumes an audience perspective located somewhere in the wings (fig. 4.6). Rooney, in "Mamãe Eu Quero," mocks his own creditable drag performance as Carmen Miranda by concluding, after a series of delicately fading repetitions of "Mama," with a shouted "Hey, Ma!" in his own voice. **<VE4.69>** And the half-minute montage that follows "Ghost Theater" overlaps and superimposes a bewildering collection of brief clips that sometimes creates a sense of coordinated motion but in itself produces no coherent narrative. Camp in each of these examples arises from the way exaggeration and discontinuity call attention to themselves and to the constructed nature of the filmic experience, and so distract from more straightforward and naturalistic presentation.

The extraordinary centrifugal force of Berkeley's camp contrasts sharply with the equally compelling centripetal force of Minnelli's camp style, which trades on a strong sense of possession deriving from framing and exquisite refinement of detail. "Possession" in this sense is not just about

Fig. 4.6: Two frame-breaking moments in the minstrel show from *Babes on Broadway*: Judy Garland at the conclusion of "Franklin D. Roosevelt Jones" (top) and Mickey Rooney's banjo choir in "Alabamy Bound" (bottom).

control; Berkeley is, after all, nearly always in control—in quasi-militaristic control, at that—of his armies of performers and multitudinous moving images. Rather, it divides into roughly equal parts of *self*-possession, evident in a strongly defined personal taste, and—through expressing that taste within clearly articulated framing and loving regard for the nuances of costuming, lighting, and camera movement—possession of the exotically rendered performances as delivered on film, which are above all to be *savored*. In contrast, one does not savor Berkeley's excesses, although one might pleasurably gorge on them. In camp's penchant for both having and eating its cake, Minnelli's emphasis is on the former while Berkeley's is on the latter.

It is in this respect that the "handoffs" between numbers in the "Ghost Theater" sequence weigh heavily in Garland's favor. Rooney's turn at Cyrano is better than might be expected, but precarious enough that one is grateful for the foreshortening of the number and for Minnelli's restrained management of Rooney's overexuberant shadow-swordplay. <IE4.70> While one might expect a more vibrant or upbeat song from Garland to succeed Rooney's Cyrano, "Mary" compels through its perfect alignment with Minnelli's style of presentation, an alignment rooted in Garland's graceful physical restraint, superb vocal delivery, and costume. The latter is suitable to both period and ghostly environment, its cobwebby fabric balanced on either side by a black feathery fan and a white diaphanous kerchief, and the ensemble topped by an elaborate, multitoned feathered headdress, all accentuated by Garland's "modeling" dance-twirls that follow the song. As the camera pans smoothly in for a close-up during the early stages of the song, the contrast of her fair face and shoulders with the surrounding darker tones of hat, gown, and background is given ample play, the brightness of the former both softened by lighting and given sharper emphasis by the tight black collar around her throat, which also draws attention to the source of her exquisite voice. The containment symbolized by the collar is then echoed during the closing bars of the number by her deployment of her shadowy fan, which alternately obscures and reveals her face before performing the same maneuver on the next poster—by way of transition, but also making a direct connection between Garland's self-framing and the sequence's basic framing device. <VE4.71>

More daring is Garland's Bernhardt/Napoleon II. To begin with, it seems an odd succession from Garland's Blanche Ring ("Rings on My Fingers"), since we expect something from Rooney given the alternating pattern. But the recitation is also odd because it is unlikely to be recognized by more than a tiny fraction of the intended audience. Hence, many assume (without actually listening to the French, apparently) that the text is drawn from "La Marseillaise"; few notice she is in drag; and fewer still recognize the text or (at least in the United States) make sense of what she is actually saying. The recitation is, in all these senses, ideal for camp expression, since the actual content is so obscure.[101] The number functions almost as pure gesture, both physical and verbal, so that it matters not a whit whether we regard the performance as "good" or "bad" in conventional terms. **<VE4.72>** As she shifts declamatory poses, we become more acutely aware instead of how much the camera movement matters to the number, how actively the camera *possesses* Garland, as indeed its caressing movements have throughout the sequence possessed Garland in a way that would simply be impossible with Rooney, given the way his cane- or swordplay threatens to break the frame in each of his turns. Indeed, Rooney's manic busyness is perhaps the only real link to the Berkeley camp aesthetic that the "Ghost Theater" sequence otherwise leaves behind.

In *The Pirate*, it is Kelly who most closely matches Minnelli's camp aesthetic, sometimes even using, as a foil, that part of Garland's comic performance style that may be understood as a legacy of her frequent work with Berkeley and Rooney, a comic style Kelly capitulates to in their burlesque performance of "Be a Clown" at the end of the film.[102] **<IE4.73>** His dances, like Garland's in "Ghost Theater," are otherwise extended poses, albeit spiced with acrobatics (which dominate his version of "Be a Clown" with the Nicholas brothers). Seen against Rooney's contributions to "Ghost Theater," Kelly's dances in *The Pirate* often seem to echo his reproach to Don Pedro ("You should try underplaying sometime"), in that Kelly lets the camera come to him rather than frantically trying to get its attention. **<VE4.74>** In this way, even Serafin's narcissism is beholden to Minnelli's overarching camp sensibility.

POPULAR MUSIC CONTRA GERMAN IDEALISM

With camp, as with minstrelsy, it has been necessary here to refocus an ongoing conversation. In the case of minstrelsy, that conversation has for a long time been concerned mainly with either racial politics or, following a positivist tradition, describing and cataloging the practices of minstrelsy while periodically acknowledging and decrying its racist basis. Without ignoring the importance of race to minstrelsy, or of knowing better what its performances and traditions entailed, I instead direct attention, earlier in this chapter, toward the rebellious attitudes that gave minstrelsy its primary sustained impetus, and for which its performance modes provided an accommodating vehicle. This is not meant to correct previous emphases but rather to provide another perspective on minstrelsy's fraught history, as partial explanation for both its tenacious hold on US American culture and, more specifically, its central role in promoting and sustaining a distinctly US American attitude toward high art and its pretensions, which in the later nineteenth century came to include the musical paradigms of German Idealism.

Engaging camp has been a more complicated project, because what I wish to offer actually *is*, in some respects, a corrective, not of particulars, but of a larger general view of the subject. To deepen understandings of camp's development, and to establish the basis for modern camp tastes in late nineteenth-century attitudes skeptical of the elevated seriousness of (musical) art, I have here differentiated two main camp categories, based respectively on the aestheticized persona of Oscar Wilde and in pirate lore, and explored a variety of attendant realms and modes of camp. Among other things, the aesthetic skepticism of camp attitudes helped reclaim music for social play within theatrical contexts and, in the late nineteenth century especially, did so largely independent of gay culture as such. Which is not to say that the large gay presence in theatrical cultures did not play a proportionately large part in the development of camp practices. Not only did it obviously do so, but those contributions also led fairly directly to camp becoming one of the central communicative modes of closeted gay men across most of the twentieth century. But importantly—important even to the success of camp in so serving closeted gay communities—camp has a broader cultural base not connected to sexual orientation, since it originated, in part, as a reaction against the more serious modes of aesthetic appreciation fostered by German Idealist thought. This reaction has especially deep roots in Anglo-American cultures, where camp has developed its most important strongholds, albeit often with strong French overtones (thus, Bunthorne's attachment for "a not too-French French bean" and his nostalgia for "the cultivated court of the Empress Josephine").[103]

Foregrounding this historical understanding of camp, as a means of making light of serious art, has made it easier to see what defines camp more generally and distinguishes it from other aspects of theatrical and cinematic creation, performance, and reception. Moreover, it inhibits the tendency to essentialize outward from the important role camp has played in (mainly closeted) gay cultures. While camp is obviously congenial to many elements in these cultures, even perhaps uniquely so, its pleasures are by no means inaccessible—and have never been inaccessible—to more mainstream (heterosexual) tastes, however seldom acknowledged and however differently camp sensibilities in those disparate populations might have been textured. In this respect, it is no accident that camp should have come to maturity in theatrical cultures, which freely mix populations of straights and gays, nor that its important early musical cultivation should have been in *operette* and operetta (along with closely related ballet traditions), nor, further, that those traditions should have flourished in cities with deeply rooted skepticism concerning the earnest seriousness of German Idealist musical aesthetics.

Operette first blossomed in Paris, which, as the seat of well-ordered (thus, mannered and surface-based) "Civilization," tended to reject depth-based German *Kultur* and the high-toned seriousness of its philosophies and art. It was thence exported to Vienna and London (as operetta), the former offering worldly Catholic resistance to more otherworldly, Protestant-friendly German Idealist thought, whereas London's embrace of its own, more respectable form of operetta was well in keeping with its high regard for sociality, its distaste for unseemly excess, its historical hedging about the specific trappings of Christianity, and its enthusiastic appreciation of civilized fun.[104] And both forms of operetta soon found ready audiences and imitators in the United States, with its impudent, New World mistrust of Europe's philosophical complexities—although, to be sure, that attitude was complicated by a nostalgic regard for Europe's Old World charms. This coupling of skepticism and affection was an ideal formula for camp's fermentation. As operetta traditions eventually blended with other musical-theater traditions to create the distinctive genre of the American musical, the latter in turn became a crucial crucible for the development of camp tastes during the middle decades of the twentieth century and beyond.

Camp and minstrelsy operate mainly within different but often overlapping class strata. Minstrelsy appealed early on chiefly to working-class audiences, but soon strove to cultivate more "respectable" audiences while trying also to maintain both its allegiance to its original audiences and its pretension to offer a recognizable if grossly mediated version of African American culture. Camp reversed this trajectory within a later timeframe, functioning most effectively within mid-to-upper-class venues and encompassing anything theatrical that might have fit within the category of the "urbane,"[105] until movies (and, later, television) made camp pleasures and appreciations more readily available to all. Even considering these reversing trajectories, and even though camp and minstrelsy might occasionally share some elements (such as cross-dressing), they have rarely seemed to inhabit the same theatrical space, owing probably to the tendency among many of camp's devotees to find minstrelsy distasteful—for its lack of refinement as much as for its racism, and perhaps also for its overt anti-intellectualism. Only in the early synchronized sound era in Hollywood, while blackface was still tolerated and camp tastes were both cultivated and (often unintentionally) encouraged, were such overlaps possible. Indeed, for many films from this period that include blackface, it is an underlying camp sensibility that serves as the larger presentational context, albeit catering more often to cruder than subtler tastes, and usually given to excess, as with the Busby Berkeley examples discussed earlier. Arguably, blackface would not have been deemed as acceptable as it was, or for as long, without the larger camp context.

Despite manifest differences, both camp and minstrelsy undermine the same key element of German Idealist musical aesthetics, and in much the same way. German Idealism's elevation of music to the highest of the arts carried with it the notion that, through contemplation, Music (that is, music true to its essence and potential) could provide deeper connections to, or even the sense of merging with, a succession of sublimely large and elusive noumenalities, such as collective consciousness, infinity, the Will, or *das Welt*. Indeed, within this paradigm, *depth* became the true content of Music. It is this conceit that minstrelsy and camp stand on its head, for it is with *surfaces* that they are most concerned, and, inevitably, the play between surfaces and whatever may be understood to lie beneath.

In late nineteenth-century minstrelsy, that play involved the use of multiple and layered masks, and a particular mode of comic trickery—often allied with "trickster" racial stereotypes, generally rendered sympathetically—that depended on the capacity of one thing to seem like another, and for truth to emerge through blatant falsity.[106] Minstrelsy's predilection for outrageous puns and malapropisms, for example, often drew on all three elements, playing on the sonic affinity of words for each other, and on the slyly oblique ways these "mistakes" could point to otherwise hidden truths, leaving at least some doubt about whether the speaker's trickster persona might be in on the jest, after all.

While puns and other verbal play can seem tiresome in real life, there is a long and successful history of exploiting them for comic effect in theatrical contexts, where they are especially effective when allied with comically sympathetic characters. In this respect, verbal play is like any other potentially annoying personality tic, in that theatrical presentation can provide a kind of societal safety valve and promote tolerance, as in Haydn's *Il Distratto* (discussed in chapter 2). Minstrelsy, whose masks and stereotypes incorporate many such traits, imbeds verbal play within racialized dialect, which, next to minstrelsy's burnt cork, clownish makeup, and exaggerated costuming, is chief among its tainted tropes for manifesting racial difference. Indeed, minstrel dialect, and much of its associated language, has seemed in many contexts as degrading as any other stereotype perpetuated by minstrelsy. But dialect, like the negative stereotypes of Zip Coon and Jim Crow, could also become a channel for something considerably more positive, and certainly more sympathetic. Arguably, it had to have done so, since all the negatively charged accoutrements of minstrelsy had to be imbued with some degree of sympathy in order for the institution to fulfill its primary function as entertainment—even if, as Eric Lott argues, sympathy was always balanced by ridicule to keep the mix acceptable to many audiences.[107]

A classic example of how this works comes from one of the oldest "chestnuts" from the early years of minstrelsy, the lecture on phrenology (fig. 4.7). **<IE4.75>** Phrenology was a then-current form of "science" dating from the end of the eighteenth century, already decried as a pseudoscience while minstrelsy was in its infancy, yet still persuasive enough to serve as one of the important bases for "scientific" proofs that some races (that is, blacks) were mentally inferior to others (whites).[108] Early on in the version of this lecture included in *Black Diamonds* (1855), the lecturer introduces his subject as follows: "Freenology consists in gittin 'nolage free, like you am dis ebening; it was fust discubered in de free schools . . ."[109] These lines are couched in a dialect now generally considered offensive, and they launch a lecture that includes much else to give offense, especially to latter-day sensibilities. Nevertheless, the quoted passage carries interesting freight,

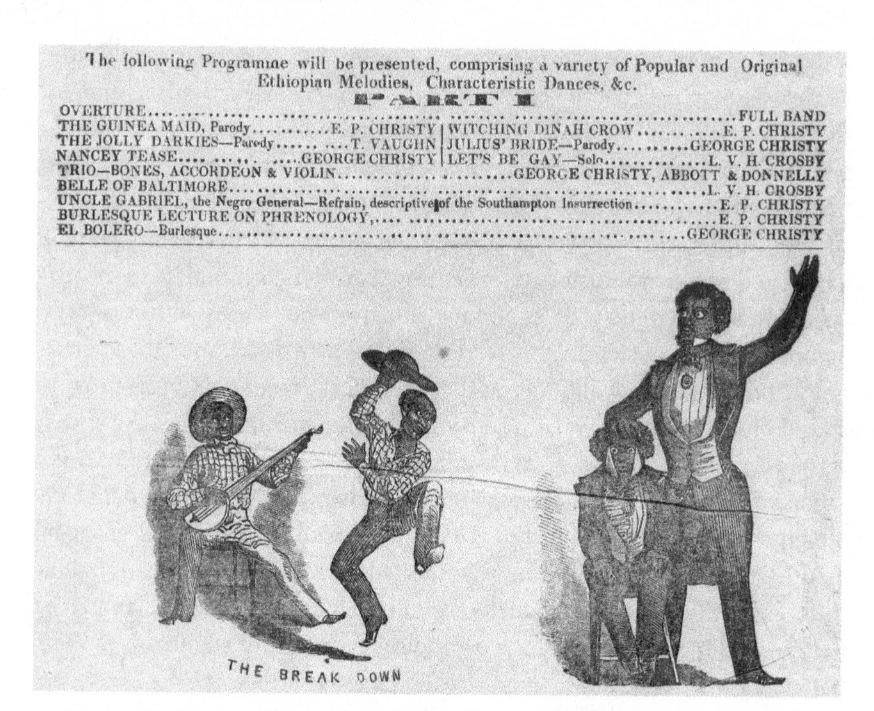
The following Programme will be presented, comprising a variety of Popular and Original Ethiopian Melodies, Characteristic Dances, &c.

OVERTURE....................FULL BAND
THE GUINEA MAID, Parody..........E. P. CHRISTY | WITCHING DINAH CROW..........E. P. CHRISTY
THE JOLLY DARKIES—Parody..........T. VAUGHN | JULIUS' BRIDE—Parody..........GEORGE CHRISTY
NANCEY TEASE..........GEORGE CHRISTY | LET'S BE GAY—Solo..........L. V. H. CROSBY
TRIO—BONES, ACCORDEON & VIOLIN..........GEORGE CHRISTY, ABBOTT & DONNELLY
BELLE OF BALTIMORE..........L. V. H. CROSBY
UNCLE GABRIEL, the Negro General—Refrain, descriptive of the Southampton Insurrection..........E. P. CHRISTY
BURLESQUE LECTURE ON PHRENOLOGY,..........E. P. CHRISTY
EL BOLERO—Burlesque..........GEORGE CHRISTY

Fig. 4.7: Caricature of Edwin (E. P.) Christy (*lower right*) delivering his "Burlesque Lecture on Phrenology." Segment of playbill from 1848 advertising performances of Christy's Minstrels at Mechanics' Hall in New York City. MS Thr 556 321, seq. 23, Houghton Library, Harvard University. Used with permission.

progressing deftly from an "ignorant" pun (phrenology / free knowledge) to bring the racially charged "science" of phrenology, which claimed a *biological* basis for the relative societal stations of blacks and whites, into close association with two institutions that attest to an *environmental* basis for mental development: the public lecture ("gittin 'nolage free, like you am dis ebening") and the New York African Free Schools, the first of which was founded by the abolitionist New York Manumission Society in 1789 to provide an equalizing education for African Americans.[110] What makes this passage "classic," qualitatively, is that it leaves in doubt whether the lecturing persona is aware that this juxtaposition is slyly inappropriate, or that the "free 'nolage" he offers is worth even less than its asking price, or, further, that among phrenology's freedoms is its complete disconnect from genuine science.

As with Gilbert and Sullivan's topsy-turvydom, the perceived butt of minstrel humor will slide willy-nilly from potential target to potential target, according to the mindset of the audience, in this case shifting from phrenology itself to the institution of the public lecture and its practitioners, to the "learned" pretensions of the blackened persona of the lecturer, to specific topical references made along the way. But however the lecture might be heard, it will cast doubt on both the scientific value of phrenology and the presumed ignorance of the lecturing persona, while reminding white listeners—and not just with reference to the African Free Schools—of the multiple ways they are kin to the black character being performed on stage.

Camp's engagement with surfaces, and with the relationship between surfaces and content, is more broadly based than minstrelsy's play with masks, although camp, too, finds masks useful. Camp may be viewed from two main perspectives, yielding distinctive modes of analysis. Most narrowly, it may be seen to be all about surfaces, not only making light of serious content but also redirecting that light to play along the surfaces and peripheries of the artwork. From this perspective, content does not matter; or, perhaps, surfaces will simply be taken to be the content. While this focus allows a rich engagement with camp experiences, and often corresponds well with specific camp tastes, it does not take camp's full measure, no more than could the practices of minstrelsy be well understood by taking its masks at "face value." The latter is indeed what our present-day revulsion for blackface urges us to do, both to evade considering minstrelsy's demeaning grotesqueries any longer than necessary, and to avoid the awkwardness of finding humor in such a repulsive institution—the very awkwardness explored in Spike Lee's *Bamboozled* (2000), until minstrelsy's "face values" reassert themselves with a vengeance.[111] But that understandable impulse directs us far from the reality of minstrelsy, which in the nineteenth century thrived on the tension between masks and what (and how) they attempt to conceal, yet inevitably reveal freshly through that very attempt—all of which happens whether the performer wishes it to or not. Similarly, any special attention paid to surfaces more broadly, as in camp, will derive *frisson* from tensions that inevitably arise between those surfaces and the content they ostensibly express; consequently, camp analyses that address the interplay of surfaces and content—the second of camp's two principal modes of analysis—will tend to be more satisfying and revelatory. Recalling Richard Dyer's previously quoted observation regarding *The Pirate,* that "it is in the recognition of illusion that camp finds reality," we may also profitably trace other dynamics between supposed opposites that camp reconfigures: between surface and content, or, in an alternative formulation, between style and substance. As Mitchell Morris writes regarding the latter pair, "Although camp is often said to have something to do with the triumph of style over substance, the aesthetic of failure suggests the opposite—that substance, when it breaks the style, is what matters most. . . . Camp claps its hands loudly to show that it believes in essences."[112]

As I claim above, an important kind of camp intensifies the blatantly artificial in order to divert from, but then bring heightened attention to, what outside a camp context would be understood as the actual content, or essence, of a dramatic event. I argue, as well, that dramatic content, in a conventional sense, is accentuated rather than denied by the camp element in *The Importance of Being Earnest* and, less consistently, in *Patience*. But how does this inside-outside relationship work in pirate camp? More broadly, how does it work in theatrical music in general after German Idealism's reconfiguration of the "content" of Music as its perceived quality of depth? And, finally, how does all this affect the development of a popular music tradition in opposition to musical idealism?

Pirate camp encourages the notion that piracy itself is more or less a good thing, since it provides welcome opportunities to enact a flamboyantly gaudy version of masculinity through makeup, dressing up, acting up, and otherwise indulging the theatrical. Like minstrelsy, it creates a mask for entertainment purposes, and so invests the masked persona—a persona incorporating elements of the evoked stereotype, the character who adopts that stereotyped role, and the performer who performs the character who adopts the stereotype—with a great deal of sympathy even though pirates, like most blackface personae, are understood to be inherently unworthy of approbation. And, as with many stereotypes of minstrelsy, the camped pirate is a trickster figure, and enjoyed as such. In both *The Pirates of Penzance* and *The Pirate*, pirates are overtly valued for their entertainment value, and characters adopt piracy as a pose. Both stories find their own means of dealing with, and containing, the realities of piracy (which involved ample doses of murder, rape, kidnapping, and human trafficking), whether through denial or confrontation. In *Penzance*, the pirate band's credentials as pirates are cast in doubt at every turn, by their ineffectiveness and soft hearts, by their reverent veneration of poetry, by their "credulous simplicity,"[113] by their devout loyalty to Queen Victoria (whose very name causes them to yield), or, in the end, by their being unmasked as "noblemen who have gone wrong." Their behavior is in each instance consistent with the fact that they, no less than the actors who play them, are not pirates but are only playing at it. In *The Pirate*, Serafin likewise acts the role of the notorious pirate Macoco, but specifically as defined by Manuela's romantic imagination, a distinction that will be put into higher relief when the real Macoco is revealed to be no more than an insecure brute, who may have once commanded a savage crew but is now incapable of commanding a stage.

In both *Penzance* and *The Pirate*, the camp element of piracy is woven into the story, and so becomes, in a sense, the content as much as it is the surface. In *Penzance*, acting the pirate is understood to be a kind of youthful hijinks, first because of Frederic's situation as an indentured apprentice who leaves the band when he reaches his maturity, and then, more explicitly, in the Major General's indulgent, conciliatory reaction upon learning that the pirates are really noblemen, alluding to the common phrase "boys will be boys": "Peers will be peers, and youth will have its fling."[114] And it helps tremendously for latter-day camp performances, which entail an assumed yet easily denied affinity for homosexuality, that each male character's transition into maturity in *Penzance* entails a move from the homosocial world of piracy to the paired heterosexuality of "unbounded domesticity."[115] To be sure, this is a standard plotline in operettas and musicals, but, significantly, it also runs closely parallel to traditional (if untenable) notions of youthful homosexual experimentation yielding to heterosexual normality in maturity—a trope also operative in *The Importance of Being Earnest*—so that piracy is well staked out, as early as 1881, as a potential youth-oriented "campground" for gay-friendly sensibilities. *The Pirate*, in its way, takes a more extreme position, linking the flamboyance of acting the pirate—seen as but one potential of theatrical entertainment—directly to the basic human impulse to imagine romantic alternatives, in both the general and the sexual senses of the term "romantic." In this, *The Pirate*, with all its outward peculiarities as a musical (only five songs, and none for the ingénue until well into the film), is by sensibility the purest of musicals, making it also, as Richard Dyer implies, one of the purest of camp outings among film musicals.[116] In consequence, the film's true content is not actual piracy or even the unmasking and bringing to justice of the real Macoco—a plotline that serves mainly as a contrapuntal sideshow—but rather Manuela's discovery of theatricality, first dreamed from the gleanings of romanticized pirate histories, then released through hypnotism ("Mack the Black"), performed in the scene leading up to "Love of My Life" (discussed above), and finally celebrated in the carnivalesque reprise of "Be a Clown."

Any attempt to analyze the camp dimension of *The Pirate* by differentiating its surfaces and content, then, will find the one collapsing into the other, and the analysis itself collapsing from the second mode identified above into the first. In Mitchell Morris's analysis of camp in Dolly Parton's performances (cited earlier), he locates camp in the failure of style to match substance; hence, in "Me and Little Andy" (the song he discusses in this connection), the sentimental substance "breaks" the style, allowing both substance and style to matter tremendously and at the same time, but in very different ways. Disconnects of this kind are the very basis of unintentional camp, and of all the instances of intentional camp I have discussed here. Even when camp's surfaces are in alignment with substance, there will be an exaggerated attention to the styling of surfaces, as if to say there is no substance worth worrying about beyond its providing an excuse to indulge camp tastes. But that, of course, is part of the urbane pose that very often informs intentional camp: a feigned disregard for matters of substance even when substance means everything.

When a film and/or musical such as *The Pirate* makes theatricality itself its culminating ideal, and shows theatricality triumphing over reality at every turn, it effectively turns the real world (or its cinematic rendering) into the backdrop of a backstage musical, displacing the real world with—or transforming it into—a world in which the show is everything. To be sure, *The Pirate*, though the purest of musicals as it turns the world itself into a mere backdrop, paradoxically also barely qualifies as a musical in the first place. But whether by initial design or through negotiated faithfulness to its dramatic conceit, *The Pirate*'s failure to follow the conventions of mainstream musicals is central to its dramatic success as a musical, in two ways. First, it is important that Manuela does not sing near the beginning of the film; that capacity must be awakened in her, as a central strand of the film's plotting. And, second, her "success" in the end is not success in "real-world" terms but nearly the opposite, since she leaves a life of material comfort and societal position (in which she has been a kind of local heroine, set to marry the rich mayor of her town) in order to become an itinerant entertainer. In these and other ways, *The Pirate* conforms to a film-musical plot archetype that I have termed the "divorce trope," in which a film that is not a musical becomes one after the heroine extricates herself from a conventionally ordered "cinematic reality," often involving a preexisting but inappropriate marriage or betrothal.[117] *The Pirate* compromises this trope slightly, since Serafin already occupies a space defined by the conventions of musicals (hence his establishing number, "Niña"), but the fact that he is forced to reconfigure his musical to accommodate Manuela's imagination makes this less of a compromise than it might seem.

One of the difficulties *The Pirate* presents, both to the surfaces-content mode of camp analysis and to its initial audience reception, is that its "content," which one would naturally assume to be related to the "real life" dimension of the story as presented, is by that association so campy as to float to the surface and evaporate. To be sure, the camp dimension of individual numbers and sequences involves readily identified discrepancies between presentation and substance, as demonstrated above. But on a broader level, such distinctions are difficult to discern, since there is little to tie the film to recognizable realities. The décor and dress of Manuela's supposedly provincial Caribbean town is less "stylized" than made up out of whole cloth (or, rather, large bolts of bright, varicolored cloth). Even the mayor, who represents the touchstone for the reality side of the film's fantasy-reality divide, cannot be taken much more seriously than Manuela's Uncle Capucho. As an unromantic "affianced" husband who is actually the real Macoco, the mayor occupies a central position in the drama, but his "reality" is undermined throughout, most notably by his "portly pirate" music cue, his ludicrous manner of "making a leg," and his often exaggerated acting style. Indeed, like Capucho, he is not really taken seriously as a man, at least not after the arrival of Serafin.

But the difficulty of parsing things in this way, in musicals, is that on some level musicals *are* camp, in toto, meant to be read that way in relation to more realist ways of bringing a story to life on stage or screen. While it is certainly common for musicals to play this element off of more serious elements within the presented story, and while failing to do so may make them more difficult for audiences to accept (as the reception of *The Pirate* shows), their legibility does not depend on it. Arguably, such internal referents can distract from, even undermine, the more radical potential of the musical as a genre. In those cases when the dramatic "content" of a musical is difficult to locate within the musical itself, that content may nevertheless be inferred to be what the world it ostensibly occupies would be like without its music, without its camp (or campable material), and without the exteriorizing that occurs through its musical and camp dimensions. The aspect of musicals that grounds and sustains such notions about their underlying content is their manipulation of the psychological realm, which redefines the relationship between an individual and the world. In being so rooted, this notion of the "content" of musicals resembles the psychological basis that is often ascribed to Wagner's *Musikdramen*—which provides a particularly relevant point of comparison and contrast for the psychological content of operetta and the musical.

Within the *Musikdrama*'s psychological world, which derives from German Idealism and reflects a grounding in *Kultur*, a character's inner life is revealed through music, which also facilitates a connection between that revealed inner life and a deep sense of the world (*das Welt*), accessed through a set of myths that, for Wagner and many others of his generation, helped compose the shared, valuable past of the German people.[118] While the psychological dimensions of operetta and the musical incorporate some of this—in particular, the notions that music provides access to a character's inner life, that it can be personally enabling, and that it can help forge bonds with a larger community—there are crucial points of difference that place in high relief the core conceits of German Idealism regarding music, and its trumpeted renovation of music's function. In Wagner, the connections forged through a musically activated psychological dimension are to be experienced through inward contemplation, whereas in operettas and musicals they are manifest on the dramatic surface and are interactively social, typically laced with a humor and wit denied to Wagner's depth-oriented art. They crackle rather than simmer. Wagner's music is calculated to move the emotions, and through them the soul, often through quasi-spiritualized expression, whereas musicals and operetta, while also seeking to move the emotions, are more obviously adept at moving the body, giving physical expression to their forged communities and psychological states, often through dance. And, while the action in a musical or operetta is grounded in a character's psychological development, it is oriented always toward the real world, toward actions to be undertaken and relationships to be pursued. Music in operettas and musicals provides a conduit from a character's inner life to the phenomenal world, and serves as an exteriorizing, enabling force in the real world, whereas in Wagner that musical conduit leads to inwardness and the noumenal.

This grounding of operetta and the musical in the social realm, in dance, in music that is spirited but also occasionally spiritual (or at least sentimental)—all presented theatrically—is something these genres share with minstrelsy, and which all entertainment-centered theatrical music in the late nineteenth-century United States depended on in its opposition to the values, beliefs, and paradigms of musical idealism. There are, to be sure, additional outlets for music of this kind, in dance venues, in music for the home, in folk- and work-based songs, in much band music, and in the kind of music that made up the core "light classical" repertory that had throughout the nineteenth century (especially in England and the United States) occupied a kind of middle ground between socially oriented music and the sterner demands of musical idealism.[119] But theatrical entertainment music, through its appropriation and redirection of the psychological dimension of Wagner's *Musikdramen*—regarded in the late nineteenth-century United States as the pinnacle of serious art music[120]—made the point more aggressively and in such a way that its brand of "popular music" could survive and thrive as a permanently viable alternative to the emergent "classical music" tradition.

Within this context, operetta and musicals encourage a supple, socially active dramatic surface, which points to both the realness of the world being evoked—real in terms of its tactile, rhythmic, and visual *presence*—and the artificial means for bringing that realness forward, through exaggerated, theatricalized emphasis on staged settings with musical accompaniment: an ideal environment for camp. But in the case of pirate camp or other camped topics that make performance and theatricality matter more than the thing being performed, the surface-content dynamic extends outward to encompass a broader perspective, in which the artificial hyperreality common to operettas and musicals provides the surface for an absent content based in some sense of normalized reality, a reality that can only be inferred as the phenomenal world that camp's artificialities shadow and enhance.

Not all backstage musicals that implicitly argue this position are as thoroughly campy as *The Pirate*. *The Jazz Singer* (1925, becoming the first commercially successful film with synchronized sound in 1927), for example, was a musical play pivotal in the development of the backstage musical on film, and more specifically regarding this notion of the show taking precedence over more conventional ideas of "real life."[121] As a film, it is famous without really being known, since both its unreflective use of blackface and its primitive presentation of early synchronized sound technologies (half "silent"–half "sound") stand as barriers for nuanced engagement. Because of this, its ample camp dimension, probably entirely unintentional, has gone virtually unnoticed, eclipsed by both the lingering shadow and shame of minstrelsy, and by its primitive technology. Apart from its odd historical situation and its unremarked campiness, the film presents a paradox regarding its actual dramatic content. Its story hinges on a wrenching conflict between a young man's generations-long family heritage of performing as synagogue cantors, and a burgeoning career that opposes his racial, religious, and family heritage in just about every possible way short of overt anti-Semitism: singing jazz in blackface with his shiksa girlfriend under an Anglicized stage name (Jack Robin for Jakie Rabinowitz). But the film's resolution flattens the conflict into Jack/Jakie's overpowering need to perform, so that singing Kol Nidre in the temple on Yom Kippur for his dying father is placed on the same footing with headlining a new Broadway musical, and in the event both performances carry the same qualities of fervent conviction—perhaps demoting the one and/or elevating the other, but in any case reducing the story's basic conflict to a nonissue.

In making the underlying dramatic content about choosing the theatrical over existing reality, operettas and musicals may be understood as fantasist and escapist, as romantic and idealist (but not German Idealist!),[122] and as many other things, but they are above all *camp*—the musical theatrical realm where, to borrow Richard Dyer's formulations, we may find reality in the recognition of illusion and, perhaps, come to know what utopia would feel like.[123] Indeed, it is an open question whether it is music or camp that provides the "crackle of difference" that Scott McMillin identifies as the musical's characteristic dramatic device.[124] Probably both, since, as I have claimed elsewhere, "the musical becomes camp the moment it actually becomes *musical*."[125] Like Wagner's *Musikdramen*, musical camp awakens the psychological realm in order to imagine and project, within a broadly subjunctive version of reality, what cannot otherwise be experienced. For German Idealism's more mysterious noumenal realm, however, musical camp substitutes a heightened reality—utopian and sometimes escapist, but in any case vividly evoked. Both *Musikdramen* and musical camp, according to this "meta" orientation, imagine musically enhanced alternatives that use the world we know as a foil, if only sometimes explicitly.

Because theatrical entertainment music in the late nineteenth-century United States plays the same game as Wagner, but from the opposite side, it is able to oppose musical idealism in ways other modes of popular musicking could not except by association. Minstrelsy and camp provided sharp attitudinal edges to this opposition, which transfers readily to other theatrical and popular musics in the United States (where these attitudes are widely prevalent), but which could probably not have originated in other venues with the same directed force. Two observations seem especially relevant regarding the early stages of popular music's opposition to the emergent tradition of "classical" music. First, theatrical entertainment was for decades the center of popular music as it developed into a distinctly US American enterprise, a position maintained through the decades of Tin Pan Alley (roughly 1890–1950), until the latter was displaced in the second half of the twentieth century by rock and roll and related types. This importance of musical theater to the development of popular music in the United States is not as widely recognized as it should be, due to the ways other historical strands have been privileged in historical narratives of popular music. In particular, historical accounts of popular music have tended to reflect the latter-day veneration of "authentic" as a category, a category that shuns theatrically based music as inherently "inauthentic."[126] The second observation—really a speculative explanation—concerns the seemingly odd circumstance that minstrelsy and camp, both of which are associated with and/or practiced by minority cultures, should have played such a pivotal role in bringing popular music in the United States into oppositional alignment with musical idealism.

German Idealism's new paradigms for Music privileged musical experiences that involved quasi-ritualistic practices of contemplation, often communal and ceremonial but in any case accompanied by attitudes of reverence (e.g., concerts in established venues such as municipal concert halls). Music thus became experientially similar to religion, most specifically like Protestant Christianity. Like religion, it imposed a purifying conformity and seriousness at the same time that it promised access to an otherwise inaccessible and mystical realm.[127] Moreover, music conceived in these terms became a political instrument, often associated not only with aspirational cultural values but also with establishing mainstream respectability as the basis for broad communality and, often, nationalist projects in which the relevant "people" are unified by a shared history and culture. Such is not an environment that might be happily embraced by marginalized groups, be they (specifically) working class, racially or ethnically "other," or homosexual. There was thus quite a lot at stake for such groups, both in undermining this top-down way of organizing who belonged and who didn't, and in furthering through theatrical representation and performance a more participatory basis for community, giving literal voice to the particularities of difference—even if often disparagingly and, in the case of minstrelsy with regard to blacks, also patently disenfranchising.

Minstrelsy, notwithstanding its inherent racism, created a space of carnivalesque inversion to attract and entertain working-class audiences, involving marginalized populations (most often Irish Americans early on, and later African and Jewish Americans) who purported to depict an even more marginalized group (everyday African Americans). Minstrelsy's music was often raucous and rhythmic, if sometimes sentimentally nostalgic, but always cutting against the grain of more serious, high-toned music. As well, minstrelsy mined a rich vein of humor grounded in the interplay of surfaces, taking the specific forms of masks (blackface), stereotyped personae, drag, and outrageous wordplay.

Camp, as it took form in theatrical cultures, became a mode of performance and appreciation that tore at the serious core of art (as espoused, for example, by musical idealism) and especially the high-art ideals of all-embracing unities (Wagner's *Gesamtkunstwerken*), by drawing attention to supposed inessentials and thus enacting an implicit metaphor for celebrating the margins. At the same time, camp established a coded means of communication through which those "in the know" might recognize each other, creating in-groups that early on might have included a variety of specific groups attracted to the theater, such as Jews and other urbanites, but came in the crucial middle decades of the twentieth century to consist mainly of closeted homosexual men.

Music within the province of either camp or minstrelsy did not necessarily lack seriousness, but it did model and otherwise encourage social discourse, celebrating the human through humor and shared predilections and prejudices—the latter a sword that cut both ways, being both inclusive and exclusionary. Because this music was designed to foster sociability, it allowed easy transfer between the stage and the everyday lives of its aficionados, thereby forging the broadly conceived tradition of US American popular music. Yet, in its opposition to classical music, popular music seemingly had to forego respectability, and long carried the stigma of association with the marginalized populations it employed, entertained, and/or depicted. Over time, however, and urged by popular music's infectious qualities, various attempts at rehabilitation reclaimed some repertories and types, generally through arguing that they were in accord with the increasingly entrenched value-standards of musical idealism. Chief among the qualities that could rehabilitate popular music was, as noted, "authenticity," however defined and applied. As I argue in the following chapter, "authenticity" thereby became the central rubric for the creation of a "high" tradition of popular music, sheared of the artificialities of the theater, untainted by minstrelsy, and thus respectable enough to be claimed as a genuine national art.

5 | "POPULAR MUSIC" QUA GERMAN IDEALISM

Authenticity and Its Outliers

The capacity of popular music to oppose the paradigms of musical idealism in the United States developed, historically and most directly, as an adjunct to the theatrical settings from which its most potent forms arose, as I argue in chapter 4; more subtly, this capacity depended as well on popular music's habitual emphasis on sociability, as reflected in its subjects, its modeling, and the activities it facilitated. As I argue in this chapter, it is in large part by distancing some types of popular music from these associations that "popular music" has more recently been understood as partially aligned with those paradigms, if not with German Idealism itself. Moreover, this partial alignment has been generally understood to be a cultural promotion, not only allowing specific traditions of popular music to transcend the stigma of being lowbrow—or even occasionally of being middlebrow, which is worse—but also allowing them to stand as vibrant emblems of US American culture, and to be more readily accepted as objects of serious study in the academy. But this promotion has been selective: the "popular music" so elevated hardly represents the full range of music that has achieved popularity in the United States, nor does it reliably encompass what has been *most* popular. Hence my use of quotation marks, which I apply in this chapter to that subset of popular music—that is, "popular music"—that has been most readily elevated in this way, to the specific types that have thus occupied a privileged position for pundits, historians, and students, and that have come to represent, through their discourse, *popular music* for those who have taken "popular music" at face value, and its colloquies seriously.[1]

Topping the list of what has facilitated the cultural promotion of "popular music" is the claim of *authenticity*, a concept and criterion, however nebulous, that has wielded enormous power over aesthetic and critical imaginations within both popular and "classical" music realms, and across similar categories that operate in other art forms, as well.[2] Often working alongside authenticity in the processes of cultural validation for specific types of music (or for at least some instances of those types) are notions of *sincerity* or of *serious intention* on the part of specific artists, qualities that are understood to carry over into their work. Underwriting all of these ascribed attributes—authenticity, sincerity, serious intention—when understood as aesthetic criteria, is the notion that art vitally expresses the artist, perhaps even intrinsically, and that compelling aesthetic value emerges from that expression. This notion, which imagines the artwork to be an extension of the artist's self, perforce casts doubt on the aesthetic legitimacy of art forms that involve either a high degree of collaboration, or the kind of theatrical pretense that arises when performers are expected, routinely, to take on roles and become actors. This is in effect a double whammy against all forms of musical theater (including its filmed versions), which become suspect according to both these measures, especially when accompanied by other modes of distancing that frequently accompany theatrical art forms, such as irony, satire, parody, spoof, *shtick*, and camp. Moreover, denying these distancing elements—say, through nonironic, sincere presentation of romantic operetta and "integrated" musicals—does not tend to mitigate this suspect status or help raise the cultural status of musical theater, even putting aside the inevitable camp readings that accrue to some audiences' reception of operetta and, increasingly, serious musicals. At best, such strategies manage to "elevate" some forms of musical theater to the aesthetic limbo of middlebrow culture, undoubtedly sincere and often serious, yet abjectly failing to achieve the elite realms of high art. (It is, indeed, this very failure that makes these types especially congenial to camp receptive modes.)

The brow-elevating concepts of authenticity, sincerity, and serious artistic intention are thus by no means in full alignment, either with each other or with German Idealism, even if their partial alignments have made them mutually empowering and especially formidable in combination. It falls to this chapter to untangle these ascribed aspects of "popular music," to show how they have served to bring "popular music" into quasi-alignment with German Idealism, and to consider the fate of those kinds of popular musicking that have not been included in the category of "popular music," particularly as that category has become entrenched in the critical press that has grown up around it, as well as in the academy. Importantly for the latter, "popular music" not only defines a broad subfield linking history, political science, sociology, anthropology, folklore, performance studies, ethnic studies, gender studies, ethnomusicology, musicology, and even literature but also embraces a set of subjects taught within many of those disciplines, subjects for which strong, now standardized narratives rooted in notions of authenticity have been developed.

This chapter follows and expands upon arguments I advance in my essay "Performance, Authenticity, and the Reflexive Idealism of the American Musical,"[3] where my concerns are (among others) the specific, usually unspoken exclusion of musicals from the category of "popular music" despite their evident popularity; the parallel roles of performance in self-formation and in musicals; and the ways in which both musicals and the concept of authenticity, as applied to popular music, do and do not conform to the paradigms of German Idealism. As I deepen, develop, and extend those arguments here, another persistent duality of US American music—also traceable to the continued influence of German Idealism—emerges more fully into view, beyond the more widely recognized divide between "classical" music and popular music. Just as Haydn has been consigned, under the sway of musical idealism, to a lesser position within high-art musical traditions, so also have some less "authentic" genres of popular music been discounted, for similar reasons: their very appeal, and the nature of that appeal, have made these genres suspect qua art, as the latter category has come to be understood. It will, however, be left to the final chapter to reconsider the categorical relationships between musical art and entertainment that have governed—and been governed by—the musical dualisms imposed through German Idealism's seductive remappings of music's legitimate functions within culture.

AUTHENTICITY, GERMAN IDEALISM, AND THE EMERGENCE OF "POPULAR MUSIC"

As Marshall Berman delineates in his pioneering 1970 study, *The Politics of Authenticity*,[4] "authenticity" as a political goal emerged in the eighteenth century as a consequence of the parallel emphases in Enlightenment thought on individual rights and personal happiness, and from the strengthening belief, expressed most urgently in France, that modern urban society, to be in better accord with nature, should be founded on freedom for all its citizens. Proponents of both capitalism and communism, in their respective early stages of political theorizing, employed the rhetoric of authenticity, as each was founded in part on the principle that individuality should be fostered and allowed free expression, and that a society hospitable to such expression would be superior both as a whole and in respect to the well-being of its citizens. In Berman's understanding, this line of thought both led to and exemplified a romantic prizing of individuality that suffered a staggering blow in the failed revolutions of the mid-nineteenth century, a blow from which it would not recover until political pessimism among the West's intellectuals in the 1950s restored authenticity as a politicized personal value. What emerged as part of *Bildung* in the early nineteenth century, the process of becoming oneself in as full a sense as possible, was in this way resurrected as a political issue after the mid-twentieth century, taking the form of a newly prized "personal authenticity," allied with such terms as " 'identity,' 'autonomy,' 'individuality,' 'self-development,' 'self-realization,' 'your own thing' "—for Berman and his generation, contemporary "vocabulary overflow[ed] with expressions which express a persistent and intense concern with *being oneself*."[5]

Contemporaneous with this resurgence of authenticity in the politically charged 1960s, many genres of "popular music"—jazz, folk, blues, rock, gospel, funk, and various hybrids—became increasingly charged with political significance, and so easily acquired the validating stamp of authenticity, in part through specifically political associations.[6] But there were at least two other relevant frames of reference for the role that authenticity played in this process of validation, both of them grounded more in philosophy than in politics, and both intertwined more intimately with musical practices and theorizing about those practices. This tripartite dimension of the term "authenticity" is a byproduct of its being always a nebulous denotative quality, definitively positive through its alliance with such ideas as *Truth* and *Purity*, yet easily appropriated for quite disparate claims within virtually any frame of reference where such ideas might be valued. Despite this nebulous aspect, however, its frequent attachment to notions of the *self* has generated a particularly strong tradition, embracing Berman's political trajectory but not limited to it.

To begin with, authenticity did not have to wait for the Enlightenment to be recognized as an admirable personal quality, a *virtue* that combines and overlaps related virtues such as honesty, personal reflection, and integrity. In this sense, the concept is ancient. As persuasively articulated in Shakespeare's *Hamlet* (ca. 1600), the virtue of authenticity is already doubly marked as extremely venerable, even antiquated. Not only is *Hamlet* itself set in the shrouded past of legend, but its definitive defense of personal authenticity is, as well, voiced by the doddering Polonius, the quintessential purveyor of dusty truths and worn-out maxims, however eloquently expressed:

> This above all: to thine own self be true
> And it doth follow, as the night the day,
> Thou canst not then be false to any man.

As Polonius's maxim argues, the idea of being true to oneself acquires moral force by promising to protect against transgressing the Ten Commandments' prohibition against bearing "false witness." But such moral grounding is scarcely needed; the modern sense of authenticity, both as a tenet of philosophy and as part of a fundamental claim regarding selfhood, derives most memorably and directly from Socrates's claim that "the unexamined life is not worth living"; moreover, this lineage also supports Shakespeare's implicit claim for the concept's ancient provenance, and provides the basis for the connection Polonius makes between self-contemplation and the manner in which one lives one's life. More specifically, these two vintage touchstones for personal authenticity, with their directives toward inwardness and self-reflection, connect authenticity directly to the intense subjectivity that underwrites German Idealism, with direct consequences for musical expression, and with a historical trajectory distinct from Berman's political scenario.

One way authenticity came to matter early on within the new paradigms of musical idealism was in the manner and approach to, and the reception of, the performance of works composed by others, a presentational mode that would become known as performing "covers" in the world of US American popular music in the later twentieth century. While the term "covers" itself acknowledges a presumptive loss of authenticity, across the late eighteenth and early nineteenth centuries, as documented and argued by Mary Hunter, such a performance could serve as a "simulacrum of Romantic subjectivity," uniting "composer and performer, originator and vessel, in an apparently single creative act," a performance-based merger echoed in turn by the merger of performer and listener "in an apparently single interpretive act."[7] The notion that music might allow one to merge one's subjectivity with that of others, especially as the latter field might itself be merged into something even larger and more definitively noumenal (that is, something not objectively or phenomenologically present, such as absolute consciousness or the *Volksgeist*), is a hallmark of music's role within German Idealist thought emergent in the early nineteenth century, as I argue in chapter 1. Moreover, as Karen Leistra-Jones argues, by the later nineteenth century, the mode of authenticity described by Hunter was attitudinally communicated in performance, by such performers as Clara Schumann, Joseph Joachim, and Johannes Brahms, through a concert demeanor projecting inwardness and seriousness—all in the service of an emergent *Werktreue* aesthetic that rejects the more theatrical, bravura performance styles of Liszt and other virtuosi, and marks the single most important difference between the practices of musical idealism and popular music, both then and now.[8]

It is important to observe—for now in passing—that this kind of antitheatrical authenticity is always itself theatrical, since it in effect "strikes a pose," constructing attitude and decorum as part of a presentational mode.[9] Moreover, this observation is equally germane to "popular music" modes of authenticity, since in both cases authenticity is, like all aesthetic programs and their foundational belief systems, based on a ritualized confidence game. In the case of authenticity in performance—however that may be understood in whatever historical period, and concerning whatever repertory or musicking tradition—the con game comes down to a tacit agreement among all concerned to act as if musical performance constitutes a genuine transubstantiation of artistic elements, that earthly bread and wine thereby become spiritualized body and blood, no matter the actual degree of belief held by the priestly performers and the individual members of their congregation/audience.[10]

This mode of musical authenticity became a linchpin both for German Idealism and for the elevation of "popular music" in the later twentieth century. As such, it distinctively combines an intensely expressed subjectivity with a deep respect for the music being performed, a respect that honors its inspirational source and invites a spiritual merging of performer with audience, who are mutually linked to that inspirational source within whatever all-embracing noumenal power is understood to undergird the union, be it *Volksgeist*, collective consciousness, some form of religious or nationalist feeling, or just a vague sense for whatever relevant slice of humanity may be envisioned and whatever noumenal space they may be imagined to inhabit as a collective. Moreover, with "popular music" as with German Idealism, the sense of a collective or community—the specifically human dimension of that larger power—depends on the notion of a "people" that is both specific in heritage and universalizing in aspiration.

Yet, by the time "popular music" discovered its own validating authenticity—roughly, again, in the 1960s, which decade's sensibilities and politics have determined the contours of most of the now-standard narratives for "popular music"—the concept of authenticity had long since slipped its moorings both in the Enlightenment and in German Idealism, becoming a central tenet of Existentialism, Idealism's seeming opposite. Intense subjectivity—the cornerstone of all personal authenticities save the *idiot savant* variety—went from being German Idealism's gateway to cosmic unity to being Existentialism's affirmation of radical alienation from such totalizing concepts. How and when this happened is much disputed. Certainly there were precipitate political events: the setbacks of the Napoleonic Wars, the failed mid-nineteenth-century revolutions, and, in the twentieth century, two devastating world wars and their associated turmoil. But there was also the odd melancholy that followed the successful nationalist quests of Italy and Germany circa 1870, brought on by the realization that the reality of achieved nationhood did not live up to its idealizing advance notices.[11] By the first decade of the twentieth century, Kierkegaard's quarrels with Hegel from early in the nineteenth century—often seen as the beginning of Existentialism, although not identified as such until much later—along with Nietzsche's broader philosophical dissent later in the nineteenth century, found echo in the expressed alienation and angst of Mahler's symphonies. But if Mahler may thus be seen as the first Existentialist composer, he was also, in parallel to Kierkegaard, also an idealist, if a sometimes disillusioned one.[12]

Mahler's double profile of an idealist/Existentialist made his music especially ripe for the renaissance it enjoyed in the United States during the 1960s and after, exactly coincident with both the similarly double-imaged appropriation of "authenticity" as a validating argument for elevating "popular music," and with Berman's scenario of authenticity's political renaissance. As with Mahler, the authenticity of "popular music" could be either that of German Idealism's quest for the Infinite through the collective, or of Existentialism's estranged individual, true only to the self—either of which could ally itself with the political dimension of authenticity. Moreover, authenticity could flip between these poles without anyone—excepting Theodor Adorno and a few others—seeming to notice.[13] Indeed, a fusion of these two notions of authenticity is well grounded in two ways, making such a fusion seem almost "natural," especially when it is at least partly unconscious. First, German Idealism and Existentialism are linked, as noted, through their mutual appeal to intense subjectivity: both begin by looking inward, locating God (or some semblance or echo thereof) within the authentic and authenticating self. Second, and more specifically musical, there is the powerful model of Beethoven: the creative loner, alienated spiritually and physically from his fellow creatures, both as an iconoclastic artist and through his increasing deafness, whose music nonetheless spoke for a nation and—depending on one's universalizing inclinations—for humanity more generally. This powerful image of the isolated genius artist, in Beethoven's case rooted in German Idealism but easily merged with Existential angst, founded a trajectory of musical modernism that led, in a fairly direct line, through Mahler and Schoenberg on the one hand and, on the other, through Charles Ives and later US American modernists who adopted Ives as their figurehead.

Ives was a pivotal figure not only for US American modernists but also, arguably, for many "popular" echoes of musical modernism. His pioneering blend of German Idealism's "collectivity through subjectivity" and Existentialism's alienation, within a specifically US American version of rugged individualism, is based in (or, perhaps, rationalized as an extension of) Transcendentalism.[14] In his *Essays before a Sonata*,[15] Ives articulates an opposition between "substance" and "manner" that reproduces the contours of *Kultur* versus *Zivilisation* (see below), a dualism he referentially personifies in the figures of Beethoven and Debussy, among others. Yet, the question of what constitutes "substance" in his own music may be answered differently according to context. Ives has been admired by many for a kind of gritty realism, for which he has been recognized as a uniquely US American modernist voice both in the United States and abroad. Equally important, however—although less likely to be fully recognized abroad or in more recent generations—is his engagement with place and people through quotation of and allusion to vernacular musical materials, often sentimental or institutional (as opposed to folk-based).[16] To be sure, it is his way of engaging these materials that constitutes his modernism, since he accompanies them with unexpected dissonance and rhythmic distortion, sometimes organizing them in brutal juxtapositions or inharmonious layers. But the familiar vernacular of his source materials nevertheless matters, as well, and in two ways.

First, his "modernist" rendering of his materials is part of a broader expression of what it means, in musical terms and according to Ives's aesthetic, to be human (or, more specifically and in accordance with his now-infamous formulation, what it means to be *masculine* and, it may be assumed, heterosexual). For Ives, this ideally includes physical involvement in music making, though often taking the musical form of visceral s(t)imulation in his compositions. This dynamic of musical involvement depends crucially on Ives's choice of materials, which are to be recognized not only as well-known tunes but also according to specific contexts of musicking, which are to some extent re-created within his music. Thus, what might well be analyzed as his gritty-realist *manner* being applied to the vernacular *substance* of his materials, becomes in combination, and within his articulated understanding of the paired terms, the actual *substance* of his music, enforcing an integrated profile that depends on his music's very lack of conventional integration between manner and substance as those terms might be generally understood. But conventional modes of understanding the distinction between substance and manner continue to signify, since they point to a way—in parallel to Mahler, as has often been noted—in which vernacular materials may transcend their roots, becoming Art through a process of defamiliarization, through the introduction of musical elements that cut against the grain of those materials as they would be presented more traditionally. It is this precise process—what Mahlerians like to call "defamiliarizing the familiar"—that creates for Ives a bifurcated musical profile, in which existential alienation simultaneously also expresses an appropriate mode of participation *within* community: aggressively muscular, and asserting an individuality that contends vigorously against complacent (and complaisant) expressions of communality without denying the importance of that communality.

The intensification of musical modernism in Europe and the United States after World War II, which included an ongoing rehabilitation of Ives's position as an authentic US American modernist voice, coincided with the full emergence of Existentialism as a credible philosophical movement, thanks to the writings of Jean-Paul Sartre, Simone de Beauvoir, and Albert Camus, among others. These coincident developments were essential to the aesthetic rehabilitation of "popular music" in two main ways. First, the sharpening divide between all kinds of popular music and the world of serious "classical" music, owing to the latter's continuing modernist development of an increasingly less accessible stylistic profile, made the alternatives that popular music offered seem increasingly viable as a more current source for concert music, either in separate events or (in some cases) alongside more traditional repertories, leading many audiences and critics to take specific types of popular music much more seriously than before. Rationalizations for this development generally took the form of claims either for a level of compositional sophistication commensurate with the classical music tradition (usually not fully convincing) or, from a different aesthetic perspective, for the "authenticity" of such music—an authenticity often especially resonant with Existentialism in that these forms of "popular music" were understood to harbor an emotional depth or angst, representing a marginalized cultural position that might too easily be overlooked. Thus were some practitioners of "popular music" elevated to the status of genuine Artists in a process of legitimization that in effect partially relocated the vitality of contemporary musicking away from "serious" composers—who were by then mainly modernists working in academia—to "popular music."

Even apart from sometimes accommodating "popular music," the more established practices of concert music became further subdivided. The divisions already enforced by musical idealism, through which concert repertories subdivide into serious and "lighter" fare, had to admit an even more stringent division between traditional (generally tonal) repertory and "contemporary" or "new" music. And, while the latter often lacked audience support, that very fact reinforced the authenticating image of the composer as a "lonely genius" who, like Beethoven—or Ives, or Mahler—might eventually be embraced by a wider public despite initial opposition.[17] In the meantime, such composers could revel in being reviled, understanding their lack of immediate or commercial success as existential proof of their authenticity as artists. This hierarchical and historical stratification, serving as a model, provided the second way to rehabilitate "popular music," whose historical trajectory could similarly be understood in quasi-evolutionary terms. In parallel to Ives's transformed vernacular musics, and perhaps also borrowing from his image as an eventually venerated iconoclast, many working in traditional genres of popular music began to adopt modernist techniques. Jazz, having already moved from swing to bop, evolved into free jazz and other forms of modern(ist) jazz, whereas some forms of rock became aggressively more "difficult," and Stephen Sondheim, following such forerunners as Marc Blitzstein and Leonard Bernstein, positioned himself as a modern(ist) Broadway composer setting more challenging dramatic subjects within a sometimes posttonal (or modernist-tonal) idiom.

AUTHENTICITY, SINCERITY, AND SERIOUS INTENTION

As "authenticity" became the most commonly evoked claim to support the elevation of "popular music" to the status of Art, it thus found fundamental grounding in the traditions and practices of musical idealism, overlapping newly emergent applications of the term deriving from Existentialism and the contemporary political scene. At the same time, the ancillary categories of sincerity and serious intention offered reinforcement and, in some respects, interference, according to their own historical contexts and trajectories of usage. Particularly interesting in this regard is sincerity; indeed, nearly coincident with Berman's *Politics of Authenticity*, Lionel Trilling linked the two terms in "Sincerity and Authenticity," his 1970 Norton Lectures at Harvard University, published as a book two years later. Within a free-ranging exploration of key texts, Trilling argued for a gradual substitution, in step with the evolution of modern society, of "authenticity" for "sincerity" as a fundamental individual virtue.[18]

According to Trilling, an emphasis on sincerity arose, almost of necessity, in response to the rise of modern theater, as an avowal that one who is sincere is not acting a role. As we may easily observe, what Shakespeare's Polonius advocates in *Hamlet*—"to thine own self be true"—runs directly counter to what actually engages audiences when those lines are spoken in a theater: actors playing roles. Yet, by the same token, stage roles such as Polonius were and are played with great sincerity and, in the case of Shakespeare's *Hamlet*, almost always supported by a serious intention that reaches for a deeper kind of authenticity grounded in dramatic expression, while perhaps also channeling something of the "authentic self" of each actor playing a role. And so, too, with roles played offstage, in "real life": the mask of sincerity, itself a kind of role adopted when interacting with others, may or may not align with an authentic self, but in any case nearly always reflects serious intention on the part of the actor, even while it may also partially obscure the full nature of that intention. Authenticity, sincerity, and serious intention, however related, thus become quite tangled in practice.

What is it that pushes these apparently related impulses so far out of alignment? In Trilling's scenario, the concept of authenticity (né sincerity) itself shifted when modern urban society displaced a prince or court as the dominating context within which people "acted," a generally gradual change that rendered society's members "individuals" in the modern sense of the word. While this understanding may certainly be reconciled with Berman's view, which also grounds authenticity within the growing importance of the individual, Trilling's emphasis finds deeper historical roots, and draws attention to two attendant conflicts that took shape within the historical background of the emergent modern city. Moreover, each of these conflicts worked itself out, in specific terms, within the rise of German Idealism, its political landscapes, and its extended musical aftermath, while also reconfiguring the relationships among authenticity, sincerity, and serious intention.

The more fundamental of these two conflicts concerns the place of the emergent individual within society, and stems from the variety of compromises or accommodations that society enforces on its members, whose effective interactions require some measure of conformance to behavioral expectations. The valorizing of the individual perspective against society's pressure to conform drives much subsequent political and philosophical thought, including German Idealism and Existentialism, along with a variety of related movements. As noted, the fundamental difference between these two, in particular, had to do with negotiating the gap between self and society (or humanity more generally). While German Idealism projects deeper connections between the self and the collective through inwardness, Existentialism (along with a plentitude of earlier thought) focuses on the conflict itself and its attendant sense of alienation. For both, society as a real-time, real-life phenomenon must be regarded to some extent as a necessary evil whose detrimental effects might be at least partly mitigated through contemplation and inwardness. And, as I argue in chapter 1, music became a vehicle for achieving that inwardness, modeled by performers and practiced by audiences. Moreover, it could also enact, especially in orchestral music, aspects of the fundamental conflict in musical terms, for example within the built-in dynamics of the concerto or in creating effects of alienated estrangement, in both cases often borrowing from the musical rhetoric of opera. Indeed, opera in the nineteenth century, especially Wagnerian opera, became a site where the artificialities of theatricality itself could seemingly be overthrown by the metaphorically authenticating "depth" of orchestral music, which acquired an enhanced sense of presence even as its production became less visible.[19]

Less fundamental but equally important to the musical profile of authenticity is the conflict over what society actually is and how it may be considered valuable. The categories of *Kultur* and *Zivilisation*, which emerged in the cultural wars between the German lands and France during the nineteenth century as an outgrowth of German Idealism,[20] address this question directly, identifying—usually from the German perspective—two quite different ways that the individual might articulate with the rest of humanity. The German (Idealist) view is that the only valuable articulation consists in that deep connection—through *Kultur*—that the self might achieve through the kind of inwardness that serious music fosters. Viewed from this perspective, French *Zivilisation* lacks depth, since it is oriented instead around the artificial surfaces of institutions, formal behavior, and sociality. Music will be understood to operate within and across these paradigms in a number of ways. If music seems to flatter its audience, partaking of a socially oriented world (through humor, some kinds of allusive or generic reference, or general accessibility, for example) rather than creating or suggesting an alternative, more demanding world that its members might immerse themselves in through contemplation, then it will be suspect. By these lights, some types of music are already suspect, such as the overtly programmatic or descriptive, or straightforward dances and marches in a popular style. To be sure, these suspect types could be rescued through appeals to authenticity, sincerity, or serious intention. Thus, authenticity is implicitly claimed through evocations of a shared valuable past (as in Beethoven's symphonic uses of the country dance or Bruckner's of the *Ländler*), sincerity through the imposition of rigorous musical processes or formal tropes (as in the marches in Beethoven's Ninth Symphony and Piano Sonata no. 28, op. 101), and serious intention through overt applications of irony (as in Mahler's use of the march in his *Wunderhorn* Lieder "Der Schildwache nachtlied," "Lied des Verfolgten im Turm," "Revelge," and "Tamboursg'sell"). The point here is twofold: not merely that these suspect types *could* be reclaimed but also that they *required* reclaiming for them to be acceptable within the new musical paradigms, and that the means for doing so was through implicit appeals to authenticity, sincerity, or serious intention.

And, as with Ives, it matters that these means allowed popular musical elements a place within serious music, even if that place also sometimes entailed an implicit critique of those elements. But it also matters that such a critique was not always necessary. Perhaps the great lesson of the "An die Freude" finale of Beethoven's Ninth Symphony is that, while Beethoven's sincerity and serious intention would call up fugue and formal complications to sustain his indulgence in simple, accessible material, that material was first of all justified by its appeal to authenticity, as representative of the folk; one must recall in this regard that the first symphonic complications of this material in the finale are overtly rejected ("nicht diese Töne").[21] Moreover, what counts as authentic will always be to some extent politically driven, as in Beethoven's use of a country dance theme in his *Creatures of Prometheus* and (using the same theme and similar variational processes) in the finale of his *Eroica*, which was not merely serving as authentic, as an emblem of the folk, but was also more directly significant politically, since the country dance itself had long served as an emblem of the democratic impulse.[22]

And here may be noted a recurring musical fissure between authenticity and sincerity, since evoking the folk as justified in and of itself differs from evoking it in order to make a democratically motivated political point. A folk hymn ("An die Freude," or the main theme in the finale of Brahms's First Symphony) may well tap into *Kultur*, gesturing toward a depth-based connection with the folk, but a dance tune is by its nature—and in the case of the country dance, also by its direct appeal to politics—oriented toward *Zivilisation*, toward how people actually interact, socially, in the phenomenal world. Although music often facilitates the fiction that these different aims and contexts might be aligned, the politics of nationalism (or something equally noumenal, such as collective consciousness) are not those of manners, if for no other reason than the former tend to be exclusionary, whereas the latter, to the extent that they reflect a democratic impulse, aspire to be inclusive. The fundamental problem is this: one's behavior, however sincere or seriously intended, will not buy a place in the exclusive club of authenticity, whose membership criteria are always based on who one is, and not—or at best secondarily—on how one acts or what one does.

Within the broad domain of popular music during the later decades of the twentieth century and beyond, this terrain maps very similarly. The historically problematic "modern urban society" becomes, for popular music, "white mainstream urban society" as reflected within the commercial sphere; whereas the "*Kultur* versus *Zivilisation*" game becomes the attempt to connect with an authenticating fan base without "selling out" to the commercially driven mainstream. A youth-oriented sense of political idealism also informs these categories in practice; "mainstream" and "selling out" become part of a network of code words that define a generational threshold between idealist youth who seek authentic musical expression, and jaded adults who fade into an inauthentic mainstream.[23] As with popular elements in nineteenth-century concert music, some types of twentieth-century popular music may easily claim a kind of blanket authenticity, whether based in populist politics (as with the folk music revival and "roots" music) or race (as with ragtime, jazz, and blues). However, some other types—such as show tunes or "easy listening"—may be safely assumed to be inauthentic except when they are appropriated as part of an authenticating milieu, as with Tin Pan Alley songs that become jazz standards. Still other types are more nebulously "in between"; these include particular artists across the continuum of pop to rock, who may be claimed to be authentic within cult followings, or may themselves foster this judgment through sincerity or serious intention. But within a commercial realm, sincerity and serious intention will always become suspect at some point, simply because they may be taken to be poses, as swerves toward the inauthentic based more on the desire to persuade than on genuine ("authentic") sincerity or artistic seriousness.

Such gestures of accommodation to appearances—which is to say, to society—reliably distinguish sincerity and serious intention from authenticity. Placing these three on a continuum based on their relation to the phenomenal world is particularly instructive. The category of authenticity cares about who one *is*, and is easily the most purely noumenal of the three terms, which is why it is so elusive not only in definition and identification but also, peeling back a layer, in its basis in something equally elusive: the self. Sincerity refers to how one *acts*; while it may indicate (or at least seek to indicate) authenticity, it can as easily be taken as a mere simulation of the authentic, one perilously small step away from an admission to inauthenticity. And serious intention identifies *why* one acts. Thus, while all three point inward, the latter two also gesture outward at least to the extent of calling attention to their inwardness, by fashioning it into a legible attitude.

Two pertinent observations may be made regarding this situation, which will, respectively, occupy the final two sections of this chapter. First, sincerity and serious intention, however tainted they might seem given their gestures toward society and appearances, play an evident role in establishing authenticity within particular types of "popular music," and it will be instructive to explore this further through considering particular situations and genres. And, second, none of these categories takes any account of what (if any) actual effect an individual self produces in the phenomenal world or in society; at bottom, all three—along with our collective judgments about them—are concerned much more with who one *is* than with what one *does*. Yet, what one does must remain an important measure of what one is, if only as a kind of "reality check"; more broadly, what "popular music" does will always remain an important aspect of what it is. For those truly sympathetic to the values of musical idealism and the classical music tradition, "popular music," like the proverbial duck, still waddles and quacks a bit too much for them to forget altogether that it also plays as *popular music*, which is especially evident whenever the mask of sincerity slips, the serious intention lapses, or the contextualizing rhetoric about authenticity is stripped away.

NEGOTIATING THE FAULT LINES OF AUTHENTICITY

It is important to remember that all types of US American popular music, not least the instrumental varieties, were in their day *popular*, and became so by entertaining audiences or by providing a useful social function (e.g., "background" music or music for dancing). For all older forms of popular music, issues of authenticity arose only later, after basic categories were established, arising in response to a number of factors: (1) to politics' increasingly overt involvement with popular music (and *vice versa*); (2) to the increasing accessibility of recorded music, which allowed multiple rehearings of the same performance, established a direct sonic link to older traditions, and increasingly allowed the "work concept" to be applicable to popular music; and (3) to the quest, emergent mainly in the 1960s and after, for a rationale that would justify taking some forms of popular music more seriously (that is, *as music*, rather than merely as a societal development). Importantly, some of this was well under way long before the 1960s.[24] But to a large extent, the politics of authenticity played out, with regard to "popular music," as a latter-day *re*evaluation of the past in tandem with a developing concern for how authenticity might be fostered in the present. This was already true regarding earlier authenticist reclamations.

Ragtime and jazz, for example, each began as a kind of musical discourse among musicians and their audiences, and both types in their early stages involved a sly manipulation of something given in order to make it more fun to play and listen to, or more pleasurable to dance to. Certainly there was already a politicized dimension to both types: the "something" was derived from white musical culture and the fun was oriented toward undermining, distorting, or destabilizing that something from an African American perspective—mainly through rhythm, but also (depending on instrumentation) through bending pitch or playing with timbre.[25] But the politics were nearly always only implicit; indeed, they pretty much had to be, given the power differential between whites and blacks especially during the early decades of these emergent types. Moreover, said politics would have come to nothing if the result did not first of all entertain, which ragtime and jazz did very well, often through impudence but more dependably and over time through a generic sense of play merging into sensuality, resulting in an experience of shared pleasure. And this sharing of pleasure, in turn, helped take the bitter edge off the politics involved, so that, even as ragtime and jazz presented a kind of interracial commentary, and were often heard in contexts in which race mattered tremendously, both types came to define a broader social world, generally understood as urban, which grew to encompass both sides of the black-white racial divide—all mostly before issues of authenticity arose, first in the 1930s and later in accordance with the changing political landscape of the post–World War II decades.

In these and other ways, ragtime and jazz were formatively oriented more toward the physical than toward the spiritual, inspiring bodily movement among both performers and audiences even absent the cakewalk or the other forms of dance they often evoked or facilitated. Nascent ragtime and jazz were thus as far from musical idealism as was blackface minstrelsy, and just as opposed to it in temperament and impulse. Yet, unlike minstrelsy—and to some extent displacing that patently inauthentic institution—both ragtime and jazz came to define a kind of US American authenticity in musical terms.[26] While this circumstance underscores the fact that authenticity and musical idealism are not always in alignment, it is equally true that claims for the authenticity of jazz can in other ways seem odd, since jazz, perhaps more than any other type of music, specifically prizes modes of *in*authenticity. The inherently inauthentic practice of transforming something given into something more enjoyable—in literal terms, making *fun* of it, or, at least, making fun *out* of it—manifests itself still today within the improvisatory idioms of jazz, which encourage and reward individual performers' ability to "fake it," aided and abetted by a large number of "fake books" that have been readily available to performers (and constantly updated) for decades, each filled with popular tunes and their chord changes.[27]

But this is only an apparent paradox, since notions of authenticity have long attached themselves to jazz with easy abandon, based on a range of attributes and historical circumstances, and with some of those notions directly related to jazz's penchant for "faking it." Even apart from arguments that may easily be made for the authenticity of improvisation, in practice and on a fundamental level "faking it" is in this context a form of "signifying," a tradition associated with African American culture that acknowledges a process of derivation in order to make a sometimes implicit personal and/or representative statement about the source material.[28] Signifying in musical terms can make something that is otherwise problematic into something more relevant or authentic, through adding an authenticating voice or attitude that inflects and reconfigures the musical flow or its significance, grounding it within a milieu that can itself provide a filter against the inauthentic.[29] If "faking it" entails getting something wrong, then, it thereby accomplishes an essential part of the authenticating work of signifying, since "getting it wrong" provides a means for refusing or denying the proffered "truth" of an inauthentic source. "Faking it" is thus the first step toward freeing something from the US American version of *Zivilisation*—what might be too white, too square, too old-fashioned, or otherwise too constrained by convention—in order to tap into its capacity to convey a domestic, contemporary form of *Kultur*, through the practices and idioms of jazz. Thus may we make at least some sense of the oft-heard—and oft-disputed—claim that jazz is "America's classical music." Even as jazz positioned itself as the antithesis of classical music—the tradition created by musical idealism, understood from jazz's perspective as something foreign—it did so through a process of signifying transformation, which allowed it eventually to be seen in the same terms as that tradition, and even regarded as its domestic equivalent.[30]

But there are other ways to understand jazz as "America's classical music" that are less fundamentally dependent on the musical paradigms of German Idealism. Most elaborately, as jazz evolved through the swing era and beyond, it began to reflect a modernist sensibility in direct parallel to modernism within the classical tradition, as many practitioners moved beyond more "commercial" forms of jazz toward more challenging idioms. To some extent, this move was a reclaiming of the tradition, or at least of its core authenticating gesture of signifying *against* mainstream musicking (in this case by nonblack jazz musicians). But while bebop and later developments were perhaps grounded in the more chaotic dimension of some earlier jazz styles, they were even more obviously modeled on developments within the classical tradition, whose modernist composers had in the previous generation begun both to extend and to challenge tradition through intensifying the level and nature of their music's difficulty. Through this means, jazz not only subsumed the historical developments of the classical music tradition, but also cycled back to the originating impetus for those developments. Jazz, like serious classical music, began to demand something akin to the kind of contemplative engagement that had long been established as the central paradigm for musical idealism, extended into a jazz-based musical modernism. Moreover, in fashioning this parallel to modernist and even avant-garde classical music, jazz musicians, through bop, hard bop, modal jazz, avant-jazz, and free jazz, renewed a claim to authenticity by continuing to signify on mainstream traditions, signaling their serious intention through their deliberate positioning relative to both commercial jazz and classical modernism, and manifesting their sincerity by channeling through their own demeanors the self-absorption exhibited by many classical composers and concert musicians.

Reclaiming jazz through signifying on a tradition that had drifted into the (white) mainstream also had a strong racial component, based not only on the origins of jazz, along with ragtime and blues, in African

American contexts but also on the controversies that arose because of frequent claims in early histories, from the 1920s, that jazz was a Jewish idiom—claims that were refuted, especially beginning in the 1930s, by counterclaims that "authentic" jazz was the exclusive purview of black musicians.[31] All of this reinforced the notion that *who* you are is fundamental to any claim of authenticity, and reflected the fact that, in the United States, race represents a fundamental fault line for identity politics, affecting, like gender (see below), any notion of authenticity grounded in personal expression.[32] Thus, a distinction is possible—and has been vitally important to some—between black jazz musicians who proactively reclaim their heritage and find their authentic voice through a kind of modernist signifying, and modernist white jazz musicians whose authenticity resides in their own birthright of deep interiority. That such distinctions were fictitious in biological terms—but not in social terms—is also important, especially for the way that their problematic basis helped reconfigure racialized stereotypes. Not only were black jazz musicians staking their own claims to deep interiority, but the inevitable reblurring occasioned by sharing practices across racial lines asserted a broader basis for jazz as well. In this way, jazz was reconstituted as more broadly *American*—and therefore more definitively so, according to US American ideologies of inclusion—whatever its historically racialized origins and development.

Jazz's claims for authenticity thus had a variety of bases, and many other forms of "popular music" either find their models for authentication among those bases or find similar bases independently, according to their own processes of remapping their respective histories according to more broadly conceived notions of authenticity or other borrowings from the paradigms of musical idealism. Charles Hamm's survey of what he terms "modernist narratives"—narratives that have served either as a form of advocacy for "popular music" or as a means to discount popular music more or less in toto—includes two kinds of authenticity narratives among an assemblage that also includes narratives based on autonomy, mass culture, classic/classical, and youth. These narratives merit attention here in part because they point to other modes of validation, distinguishable from authenticity as a category but related to it. Hamm's purpose in delineating his collection of "modernist narratives" was to demonstrate the ways in which much popular music is *excluded* from being taken seriously. But his narratives also provide key examples of how some repertories might be elevated to a higher status, and this potential has over time brought more popular music into the more exclusive ranks of "popular music" than his argument suggests. (To be sure, much of this realized potential was achieved in the years following his essay, and almost all of it since he began to write about popular music.)

For example, Hamm's narratives of musical autonomy, mass culture, and classic/classical, when considered together with his "first narrative of authenticity," point ultimately to a broadening of one of German Idealism's early projects, advanced most strenuously by Herder: the enshrining of folk music as the emblem and expression of a people's shared heritage. Hamm's "first narrative of authenticity" is fully congruent with Herder's project, joining "authentic" (as opposed to commercialized) ragtime and jazz to the emblematic status of genuine folk music. But once that basic, limited move is accomplished, it provides a conduit by which other forms of ragtime and jazz might be authenticated, as well, especially with the passage of time (activating Hamm's classic/classical narrative), and despite the accumulated weight of critical scorn that has accrued to the commercialized extensions of these "folk" types. Indeed, as more and more of this "commercialized" (or, to be more narrowly Marxist, "commodified") music finds new audiences through vintage recordings and new covers, and as lesser items fall away into obscurity, notions of "timeless classics" and even autonomy start to cling to what remains in play, distilled into a "repertory" or "canon" akin to those that have developed in idealist concert traditions—which markets also once included large quantities of music that has not survived the "test of time." And what, in the end, is the most persuasive argument advocating for something's timelessness, if not the persistent approval of a large audience? And how might this persistence be distinguished from the processes of natural selection that govern folk music? That these rhetorical questions can be at least partly answered matters in the end far less than that they nevertheless retain their rhetorical force,[33] especially to the youth markets to which much of this music first appealed, whose consumers grew into maturity with musical tastes intact, and who have been more than ready to rationalize those tastes as a response to authenticity.

Despite some recent broadening of Hamm's narrative categories to admit a wider swath of popular music into the more elite category of "popular music," those categories nevertheless continue to set limits on what can count and what cannot. In order to count, popular music must be at once grounded in an authenticating tradition and not overly tainted by either its commercial appeal or its perceived level of calculated pandering to achieve popularity in the first place. There are three main bases that have served most reliably to provide this kind of grounding authenticity: (1) relatively early forms of African American musicking (spirituals, ragtime, blues, and jazz); (2) regional (mostly white) folk traditions (a category in recent times usually extended to include the politically charged "folk music" composed by such figures as Woody Guthrie, Pete Seeger, Joni Mitchell, and Bob Dylan, with the narrower category of "roots" music reserved for music that has a more secure claim to the basic category); and (3) youthful rebellion, which may be understood as a species of personal authenticity. All three bases (along with their various blends), have allowed respect to be accorded something previously considered low-brow, with at least some special claim to the status of primitive.

The category of the primitive has itself played a complex role in cultural hierarchies, especially in the negotiation of brow. That the primitive has so often served as a sign of the authentic is probably due primarily to its presumptive home among the lower brows and its seeming resistance to artifice, notwithstanding that important aesthetic use has been made of the artfully simple or even brutish. "Primitive" also has an implicit racial dimension—as does the notion of relative "brow," after all—according to which non-European-based (that is, nonwhite) cultures are understood to be inherently more primitive, albeit valuably so in this context. Moreover, this implicit dimension has often enough been made explicit, especially during the Harlem Renaissance, whose cultural products often laid claim to authenticity through a forceful, aspirational fusion of race and the primitive.[34] Moreover, this potential had already been hinted at, through manifestly inauthentic appropriation, by the Société des Apaches ("Les Apaches," whose members included Stravinsky, Ravel, de Falla, and Viñes) in Paris during the fin de siècle, where the reference was in part a local one, to street gangs of hooligans who had been dubbed "Apaches" by the press.[35] Already for this generation, the primitive served not only as an authenticating badge of individualized nonconformity but also as a complex aesthetic category, allied with modernism but also serving at times as a counter to modernism's complex artifices, especially, in Paris, those strains that arose as a late-stage extension of German Idealist aesthetics. Finally, we may note that the category invokes not only racial fault lines, as noted, but also gender and class, since the masculine and the lower classes have long seemed more naturally aligned with the primitive, in sharp distinction to the feminine, the genteel, and the aspirational aspect of the middle classes.[36]

Equally important is the dynamic through which such understandings about authenticity and its bases take shape. Typically, that dynamic unfolds along a fault line or two that act as divisions between the authentic and the inauthentic, with inevitable controversies occurring both over where and how firmly the line should be drawn, and regarding which side of the resulting divide has the stronger claim to authenticity. With jazz, the most obvious generic fault lines, historically, have been between and among traditional (Dixieland) jazz, swing, and bop; notably, the bases for the authenticity of Dixieland and bop have had opposing footings, the one in tradition and collectivity, the other in personal expression. Moreover, each basis reflects a different, equally prominent component of jazz as a practice more generally: jamming together as a group within established interactive modes versus individualist expression through improvisation. Folk music has a somewhat different set of generic fault lines, but again with opposing sides each claiming a distinctive authenticating basis. Along the most familiar fault line, one side adheres to a traditionalist approach based in long-venerated generic conceptions of folk music (deriving from Herder), the other to politically committed, newly composed (or adapted) songs that promote a (generally leftist) political message, including "protest" songs. Moreover, as with jazz, there is a "swing" position in the folk spectrum with weaker claims for authenticity, which might encompass performing a more "commercialized" version of folk music in large venues, teaching folk music in public schools or youth-oriented groups, or adapting a folk style to promote or express generalized grassroots cultural affinities, along the lines suggested by Beethoven's "Ode to Joy" in the finale of the Ninth Symphony. Within this type—or, really, these *types*—of musicking, politics may seem less overtly important but actually move to a more basic level and often reverse field, favoring conservative causes, or promoting nationalism and its domesticated cousin, patriotism. Within this swing category, the clash of overt and implicit politics can produce odd and even amusing results, as when conservative public school folk canons blithely include such decidedly leftist "folk" songs as Woody Guthrie's "This Land Is Your Land" or Pete Seeger and Lee Hay's "If I Had a Hammer," the former overtly disclaiming private property and the latter, more subtly, pairing symbols associated with the Soviet Union and the United States.[37]

As with these kinds of factional divisions within traditions, fusions of traditions also engage a system of generic fault lines, with disputes regarding authenticity again residing in the opposed authenticating bases of tradition and personal expression. Folk rock, for example, was initially rejected by those folk musicians (along with their audiences) who valued tradition over youth-driven politics; yet, since the political in this case derives its authenticity from the commitment of the individual artist, a natural alliance formed between politicized folk song and youth-oriented rockers, whose authenticity was already also grounded in personal expression.[38] Indeed, the backstory for that grounding involved a similar fusion, since rhythm and blues (shifting into rock and roll, and thence into rock, mainly by designation) also originally outraged purists who located authenticity in the folk-based dimension of blues practices, a reaction that was inevitably swamped by the investment in individual expression that was also part of those practices, so that the infusion of energy enabled by an up-tempo rhythm section was generally welcomed.

It is easy to be drawn anew into these disputes, given the importance of authenticity in imputing value to "popular music." But if we step back from the authenticity wars, we might come to better terms with what reinforced both of these fusions on a more basic level: their capacity to accompany dance. From this perspective, establishing the authenticity of each new type is a matter of rationalizing a foregone popularity, based on its ability to generate physical excitement and engage the social, which are key to achieving popularity in the first place. While this task is easier for some fusions and factions than others, at bottom these and all similar claims of authenticity reduce to rationalizations on the behalf of personal preference, absent more objective criteria than the cherry-picked traditions and subjective "truths" that claims of authenticity ultimately rely on. But "rationalization" is only one way to describe these kinds of authenticating processes. Because they create and invest belief systems that are crucial to the performance and receptive modes that support "popular music," they allow "popular music" to partake, even if often irreverently, in the kind of religiosity more often associated with the classical tradition.

But religiosity is risky to claims of authenticity, since religion tends strongly toward the middlebrow, especially in US American culture. In a combination typical for middlebrow, religiosity frequently supports the aspirational but rarely generates the complexities or subtleties that might elevate its artifacts to a higher brow. Indeed, in this context it is often aspiration itself that is suspect, since it seeks to pull away from a given identity and station, an effort that is by its nature doomed both to fail and to taint the aspirant with the stain of being inauthentic, of trying to pass for something higher than his or her true cultural station. And, while authenticity—which can redeem the lower brows, as noted—might be claimed for the tokens of religion, they are too often consigned by their aesthetic nature to the category of kitsch, which can be an irredeemable stigma in this context.

Religion is a fault line of a different order than the generic fault lines considered just above, which involve the sometimes-conflicting claims of authenticity based on tradition and personal expression. We might consider religion, like politics, to be operating as a subordinate or more subterranean fault line that nevertheless exercises a strong influence over the more generic tug of war between tradition and personal expression. The fault lines of race, gender, and class—each of which connects readily to politics, and almost as reliably to religion—also operate on this subordinate level, although somewhat differently.

For example, jazz and rock have traditionally privileged men over women, to the extent that the authenticity of women performers in these categories (excepting jazz vocalists), even today, will often require special pleading, especially for an older generation. To be sure, there were always exceptions, and a few of them had a communal component. In the 1960s, Motown's girl groups sometimes broke down this barrier, with the default authenticity of blackness, combined with considerable radio play, producing the persuasive combination of authentic racial roots buoyed by an initially hard-won popularity (a combination that was often also sabotaged, in terms of authenticity claims, by an abiding middle-class sensibility). And a few other women songwriters/vocalists did so as well, with some already "authenticated" women folk artists riding out the fusion with rock, and other women musicians aided by the later splintering of rock into a variety of competing subgenres, with the gender-bending of glam rock serving as an important catalyst along the way,[39] and punk evolving into a reliably welcoming space for women. But in broadly generic terms, jazz and rock followed the classical music scene in establishing and enforcing a predominantly (and outwardly heterosexual) male domain, excepting women singers, supported by a prejudicial sense of a gendered basis for authenticity, and depending (in some vocal genres) partly on the culturally reinforced habit of equating lower vocal registers with authority and depth.

Class, too, has sometimes figured importantly in establishing authenticity, especially in the broad categories of country and bluegrass music, which, like folk music, are generically suspicious of sophistication and relish the twang of a class-based (and thus authenticating) musical accent. Perhaps because of their greater historical distance from the practices and sensibilities of musical idealism, country and folk (especially the former), have been quicker to invest the feminine with authenticity. Moreover, country (again like folk) has historically been understood to be the province of lower-class whites, providing a path to authenticity that privileges a group that is otherwise rather underprivileged in terms of the respect it is accorded. Yet, country, unlike much folk music, has not generally played as authentic to urban sensibilities, which see artifice in the exaggerated country accents and maudlin sentimentality, as well as in country's predilection for slick presentation and rhinestones. This urban tendency to reject country music out of hand may be traced in part to a tendency to take the bumpkin act at face value, rather than as an act deliberately contrived to tweak ostensibly more sophisticated outsiders, which may perhaps be recognized as a species of camp by those in the know, but in any case poses no barrier to fans who will recognize the core of authenticity beneath the mask.[40]

But it does matter who writes the histories, and for whom, and it is only fairly recently that country has been taken seriously beyond its core fan base, through increasing mainstream exposure and, more recently, serious scholarship.[41] Moreover, mainstream exposure often comes at a price, for example in films that indulge in a kind of "hickface,"[42] even if there has also been more celebratory exposure, with little sense of slumming, as in Peter Bogdanovitch's *They All Laughed* (1981). But however much country's modes of authenticity may have mattered to fans, it has had until very recently little currency among those who write about "popular music," who have taken its evident posing at face value, as a sign of insincerity and lack of authenticity. In this it may be usefully contrasted with many of the offerings of Motown; although there was always a bit of the assembly line in Motown's output, it managed to foreground its frequent basis in religious musical types in a way that seemed sincere (thus, soul as a descendent of gospel), at the same time capitalizing on race as a marker for authenticity, especially effective when considered alongside the emergence of the Black Power and Black Pride movements, with which Motown helped forge a distinctive, up-to-date black musical sensibility.[43] Moreover, these blends also managed often enough to find a prominent place for women, whether through the authenticity of gendered racial difference or deriving from religious expression. Of particular significance in regard to parallel developments in country music is the relative place for religion in the mix, which has fared better—both in terms of respect and mainstream popularity—on the black side of the street.

OUTLIERS: CAMP, THEATER, COMFORT, SOCIALITY

As noted, signifying in early jazz often took the form of making fun of white folks' music, not only in the sense of ridiculing it but also in the literal sense of making it fun. This suggests a striking correlation between jazz and camp, following Christopher Isherwood in his oft-noted harbinger to Sontag's "Notes on Camp," from *The World in the Evening* (1956): "High Camp always has an underlying seriousness. You can't camp about something you don't take seriously. You're not making fun of it; you're making fun out of it. You're expressing what's basically serious to you in terms of fun and artifice and elegance."[44] Like camp, many forms of jazz exhibit a gradient in their expressed attitudes toward the object of its fun, while never rejecting that object outright. This bond of affection, occasionally even shading toward veneration, also enables a cumulative process, in which jazz—again like camp—may playfully engage a full range of aesthetic experiences, at any level, even embracing the overt processes of jazz themselves, all without losing affection for the inspirational content, or even creating an aesthetic distance from it. Reversing the field, we may find in camp a mode of *signifying*, albeit differently proportioned between performance and reception than is the case for jazz. If camp, like jazz, may best be understood as a verb rather than a noun (cf. Isherwood, just above), then musical camp, like jazz, is something done to and with more serious music and musical styles, mocking the seriousness but not the substance, which it honors by worrying its surface details. In these ways, the inaugurating spirits of jazz and musical camp hold substance and surface interactive processes in careful balance, protecting the former but with an overriding and generically distinctive investment in the latter. From this perspective, jazz and musical camp are most immediately concerned not with what music *is*, but with what it *does*, in direct parallel to the distinction made above regarding the self and its relationship to the phenomenal world.

Given these parallels, it is worth considering how differently musical camp, especially in theatrical genres, has fared compared to jazz, in terms of critical and academic attention and esteem, and, more generally, in terms of how seriously those who partake of it tend to regard what it has to offer in aesthetic terms. Because serious discussions of camp, seen in a positive light,[45] have most often framed it as an adjunct to gay subcultures, it is mainly regarded in terms of its societal and cultural dimensions, and less often analyzed in aesthetic terms (which is especially true for musical camp, although that is changing). And, because of an abiding societal tendency to see homosexuality as abnormal and even abhorrent—with the backing of some religious and legal authorities and, until all too recently, official medical and psychological authorities, as well—there has been little incentive to find authenticity within the aesthetic predilections of gay subcultures. Thus, despite the obvious attitudinal parallels between jazz and musical camp—especially evident within the performance personae of jazz artists such as Fats Waller and Cab Callaway—the one has been cast as authentic and the other outcast by the persistent taint of association.[46]

But this is only part of the problem for musical camp. Because camp functioned so long in association with "passing," providing a means for gay men to engage with mainstream culture—often swimming against the current, as it were, but subtly enough that their ripples would be noticed only by insiders—any claims it may have to authenticity are fundamentally undermined. The fact that racial difference is (usually) visible has thus paved the road to authenticity for jazz and other race-associated genres of "popular music," making "authentic" the latter-day default category for most music associated strongly with African American cultures. Race can't (usually) hide, making the honesty of its artifacts self-evident, whereas homosexuality, which can more easily disguise itself by passing for straight, undermines the authenticity of its artifacts as part of a process of self-protection. Moreover, not only is passing by definition *in*authentic, but camp attitudes will also, in themselves, proscribe the essentializing claim of authenticity. Camp insists on quotation marks; the authentic simply *is*.

Musical camp has thrived most vibrantly in the realm of theatrical music, which entails its own set of problems regarding authenticity, even apart from its prevalent camp dimension. And those problems are most severe for *commercial* theatrical music, ranging from revues to musicals, operetta, and the operatic musical. In all of these genres—as in opera, but with a higher degree of pandering to audience tastes—actors sing while playing roles in costumes and makeup in front of elaborate scenery. Every aspect of this situation—indeed, the very basis of musical theater—announces a full-frontal embrace of artifice, and thus effectively forecloses claims of authenticity within the paradigms established for "popular music." Moreover, part of the lasting historical appeal for most of these genres, but especially for the Broadway musical, has been their comforting and often escapist generic profile, with a manifest tendency toward setting up solvable problems and delivering happy endings (notwithstanding prominent exceptions and partial exceptions). But music that mostly comforts will never seem as authentic as music that discomfits, since to comfort is to coddle, to indulge fantasy and sentimentality, perhaps even to infantilize. In this sense, musicals will seem, for many invested in "popular music," to share the stigma of easy listening, smooth jazz, mainstream country, innocuous pop, much dance music (including especially disco), and many other kinds of music that seem uninterested in engaging deeper, more contemplative dimensions of human existence.

Part of how such music offers comfort is through its very sense of assurance, conveyed compositionally through its mastery of conventions, and performatively through a particular kind of virtuosity, more often of tone than of passagework, a kind of courtier virtuosity more invested in pleasing than in calling attention to itself as such. The complacency of these kinds of music marks them as middle-class and lower-brow (if not simply lowbrow), with aspirations that may sometimes reach upper-middlebrow, but only if they can overcome the sense that they routinely pander to their audiences. Stripped of some sort of claim to authenticity, whether through race or some other means, these modes of musicking will seem to forsake authenticity for mere "chops," achieving a level of craft that may take them well beyond the primitive but never all the way to Art. Their reliance on convention, even (especially) conventions borrowed from traditional concert music, bars them from the ranks of "popular music," with its assorted pathways to authenticity and a strong tendency to disavow (at least some kinds of) convention.

There are many catchwords and catchphrases in the above descriptions that both underscore and devalue the links between musical creators and consumers within an economy of value based on authenticity: coddling, indulging fantasy and sentimentality, pleasing, pandering, complacency, convention. Yet what these terms have in common is that they help constitute a set of *social* understandings that govern many musical practices. And not just among the outliers; many forms of "authentic" musicking also value the social dimension of music, even though it is also true that a marked emphasis on the social may undermine even an established authenticity through implicit gestures toward commerciality and commodification. It is not (quite) that the antisocial maps directly onto the authentic within the select category of "popular music," but these categories are nevertheless often mutually reinforcing, so that gestures toward the social in music are easily read as tokens of inauthenticity. It is this correlation, as much as anything, that strands many aspirational types of popular music within the aesthetic limbo of middlebrow, along with "lighter" classical music and related genres, such as jazz or movie music performed in the concert hall.

Crucial to the way these distinctions are often thought and talked about are the families of terms that point toward either side of the divide between the social and the deeply personal—the "doing" and "being" dimensions of music—a dichotomy that implicitly denies the collective potentials of German Idealism even as it allows distinctions pertinent to the quasi-idealist category of "popular music." True *beauty* is deeply personal, whereas the *pretty* is merely social. Souls unite in *love*, whereas members of social groups *enjoy* one another's company.[47] *Art* is to be contemplated; *entertainment* is more effective when it is shared with others. The social's musical sublime—to be found in the rave, the Beatles' appearance in Yankee Stadium, the rock concert more generally, or any other musical mob scene—is not sublime at all in the evolved high aesthetic sense but is rather a kind of aesthetic negation achieved through the obliteration of the self within an indistinguishable multitude. In this way, the vocabulary of the social, through its pastel shadowing of more idealist categories, systemically reinforces the idealist hegemony, which is in any case fully manifest within the rhetoric and categories of "popular music."

§

The four broad categories of popular musicking I identify here as "outliers"—musical camp, theatrical music, comfort music, and social music—have been systematically excluded from the exclusive club of "popular music," except when specific instances or types find shelter within authenticist categories, or through grounding in "authentic" origins such as race or folk. This carries some irony, since these categories were the very basis of US American popular musicking during the later nineteenth century, the era that saw the first confrontations between musical idealism and the emergent extreme popularity of popular music in the United States. There are many reasons for this development, ranging from politics to societal tastes, from the steadily augmenting taint of minstrelsy to the shifting of tastes away from the sentimental style of Foster and others to the ever-changing arenas of public and private dance music, in the latter two cases driven in large part by the transformative effects of the rhythmic and harmonious intoxications of successively emergent African American musical styles. These quasi-visceral explanations may well be compelling alternatives to the central argument of this chapter, but they nevertheless point to the same persistent emphasis on the physical and social dimensions of musicking that characterized popular music's early opposition to German Idealistic musical paradigms. To a large extent, latter-day justifications for taking "popular music" seriously routinely cut off the early stages of that opposition at the root, focusing especially on the transformative African American innovations in order to forge and enforce, mostly after the fact, an imagined affinity between "popular music" and musical idealism, based on newly configured, generationally resonant authenticist paradigms.

Authenticity in its modern form has represented a form of self-empowerment that arose in parallel to German Idealism, driven by similar currents, easily intertwined but not identical in its implications for how selfhood matters, neither in the real world nor in art. In German Idealism, the point of it all, and especially of music, was to forge a resonance between the self and some deep sense of the world. While this has remained a possibility for authentic musical expression in "popular music" of the later twentieth and twenty-first centuries, it has certainly not been the only one, nor the easiest. Much more prevalently, what counts as authentic for "popular music" has been a combination of an existing connection to a larger condition (often enforced, to a large extent negatively, through race or class) and the self-expressive, a category that has tended sharply toward something considerably more self-indulgent than German Idealism would ever allow without significant rationalization. As I argue in my "Performance, Authenticity, and the Reflexive Idealism of the American Musical," there is a special irony in this, since American musical theater, with its dual dynamic impulses of self-realization and the desire to merge with something larger, both to be achieved through music, has run closer to German Idealism than the modes of authenticity that ended up mattering most for "popular music." But more centrally important here is the *fact* that this and other types of theatrical or social music were cast aside as insufficiently authentic, in much the same way as those qualities that most distinguished Haydn's symphonic and chamber music were increasingly devalued by an evolving musical idealism across the nineteenth century. As I will explore in the final chapter, this parallel points to an underlying aesthetic commonality that has potentially large implications for our understandings and reappraisals of these—and perhaps other—devalued repertories.

6 | MUSICAL VIRTUES AND VICES IN THE LATTER-DAY NEW WORLD

I want to make this artistic movement the basis for a new civilization.

—OSCAR WILDE

I start with the notion, already well supported in chapter 4, that the underlying aesthetic of high camp has a longer and more diverse history than is generally supposed. This claim is not as straightforward as it may seem, for it calls up several areas of uncertainty and possible contention involving camp and its history, which taken together entail certain obligations. Because the claim suggests that we can identify "the underlying aesthetic of high camp" well enough to trace its "diverse history," it obliges us to do both. And, for the sake of credibility and establishing relevance, it also obliges us to explain why this longer history has not previously been made much of, and how it might nevertheless matter to both our understandings of the past and our receptive practices and valuations today—in particular regarding Haydn, who belongs in this history but now has little if any camp currency.

My opening proposition thus lays out a specific agenda for my final chapter, but I will pursue this agenda with a parallel set of goals in mind. As the title for this chapter suggests, I wish in this context to revisit ethical questions raised by German Idealism's formidable incursion into musical aesthetics, especially as they apply to the persistent dualities of music in the New World. And this will in turn lead me to take up anew the aesthetic challenge Oscar Wilde broached during his own expedition to the New World (in the epigraph to this chapter)—I do this not to stipulate how his "new civilization" might be constituted, but rather, borrowing Richard Dyer's formulation, to imagine "what it would feel like."[1]

THE UNDERLYING AESTHETIC OF HIGH CAMP

In one prevalent account, camp involves a pleasurable diversion of attention away from the supposed *content* of an artwork or performance to some element or elements that are generally understood to be more on the surface or periphery, making them less essential to the aesthetic experience as generally understood. With camp, attention either focuses more on the "how" than on the "what" of the art or performance in question, or, often enough, focuses more on the periphery of the "what" than on its center. High camp may be distinguished from low camp by the balance maintained between content and the surface/periphery. Whereas all camp maintains affection for the object being camped—that is, the artistic construction that supports the ostensible content of the art work—*high* camp will insist that such content and its supporting structures are also taken seriously, at least on some level. The high-camp sensibility understands that one may relish the surface and peripheral distractions of aesthetic experiences (including imperfections) without devaluing the art or the performances involved, their appreciation, or the deeper thoughts and emotions that they may stir; indeed, high-camp experiences teach us that those deeper thoughts and emotions may well intensify through camp engagements.

Another account of camp finds aesthetic failure at its heart, often expressed in the simplistic formula "it's so bad, it's good," but extending as well to the more negligible flaws that bedevil even the greatest of artworks. Failures can range, too, from the deliberately staged to the unwitting, and even to the hapless. They can motivate camp's diversion of attention as described just above. Or they may be noticed only because of a camp receptive strategy that, figuratively, prowls the periphery of the aesthetic experience, constantly tracking the infrastructure of the artwork or performance, ever on the alert for such failures and ready to recognize them either as winks across the proscenium of aesthetic artifice or as the tokens of humanity that must always accompany art's divine aspirations.

The basis for the aesthetic failures relished by camp tastes may also be various. One kind of failure is an incommensurability among the parts, as when a film or stage show moves erratically from one style to another without sufficient (or sufficiently organic) motivation. A broader kind of aesthetic failure involves an inadequate match between means and content, which immediately enforces an aesthetic separation of these elements. Overelaborate means may draw attention away from the content even when the intention is to intensify it, an effect often described as "over the top." Or the means may simply seem ill suited or distractingly "off," as happens when a camp sensibility encounters older films, whose presentations—whether of fashion, filmic technique, acting styles, attitudes, or some other dimension—may seem dated or mannered. Aesthetic failure often resides in the area of performance; thus, performances by otherwise venerated stars—especially divas—may register as flawed from some combination of inadequate acting or vocal technique, miscalculated aspects of appearance (e.g., being too old or too young for the role), or idiosyncratic performing habits ill-suited to the material or character being performed. Or, perhaps, a performance may simply draw too much attention to itself *as* a performance, distracting attention from what is being performed.

Aesthetic failure may also register more basically, on the level of tone or sensibility. Camp will often be understood to be at play when an artwork takes trivial subjects too seriously, or seems to make light of serious ones, forcing an aesthetic separation between the content and the manner or mode in which it is presented. In the case of taking serious topics too lightly, as well as with excessive presentational styles, aesthetic failure will frequently register as a manifestation of bad taste and will present itself most immediately as low camp. Yet, a well-wrought "over-the-top" performance of some element may elevate the camp level, whereas, with trivial treatments of serious topics, a high-camp engagement might still be possible if the seriousness lacking in the mode of presentation is evident in some aspect of the delivery or content. Craft, on all levels, always tends to enable high camp.

A well-known example will illustrate some of these camp elements, from both perspectives and on multiple levels. In Mel Brooks's 1967 film *The Producers*, the title characters Max Bialystock and Leo Bloom decide to produce *Springtime for Hitler* on Broadway from a script carefully selected to be a surefire flop, part of a scheme to oversubscribe investors and not have to pay them off. **<TE6.1>** To hedge their bets, they hire the flagrantly gay Roger de Bris to direct it, decide to make it a musical, and entrust the role of Hitler to one Lorenzo St. DuBois (LSD), who plays him as a version of his own persona: a whiningly ineffective, drugged-out flower child.[2] The title song, which opens the show, is a pastiche vaudeville presentation of content that is every bit as appalling as the subject suggests, staged with all the accoutrements of a Ziegfeld Follies number, with a touch of Busby Berkeley added for the climax, when a group of black-uniformed and black-capped Nazi officers (both male and female) form a rotating swastika as seen from above. The audience watches aghast—all except the gleeful author, Franz Liebkind—and, as the number concludes, most begin to walk out after a lone audience member attempts to applaud and is stifled by those around him. Max and Leo, satisfied that their scheme has worked, also head out, to celebrate. But LSD's flower-child Hitler immediately thereafter strikes the audience as hilarious, apparently unlocking the camp receptive sensibility that will allow them to enjoy even "Springtime for Hitler" in retrospect. At intermission, Max and Leo's celebration at a nearby bar is cut short by an influx of theatergoers delightedly reliving their experience of the first act, with one of them singing the opening phrase of the song as they all leave the bar in eager anticipation of the second act.

The most obvious basis for camp here is the number's failure of sensibility: Hitler and the Holocaust will seem, by default, inappropriate for either musical celebration or comedy. But there are many other camp bases, as well. The follies-style presentation is itself dated, so that the number re-creates part of the camp appeal of older revues and film musicals. The number also includes abrupt internal transitions into different styles, both with the Busby Berkeley bit toward the end and earlier, when crude spoken lyrics introduce a faster dance break (rhyme-impaired Rolf from Düsseldorf; then Mel Brooks himself recruiting on behalf of the Nazi Party). For its part, the rotating swastika is a specifically cinematic device that would not work for audiences within the constructed theater space.[3] Besides the chilling and ludicrous spectacle of a quintessential US American device being used to reproduce the familiar Nazi symbol, rotating cheerfully as if on a pinwheel, the sequence is thus doubly allusive to Busby Berkeley, both to his frequent use of bodies deployed in mobile formations, and to the way his elaborate numbers break the illusion of representing an actual stage show on film. In this way, the climax of "Springtime" reproduces part of the specific "over-the-top" camp appeal of Berkeley's most famous film sequences.

More subtle is the number's use of the interstitial moments between the broadly scaled phrases of the song itself, starting with a small but strategic camp deflection of attention toward the musically inconsequential. The song begins with a series of campily broad strokes, introduced by exaggeratedly dressed, operetta-styled peasantry in front of the curtain, <IE6.2> then proceeding with a front man in formal attire singing the first chorus as he presents a parade of "elegant" women in various showgirl attire and poses, with the vulgar German kitsch of their costumes sabotaging what would like to be a dazzling display of feminine beauty and high fashion. <IE6.3> While all this is undoubtedly camp, the first overtly campy dance move comes in the middle of the first phrase of the chorus, when the lead singer abruptly breaks from his established manner of stately elegance to perform a prancing back-and-forth hopping motion to accommodate a spritely four-note dotted figure from the winds, then snaps back to his (more or less) dignified presentational mode for the rest of the phrase. This key deflection, delightfully quirky in itself (and repeated within the a-b-a-c structure of the chorus), then becomes, with the instrumental second iteration of the chorus—the faster "dance break" referred to above—the occasion for the two verbal interjections already mentioned. Finally, third time around, with full chorus goose-stepping across the stage, these interstitial moments are expanded to include the sounds of artillery, gunfire, and bombs falling, setting up the rotating swastika with a bolero-inspired drum tattoo, and leading to the final verbal turn, when the original concluding phrase ("Come on, Germans, go into your dance") becomes "Soon we'll be going . . . we've got to be going . . . you know we'll be going to war!"—accompanied by an exaggerated form of the same prancing hop that had first opened the door to the escalating interpolations, now performed by all and with jazz hands. <VE6.4>

Although the swastika climax of the number well warrants the exclamation of the first departing couple—"Well! Talk about bad taste!"—this reflexive reaction is then immediately deflected through another campy switch of mood, quickly reclaiming most of the departing audience. As the exodus begins, Eva Braun's nasal Brooklyn accent intones, "Er liebst mir, er liebst mir nicht," drawing most of the audience back to their seats as we are suddenly plunged into a *Mischmasch* of Third Reich and contemporary 1960s sensibilities, with LSD's Hitler performing a New Agey blues number about his invasion plans. Since the only transitional continuity from the opening number substitutes Eva Braun's twirling of a flower for the rotating swastika (which isn't really given any emphasis), the abrupt shift from the presentation style of "Springtime" indirectly highlights, through juxtaposition and after the fact—and for those inclined to notice such things—that the title song was actually faithful to its era, reminding alert observers that Berkeley's signature cinematic evocation of the vaudeville production number developed in the early 1930s, precisely in step with Hitler's rise to power.

Moreover, a still deeper level of engagement lurks just beneath the camp façade. The evocation in "Springtime" of the familiar device of creating symbols through the shifting patterns of choreographed, interchangeable human bodies is more than just campily inappropriate; it may also register, if for only a few, as grim satire, since the control and regimentation of bodies in musical films—and, more relevant for the 1960s, in marching bands on football fields—provides a ready symbol for totalitarian political and military organizational principles. Indeed, the specificity of the swastika symbol here displaces the point of reference for that part of the routine from Berkeley to more contemporary marching-band displays, both because of the military uniforms that provide the black basis for creating the image of the swastika, and because Berkeley preferred more abstract arrangements in his mobile human sculptures, such as the vaguely floral, the fountain-like, or the wave.[4] As well, most 1960s audiences would have been more likely to see contemporary Las Vegas than Ziegfeld in the follies pastiche, offering another cross-historical reference between the 1930s and the 1960s that anticipates LSD's mapping of a whining flower child onto Hitler's persona. If the latter invites a jaundiced comparison between the 1960s and the 1930s, the deft linkage just before, of US American styles of presentation from the Hitler era to their contemporary extensions in Las Vegas and televised halftime shows, reinforces that comparison while providing a pointed contrast between LSD's "free spirit" Hitler and the regimentation of the American marching band executing formations—the latter one step away from soldiers training for deployment to Vietnam.

If these fairly subtle aspects of the cross-referencing between the 1930s and the 1960s probably don't register for very many viewers of the film, neither do the specific camp dimensions identified above register, *as camp*, for most of the characters *in* the film. Which speaks to a larger issue: who gets what out of camp opportunities depends hugely on circumstances and predilection. In this case, we are hard-pressed to discover anyone in the film who actually models a true camp reaction to "Springtime." De Bris and LSD are presumably "in" on its camp dimension, as would be the young men in the chorus, but we see no direct confirmation of this, even if they are all either overtly gay or coded as gay—historically the most important group to foster camp sensibilities, as was already fairly well known by the mid-1960s through Susan Sontag's "Notes on Camp" (see chapter 4). Perhaps we may also assume that the lone clapper gets the number as camp; despite the fact that he seems to have a female date (or possibly two—both women adjacent to him seem to be otherwise unattached), his look and attitude are as one with the chorus boys, and his very enthusiasm suggests that he has thoroughly enjoyed the number without the least concern for its problematic subject matter. In so doing, he is displaying a quintessential camp reaction, delighting fully in the presentation and performance, while oblivious to its content. For this to be fully plausible in that moment, the performance itself must be expertly realized—as indeed it is, with only the faintest exaggeration of the type to underscore the camp intention. It also matters, if only subliminally for most, that there is a deeper text available, as sketched above: sensibilities attuned to high camp are always gratified to sense serious content simmering beneath the distractingly campy surface. And, from a very different perspective, it is crucial that the last scenes we see from the play, after Max and Leo return to the theater, no longer pretend to celebrate the Nazi project but rather celebrate its demise by rendering its later stages as farce, with Hitler and Goebbels adopting the behavior of a drugged-up, jazz-scatting parody of a sixties-era standup-comedy duo.

The potential for the high-camp aesthetic to enable an enjoyable engagement with problematic content is thus well displayed in what we see of *Springtime for Hitler*, yet the audience, as a whole, does not respond with a camp sensibility. Rather, when they do embrace the show after their initial mystification, they understand it as a spoof, ridiculing with one extended riposte the Nazis, outmoded styles of presentation, and the contemporary hippie as projected by LSD—whose whining, mannered performance in the end reduces both hippie and Hitler to little more than spoiled children. As many other artifacts of the 1960s showed—especially on television—spoofs line up very well with camp, due in part to the long-standing association of camp with both musicals and older films, which often come across as self-parodies, since, like spoofs, they habitually draw embarrassing attention to sometimes bizarre generic conventions.

But if few characters *in* the film seem attuned to camp tastes, the film itself has much to offer a camp audience. And, while the show-within-a-show is the most obvious site for this, the peculiar circumstances of that show's premiere are no less useful for triggering camp responses. We may well wonder why there is an audience at all for this premiere, which apparently didn't even bother with an out-of-town tryout. And we may also wonder what that audience might reasonably have expected from a show named *Springtime for Hitler*. Here, the lone clapper, assuming he is responding to the camp element, is the only one in that audience whose presence could really be accounted for; probably, he is already a de Bris fan or has dear friends in the chorus, and thus knows full well what to expect. For the rest (excepting the show's gleeful author), it takes a leap of faith to believe there is any kind of mainstream audience present for the premiere, or that there wouldn't be at least a few more audience members well used to the workings of camp—after all, this is a Broadway musical directed by noted gay director Roger de Bris. But audiences for the film easily forgive this lapse in a logic that would, if adhered to more rigorously, deprive them of the opening number's much-anticipated collision between mainstream and camp tastes.

Arguably, however, de Bris's presence in the film is not really about the camp element he brings to the script and staging of *Springtime for Hitler*—we don't actually see him in action on this front, and are left to imagine that it is all due to him. Rather more important to the larger workings of the film is the gay foil he provides for the ostensibly straight Max and Leo, whose romance serves as the central plotline of the film, replete with an earlier "dating" montage and a celebratory kiss during "Springtime." **<IE6.5>** Their heterosexual "beard" is pretty thin, consisting of Max's stable of little old ladies (whom he obviously loathes) and their secretary Ulla (who at one point suggests with a giggle that the two men go to a hotel together), so that showing us de Bris and his bitchy paramour reassures us that Max and Leo are (at least relatively) straight. Indeed, *The Producers*, like other campy artifacts from this era, seems extraordinarily nervous about the association of camp with gay theatrical subcultures, which is why there is so little gay presence in the audience, and why the category of spoof becomes so important, as a heterosexual beard for camp tastes.[5] In the end, these features function much like the heterosexual plotting of most Broadway musicals, with camp tastes unlocking the gay subtexts for those in the know, while also allowing them to fly beneath the radar of mainstream straight audiences, for whom the official heterosexual content provides an adequate screen. Spoof, like the overtly heterosexual plotting of musicals, tends to face in only one direction, whereas high camp—as any coded language must—tracks several perspectives at once.

This is the dynamic that has, for many, made camp's utility for gay subcultures its most salient feature, but that utility is based in an aesthetic that has a potentially broader base. Even aside from that broader base's precamp history, the notion of gay exclusivity regarding camp has been steadily and increasingly undermined by the general awareness, since the mid-1960s, of camp as a specifically gay sensibility, which has (with some irony) eliminated camp's protective cloak and made camp itself more generally available as a receptive strategy. Moreover, there has been a parallel (though still woefully incomplete) easing of the need for the closet after the Stonewall rebellion helped launch the gay pride movement in 1969. For the present argument, what has been especially interesting to observe, as part of these processes, is the way in which camp-based aesthetics have functioned socially, as an extension of camp's aesthetic basis. It is this social function that made camp central to gay theatrical subcultures in the first place, and that social function not only has survived camp's outing by Sontag but may also allow for a more secure connection to the aesthetic prehistory of camp, which similarly was not exclusively connected to identifiably homosexual tastes and aesthetic predilections.[6]

One of the reasons the camp aesthetic has flourished in theatrical contexts is that those contexts necessarily involve a social dynamic beyond whatever more abstract aesthetic experience they may provide, despite the ways that art—and especially musical art—has been enshrined as a purely aesthetic experience in the wake of German Idealism. In a theater, there is an audience, and that audience affects both the performance itself and the experiences of individual audience members, specifically in terms of appreciation and the various expressions given to that appreciation. To be sure, there is some slippage during any live performance regarding what exactly is being appreciated at any given time, and by whom, and why. But that in itself is useful, allowing audience members to share a general feeling of approval without confronting the fact that, often enough, they are approving quite different things, for quite different reasons, that happen to coincide temporally. This allows many camp appreciations to "pass" as straight, while at the same time allowing—perhaps over time, or through various covert indications—those attuned to camp responses to recognize each other.

Being in an audience allows one to join a community based on shared appreciations and perceived affinities. But within this larger community of approval, there can also be recognition of difference, of affinities shared by some but not others, so that within the larger group may form a smaller, more select community whose appreciations are perhaps more subtle, and certainly more various. In camp's gay golden age (that is, post-Wilde and pre-Sontag), camp attitudes thus had several pleasurable payoffs for gay men: (1) a richer, more diverse aesthetic experience; (2) a sense of being part of a secret in-group, more sophisticated than the larger audience; (3) a way to defend against the inevitable flaws of theatrical performances, which might be appreciated as unintentional camp without interfering with the proffered pleasures of the performance; and (4) a sense that the difference in sensibility of those on the inside, by mostly aligning with the appreciations of the larger audience, ensured a legitimacy for them within that larger audience. The latter sense could establish a powerful lived analogue of societal acceptance (a sense of "what utopia would feel like"), even while the second payoff allowed fellow gay camp enthusiasts to forge clandestine relationships in full recognition that this utopian experience was illusory. Much, but not all, of this remains in the post-Sontag camp environment, and we may reasonably expect a similar profile for earlier manifestations of a camplike aesthetic.

HAYDN'S DIFFERENCE REVISITED

In chapter 4, I trace the early history of camp sensibilities by considering some of the early operettas of Gilbert and Sullivan, in particular, *The Pirates of Penzance* and *Patience*; arguably, these shows, together with *Pinafore* (and perhaps *Iolanthe*), represent the tipping point, the historical moment when spoof transforms into camp, or at least protocamp. What makes Gilbert and Sullivan more than spoof, if perhaps not yet fully camp, is their approach to the aesthetic profile of what would later be termed "high camp." This approach to high camp elevates spoof by fostering an inclination and capacity to take content seriously despite the apparent frivolousness of the enterprise. Gilbert and Sullivan bring about this elevation through a high level of musical and verbal craft, coupled with a deft confusion of elements through clever parody that, by cutting both ways, allows for multiple readings that extend to the serious. It was after all no small thing, in Victorian England, to critique the British Navy as effeminized through political opportunism while flirting with democratic notions in the military (*Pinafore*), to equate nobility with piracy while maligning the bravery of the police (*Pirates*), to call out whole literary movements as pretentious frauds while lampooning careerist military officers as poseurs (*Patience*), or to transform the House of Peers into the "House of Peris" (*Iolanthe*). But just as the conflation of the US American 1960s with the German Nazi era in *Springtime for Hitler* cuts both ways, so also do Gilbert and Sullivan's more daring conceits, since it remains deliberately unclear, in each case, which side of the coin is being impugned through association with the other. Gilbert and Sullivan's nimble negotiation of this kind of political tightrope, managed while simultaneously mounting exquisitely wrought musical numbers that both underscore their audacity and exempt it from censure, transforms their operatic spoofs-cum–political satire into something that easily plays, still today, as high camp.

Contrariwise, Haydn's symphonies and quartets, discussed in chapters 2 and 3, do not fit directly into the history of camp. As far as I know, they do not function as a basis for camp today, nor did they do so in earlier phases of camp's development. And I do not propose to argue here for reconsidering this situation, for trying to understand them in specifically camp terms. They are not "so bad that they're good"; rather, they are generally understood to be highly sophisticated and well-wrought music, despite the fact that their audience today—their "fan base"—is relatively small. Nor do the amusements they provide—apart from the inadvertent situational quirks that can intrude on any live performance—stem from the surface or the periphery of their "content," since Haydn manages surface and peripheral amusements *as content*, and often enough makes them central to the musical developments that occupy the main focus of a movement or work. Nor can these works follow the path of Gilbert and Sullivan's operettas toward camp, since they are not spoofs. They mean to be—and certainly are—full-fledged symphonies and quartets, understood by Haydn's contemporaries as the finest specimens of their type, and still venerated for their effectiveness in performance and the quality of their musical working-out.

Nevertheless, Haydn's ensemble instrumental music shares much with the aesthetic that governs high camp, if not with its specific structures and social context. For example, the inside-outside social dynamic involved in Haydn's string quartets, as detailed in chapter 3, foreshadows high camp in creating tiers of aligned receptive environments, some of which are more "inside" than others, and thus closer to the complexities of the originating spirit. And, as discussed in both chapters 2 and 3, Haydn often trades in incongruity, in the triumph of the odd surface detail over more conventional substance, in making light of serious things and vice versa, and in what may fairly be termed aesthetic "failure," at least on some level. All of these elements, preeminent in Haydn, are also hallmarks of high camp. To be sure, despite their many salient differences, it should not surprise us to find Haydn anticipating some of the sensibilities of high camp, since, as I have argued, Haydn and camp may be considered oppositional bookends to the aesthetic paradigms of German Idealism. But considering their commonalities more closely will clarify how, in more specific ways, they may be seen to frame German Idealism, together manifesting a shared opposition to German Idealism's musical paradigms on a fundamental aesthetic—and even philosophical—level.

It may seem no more than oddly coincidental that my central examples in chapters 2 and 4 involve placing a fearsome marauder—the Turk and the pirate, respectively—at stage center, reconceived as a figure whose colorful excess is to be more savored than feared. But this point of similarity between Haydn and camp is highly emblematic of their respective distances from and implicit attitudes toward German Idealism. With Haydn's Janissary indulgences in the "Military" Symphony, as with later pirate camp, the source of fear is in effect domesticated; indeed, this is precisely how I read the overall trajectory of Haydn's "Military" Symphony in chapter 2. But in E. T. A. Hoffmann's famous essay, "Beethoven's Instrumental Music"—which may for us serve as a kind of idealist manifesto—he finds the key to Beethoven's heightened romanticism to be the way Beethoven uses fear quite differently, as a means of calling up the sublime and thereby providing a potential passageway to the longed-for Infinite:

> [Instrumental music] is the most romantic of all the arts, one might almost say the only really romantic art, for its sole object is the expression of the infinite. . . . Music discloses to man an unknown kingdom, a world having nothing in common with the external sensual world which surrounds him . . .
>
> Beethoven's instrumental music discloses to us the realm of the tragic and illimitable. . . . And only through this very pain in which love, hope, and joy, consumed but not destroyed, burst forth from our hearts in the deep-voiced harmony of all the passions, do we go on living and become hypnotized seers of visions! . . .

Haydn conceives romantically that which is distinctly human in the life of man; he is, in so far, more comprehensible to the majority.

Mozart grasps more the superhuman, the miraculous, which dwells in the imagination.

Beethoven's music stirs the mists of fear, of horror, of terror, of grief, and awakens that endless longing which is the very essence of romanticism.[7]

In domesticating fears rather than amplifying them into a semblance of the sublime, Haydn and pirate camp insist, as Hoffmann would have it, "on that which is distinctly human." Moreover, both high camp and Haydn insist as well on a perspective broad enough to encompass both laughter and seriousness, even simultaneously, as appropriate responses to music. It is not that Haydn's Turks are not, in context, "real" in the "Military" Symphony, but that they are *precisely* that, in Haydn's terms: they are *human* rather than *superhuman*, and so engender not only fear but also recognition and, eventually, laughter. Making light, in this sense, is to make human. Haydn's musical realms, like those accessible through high camp, remain tied to "the external sensual world"—and so are quite unlike those fantastic realms that Hoffmann essentializes as music's "unknown kingdom," whose calling up he understands to be instrumental music's "sole object." In encompassing both laughter and seriousness, Haydn and high camp embrace a totality of human experience, a great deal of which Hoffmann and the other German Romantics, in their quest for German Idealism's noumenal, set aside as the mere phenomenal world. Haydn and high camp thus stand apart from German Idealism on a fundamental level, forging an opposition based resolutely in a strongly stated philosophical difference.

MUSICAL VIRTUES—FIELDS OF PLAY

My consideration of "Haydn as Philosophical 'Other'" in chapter 2 seeks to extend David Schroeder's pioneering discussion of Haydn's philosophical tendencies in *Haydn and the Enlightenment*, which he bases on speculations by Thomas Twining and others during Haydn's London trips. In extending Schroeder's discussion, I also build on Alasdair MacIntyre's *After Virtue*, where he traces an Aristotelian ethical tradition based structurally on a hierarchical conception of *virtues* that may be understood to support human flourishing, of which, with regard to Haydn's symphonies, Schroeder's identification of tolerance serves as a salient example. Within the complex negotiations that occur during the musical argument of a Haydn symphony, and within the negotiated understandings that informed and regulated public performances of those symphonies in his lifetime, Haydn sought what Aristotle might have termed a "golden mean" between many sets of poles: between dramatic narrative and musical argument, between eccentricity and functionality, and between entertainment and edification, among others.

Mitchell Morris's assessment of the (still) current state of American musicology, in "Musical Virtues," pursues two intertwined threads of MacIntyre's delineation of a virtue-based understanding of ethics, within two intertwined fields. Specifically, Morris shows how the concepts of "practice" and "tradition" might serve, within musicological enquiries, as a framework for understanding the virtues advanced through musicking's varied cultural contexts, and how the discipline of musicology itself might be understood, and improved, through application of these concepts, as well.[8] In line with Morris's argument, we may understand Haydn as participating in a set of practices within a tradition, much of which changed quickly and profoundly after his London visits in the early-to-mid 1790s. Within the less human-centered musical practices encouraged by German Idealism and its evolving aesthetics, much of what energized Haydn's practices became devalued and even irrelevant. And, within musicology—a discipline that took definitive shape in response to the needs and practices associated with the new musical paradigms—most discussions of Haydn, however often they may be motivated by responses consistent with Haydn's actual practices, focus primarily on aspects of his music that fit comfortably within the new practices that emerged in the nineteenth century, and that came to dominate the "classical" concert tradition that Haydn has been understood to belong to.

Musicology, when it pays attention to Haydn at all, thus focuses, within the above listed dichotomies, on musical argumentation, functionality, and edification, leaving aside or decentralizing dramatic narrative, eccentricity, and entertainment. In the process, the former aspects of his music, which within Haydn's practices took part in dynamic negotiations with the latter aspects, have been sheared away from the sustaining energies those negotiations produced. Deprived of their dialogic moorings, these aspects of Haydn's music have thereby been cast adrift within an abstract ether vaguely understood as "compositional craft," to be readily reclaimed by Beethoven and others to serve new purposes within the emergent paradigm of musical idealism. Meanwhile, Haydn, having earned the sobriquet "Papa Haydn" as a virtuous forbear who developed the requisite techniques but lacked the vision for how they might serve a new musical order, has been unfairly but inevitably cast into an ancillary historical role. This historical hierarchy, in turn, has reinforced musicology's preoccupation with the "serious" dimensions of Haydn's dynamic polarities, in effect focusing not on Haydn but only on that part of him legible from the perspective of a set of musical practices and understandings that evolved only after his career ended, and which left no place for the central dynamic that energized his musical practices.

High camp, however, may be understood to reconstitute, in its receptive practices, a Haydn-like set of relationships and negotiations that set up high-art seriousness in dynamic opposition to the quotidian, and then seek something like Haydn's golden mean between these poles. High camp relishes the tension between what an artwork or performance aims to be and what its flaws reveal it to be, between its aspirations and its realities, between its promised infinities and its grounding in the human. Whereas musicology's dominant approach to Haydn has led to a kind of amputation, isolating specific "serious" qualities from the dynamic oppositions that originally vitalized them, high camp establishes a similar dynamic opposition as the basis for its own complex negotiations, which, in reception, insists on placing high art's aspirations, pretensions, and signal achievements within a more everyday human context.

As a practice, high camp encourages human flourishing in myriad ways, not all of which relate easily to the practices of Haydn and his associates. For instance, camp's historical importance to gay subcultures has no obvious parallel in Haydn reception, although both are based in shared appreciations that, while recognized as mutual, were not often analyzed as such. Yet, latter-day high-camp receptive strategies and Haydn's initial reception nevertheless have something fundamental in common, which structures their respective aesthetic bases. Both set up, and relish, a dynamic opposition between distinctly different frames of reference, which between them and in possible combination with other paired frames of reference define the scope of their respective fields of play. And "play" here is indeed the operative word, for both Haydn and high camp depend to some extent on an awareness of this tension and of how one pole plays off the other. Both take considerable pleasure in this awareness, without in the process sacrificing investment in either referential frame, preferring to hold them in some kind of mutual balance. And both employ such oppositional poles to widen the perspective on musical experiences as much as possible, enhancing the various meanings and values that may be derived therefrom, including enjoyment and other pleasures and amusements, access to deeper feelings, and a fostering of connections to others who partake in the practice.

Musical idealism, on the other hand, has never been about stretching our conception of what constitutes a musical experience, but rather the opposite. If we are to value music primarily because of what we imagine it might accomplish in the metaphysical realm, we will tend to see anything that interferes with that as problematic; in reaction, we will seek to rarefy the musical experience through purging unwanted elements, or develop listening strategies for bypassing such interferences. This is precisely the opposite of Haydn and high camp's response to such problematics, which, as I've argued here, has been to harness them so as to expand music's purview. Moreover, if German Idealism leads us to understand music's unique metaphysical capacities as stemming from music's *lack* of ties to everyday reality—the specifically social, the descriptive, the quotidian—we will effectively shut down what matters for the more robust of Haydn's musical practices, even while we by the same token inadvertently give camp reception a deliciously broad field of action.

Which is not to say that musical idealism, as a practice, does not have distinctive virtues, such as the encouragement of reverence and its attendants, respect and valuation; the enhancement of deep emotions; and the intensification of receptivity through listening to complex human creations and comprehending them as such through contemplation. Moreover, the *actual* practices of musical idealism quite often include many of the virtues we might more readily associate with other, less idealistic musicking practices, such as furthering sociability and fellowship through the sharing of mutually valued experiences. After all, musicking will be musicking, no matter how we might want to dress it up and take it to Sunday Meeting. But idealism also encourages the suppression of these hierarchically lesser virtues should they intrude on the holier, more purely metaphysical domain music is aspirationally seen to occupy, and its inclinations when provoked are less than generous to precisely those elements that might produce the poles of opposition relished by Haydn's original audiences, or by latter-day high camp.

It is a difficult thing, to be sure, to reawaken an aesthetic sensibility when the conditions that support it have vanished, particularly when something that approximates many aspects of those vanished conditions has developed to take its place. Such is the fate of the sensibilities that responded to Haydn's music in his day, whose traces we may find in his ensemble instrumental music but rarely experience in their fullness within the public space of the concert hall or the semiprivate space of the chamber (although the latter is likely to come closer more often). But we might hopefully imagine that musical performance of scripted works with Haydn's practices in mind will, over time, reawaken such sensibilities. Such hopes will be particularly strong if we hearken to one of the great lessons offered by the historically informed performance movement, which is that such scripts, properly understood within a nurturing performance environment, can retrain our latter-day practices so as, in a sense, to regrow long-atrophied receptive practices.

Indeed, if we look closely enough at the near train wreck that occurred to the historical performance movement a quarter century ago—back when it liked to call itself "authentic"—we might even derive more encouragement from that movement's continued flourishing. When Richard Taruskin called out the movement for playing more to modernist, antiromantic tastes than to the historical authenticity it claimed, he was also pointing to the very thing that gave the movement a secure foothold in an otherwise fairly hostile receptive environment. Playing to existing elements in a receptive field is precisely what the movement needed to do, as a first step to retraining that field, and reclaiming at least some of the dormant aesthetic of its treasured historical traces.

It is just this sort of foothold that high-camp receptive practices may provide for Haydn. But it will not be an easy path, for many reasons.

MUSICAL VICES—HONOR THY PAPA

A crucial difference between high-camp receptive modes and the original receptive practices for Haydn's music is simply historical. One of the main musical foils for high camp—as, indeed, for minstrelsy, as laid out in chapter 4—is the receptive environment fostered by musical idealism, an aesthetic barely in its infancy in Haydn's day. Moreover, the relationship of high camp to musical idealism resembles that between a parasite and host, which may even be seen to reverse the historical relationship of Haydn to musical idealism. Idealism took over a musical receptive environment fostered by Haydn and turned it to new purposes. But, as the aesthetic environment for serious music began, under the sway of German Idealism, to impose standards that any particular musical work or performance would in some way fail to meet, it also guaranteed that musical camp's appetite for aesthetic pretensions and failures would never be starved. Moreover, while these essential camp commodities will be omnipresent in any aesthetic tradition invested in artistic seriousness to such an extent that it seeks to suppress the quotidian altogether, musical idealism constitutes an extreme case, since it is founded on a metaphysical impossibility, however fervently it might be believed by its adherents.

As with all belief systems that push into the realm of what will seem absurd and nonsensical from a commonsense perspective, German Idealist musical practices entail not only the advancement of specific virtues but also the suppression of specific vices, as the inevitable recourse for those who would control unruly impulses. Such impulses will generally include the urge toward reason, evidence, and logic, an urge that certainly comes into play in response to claims, such as E. T. A. Hoffmann's, that music expresses "the infinite" (which is by definition unknowable), or that listening to music can transport us to "an unknown kingdom, a world having nothing in common with the external sensual world which surrounds [us]." It may well be that we are to understand such claims as merely figurative, or cast in an implicit subjunctive mode. But the urgency with which musical idealism fosters an environment where such claims will seem plausible (or at least *feel* plausible) indicates otherwise, as does the idealist tendency to police such environments. Sooner or later, there will be an uncomfortable moment (we might call it the "Scriabin moment") when we can only wonder where figurative aspiration ends and literal belief takes over, and whether idealism doesn't stand a little too close to the edge of lunacy for comfort.

Hoffmann's language in his Beethoven essay is often understood to be a manifestation of Romanticism's feverish excesses, which we may well raise our eyebrows at but need not take seriously except as an expression of the Zeitgeist. Yet his words—and their literal meanings—were clearly meant to have at least one real-world effect: to elevate the prestige of music. As I argue in chapter 1, his claim quoted just above, that music "is the most romantic of all the arts, one might almost say the only really romantic art," is a mere step away from claiming music to be the highest of the arts. And these are very high stakes. Once that step was taken, the cult of serious music became a religion, and to secure its newly claimed high ground it was soon replete with a set of prohibitions and vices such as all religions must enforce and purge if they are to compel adherence to their catechisms.

And what are these musical prohibitions and vices, according to musical idealism? Not surprisingly, many of them shadow Judeo-Christianity's Ten Commandments in requiring that due reverence be shown to the sanctities and hierarchies of belief, ritual, and lineage. And, in parallel with the evolution of churchly protocols, the identification of musical vices is concerned importantly with self-regulation, according to the belief that Music—that is, *true* music, properly apprehended by a contemplative listener in full receptive mode—ought to move the soul but not the body. Stillness, regarding both movement and distractive noise, fosters the ideal receptive environment. Displays of approbation are carefully regulated; applause, while it rightfully acknowledges the performers (and sometimes composers), must not intrude on a space commanded by the sacred text, *especially* (because of its symbolic value) during those silent intervals between movements in a symphony, concerto, or other multi-movement work. Performers' bodies must of course move, but only as necessary to execute the music and convey its sense, and certainly not in such a way as to call undue attention to the performer. The latter vice, the vice of undue display, may take various forms, such as extravagant dress, improper decorum, or flamboyantly gestural execution. But no matter how common and even expected this vice may be among concert soloists, it nevertheless counts as a vice within the practices of musical idealism, whereas its absence, however rarely encountered, may be admired as an exceptional virtue.

One of the most policed vices of musical idealism—and here we return to the anecdote that opens chapter 1—is laughter. But laughter may also be the (sometimes silent) accompaniment not only to high camp but also, as my anecdote attests, to Haydn. There are several consequences of this locus of conflict, all of which tend to drive a wedge between camp receptive strategies and their capacity to influence Haydn reception.

Despite its dependency on idealist aesthetics, camp tends to leave the core practices of musical idealism well enough alone. High camp, in particular, comes from a generous and affectionate place that will tend more to respect than mock (or both respect *and* mock) the protocols and prohibitions of the concert hall, and especially will refrain from interfering with the concentration of the performers or the contemplation of the audience. This is why camp, however serious its foils, is most at home within less regulated environments, such as comic-theatrical events or in watching films that are either intentionally comic or otherwise not likely to be taken too seriously. But the theatrical side of concert traditions—the staged presentation, the dramatic lighting, the extravagant regalia, the specialized rituals—is nevertheless ripe for camp appreciations, and there is fairly dependably an air of shared amusement regarding this side of concert life, especially among performers, even as it is indulged and allowed to do its quasi-religious work toward idealist appreciations for and participations in the hallowed traditions of serious music. This blend of amusement and respect is typical for a sensibility attuned to high camp, and like other indulgences in this receptive mode will in the end generally serve to intensify the experience of the event's earnest core. Importantly, this receptive dynamic respects the sanctity of the performance itself, during which even subdued mirth will be held in check, even (usually) for Haydn.

Within this dynamic environment, in which camp sensibilities tend to focus on the accoutrement of the event rather than its actual music, camp is essentially fenced off from engaging, at least outwardly, with most of Haydn's sometimes camplike extravagances, since these are always musically based. And, too, Haydn has been an unlikely focus for camp, since he belongs to an earlier aesthetic not as prone to pretension, even if we might imagine the very quaintness of some of his conceits having a certain camp appeal.

From the beginning, the path Haydn's music took to survive in a world dominated by the creed of absolute music was to learn something like the self-regulatory behaviors demanded of its audiences. If Haydn was to remain in the repertory within the evolving culture of serious music, the focus had to be on the serious side of what his music had to offer. However entertaining his music, and whatever its eccentricities, Haydn's admission ticket to the new order was the serious rigor of his craft, the earnestness of his intentions, and, in the end, his importance to the tradition itself. The latter has proven to be his ace in the hole in a religious order bound to respect its elders. Honor thy Papa.

BRIDGING PERSISTENT DUALITIES

Musical idealism—the set of musical practices that developed in response to German Idealism—has always been a fragile construct. The practices and uses of musicking are too varied, and that variety too entrenched in human life, for idealism to enforce, even in the concert hall, its narrow vision of what music *must* be owing to its essential nature. But the profit margin of this fragile construct was huge, in terms of prestige, and so the bargain was struck, and the lines were drawn. It is in drawing and redrawing those lines around what counts as "serious music" that the dualities noted in chapters 1 and 5 became first operative and then seemingly intractable, although with sometimes shifting boundaries: between serious (German) music and all other musics, between classical and popular music, between classical and "light" classical music, and between "authentic" popular music and music that is merely popular. Camp loves boundaries like these, generally parking itself just across the border on the louche side of whatever fence is operative, and taking its amusements from the border skirmishes while also eagerly taking in as much else as it can from both factions.

But although camp can partake of either side of these persistent dualities, it will always seem to *belong*, according to the high aesthetic border patrols, to the lesser. It is too easily entertained by spectacle, especially as provided by serious aspirations and their inevitable failures, to itself pass as serious, too Algernon to pass as earnest. Further, because of high camp's affinities with low camp, whose eagerness to find pleasure in the patently unworthy can appear unseemly, it carries the taint of association, even on the categorical level. This is to be expected; if camp, with all its heightened sensibilities, nevertheless sees and applauds the inadequacies of not only pretension but also sheer ineptitude ("it's so bad it's good"), how can one know for sure that this kind of sensibility slumming doesn't betray an ill-concealed "guilty pleasure" that accepts the aesthetically bad on its own terms? These are slippery distinctions. And they are not made easier by the history and practices of camp, which managed before Sontag's essay to guard well the secret of its specialized sensibilities in order to pass for straight, and has since maintained some of those precautionary habits.

Haydn, meanwhile, has had his own flirtations with the redrawn borders of these persistent dualities. The veneration accorded him as "Papa Haydn" has faded considerably after more than two centuries of familiarity, so that his playful musical demeanor registers increasingly as an irritant within the practices of serious art music, despite well-entrenched habits of hearing past his jokes to his unassailable craft. Yet despite Haydn's occasional appearances in "light classical" concerts, he has never really been at home there, either, and increasingly less so. Regarding the "Farewell" Symphony, for example, audiences will be not only impatient for the sweetly comic payoff but also potentially mystified by the turgid ferocity of the opening movement. They will, in fact, tend to be happier with "Pops" than with "Papa," since the Pops side of the "light classical" repertory will often enough be based on actually popular music, as with film scores, classicized pop tunes, or concert pieces derived from musicals. On the other hand, Haydn has over the last generation attracted renewed attention in the academy, some of it extremely responsive to what makes him so remarkable a composer and musical thinker.[9] But despite this more serious attention to his lighter side, within the more earnestly serious spaces of musical idealism Haydn will too often seem the unruly child who hasn't learned to regulate his impulses. Here, the finale to the "Farewell," the second movements of the "Clock" and "Surprise" Symphonies, and above all the "fart" movement in no. 93, will for many seem silly and inappropriate, as will the returning Janissary instruments at the end of the finale in the "Military" Symphony.

There are, to be sure, other "serious" composers whose sometimes saucy insouciance has made them uneasy entrants in the idealist tradition. Many of these are French, and a few Russian, but many others are US American, working in increasing numbers within a more modern, avant-garde, or postmodern idiom whose difficulty, aesthetic pretension (or conceit), and/or exotic novelty offer a sufficiently serious credential whatever playful elements they might also introduce. In earlier generations of the twentieth century, when such insouciance was likely as not to stem from offshore sources, it might be taken within a New World context as an aspect of foreignness, as with Stravinsky's angular modernism, Prokofiev's "sarcasm," Ravel's and Milhaud's oddly construed "jazz" idioms, or Poulenc's impudence. US American entrants to this kind of "insouciant" list, for their part, will often seem attitudinally self-conscious as "Americans"; such a list will probably begin by default with Charles Ives, and might also include Henry Cowell, Aaron Copland, Virgil Thomson, John Cage, Milton Babbitt (who can be hilarious despite his reputation as a "difficult" composer), John Zorn, Laurie Anderson, and Andrew Norman, among many other aspirants. Some of these even have a pronounced camp appeal, such as Poulenc (e.g., *Les mamelles de Tirésias, Banalités*) and Thomson (*Four Saints in Three Acts*).

These campy intrusions into the concert hall—especially, say, with Milhaud's or Poulenc's concert pieces—do muddy the water considerably. True enough, musical camp, like all camp engagements, can always be denied; this is after all one of its most useful features. But much of this music comes across oddly in serious venues, with those audience members not "in the know" getting the uneasy feeling that their legs are being pulled in some way, or that the music carries more than a whiff of mockery directed toward its august setting. While it may well be that this still-growing repertory will succeed on its own in opening up the concert hall to less religiously regulated experiences, it more often seems to provide no more than the exception that proves the rule, that tests—and is defeated by—the continued sway of musical idealism. The result is that within the concert hall, for the most part, this mode of camp remains closeted, and is likely to remain so for the foreseeable future—unless, perhaps, it gets outed by a latter-day Sontag.

All this activity, including the play of high camp around the edges of serious musicking, has thus had little effect on Haydn's reception in the concert hall. But the potential bond between Haydn and high camp, grounded in the dynamic created by insisting on holding laughter and serious feeling in equal regard within a productive, human-based tension, remains tantalizing. In thinking long about Haydn, high camp, and German Idealism's musical paradigms, I have been especially struck by a number of considerations, which together may point to a more productive actualizing of that bond:

1. For much of this book, I have adopted William Weber's term "musical idealism" as a replacement for longer constructs such as "German Idealism's musical paradigms," which seems eminently warranted by historical realities and linguistic ease. But one problem with this

substitution is that it fosters the misleading impression that serious music was essentially a result of internal developments within musical traditions. Certainly it was an internal development, to a large extent. But the musicians who led this line of development were enticed to do so by an aesthetic movement dominated by poets and based in the newly evolving philosophy of German Idealism, which promised—and delivered—a new hierarchy of the arts with music on top.

2. This demonstrated power to shape musical practices and traditions from outside, to steer internal developments by what we say about them, might well be harnessed to different ends. The operative "we" in this case includes any and all who might be willing and able to theorize musicking in terms of human flourishing, who might recognize the potential to reconceive the concert hall as something other than a portal to infinity, who might reimagine it also as a venue grounded in what music has to offer humans whose focus remains the human, who still care about the contemplative possibilities of the venue and its established repertories while also wanting to celebrate, simultaneously, other potentials, founded on other musical practices and traditions.
3. In some areas of the academy there are already significant beachheads establishing this line of advocacy, from scholars and critics whose work might be extended to embrace potentials of the concert hall that have remained categorically off limits, sometimes through habit but probably oftener through the agency of institutions (including those of the academy itself). Most relevant, in my view, are the writings of Richard Dyer and Mitchell Morris, who have worked to free categories such as "entertainment," "camp," and "sentiment" from the stigma that idealist habits of thinking have attached to them, a stigma that popular music studies and most other branches of cultural studies have tended to leave in place.
4. The concert hall's latter-day cultural role, as a kind of museum, is not actually coextensive with its function within idealism, since the latter acts as a filter for the practices represented through the former function. If the concert hall would like to embrace more fully its role as a museum, it would have to endeavor to reconstitute the practices and traditions that produced repertories that predate idealism and have a significantly different philosophical basis (such as

Haydn), as well as to consider how to host more appropriately those latter-day repertories that stand apart from idealism (such as Prokofiev and Poulenc). This would make of the concert hall a more generous space, refusing to enforce—as idealism currently does—the suppression of those modes of reception that insist on embracing humanity rather than (just) the infinite.

5. Such an approach would also admit easily to high-camp sensibilities, which are often driven by a determination to take flawed things seriously, and know how to acknowledge and even savor such flaws without threatening the seriousness that lies beneath the flawed surface. It would presumably be at such a juncture, when mainstreamed high-camp sensibilities extend with a greater sense of presence into a more welcoming concert hall, that Haydn and related repertories, both pre- and postidealist, could speak to their full dynamic range.

To be sure, some of this has already been happening, in modest ways, usually propelled by fears that the concert tradition is dying and that ways must be found to make it more appealing to new audiences. This fear, and these initial moves in the direction of making concert life more entertaining, mark this as a propitious historical moment for critics and others in the academy to provide a well-grounded rationale for this kind of shift, basing a potential sea change on specifically human needs rather than on the pragmatic financial needs of dying institutions. In this way, we may hope that an artistic movement can indeed provide the basis for a new civilization, or at least allow us to imagine what that new civilization, that new world, might feel like.

Appendix A | More Extended Musical Examples

The following extended musical examples are discussed in chapters 2 (ex. 1) and 3 (exx. 2 and 3).

Appendix A Ex. 1 Haydn, "Military" Symphony, mvt. 2, mm. 70–80

Appendix A Ex. 1 continued

Appendix A Ex. 1 continued

Appendix A Ex. 2 Haydn, String Quartet, op. 64, no. 3, mvt. 1, mm. 1–69

Appendix A Ex. 2 continued

Appendix A Ex. 2 continued

Appendix A Ex. 2 continued

Appendix A Ex. 2 continued

Appendix A Ex. 2 continued

Appendix A Ex. 2 continued

Appendix A Ex. 3 Bartók, String Quartet no. 2, mvt. 2, mm. 1–43

Appendix A Ex. 3 continued

Appendix A Ex. 3 continued

Appendix B | Listing of Video Examples from Films

Clips from the following films are available on line at knappmakinglight.net, keyed to the indicated symbols next to where these clips are discussed (please see explanatory note on p. xxi). Because online video streaming has sometimes proven unreliable, I provide the following listing according to when they are discussed in the book, with the approximate timing indicating the beginning of each clip within the specified DVD release.

Show Boat (James Whale, 1936). Classicline, 2003 (also available Warner Archive Collection, 2014).

<VE4.7> p. 153 56:45

Swing Time (George Stevens, 1936). Warner Home Video, 2005.

<VE4.8> p. 154 1:14:00/1:15:20 /1:20:25

Holiday Inn (Mark Sandrich, 1942). Universal Studios, 1999.

<VE4.9> p. 156 44:55

Babes in Arms (Busby Berkeley, 1939). Warner Home Video, 2007.

<VE4.10> p. 158 1:09:45

<VE4.12> p. 160 1:12:30

Babes on Broadway (Busby Berkeley, 1941). Warner Home Video, 2007.

<VE4.11> p. 160 1:44:15

<VE4.13> p. 160 1:46:45

<VE4.14> p. 161 1:51:50
<VE4.15> p. 161 1:49:10
<VE4.68> p. 198 1:18:20
<VE4.69> p. 200 1:34:45
<VE4.71> p. 202 1:23:55
<VE4.72> p. 203 1:26:35

The Pirate (Vincente Minnelli, 1948). Warner Home Video, 2007.

<VE4.52> p. 191 32:50
<VE4.55> p. 193 1:34:45
<VE4.56> p. 193 32:30
<VE4.57> p. 195 18:50
<VE4.58> p. 195 5:35
<VE4.59> p. 195 23:05
<VE4.60> p. 195 25:10
<VE4.61> p. 196 37:15
<VE4.62> p. 196 58:05
<VE4.63> p. 196 1:06:45
<VE4.74> p. 203 52:30

The Producers (Mel Brooks, 1967). MGM Home Entertainment, 2002.

<VE6.4> p. 257 58:15

Notes

1 | IDEALIZING MUSIC

1. "'A Clever Orator': Colloquies and Performances Exploring Rhetoric in Haydn's Chamber Music," Clark Library, UCLA, April 20–21, 2001 (organized by Tom Beghin, Raymond Knapp, and Elisabeth Le Guin, under the auspices of the UCLA Center for 17th- and 18th-Century Studies, directed by Peter Reill). The "extraordinary moment" occurred during a performance of Haydn's Trio in A♭, Hob. xv:14, performed by Tom Beghin (piano), Lisa Weiss (violin), and Elisabeth Le Guin (cello).
2. Regarding the depth metaphor—a central signpost of German Idealism's sway over discourses on music—see Fink, "Going Flat"; and Watkins, *Metaphors of Depth*.
3. Four recent studies run in close parallel to the project of this book. Berthold Hoeckner's *Programming the Absolute* offers a groundbreaking critique of German music during precisely the period I discuss in this chapter, and from a perspective informed by philosophies of both that era and our more recent past. Melanie Lowe, in *Pleasure and Meaning*, seeks to recapture modes of engaging with late eighteenth-century symphonic music that were displaced by the doctrine of absolute music. And Mark Evan Bonds, in both *Music as Thought* and *Absolute Music*, traces, as does my first chapter, the transformation by German Idealism of musical practices and associated beliefs across the nineteenth century. Although the roots of my own project predate these, they have nevertheless been seminal, since I seek to accomplish something like Lowe's reclamation project through understanding more fully the transformation that Bonds traces, from the perspectives that Hoeckner explores. Yet, my emphasis is in the end not,

like Hoeckner's and Bonds's, on German traditions themselves, but on their consequences, specifically on the effects of German Idealism on receptive practices regarding earlier and subsequent repertories that do *not* fit easily into its modes of engagement. And while I, like Lowe, am much interested in the objectifying dimension of absolute music, based on its theoretical separation from referents to the real world, I am even more interested in the motivation for this dimension: by imagining music as disconnected from everyday reality, German Idealism enables music to serve more effectively as a link to something beyond that reality. See chapter 1 (especially 8–11) for Lowe's principal discussion of the idealist dimension of absolute music. (See also Weber, "Musical Idealism," which I discuss in chapter 4.)

4. Proksch, *Reviving Haydn*, 7. See also Botstein, "Consequences of Presumed Innocence" (an expansion of Botstein, "Demise of Philosophical Listening"); both Proksch and Botstein trace Haydn's "demotion" through writings by, among others, E. T. A. Hoffmann (1813), Robert Schumann (1839 and 1841), Franz Brendel (1852), Eduard Hanslick (1856), Adolf Bernhard Marx (1857), Hans von Bülow (1858), Adolph Kullak (1860), Ludwig Nohl (1866), and Nietzsche (1880s). Botstein notes, across the nineteenth century, a muted regard for Haydn that cuts across conflicts surrounding Wagner and program music, and finds this attitude of a piece with the rise of romanticism and the "work aesthetic," along with habitual veneration of Beethoven and Mozart, for whom Haydn's role as a precursor was seen as his central contribution to history. Botstein also notes ("Consequences of Presumed Innocence,"16–17) the dissenting view of Hermann Kretschmar (1919), who sets the tone for later twentieth-century musicology by extolling Haydn's profundity as a counterargument to his "presumed innocence" during his century of wholesale demotion.

As counterweight to these arguments, see Head, "Music with 'No Past?,'" which focuses on the complex receptive environment for *The Creation*. For other overviews of Haydn's vacillating reputation, see Geiringer, "Portrait of Haydn"; and Garratt, "Haydn and Posterity," the latter additionally valuable for its survey of other writers dealing with this topic. Lawrence Kramer, "Kitten and Tiger," finds Tovey's championing of Haydn as a musical master emblematic and anticipatory of others in the twentieth century who attempted to rescue Haydn's reputation by showing Haydn's conformance to Kantian virtues (without, typically, mentioning Kant). Elsewhere in Clark, *Cambridge Companion to Haydn* (which includes both "Haydn and Posterity" and "Kitten and Tiger"), Webster, "Haydn's Aesthetics," makes that case explicitly (see note 74).

5. The "we," "us," and "our" that I use throughout this book, perhaps presumptuously, refer most directly to those who share my inherited US American culture, but will, I hope, often embrace those for whom Haydn or US American popular musics have mattered, as well. I use these collective terms invitationally, and to signal what I hope to be a broad base of shared interests, concerns, and experiences among readers of this book.
6. The term "musicking" and the critical context for much of the argument in this chapter derive from the work of Christopher Small, especially *Musicking*. Regarding the difficulty of performing surgery on the concept, history, and legacy of "absolute music" from within the operating theater of musicology, see Daniel Chua's often-devastating *Absolute Music and the Construction of Meaning*, especially the final sentence of chapter 1: "To write a history of absolute music is to write against it" (7).
7. The metaphoric basis of this section in chemistry predates the "chemical experiment" described in Chua, "Haydn as Romantic"; the intriguing "chemistry" between his evocative discussion and the issues I raise here resonates more specifically with other parts of my argument, however.
8. Hanslick, *Vom Musikalische-Schönen*. Geoffrey Payzant's translation (1986) usefully includes a historical overview and survey of later editions. See also Dahlhaus, *Idea of Absolute Music*; and Bonds, *Music as Thought* and *Absolute Music*.
9. This entrenched view of music as essentially abstract, most famously articulated in Stravinsky's claim that music expresses nothing, has been under increasing attack in recent decades by many scholars, most influentially by Susan McClary, Anthony Newcomb, and Lawrence Kramer. Regarding the period under discussion, see especially McClary's "Pitches, Expression, Ideology," "Musical Dialectic," *Feminine Endings*, "Narrative Agendas," "Narratives of Bourgeois Subjectivity," "Constructions of Subjectivity," and "Impromptu"; Newcomb's "Once More," "Schumann," "Narrative Archetypes," and "Polonaise-Fantasy"; and L. Kramer's *Music as Cultural Practice, Classical Music and Postmodern Knowledge*, and *Musical Meaning*.
10. See Pederson, "A. B. Marx"; especially relevant is her discussion of the agendas of those promoting this rise (especially Marx), and of the resulting shift in the audience's role, from an appreciation of the performance to a contemplative engagement with the work being performed. Pederson's linking of these efforts with nationalism has been challenged by many who make a careful, if slippery, distinction between cultural and political nationalism. See, for example, Celia Applegate, "How German Is It?"; in positing a less central role for political nationalism in the elevation of music, however, Applegate neither denies the place Marx and others claimed for "serious" music within the

context of a developing German nationalism, nor argues effectively against either the gravity of the consequences or the often pernicious tenacity of this coupling. Related accounts may be found in Applegate and Potter's *Music and German National Identity*; Gramit's *Cultivating Music*; and Bonds's *Music as Thought*.

11. This despite the importance of one aspect of that history—the national origin of a particular piece—to many of those who promoted a work-oriented aesthetic.
12. "Who Cares If You Listen?" was originally published in *High Fidelity Magazine* and has been frequently reprinted. That the title was not Babbitt's own scarcely detracts from its aptness in describing his often belligerent firsthand account of the estrangement between the modern composer and his or her audience. Regarding this estrangement in general, see McClary's "Terminal Prestige."
13. Cf. Richard Taruskin's related observation, from the performer's perspective: "Modernist performance ethics, serving the idealization of the objectified work and seeking by the proscriptive use of research evidence to keep the threateningly contingent subjectivity of the performer at bay, has received a great boost from modern technology. In broadcast and recording situations, where the physical presence of the audience has been (or can be) removed from the scene, the audience, and any responsibility owed it, can be all the more easily forgotten" (Taruskin, *Text and Act*, 23). The ludicrous (and rather sad) picture that emerges is of performer and audience strenuously pretending the other does not exist in order to project a mystical communion with "the work itself." For once, we may be grateful to the commerce-driven star system for keeping the relationship between performer and audience in the foreground, if frequently at the expense of artistic prestige.
14. I have written in a different context about how successful performance welds performer and her or his material into a single event, as an expression of personal identity (Knapp, *American Musical and Personal Identity*; for related arguments, see Wolf, *A Problem Like Maria*). That this central position for the performer is also fundamental to the "classical" tradition has occasioned considerable uneasiness regarding the relationship between performing stars and the most revered works in the canon. We must remember, however, that in the eighteenth century, performers eclipsed composers more often than not, both in prestige and in their capacity to attract audiences.
15. As Taruskin argues (*Text and Act*, 10–11), "interpretation" has become anathema within the historical performance movement, which assumes a hierarchy he likens to that of Wagner's *Ring*: "The producers of timeless works are the gods, exulting in their liberation from the world of social ("extramusical") obligation and issuing peremptory commands. The recipients of the

commands are the Nibelungs, bound scrupulously to carry out the masters' intentions for the sake of their glory, their own lives pledged to a sterile humdrum of preservation and handing-on. . . . There is also a class of Alberichs, of course, Nibelungs (chiefly of the podium, the keyboard, and the larynx) who aspire to godlike power, and who are dependably crushed for their hubris by critics and pedagogues, the priests of the *Werktreue* faith, though their fellow Nibelungs secretly egg them on and they enjoy wide sympathy among the mortals in the outer darkness of the hall." If the need for at least some interpretation is more typically felt with regard to traditional modern performance, these hierarchies are nevertheless maintained with some rigidity. To cite a typical example: a thoughtful review by Chris Pasles, of a performance of Beethoven's Seventh Symphony and Brahms's Second Concerto by the Los Angeles Philharmonic (conducted by Mark Wigglesworth, with Stephen Kovacevich as soloist) sums up the performance of the Beethoven as "not a performance in which the conductor ventured an individual interpretation. . . . It was, however, an exciting realization of Beethoven's music." The implication that more interpretive license might be welcomed is amended at the end of the review, as if to conform to Taruskin's claims about historical performance: "The conductor may yet decide to offer more personally distinctive 'interpretations.' . . . Right now, though, he can offer something better: the composer's music." The discussion of the Brahms concerto addresses the other dimension of this hierarchy: "Simply radiant was Ronald Leonard's cello solo. . . . But so too was the playing of the whole section at that point. Add the sensitive pianissimos in the violins and you come full circle back to Wigglesworth balancing the orchestra and how important that is." We do not even hear of "interpretation" from such menials as the individual players; all—even "simply radiant" solo playing—is to be understood as an extension of the conductor, who is to be understood as, most importantly, a servant to the composer (Pasles, "Wigglesworth").

16. See chapter 5 of Gramit's *Cultivating Music* for an account of the public concert's ascension, especially (regarding Beethoven) 158–160.
17. Even Theodor Adorno finds that Mahler approaches "chamber-music procedures" in his Fourth Symphony, stemming in that case from his severe reduction of the orchestra but also providing a model for many of his later works (*Mahler*, 53). The care with which Adorno circumscribes his claim for a chamber affinity—he is quick to point out that the Fourth does not remain chamber music, and that, when needed, "chamber complexities are joined as an element" to "massive tutti effects"—is, however, exceptional, so that hearing Mahler's symphonies as a kind of chamber music has now become commonplace. The contrast between the "chamber" qualities of Haydn's and Mahler's symphonies—Haydn's based in practical matters, and Mahler's in

an idealized (thus manufactured) sense of intimacy—stems first of all from the fact that Haydn's symphonies were composed before conductors as we now think of them became fixtures of concert orchestral performance.

18. Knapp, "Suffering Children," revised as chapter 7 in *Symphonic Metamorphoses*.
19. Five excellent accounts of the rise of German Idealism, from quite different perspectives, are chapter 12 of Randall Collins's *The Sociology of Philosophies*; chapters 14–15 of Alasdair MacIntyre's *A Short History of Ethics*; part 1 of Friedrich Kittler's *Discourse Networks, 1800/1900*; and, most comprehensively for the first generation, Dieter Henrich's *Between Kant and Hegel* and George di Giovanni's *Freedom and Religion in Kant and His Immediate Successors*. The latter is the most systematic account available of the specific contributions of the many philosophers involved in this development, including most of those I include in my own brief sketch. For a comprehensive account of the aesthetic tradition that developed in conjunction with German Idealism, see Bowie, *Aesthetics and Subjectivity*; see also Hammermeister, *German Aesthetic Tradition* (for which, however, musical aesthetics plays only an incidental role).
20. See Özkirimli, *Theories of Nationalism*, for a representative survey of how nationalism has been theorized and critiqued.
21. As Dieter Henrich notes, "In Johann Gottlieb Fichte's *Science of Knowledge*, the romantic theory of art and poetry originated. . . . The early romantics considered themselves to be students of Fichte" (*Between Kant and Hegel*, 3; see also chapter 15).
22. A. MacIntyre, *Short History of Ethics*, 197; see also A. MacIntyre, *After Virtue*.
23. Among many studies that place aesthetics, and especially poetry, at the center of the rise of German Idealism, see especially part 1 of Kittler's *Discourse Networks*.
24. Collins, *Sociology of Philosophies*, 628–630.
25. "Kurz wir verlangen, daß jede poetische Komposition neben dem, was ihr Inhalt ausdrückt, zugleich durch ihre Form Nachahmung und Ausdruck von Empfindungen sei und als Musik auf uns wirke" (Friedrich Schiller, "Über Matthisons Gedichte," quoted in *Schillers Werke*, 272).
26. See Riggs, "On the Representation of Character."
27. For a more extensive discussion of this flow of ideas, from idealism to perceiving untexted music as the highest art, see Bonds, *Music as Thought*, especially chapter 1. Bonds's project, along with my own, runs in parallel with that of Michael P. Steinberg's *Listening to Reason*; all three are concerned, from different perspectives, with the transformative consequences for music and its place in culture across the nineteenth century accruing from the valorization of subjectivity. Lydia Goehr offers a related discussion, tracing music's rapid ascent to aesthetic preeminence in this period; see Goehr, *Imaginary*

Museum, especially chapter 6. See also Gay, "Bourgeois Experiences, IV: The Art of Listening," in *Naked Heart*, 11–35; and Bowie, *Aesthetics and Subjectivity*.

For a broader treatment of the developments traced in this section, extending from Johann Mattheson through the 1820s, and placing philosophical inquiry against a background of developing musical aesthetics and practices, see chapter 2 of Applegate, *Bach in Berlin*. Two other studies illuminate specific developments traced here. Chapter 15 of Henrich's *Between Kant and Hegel* delineates the dynamic transmutation of Fichte's arguments about imagination and longing (*The Science of Knowledge*, 1794–1795) into the work of this generation of German romantic poets—specifically, Schlegel, Novalis, and Hölderlin; whereas Chantler, *Hoffmann's Musical Aesthetics*, explores the basis and development of Hoffmann's approach to musical hermeneutics (see especially chapter 3).

Hoffmann's review of Beethoven's Fifth Symphony is a classic text available in many sources, most usefully (in English) in *Hoffmann's Musical Writings*.

28. While Hegel elevated music to a romantic art—purely inward through being nonspatial—he betrayed his conservative bent by ranking it below poetry, owing to its lack of content; see Hammermeister, *German Aesthetic Tradition*, 100. Regarding especially Schelling's importance in these developments, see chapter 4 of Bowie, *Aesthetics and Subjectivity*.
29. Regarding Wagner's shift, see Dahlhaus, "Twofold Truth in Wagner's Aesthetics." For Wagner's original argument, see Wagner, *Richard Wagner*, vii; in Wagner, *Richard Wagner's Prose Works*, ii, see especially part 1.vii.106–111, and part 3.iii.289–290. Regarding Wagner's problematic argument about Beethoven's Ninth Symphony, see Knapp, "Reading Gender in Late Beethoven."

    Wagner's pronouncement indirectly underscores how oppressively male-centered the histories recounted in this chapter are—histories, we may note, that mainly concern the ways male philosophers, aestheticians, and composers redefined the importance, role, and practices of music. Wagner echoes a longstanding understanding of music as a feminine realm, which remained a source of deep anxiety throughout this evolution of (male) thought. Moreover, that anxiety continues to express itself today in many ways, for example in persistent gender-based protectionist attitudes (and sometimes policies) about women participating in various aspects of musicking, from performing in orchestras, jazz bands, and rock groups to composing to conducting research and writing about music.
30. Regarding Schopenhauer's elevation of music to the highest of the arts, with metaphysical significance, within a wider consideration of German Aesthetics, see Hammermeister, *German Aesthetic Tradition*, 124; and Bowie, *Aesthetics and Subjectivity*, 264–270.

31. Knapp, "*Selbst dann bin ich die Welt.*"
32. See Pederson, "A. B. Marx," regarding Marx's direct contributions to this shift in understanding.
33. For related discussions, see Chua, "Haydn as Romantic"; and Bonds, *Music as Thought*, 10–12. Regarding Hoffmann's essay, see Bonds, *Music as Thought*, chapters 1–3; and Chantler, *Hoffmann's Musical Aesthetics*.
34. Bonds, *Music as Thought*, prologue and chapters 4–5.
35. Bonds, *Music as Thought*, 65.
36. See chapter 6 of Knapp, *American Musical and National Identity*, regarding this specific theoretical derivation for European nationalism. Regarding Schiller, see Solomon's *Beethoven Essays*; Nelson's "Fantasy of Absolute Music"; and Alpers's "Schiller's Naive and Sentimental Poetry."
37. For a delineation of Schiller's theories as applied to composing music, see Nelson, "Fantasy of Absolute Music," 164–205.
38. Bonds, *Music as Thought*, chapter 5, argues that culture rather than land is the issue for early German nationalists. Yet, in detailing an idealist core of nationalist thought back to Herder that distinguished between nation and state (82–83), Bonds also traces an alarming strand of xenophobia that developed alongside this core (84–87). Arguably, land and who it belongs to by cultural heritage will inevitably emerge as the ultimate concerns of nationalist ideology, however lofty its initial aims, although the essentializing of race as a basis for culture is perhaps more directly a consequence of behavior learned independent of nationalism.
39. I am indebted to Eva Sobolevski, Stuart de Ocampo, and Ewelina Boczkowska, whose work has heightened my awareness of this dimension of Chopin's music.
40. In Richter, *Vorschule der Ästhetik*, see section 22 of "V. Programm: Über die romantische Dichtkunst": "Wesen der romantischen Dichtkunst—Verschiedenheiten der südlichen und der nordischen" (The Nature of Romantic Poetry—Differences between the Southern and Northern Types), 86–92. Readily available English translations may be found in Willson, *German Romantic Criticism*, 49–54; and Strunk and Solie, *Source Readings in Music History*, 6.14–18.
41. Forbes, *Thayer's Life of Beethoven*, 956; the anecdote comes from Karl Gottfried Freudenberg's *Erinnerungen eines alten Organisten*.
42. Pederson, "A. B. Marx."
43. Schumann, without directly denouncing Brendel, who succeeded him in editing the *Neue Zeitschrift für Musik* in 1844, resisted invitations to contribute to the journal until "Neue Bahnen" (1853), in which he championed newcomer Brahms as a rising star among a list of twelve others, while point-

edly leaving Berlioz, Liszt, Wagner, and other favorites of Brendel off the list. (Schumann's early admiration for Berlioz had by then faded, although he remained an admirer of his conducting.)

44. Brahms himself remained at heart a German, not an Austrian. Regarding his attempts to recruit Dvořák for Vienna, see Beveridge, "Dvořák and Brahms." Regarding Dvořák's Viennese reception, see Brodbeck, "Dvořák's Reception in Liberal Vienna," and chapter five of Brodbeck, *Defining "Deutschtum."*
45. La Grange, *Gustav Mahler*, 2:172–174.
46. Chopin would also eventually be "adopted"—by no less than Heinrich Schenker, who "elevated" Chopin to his list of "great German masters," arguing that, "for the profundity with which nature has endowed him, Chopin belongs more to Germany than to Poland." Schenker, *Masterwork in Music*, 1:81.
47. Taruskin, "Nationalism," 2006.
48. Regarding the turn to romanticism in Italian opera, see Tomlinson, "Italian Romanticism."
49. As Richard Taruskin puts it, "Yet under that rubric [*Ars gallica*], the society fostered the most thoroughgoing Germanification (or 'New-Germanification') French music ever endured" (Taruskin, "Nationalism," 2006, section 8).
50. Regarding "utility," see Pasler, *Composing the Citizen*, especially chapter 1 and part 4.
51. Regarding the shared epistemological basis of Impressionism and Expressionism, see Dahlhaus, *Realism in Nineteenth-Century Music*, 114–120.
52. For a cogent explanation for how the Germanic center of this enterprise survived World War II stronger than ever—ironically, largely through the work of a generation of US American musicologists who had fled Germany in the years surrounding the war—see Josephson, "German Musical Exile"; see also Brinkmann and Wolff, *Driven into Paradise*.
53. Regarding Mendelssohn's performance and its background, see Applegate, *Bach in Berlin*.
54. Forkel, *Über Johann Sebastian Bachs Leben*, 124.
55. Taruskin, "Nationalism," 2006, section 2; and Taruskin, *Oxford History of Western Music*, 2:237–238 and 2:313–327; see also Smith, *Handel's Oratorios*.
56. The phrase "holy German art" is sung by Hans Sachs near the end of Wagner's *Die Meistersinger von Nürnberg*, and echoed by the *Volk* just before the final curtain: "Ehrt eure deutschen Meister, / dann bannt ihr gute Geister; / und gebt ihr ihrem Wirken Gunst, / zerging' in Dunst / das heil'ge röm'sche Reich, / uns bliebe gleich / die heil'ge deutsche Kunst! / Heil! Sachs! / Nürnbergs teurem Sachs!" (Honor your German Masters, / if you would conjure their good spirits; / and if you favor their works, / even if in mist vanishes / the Holy Roman Empire, / for us would yet remain / holy German Art! /

Hail! Sachs! / Nuremberg's dear Sachs!) The opera premiered in 1868, but this phrase dates to 1851 (just after the Bach Edition was launched), where it concludes an early prose sketch of the opera.

57. Handel, too, was reclaimed early on as a giant of German music, but his association with Italian opera and his career in England, coupled with a perceived lack of depth relative to Bach (thus, substituting large effect for contrapuntal rigor), led to a declining reputation in the German lands, running roughly in parallel to Bach's ascent.
58. Knapp, "*Selbst dann bin ich die Welt.*"
59. For Nietzsche's arguments, see his "On Music and Words," included as an appendix (trans. Walter Kaufmann) in Dahlhaus, *Between Romanticism and Modernism.*
60. Mendelssohn's *Die erste Walpurgisnacht* (1832, rev. 1842–1843), *St. Paul* (1836), *Lobgesang* Symphony (no. 2, 1840), and *Elijah* (1846); Schumann's *Das Paradies und die Peri* (1843) and *Scenen aus Goethes Faust* (1844–1853); and Brahms's *Ein deutsches Requiem* (1865–1868) and *Schicksalslied* (1868–1871), among others.
61. Among other writings, see McClary, "Blasphemy of Talking Politics"; Chafe, *Tonal Allegory*; and Taruskin, "Facing Up."
62. Thus, Michael P. Steinberg's brilliant reading of *Don Giovanni* in terms of a Protestant-Catholic/modern-Baroque dialectic (Steinberg, *Listening to Reason*, 23–39) cannot account for this ending as other than a lie, concluding that "the nineteenth-century performance convention that omitted the *lieto fine* may have been onto something: notably, the possibility of the work's mendacity along with that of its characters, its indulgence of the survivors' advocacy of an exhausted social ideology" (39). Here Steinberg seems oddly less willing than in his later discussion of *Così fan tutte* (51–58) to confront how Mozart's basic conservatism intertwines with his dramatic and formal sensibilities.
63. Cf. Charles Rosen's discussion of finales in Rosen, *Classical Style*, 274–280.
64. Regarding how musical conventions signify, see McClary, *Conventional Wisdom.*
65. See McClary, "Musical Dialectic," regarding the dynamic between the individual and the larger order as it unfolds in the middle movement of Mozart's Concerto in G Major, K. 453.
66. Regarding the emergence of "Wolfgang Amadeus" as Mozart's definitive name, see Solomon, *Mozart*, chapter 18.
67. Anderson, *Letters of Mozart*, 769.
68. Lowe, *Pleasure and Meaning*, provides a wide-ranging discussion of the entertainment culture that supported the public concert in the eighteenth century. Tracing the same fault lines from a different perspective, Chua,

"Haydn as Romantic," proposes an alternative delineation, between the eighteenth century's (mechanical) body and the nineteenth century's (organic) soul.

69. See Proksch, *Reviving Haydn*, regarding Haydn's continued popularity across the nineteenth century, often against the grain of routine critical dismissal of his music. Noting the persistent respect among many composers and critics for Haydn's *Creation* and the long-persistent popularity of his symphonies among audiences, Proksch also discusses the strategies of Hans von Bülow, which would serve as a kind of model for others, who came to use Haydn as "the musical equivalent of an appetizer" (*Reviving Haydn*, 44).
70. Regarding Mozart's difficulty with the "Haydn" quartets, see Rosen, *Classical Style*, 265. Regarding the development of Beethoven's op. 18, including speculations regarding his second thoughts, see Forbes, *Thayer's Life of Beethoven*, 261–264.
71. Rosen, *Classical Style*, parts 2 and 3.
72. See, for example, Rosen, *Classical Style*, part 6, chapter 3, especially, 367–368.
73. As James Webster argues, Haydn's (and Mozart's) "sublime" partook of an earlier paradigm, which shifted, with Beethoven, from a rhetorical domain to a Kantian category, with Haydn's *Creation* functioning, in reception, as an important hinge; see Webster, "*Creation*," 57–60.
74. "Lieber Beethoven! Sie reisen itzt nach Wien zur Erfüllung Ihrer so lange bestrittenen Wünsche. Mozarts Genius trauert noch und beweinet den Tod seines Zöglings. Bei dem unerschöpflichen Haydn fand er Zuflucht, aber keine Beschäftigung; durch ihn wünscht er noch einmal mit jemandem vereinigt zu werden. Durch ununterbrochenen Fleiß erhalten Sie: Mozarts Geist aus Haydns Händen" (Beloved Beethoven! You are going to Vienna in fulfillment of your long-frustrated wishes. The Genius of Mozart is mourning and weeping over the death of her pupil. She has found a refuge but no occupation with the inexhaustible Haydn. Through him she wishes to form a union with another. With the help of assiduous labor you shall receive: Mozart's spirit from Haydn's hands). James Webster argues, from a different perspective, that Haydn, through being original, satisfied Kant's definition of genius—without, however, explaining the discrepancy between this finding and Waldstein's condescension, which also reflects German Idealist standards (Webster, "Haydn's Aesthetics," 43–44).
75. Rosen, *Classical Style*, part 7.
76. See Schroeder, *Haydn and the Enlightenment*, especially chapter 1.
77. Chapter 5 of Melanie Lowe's *Pleasure and Meaning* gives an excellent account of how Haydn's "fart joke" is absorbed into the processes of the movement. Gretchen Wheelock provides an extensive exploration of Haydn's comic side in her *Haydn's Ingenious Jesting with Art*. And Scott Burnham offers a useful

overview of expressed perspectives on Haydn's humor as part of his own exploration of the topic ("Haydn and Humor").

78. Forbes, *Thayer's Life of Beethoven*, 1044.
79. This phrase achieved notoriety from an essay on Beethoven published in *Reader's Digest* (Peattie, "Beethoven"), which was then included with a set of recordings of the nine symphonies released by *Reader's Digest* in 1962, under the title "Beethoven: The Man Who Set Music Free."
80. Regarding Beethoven's "nobility pretense," see chapter 3 of Solomon, *Beethoven Essays*.
81. Blume, *Classic and Romantic Music*; and Rosen, *Classical Style*.
82. See Knapp, "On the Inner Dimension" and "*Selbst dann bin ich die Welt.*"
83. Weber, "Musical Idealism."
84. Precursors for this divide included, most importantly for the nineteenth century, what Carl Dahlhaus called the Beethoven-Rossini *Stildualismus* (see Dahlhaus, *Nineteenth-Century Music*, 8–9), and, along related lines, A. B. Marx's more generalized insistence on Beethoven over Italian opera. The former is explored from a variety of perspectives in Mathew and Walton, *Invention of Beethoven and Rossini*, the latter in Pederson, "A. B. Marx."
85. See Weber, *Music and the Middle Class*.
86. See Knapp, *American Musical and National Identity*, 63–66, and chapter 4 below for further discussion of this confluence. Christy's Minstrels first performed at St. James's Hall (in Piccadilly Circus) in 1857, where they appeared intermittently until disbanding, whereupon an entirely new group formed, initially under the same name, beginning their thirty-five-year run there in 1865.
87. Concerning the cultivation of European music in the United States during the later nineteenth century, see Baur's "Let Me Make the Ballads"; Horowitz's *Wagner Nights*; and Locke and Barr's *Cultivating Music in America*.
88. Still others catered to foreign-language-based immigrant communities, ranging from the serious to the considerably less so. The most influential of these were German-based and, slightly later and overlapping, Yiddish-based. Regarding the former, see Koegel, *Music in German Immigrant Theater*; regarding the latter, see Sandrow, *Vagabond Stars*. The desire of these constituent populations to assimilate, at least outwardly, led both these traditions to merge with a variety of English-language traditions, especially vaudeville (including blackface) and the American musical. Regarding the assimilationist dimension of the latter, see Most, *Making Americans*, and, more generally, Knapp, *American Musical and National Identity*.
89. When the separateness of those worlds was not enforced, partial assimilation was the more likely outcome, as when, occasionally, African-descended musicians achieved distinction within European traditions (for example,

the Chevalier de Saint-Georges, né Joseph Boulogne, or, in the United States, Francis Johnson). Assimilation, too, resulted in some musical crossbreeding, but precisely because of the more generally enforced racial segregation, which affected all forms of musicking.

90. For an overview of this symphony's mix of spirituals, Indianist idioms, and European traditions, see Beckerman, *New Worlds of Dvořák*. The Russian "magic" harmonic practices I refer to include octatonic passages (based on what contemporaries called the "Rimsky" scale) that occur in the evocative introductions of both the first movement and the second, and in reprises of the latter's chordal passages later in the movement. The Russian orchestral manner, of repeating short themes with different orchestral color (described in Taruskin, "How the Acorn Took Root"), is most evident in the finale.

91. See Hamm, "Dvořák in America." Easiest to construe as naïve was Dvořák's equivocation among the musics of different ethnic or racial groups in the United States. Thus, as part of his discussion of the "New World" Symphony (*New York Herald*, December 15, 1893; as given in Tibbetts, "Appendix A," 363), he claims (astonishingly, if taken out of context): "I found that the music of the Negroes and of the Indians was practically identical." Here, he was writing specifically about their use of a gapped or pentatonic scale; later, he was more careful: "A while ago I suggested that inspiration for truly national music might be derived from the Negro melodies or Indian chants," he said, following this with a discussion of how authenticity might be judged considering the mixed origin of the former, and along the way concluding that "it matters little whether the inspiration for the coming folk songs of America is derived from the Negro melodies, the songs of the creoles, the red man's chant, or the plaintive ditties of the homesick German or Norwegian. Undoubtedly the germs for the best in music lie hidden among all the races that are commingled in this great country" ("Music in America," *Harper's New Monthly Magazine*, February 1895; as given in Tibbetts, "Appendix A," 376, and 377). The musical commingling that Dvořák projects in this interview is evident in the "New World" Symphony, offered as a prototype.

92. Michael Beckerman's about-face regarding the second movement's basis in a spiritual idiom represents a partial exception to this kind of denial, since his position of denial was based not on an essentialist argument but on strong documentary evidence for an alternative programmatic basis, which he later amended because of new evidence (and a reconsideration of older evidence and testimony); cf. Beckerman, "Dvořák's 'New World'"; and chapter 9 of Beckerman, *New Worlds of Dvořák*.

93. For a concise and balanced account of Copland's quest for an "American" music, and of its reception, see Pollack, *Aaron Copland*, 526–531. For a related

discussion of this period, see Levy, "From Orient to Occident." For a reconsideration of the entrenched view that the "open-plains" idiom originated with Copland, see Hubbs, *Gay Modernists*.

2 | ENTERTAINING POSSIBILITIES IN HAYDN'S SYMPHONIES

1. Thanks to Elisabeth Le Guin for pointing out the relevance of the etymology of "entertain" in this context.
2. For related discussions, see Brown's "Haydn's Chaos"; L. Kramer's "Haydn's Chaos, Schenker's Order" and "Music and Representation"; R. Kramer's "Haydn's *Chaos* and Herder's *Logos*"; B. C. MacIntyre's *Haydn* (especially 67–80); Solomon's "Some Images of Creation"; Temperley's *Haydn: "The Creation"* (especially 47–51); Webster's "*Creation*"; Holloway's "Haydn," 333–334; and Head's "Music with 'No Past?'"
3. Howard E. Smither calls this pizzicato stroke "priceless" and a "typically Haydnesque touch" (*History of the Oratorio*, 3:506), noting that what makes it so is its rationalist, mechanistic basis (personal communication, May, 1984). Lawrence Kramer likens this moment to "a biblical 'siehe!'" ("Music and Representation," 29). And Richard Kramer observes that it betokens "the happy accident of unexpected discovery—God finds the light switch, as someone once put it," observing that Haydn thus "humanizes the act of creation" ("Haydn's *Chaos* and Herder's *Logos*," 160 and 168).
4. In such movements, there is generally at least one other clearly differentiated theme, often appearing after the second group is well under way and confirming the new tonic. Bonds, "Haydn's 'Cours complet,'" argues that Haydn's employing a version of the main theme to articulate the second thematic group solidified around 1772, as part of a "complete course in composition" then under way. Regarding Haydn's "departures from conventions" in recapitulations (as defined later, according to Beethoven's and Mozart's usual practices), see Edwards, "Papa Doc's Recap Caper." For an argument against some standard explanations for such departures, see Neuwirth, "'Monothematic' Expositional Design."
5. Regarding Haydn's "false recapitulations," see Bonds, "Haydn's False Recapitulations"; and Hepokoski and Darcy, *Elements of Sonata Theory*, 226–228.
6. Regarding Haydn's "named" symphonies, see Walter, "Über Haydns 'Sharakteristische' Sinfonien."
7. The nickname "Military" became attached to the symphony soon after its premier, after its warlike gestures were recognized as such in early reviews; see Landon, *Haydn*, 3:247 and note 22 below.

8. Regarding the *ombra* topic, see Ratner, *Classic Music*; Allanbrook, *Rhythmic Gesture in Mozart*, 197–198, 292–319, and 361; McClary, "Narratives of Bourgeois"; and McClelland, *Ombra*.
9. See Rosen, *Classical Style*, 345–350, regarding introductions in the first movements of classical-period instrumental works.
10. Haydn's *Symphonie concertante* employs a mixed four-voice solo group: violin, cello, oboe, and bassoon, situating an independently viable chamber ensemble as a smaller group within the larger group. The mix of chamber and orchestral textures is as important as the mix of symphonic and concerted formal conventions, recalling the similar mixes that occur in some of Haydn's early symphonies (e.g., in the "Morning" Symphony no. 6 in D, from 1761), or the trio-sonata episodes in the symphonies of C. P. E. Bach.
11. Regarding the public concert practices in London in the decades prior to Haydn's visits, see Weber, *Music and the Middle Class*; McLamore, "Symphonic Conventions"; and McVeigh, *Concert Life in London*.
12. I borrow the term "purple patch" from Donald Tovey to describe a common feature in many sonata forms, in which the second group of the exposition includes an episode of harmonic uncertainty, often—as here—just before the closing group.
13. The concerto (Hob. vii h:3), which like the symphony, is in G Major, is included in Haydn, *Concerti mit Orgelleiern*, 141–174. Regarding the *lira organizzata* and the origin of these works, see Edwall, "Ferdinand IV." Regarding modern performance options for the lira organizzata, see Mahling, "Performance Practice." Regarding the transformation of this particular movement, see McCaldin, "Haydn as Self Borrower," who notes, besides the Janissary instruments and the coda, additional wind parts, countermelodies, and links between phrases, arguing (like Dolan, "Haydn," 346) for a more transformative reorchestration than what I claim.

    The frequent assertion that the theme for this movement derives from the French folk song "La gentile et jeune Lisette"—the basis for the slow movement of "La Reine," Symphony no. 85 (discussed below regarding a different self-borrowing)—seems forced, although the similarity may be heard to reinforce the exaggerated *semplice* of the movement's opening (cf. Geiringer, *Joseph Haydn*, 129).
14. Compositionally, of course, the reverse probably occurred, with Haydn reserving this most complacent version of the ubiquitous turn figure for this moment in the first movement and no other.
15. Raymond Monelle (*Musical Topic*, 164) identifies the trumpet call as the *Generalmarsch* of the Austro-Hungarian Army, although the parallels with the

second siege of Vienna (see note 17 below) suggest it is meant to indicate the arrival of Polish troops, using the same system of calls.

16. Landon and Jones, *Haydn*, 174.
17. Regarding the relationship between this symphony and the second siege of Vienna, see Al-Taee, "Sultan's Seraglio," 134–220, especially 181–196. Al-Taee argues that Haydn may have intended the "Turkish" connection already in the concerto version of the movement, as an acknowledgment of the King of Naples' family connection to Vienna, and discusses other instances of scholars finding references in Haydn's symphonies to the Turkish invasions, including nos. 63 and 103.
18. Regarding the "Turkish" or "Janissary" topic, see Meyer, "*Turquerie*"; Griffel, " 'Turkish' Opera"; Obelkevich, "Turkish Affect"; Said, *Orientalism*; T. D. Taylor, "Peopling the Stage"; Hunter, "*Alla Turca* Style"; L. Kramer, "Harem Threshold"; Al-Taee, *Representations of the Orient* and "Sultan's Seraglio, 134–164; Head, *Masquerade and Mozart's Turkish Music*; T. D. Taylor, *Beyond Exoticism*; and Avcioglu, *Turquerie*.
19. H. C. Robbins Landon (*Haydn*, 1:21) provides a suitably grim account of the brutal legacy of the Turks in this area, noting that Haydn's grandfather was "one of the very few [in Hainburg] to hide successfully" from the invading Turks. As noted in Geiringer (*Joseph Haydn*, 5), the Turks were not the only invaders who victimized Haydn's forebears, as his maternal grandparents lost their home a second time in 1707, this time to anti-Hapsburg insurgents.
20. Regarding Haydn's departures from the generic elegance of the minuet in his symphonies, see Lowe, "Falling from Grace"; see also chapter 4 in her *Pleasure and Meaning*.
21. Conventionally, minuets and trios are binary-form dances arranged within a ternary structure with the trio in the middle. This is but one of many instances when a composer will write out the (varied) repeat of a section instead of using repeat signs; most typically, as here, this will occur with the opening, shorter phrase of the minuet. Modern practice has long been to drop the minuet's repetitions in the da capo, although historically informed performances often restore them.
22. A much-quoted review after the first performance of the symphony, from the *Morning Chronicle* (April 9, 1794), indicates that audiences both took the movement's evocation of war seriously and were entertained by it. Thus, "the middle movement was again received with absolute shouts of applause. Encore! encore! encore! resounded from every seat," and "It is the advancing to battle; and the march of men, the sounding of the charge, the thundering of the onset, the clash of arms, the groans of the wounded, and what may well

be called the hellish roar of war increase to a climax of horrid sublimity!" (Landon and Jones, *Haydn*, 248). A later reviewer in the *Morning Chronicle* (May 5, 1794) distinguished between the Janissary intrusion in the second movement and the recollection of these instruments at the end of the finale (which was deemed "grating and offensive") by noting that the earlier use is programmatic: "They inform us that the army is marching to battle, and, calling up all the ideas of the terror of such a scene, give it reality. Discordant sounds are then sublime; for what can be more horribly discordant to the heart than thousands of men meeting to murder each other" (Schroeder, *Haydn and the Enlightenment*, 183).

23. This reflects, to be sure, a contemporary, Eurocentric view of things, able to see the "higher" level of sophistication of European culture much more readily than the barbarous realities of Europeans subduing conquered peoples in Africa, the New World, and Asia. Although it would not have fit the stipulations of my rhetorical question for European audiences in the eighteenth century, European-based conquerors had long been avid pupils of their vanquished, in both music and dance, hungry to feed their taste for the exotic in ways that would later be understood as Orientalist.
24. Head, "Haydn's Exoticisms," 82–85, makes a similar argument about Haydn's use of the gypsy topic, which in extension meshes well with my discussion of *Il Distratto* below.
25. Webster, "Haydn's Symphonies," champions an earlier group of Haydn symphonies with special reference to the categories of "comedy" and "entertainment" (as opposed but not irreconcilable to "art"). Webster cites parts of some later works, as well, including the returning Janissary instruments in the finale of the "Military" (231).
26. Schroeder, *Haydn and the Enlightenment*, 13–20.
27. See, in this regard, Elias, *History of Manners*, 1–34; and Hartman, *Fateful Question of Culture*, 205–224. See also Knapp, "*Selbst dann bin ich die Welt.*"
28. Carl Dahlhaus elaborates the category of "musical prose," derived from Wagner's *Oper und Drama*, in "Musical Prose"; "Issues in Composition"; *Nineteenth-Century Music*, 199–200; and *Realism in Nineteenth-Century Music*.
29. Knapp, "*Selbst dann bin ich die Welt.*"
30. A. MacIntyre, *After Virtue*, 146.
31. Schroeder, *Haydn and the Enlightenment*, 115–116.
32. A. MacIntyre, *After Virtue*, 121.
33. Regarding the latter, see Knapp, "*Selbst dann bin ich die Welt.*"
34. A. MacIntyre, *After Virtue*, 187–191.
35. Morris, "Musical Virtues."
36. Small, *Musicking*.

37. Of particular interest is the persistence of the Germanic bent of American musicology, which Josephson ("German Musical Exile") explains in terms of population shifts related to World War II; see also Brinkmann and Wolff, *Driven into Paradise.*
38. Pederson, "A. B. Marx."
39. Hence the conference described at the opening of chapter 1, "'A Clever Orator': Colloquies and Performances Exploring Rhetoric in Haydn's Chamber Music." Beghin and Goldberg's *Haydn and the Performance of Rhetoric* includes many essays deriving from that conference.
40. McClary, "Musical Dialectic."
41. This view of things finds ample resonance in Haydn's time, and, as Elaine Sisman has shown, with specific reference to *Il Distratto*. Thus, regarding the play this music was originally written for, in its originally French version, Sisman writes, "[Gotthold Ephraim] Lessing [writing in 1769] even dealt with the question of the morality of making a particular character, an absent-minded person, the object of a comedy, as Regnard did in his *Le distrait* (1697). . . . Lessing disagreed with those who believed comedy should concern itself with faults that can be improved and therefore that absent-mindedness should not be ridiculed because it cannot be remedied and is only a malady, not a vice. He claimed that, to the contrary, the fault can easily be remedied, and, in addition, that the character himself is a virtuous man whose character may otherwise be admired; he becomes, in a sense, a moral character with a comic flaw" (Sisman, "Haydn's Theater Symphonies," 311; based on Lessing, *Hamburg Dramaturgy*).
42. Three valuable considerations of *Il Distratto* are available. Sisman ("Haydn's Theater Symphonies," 311–321) probes the ways in which the work, as a symphony, strongly reflects its theatrical background and function. Wheelock (*Haydn's Ingenious Jesting with Art*, 154–173) considers its comedic aspect in terms of both its original theatrical presentation and its critical reception. And Angermüller ("Haydns *Der Zerstreute*") details the symphony's specific derivation from the entr'acte music for the opera *Der Zerstreute*. The work's theatrical origin should not be construed as evidence that the symphony is not a "true" symphony, for not only did Haydn himself so declare it, but also it seems at least possible that the symphony, as a genre, stood as an originary model for the "reasonable" progress of the music (hence, an *allegro* followed by a slow movement and a minuet), from which the symphony willfully departs, in much the same way that *The Creation*'s opening "Chaos" derives from more normalized sonata procedures. Regarding the general tendency for latter-day critical judgments against symphonies that derive from the stage (as pastiche, or what Landon terms "potpourris"), see Webster, "Haydn's Symphonies."

43. A similar dynamic of correction governs the first movement of Haydn's String Quartet in B♭, op. 64, no. 3, composed much later; see chapter 3.
44. Sisman ("Haydn's Theater Symphonies," 315–316) hears this movement, within its theatrical context, as depicting events in the third act, including an abortive dance and an argument between the female protagonists.
45. This fanfare, in the original theatrical context, was probably meant to lead directly into the final act (Sisman, "Haydn's Theater Symphonies," 316–318).
46. Revisiting the previous tonic, recast as an extended cadential subdominant, is a familiar device in the closing sections of Haydn's expositions. In the first movement of *Il Distratto*, in fact, this device provides the most elaborate moment of distraction, when the string choir becomes "stuck" on a C-major chord during the approach to the exposition's close in G (this passage is the main focus of Sisman's discussion of this movement in "Haydn's Theater Symphonies," 312–313).
47. The "Farewell" Symphony is analyzed at length, and to impressive ends, in Webster, *Haydn's "Farewell" Symphony*. I take it up here, more modestly, to extend Webster's discussion to an aspect of the symphony that he does not consider as such, although our readings are by and large compatible.

The term "Sturm und Drang," used in connection with Haydn, refers either to a period in the early 1770s when he was prone to writing in an angst-ridden minor mode, or to the associated musical style and its textures. The term is based on a mistaken conjecture that this compositional phase was a response to Goethe's Sturm und Drang (referred to in chapter 1), which it in fact preceded. Use of the term has persisted because it is too useful to relinquish; it remains apt as a descriptor, and there has been no explanation forthcoming for this short-lived compositional tendency compelling enough to displace the association with Goethe, an association that suggests, without firm basis, that Haydn and Goethe were both in some way responding to the Zeitgeist. For a useful survey and critique of earlier writers regarding Haydn's Sturm und Drang, see Grim, "Coining of the Term."
48. See Webster, "D Major Interlude," which becomes the basis for his discussions of this passage in Webster, *Haydn's "Farewell" Symphony*. What to call this passage has been as problematic as what to make of it; in calling it an "interlude," Webster (*Haydn's "Farewell" Symphony*, 39–45) takes issue with both Landon's describing it as a displaced second subject (Landon, *Haydn*, 2:302) and Rosen's terming it a "trio" within a sonata-form movement (Rosen, *Classical Style*). In my view, it becomes a matter of emphasis; Webster refuses the "trio" designation because the passage remains unbalanced in context, whereas I retain the term, equivocally, because of the passage's character of respite from its surroundings (a frequent function of trios within minuets), and because of its style and meter, through which the passage would like,

seemingly, to convert the movement's driving triple meter into something more pleasant.

49. Regarding this use of the ♭ VI key area, see McClary, "Pitches, Expression, Ideology." Regarding the idea of a "musical subjunctive," I am much indebted to the as-yet unpublished work of Stuart Deocampo.

50. Charles Rosen cites the opening passage from Haydn's String Quartet in B Minor, op. 33, no. 1, as "the true invention of classical counterpoint" for displaying just this kind of transformation from accompaniment to principal melody: "The opening page of this quartet . . . affirms the distinction between melody and accompaniment. But it then transforms one into the other" (*Classical Style*, 116–117). Regarding this kind of interplay between melodic and supporting voices, see also my discussion of op. 64, no. 3 in chapter 3, and Mary Hunter's discussion of op. 64, no. 2 in "Quartets," 120–122.

    For parallel discussions of "La Reine," see Larsen, "Sonata Form Problems," 276; Feder, "Similarities," 191–192; Harrison, *Haydn*, 69–88; and chapter 8 in Haimo, *Haydn's Symphonic Forms*, especially 181–194.

51. Harrison (*Haydn*, 1 and 113n8) observes that "it is not inconceivable" that Haydn expected his Parisian audience to recognize his allusion to the "Farewell," since the latter had been performed and published in Paris just before. But Harrison's caution seems misplaced; given Haydn's careful thematic manipulation as traced here, he clearly expected his allusion to be recognized, and even staged a kind of teasing game regarding *when* it would be fully recognized, with its emergence in the development confirming his intentionality regarding what many in his audience would have by then at least suspected. In arguing similarly, Ethan Haimo finds Haydn's handling of the allusion, already in the exposition, extravagant enough to call attention to itself: "That Haydn meant the quotation to be heard as a detour is made perfectly plain by the continuation" (Haimo, *Haydn's Symphonic Forms*, 183).

52. "Jupiter" may in some sense be taken as this kind of descriptor, and may be considered the exception that proves the rule. Thus, notably, this now popular title for Mozart's Symphony in C (K. 551) originated with none other than Salomon, the impresario who brought Haydn to London. The common German-language name for this symphony has long been "Symphonie mit der Schlussfuge" (Symphony with the Fugue at the End).

3 | HAYDN, THE STRING QUARTET, AND THE (D)EVOLUTION OF THE CHAMBER IDEAL

1. Haydn's symphonies were numbered according to different systems until the standardization of 104 authenticated symphonies by Eusebius Mandyczewski in 1908, ordered chronologically according to scholarship then available.

Despite many corrections, Mandyczewski's numbering became so widely used that Anthony van Hoboken adopted it as Series I within his catalog of 1957. An older habit has persevered regarding the quartets, which are generally referred to by opus number (long standardized), and by quartet number within each opus (thus, op. 33, no. 3). Since all of Haydn's known quartets were published with opus numbers, most often in groups of six, this method has the advantages of clarity and chronological accuracy. With the quartets, using Hoboken's catalog numbering obscures their presentation within sets and presents a possible confusion with the once prevalent collection of "30 Famous Quartets" (Haydn, *30 berühmte Quartette*).

2. See Sisman, "Haydn's Career," regarding Haydn's strategies for pleasing players, patrons, subscribers, and the public.
3. Weber, "Mass Culture," 177.
4. Weber, "Mass Culture," 178–180.
5. Mary Hunter ("Haydn's London Piano Trios") argues for, and describes particularly well, the social dimension of Haydn's chamber music, and makes a cogent distinction between the ways that his quartets do this relative to his trios. In particular, her demonstration that "the trios model the act of performance as more continuous with the act of composition than do the quartets" (110) meshes particularly well with the inside-outside dynamic I detail below.
6. Regarding the complex of traditions, innovations, and interactions that yielded the "classical string quartet," see David Wyn Jones's "Origins of the Quartet" and W. Dean Sutcliffe's "Haydn, Mozart and Their Contemporaries." Jones exposes the disingenuousness of Haydn's own recollections regarding his contribution (relayed through Griesinger), whereas Sutcliffe details some of the contributions of Haydn's contemporaries, in order to probe the practices and habits of thought that have established Haydn and Mozart as the genre's only important early figures, as well as the growing mystique of the genre both as an emblem of the period and as a "proving ground" for composers. Sutcliffe argues against privileging the quartet as the musical expression of sociality: "Yet the implied distinctions from other genres are at least partly fictional. Almost all later eighteenth-century instrumental music can be understood as having conversational aspects . . . and all instrumental genres can be understood as metaphors for social relations" (186).

   As Ludwig Finscher notes ("Die Theorie des Streichquartetts," 298–299), an indication of the emergent importance of the string quartet as a genre, and of Haydn, Mozart, and Beethoven as the genre's most important composers, was the appearance of these works in study scores, beginning with Pleyel's publication of Haydn's quartets in ten volumes (1798–1802), followed soon after by Mozart's "Haydn Quartets" (1804). Beethoven's late quartets were published in score and parts together, and his earlier quartets were published in score soon after his death.

7. Haydn claimed to have written the op. 33 quartets "in an entirely new and special style," and the two sets employ exactly the same set of keys. For an astute discussion of the development framed by these two sets, including other musical connections between them, see Rosen, *Classical Style*, 115–141, especially 115–120 and 138–141 (quotation as given 116).
8. For this later brief survey, I choose my examples in part to trace a particular line of development with its primary roots in Beethoven; for more comprehensive surveys, see chapters 10–14 of Stowell, *Cambridge Companion* (Stephen Hefling's "Austro-Germanic Quartet Tradition"; Robin Stowell's "Traditional"; Jan Smaczny's "Nineteenth-Century National Traditions"; and Kenneth Gloag's "String Quartet").
9. Roger Hickman, "Haydn," sees the increasing symphonic power in quartet writing as a response to the growing practice of performing them in larger halls during the 1790s, between Haydn's op. 64 and op. 71.
10. Rosen (*Classical Style*, 137–138) offers a cogent argument along these lines: "The string quartet—four-voice polyphony in its clearest non-vocal state—is the natural consequence of a musical language in which expression is entirely based on dissonance to a triad." Finscher, "Die Theorie des Streichquartetts," surveys theoretical understandings of both four-part string writing in general and the string quartet in particular, and considers how "chamber music" came to denote a type of music rather than (merely) a performance venue. Finscher initially stresses the harmonic realm (like Rosen), but then gives greater stress to the contrapuntal dimension, deriving from a perceived differentiation among the four players (as in the "conversation" analogy).
11. Regarding the conversational dimension of Haydn's quartet writing, see especially Finscher, "Die Theorie des Streichquartetts"; Rosen, *Classical Style*, 141–142; and Hunter, "Quartets," 119–122.
12. Martin, "Quartets in Performance." For another "insider" perspective on string quartet playing, often with a more technical orientation, see Waterman, "Playing Quartets." Both Martin and Waterman are cellists.
13. Kerman, "Beethoven Quartet Audiences."
14. Wheelock, *Haydn's Ingenious Jesting with Art*, 90–91. What Wheelock proposes is similar to what Sisman ("Rhetorical Truth") terms "tertiary rhetoric"; regarding the latter, see also Somfai, " . . . *They Are Full of Invention.*"
15. Hecker, *Briefwechsel*, 3:246; see also Botstein, "Patrons and Publics," especially 80–91.
16. Rosen, *Classical Style*, 140. Mirka observes a parallel subterfuge in this opening's manipulation of meter ("Metre," 90–94 and 105–106).

17. The relationship with the Fifth Symphony is closer in technical terms, since the ambiguities of the opening of the Ninth are not between the tonic and its relative, and since the exposition of the latter moves not to the relative but to the submediant.
18. See Knapp, "Tale of Two Symphonies."
19. This is the same rhythmic ambiguity Haydn used in the first movement of *Il Distrato*, and he would later use the same "normalizing" rhythmic impulse to stabilize the exposition in the "Military" Symphony (both discussed in chapter 2).
20. That such an important marker for the secondary key of the exposition should not reappear in the recapitulation is highly unusual. Rosen (*Classical Style*, 72–78) notes how the relative length of recapitulations relates to both Haydn's sense of balance and the need for resolution, citing this movement as an extreme case (73). Edwards ("Papa Doc's Recap Caper," 304) discusses this passage as part of Haydn's subversive approach to recapitulations in general. Hughes (*Haydn String Quartets*, 40–41) sees the early return of the secondary theme as a means for Haydn to revert to a "monothematic" recapitulation despite the exposition's clearly differentiated second group. For a general discussion of Haydn's approach to sonata form, see Chua, *Absolute Music*, chapter 26.
21. See LaRue, "Bifocal Tonality," regarding oblique harmonic approaches to the recapitulation in Haydn's sonata forms.
22. Hunter ("Quartets," 120–122) traces a similar cycle in the final section of the first movement of op. 64, no. 2 (discussed above in the context of its opening harmonic ambiguity), in which a secondary idea emerges into prominence before yielding to the prior leading voice. She characterizes this temporary emergence as a "mere sidekick" becoming "the co-leader of the conversation," and finds the passage emblematic of the conversational dimension of Haydn's quartet writing generally.
23. Martin, "Quartets in Performance," 140–141.
24. Mozart took three years to compose his six "Haydn Quartets," and wrote in his dedication of the "long and laborious effort" they exacted from him. See Bonds, "Replacing Haydn," regarding the complex genesis of Mozart's "Haydn Quartets"; and Bonds, "Listening to Listeners," 41–47, which extends that discussion to consider the initially difficult reception of these quartets. For his part, Beethoven withdrew at least two quartets from his op. 18 set after sharing them, as he claimed to have "just learned to write quartets properly" (Forbes, *Thayer's Life of Beethoven*, 224–225 and 262–264; see also Brandenburg, "First Version"; and Lockwood, *Inside Beethoven's Quartets*, 6–13). Kerman (*Beethoven Quartets*, 9) notes numerous parallels between Mozart's and

Beethoven's struggles with writing quartets, including the similar ages of the composers when these two sets were launched and their gestation periods.

25. Thus Haydn's obfuscating "explanation" for the passage—"If Mozart wrote it so, he must have had his reasons"—which he offered in response to puzzled inquiries after Mozart's death from those who believed there were printing errors in the published score (as quoted in Jahn, *Life of Mozart*, 3:4).
26. See Forbes, *Thayer's Life of Beethoven*, 261; and Kerman, *Beethoven Quartets*, 36–42.
27. See Kerman, *Beethoven Quartets*, 76–82; and Lockwood, *Inside Beethoven's Quartets*, 19–21. A hypothesis offered in Caldwell, "La Malinconia," that Beethoven meant to set the cycles of melancholia rather than to contrast melancholia with its opposite mood, has not been given sufficient consideration by musicologists. Jones ("Beethoven") suggests that Beethoven's model for this movement may have been C. P. E. Bach's Trio Sonata in C Minor, H. 579, presented as a "Conversation between a Sanguineus and a Melancholicus"; Jones conjecturally applies Bach's comment on the second movement, "Melancholicus gives up the battle and assumes the manner of the other," to Beethoven's coda (214).
28. Bonds, "Rhetoric versus Truth"; see also chapters 2 and 3 in Bonds, *Music as Thought*. For a defense of rhetoric *as* truth, see Sisman, "Rhetorical Truth." Arguably, this distinction lies at the heart of Kerman's judgment that this movement is an extremely accomplished failure, due largely to its overindulgence in sentimentality.
29. Because the quartet version occasionally omits important material, it seems possible that it was arranged by someone else and then approved by Haydn, as is known to be the case with the keyboard arrangement.
30. Le Guin, "Visit to the Salon." Regarding the importation of salon culture to the German lands in the 1770s during the reign of Maria Theresa, and its probable impact on Haydn's quartet style, see Melton, "School, Stage, Salon," 103–107.

    Le Guin's focus on the keyboard trio, rather than the string quartet, was in part an artifact of the conference for which she first presented this work, which was from the beginning to feature performances of a selection of these works by her and coorganizer Tom Beghin (see the anecdote with which this book opens). The hierarchical model Le Guin elaborates for directed conversation (that is, with someone who leads, and others who listen more than speak), is more apparent in a trio, where the keyboardist can be seen to preside. Yet much the same function falls to the first violinist in a string quartet, with nearly as audible a result. Le Guin also addresses the more familiar claim that the string quartet models conversation, by including, in full, Giuseppe Carpani's oft-cited elaboration of this metaphor (Carpani, *Le Haydine*, 96–97; quoted in Le Guin, "Visit to the Salon," 26n27).

31. Necker, *Mélanges extraits*, quoted in Le Guin, "Visit to the Salon," 18.
32. Regarding Schenker's admission of Chopin into the German canon, beginning explicitly in 1921 but implicitly from at least 1906, see Bent, "Heinrich Schenker." Regarding Schenker's thought, contextualized within his generation, see Blasius, *Schenker's Argument*; and Snarrenberg, *Schenker's Interpretive Practice*.
33. See Rothenberg, "Thus Far, but No Farther." For a revisionist reading of this situation, see Kimber, "'Suppression' of Fanny Mendelssohn." For a fuller accounting of her life as a musician, including her continuing determination to publish under her own name, see Todd, *Fanny Hensel*.
34. Notwithstanding this distinction, compositions by both Felix and Fanny were performed at the latter's *Sonntagskonzerte*.
35. Historically, this attitudinal change derives directly from German Idealism. Finscher ("Die Theorie des Streichquartetts," 287) notes a shift from describing chamber music as a convivial conversation among equals, stimulated by the individual character of each participant, to describing it as a "philosophical argument" (*philosophischer Ideenreihe*), and traces the new characterization to Friedrich Schlegel, writing around the turn of the nineteenth century (in *Athenäumsfragmente*).

4 | POPULAR MUSIC CONTRA GERMAN IDEALISM

1. Sontag's "Notes on Camp," first published in *Partisan Review*, has been reprinted often, for example in Sontag, *Against Interpretation*, 275–292; and Cleto, *Camp*, 53–65.
2. For useful summaries of camp's emergence within mainstream culture and as a topic for academic discourse, see Ross, "Uses of Camp"; and Cleto, introduction; for more specific documentation, see also Cleto, "Digging the Scene."
3. Dale Cockrell's *Demons of Disorder* argues that minstrelsy in its early stages was both a more honest attempt to celebrate elements of black culture than would be evident later, and a means, through that celebration, to inspire a common feeling between working-class whites and blacks. In this view, common in musicological studies, minstrelsy was once a mechanism for pricking the conscience of a nation that had become dependent on slave labor (see, e.g., Cockrell's discussion of antislavery verses set to "Jim Crow" in 1833, 89). Cockrell also traces some of the steps by which the transformation occurred, through the development of the minstrel show as an institution by such figures as Dan Emmett and Edwin Christy (chapter 5). See also Robert

Nowatzki's *Representing African Americans in Transatlantic Abolitionism and Blackface Minstrelsy*, which provides a more extended analysis of minstrelsy's association with abolitionist sentiment, focusing on its early stages, before it became "more consistently proslavery and racist" (3), and which argues a shared discourse in these elements between England and the United States. W. T. Lhamon, Jr.'s *Raising Cain* probes minstrelsy's simultaneous engagement in and resistance to racism through a close reading of its materials, lore, tropes, and settings.

Nuanced as these accounts are regarding minstrelsy's potential for inverting or subverting its overt racism, a strong case may be made that minstrelsy was intrinsically and overtly racist from the beginning, and that its political agenda was always white-supremacist and, before the war, anti-abolitionist. For a forceful argument along these lines, taking full account of the predominant politics of those who practiced the art, see Alexander Saxton's "Blackface Minstrelsy and Jacksonian Ideology," which locates minstrelsy's origins firmly within the nationalist/expansionist, antimonopoly, antitemperance, and white-supremacist Jacksonian democratic tradition, with its strong basis in the urban working class: "It was linked from its earliest beginnings to Jacksonian democracy. The rise of the first mass party in America and the dominance of the minstrel show as mass entertainment appear to have been interrelated and mutually reinforcing sequences. . . . [Regarding] the ideology of minstrel shows, the interpenetration of form and content is relentlessly at the crux of the matter" (4).

4. That this was true more or less from the beginning is argued, indirectly, in Eric Lott's *Love and Theft* ("Popular Counterfeits," 100–105). Also relevant to this claim is a relatively early study of minstrelsy, Hans Nathan's *Dan Emmett and the Rise of Early Negro Minstrelsy* (1962), which, much more than later book-length treatments, considers minstrelsy's English roots and earlier New World precedents.
5. For further discussion of minstrelsy's later role in negotiating black-white relations in the United States, see especially Ann Douglas's *Terrible Honesty*, 75–77 and 99–100; particularly evocative is her recitation of the early stages of the process: "Blacks imitating and fooling whites, whites imitating and stealing from blacks, blacks reappropriating and transforming what had been stolen, whites making yet another foray on black styles, and on and on: this *is* American popular culture" (76). See also the "Minstrelsy" section in Knapp, *American Musical and National Identity*, and the discussion of *Stormy Weather* and *Bamboozled* in Knapp, *American Musical and Personal Identity*, 79–94.
6. The strong association of camp with gay males, which "Notes on Camp" already draws attention to, has been one of the most dominant ideas regarding camp, although not without controversy. Typical is the succinct description

of camp in Richard Dyer's "Judy Garland and Camp," which is not quite a definition but reads like one, and which leads off by locating camp within the gay community: "Camp is a characteristically gay way of handling the values, images and products of the dominant culture through irony, exaggeration, trivialization, theatricalisation and an ambivalent making fun of and out of the serious and respectable" (107). At the end of this essay, Dyer hedges regarding wider associations, but not regarding the specific connection between camp and gay male subcultures: "Play on illusion and reality does not have to be seen as camp or gay. . . . I am neither claiming that only gay men could see it this way or that these aspects need be understood as camp or gay" (112). Among the most persuasive discussions linking camp *essentially* within gay sensibilities is Jack Babuscio's "Camp and the Gay Sensibility." Among related discussions, Ross, "Uses of Camp," details how camp tastes articulate with gay subcultures; Cleto (introduction, 4–6) rehearses the controversies attending this association; and Chauncey, "Double Life," grounds camp within the social milieu of double lives and double entendres created by homosexual men in New York.

7. The Stonewall rebellion is generally seen as a decisive moment in the then-emergent gay rights movement. It began as a routine confrontation between police and homosexuals at the Stonewall Inn on Christopher Street in Greenwich Village, New York City, shortly after 1 AM on June 28, 1969, and became a riot/siege that lasted three days, sparking demonstrations in major cities across the United States. Among many accounts of Stonewall and its place in the history of gay rights, see Duberman, *Stonewall* (especially part 6); and Carter, *Stonewall.*
8. There are, aside from the arguments I advance here, two dating issues that affect the precise ways in which we might imagine, or refer to, such an intermingling of camp tastes among gays and straights in the later nineteenth century. First, there is the emergent designation of the term "homosexual" to mean a type of person, displacing the earlier practice of referring to the sexual activities involved (e.g., sodomy). Controversies remain concerning when this usage shifted, and the ways in which this usage actually mattered, but there is some consensus that the term was entrenched by the late nineteenth century, having already come into some play by the time of the earlier of the examples I consider below (*The Pirates of Penzance* and *Patience*), with Krafft-Ebing, *Psychopathia Sexualis,* acting as a kind of watershed, after which the designation became common. Second, there is the use of the term "gay" to describe a homosexual man and his mannerisms. Charged but still easily closeted uses of the word "gay" have been traced back from fairly common instances in the 1940s to occasional appearances in novels of the 1920s, suggesting that already by then there was some "street" history for this usage;

see Chauncey, *Gay New York*, 14–23. Katz, *Gay/Lesbian Almanac*, speculates on the possibility that the coded use of "gay" may have had some currency "as early as 1908–1912" (405); elsewhere, Katz notes the lines from the 1929 Noël Coward operetta *Bitter Sweet* (sung by a male chorus): "We are the reason for the nineties being gay" (437), a daring appropriation of a commonly used designation, which implicitly claims, without evidence, that the word already had a double meaning even in the "Gay Nineties." See also Russo, *The Celluloid Closet*, 6. I have found it in general both convenient and less confusing to use the term "gay" across the entire period I discuss, which runs some risk of my being found ahistorical in my usage, but does not, I think, affect the substance of my argument.

9. See Baur's "Let Me Make the Ballads" for an exploration of both sides of this emergent divide, which I found inspirational at an early stage of my work on this period. Among more general histories of music in the United States, see especially Crawford, *America's Musical Life*; Hamm, *Music in the New World*; and Hitchcock, *Music in the United States*. Regarding the historiography of music in the United States, see chapter 1 in Crawford, *American Musical Landscape*.
10. Weber, "Musical Idealism."
11. Weber, "Musical Idealism," 87, 93, and 97.
12. "You're putting me on" is a specifically US American construction, roughly equivalent to the United Kingdom's "You're having me on."
13. Berlin's rewrite of the song specifically edits out elements that point to African Americans. Thus, "Harlem sits" becomes "Fashion sits"; "Spangled gowns upon a bevy / Of high browns from down the levee" becomes "Diff'rent types who wear a day coat / Pants with stripes and cut-away coat"; and "Come with me and we'll attend / Their jubilee and see them spend / Their last two bits" becomes "Come let's mix where Rockefellers / Walk with sticks or umbrellas / In their mitts." For more on this dimension of the song, see Knapp, "Music, Electricity," 13–15. Regarding Zip Coon, see especially chapter 4 in Cockrell, *Demons of Disorder*.
14. McMillin, *Musical as Drama*, 2.
15. Another aspect of interpretation, as it is generally understood regarding performed musical works, couples the performer's perspective with the text being performed, so that the interpretation becomes an embodied reading. A closely related aspect of interpretation more generally (and as discussed in Sontag, "Against Interpretation") regards interpretation as a kind of translation, a means to make a work accessible or relevant for an audience and context different from its original audience and context. For both these additional meanings, at least with regard to musical interpretation through

performance (which Sontag does not discuss), the interpreter remains answerable to the text itself, so that a performance may be judged capricious or self-indulgent if it inappropriately places the performer ahead of the work being performed. Sontag, in disparaging interpretation for reductively turning "*the* world into *this* world" (7), at the same time identifies the precise stakes involved regarding the German Idealist paradigm for music; similarly, her extolling of "*transparence*" (13) may be readily adapted as a guideline regarding the interpretation of music through performance (as, indeed, it often is; see the related discussion in chapter 1).

16. Amy Fay, contrasting the concert comportment of Franz Liszt and Joseph Joachim, provides a particularly revealing contemporary description of how such distinctions in demeanor once manifested themselves in performance; see Fay, *Music Study in Germany*, 248. Regarding how the distinction between authentic and theatrical musical performance emerged in the later nineteenth century, see Leistra-Jones, "Staging Authenticity."
17. Oscar Wilde, *An Ideal Husband*, in Wilde, *Complete Works*, 487. Wilde has long been a touchstone for camp tastes. Thus, Sontag sprinkles several Wilde quotations, as epigraphs, into "Notes on Camp"—a practice I will pay homage to below as part of a brief exploration of prototypical camp tastes in Wilde's *The Importance of Being Earnest*.
18. Knapp, *American Musical and National Identity*, 56. For a somewhat different perspective on how this dynamic has operated then and since, see the growing literature on cultural hierarchies, usually delineated as highbrow, middlebrow, and lowbrow, including especially Woolf, "Middlebrow"; Macdonald, "Masscult and Midcult"; Gans, *Popular Culture and High Culture*; Levine, *Highbrow/Lowbrow*; Rubin, *Making of Middlebrow Culture*; and Savran, *Highbrow/Lowdown*. Regarding the cited programs, see Mahar, *Behind the Burnt Cork Mask*, 12.
19. The long legacy of minstrelsy's affront on notions of respectability, allied perhaps with the "trickster" figures of the minstrel stage, overlaps "the dozens," a game of traded insults most often centering on the opponent's mother; see Wald, *Dozens*. For another wide-ranging exploration of similar (or at least overlapping) territory, see Strausbaugh, *Black Like You*.
20. Mahar, *Behind the Burnt Cork Mask*, 195–267.
21. Bakhtin, *Rabelais and His World*. For an extended consideration of Bakhtin's carnival in connection with minstrelsy, see Cockrell, *Demons of Disorder*.
22. In the first half of the nineteenth century, the infectious songs of the minstrel stage were not highly regarded as music, although these songs, understood as deriving from and/or representative of African Americans, arguably provided the foundation for minstrelsy's sustained vitality as an institution. More

immediately, however, it was African American dancing that first captured the imagination of whites and helped create the mythos of blacks' innate musicality; see, for example, Eric Lott's discussion of Master Juba (William Henry Lane, ca. 1825–ca. 1853), the most famous of black dancers, described by Charles Dickens with picturesque hyperbole in *American Notes for General Circulation* (1842), and whose abilities and mystique were unmatched by white dancers in blackface (Lott, *Love and Theft*, 113–116). By 1855, under the influence of minstrelsy, a mythologized appreciation of "black" singing was becoming widespread; see "Negro Minstrelsy—Ancient and Modern," *Putnam's Monthly* 5, no. 25 (1855): 72–29, quoted and discussed in Lott, *Love and Theft*, 58. Also contributing to the conceit of inherent musicality was the figure of "Blind Tom" (1849–1908), born a slave and, according to *Dwight's Journal of Music*, "without even ordinary intelligence," but nevertheless exhibiting already as a child extraordinary musical capabilities (Radano, *Lying up a Nation*, 175–177). Such appreciations, already reinforced by minstrel shows, would be amplified after the war by blacks performing in "colored" minstrel shows and, even more dramatically, by the Fisk Jubilee Singers, whose tours began in 1871; already in 1866 the all-black Georgia Minstrels were outdrawing all other minstrel troupes (Toll, *Blacking Up*, 199).

23. Baur, "Rhythm"; see also Baur, "Let Me Make the Ballads," 162–226.
24. Douglas, *Terrible Honesty*, 75–77 and 99–100. Regarding the back-and-forth ethnicity of blackface minstrelsy, see also, among others, Toll, *Blacking Up*, 42–46; Lott, *Love and Theft*, 93–97; and Cockrell, *Demons of Disorder*, 86–89. Particularly relevant, and resonant as well with my discussion of minstrelsy as primarily about entertainment, is Lott's discussion of P. T. Barnum's improvisation when his blackface dancer ("Master" John Diamond) left the show in 1841: as related by Thomas Low Nichols, Barnum replaced him with a black dancer in blackface, who thereby passed as white, perhaps the first important instance of this recourse. This replacement seems to have been none other than Master Juba (William Henry Lane), who in 1844 bested Master Diamond in a dance competition. At this early stage, as Lott notes, a black man imitates a white man who imitates a black man, the discernible trace of a long succession of interracial imitations (Lott, *Love and Theft*, 112–116; see also Nichols, *Forty Years*, 369–370).
25. Regarding the broad success of blackface minstrelsy in London, and in England more generally, see Pickering, "White Skin, Black Masks," "Jet Ornament to Society," and "Mock Blacks and Racial Mockery"; and Scott, "Blackface Minstrels." Scott reports the relative lack of success early on of such acts in Liverpool and Manchester, and of persistent resistance to minstrelsy there, at least in the press (which may itself be indicative of actual commercial success). Although most often based in London, many minstrel

companies, including both professional and semiprofessional performers, toured across England, with many amateur shows, as well.

26. The borrowing is from "Johnny Get Your Gun," a fiddle tune most familiar as the dance-postlude to Monroe H. Rosenfeld's song of the same name. I discuss this derivation in Knapp, *American Musical and National Identity*, 64–65, where I include a musical comparison between the two; see also 322n11 for a brief summary of the tune's derivation and subsequent history.
27. Instruments are not specified in the printed libretto, but Gilbert's rehearsal manuscript of the libretto (Wolfson, *Final Curtain*, 192) reads, "(*Capt. Fitzbattleaxe has his banjo. Mr Blushington takes a set of bones out of his pocket. Mr Goldbury finds a tambourine on his chair.*)," whereas a review of the first performance (*Staffordshire Sentinel*: "*Utopia Limited*") describes the scene thus: "The Cabinet Ministers suddenly produce musical instruments and, to a rattling solo for the King, they give one of the most perfect burlesques of the Christy Minstrel Chorus that has ever been written." The *Daily News* reported "banjos and fiddles" in addition to "tambourines and bones," as well as a "breakdown" danced by King Paramount (Allen, *First Night Gilbert and Sullivan*, 379).
28. Quotations from *Utopia Limited* are as given in Gilbert and Sullivan, *Complete Plays*.
29. Walbrook, *Gilbert and Sullivan Opera*, chapter 15. The royal umbrage may have been exaggerated; Allen (*First Night Gilbert and Sullivan*, 380) quotes Thomas Dunhill as follows: "The only matter to which the Prince of Wales . . . took exception . . . was the appearance of King Paramount in a British Field-Marshal's uniform, wearing the Order of the Garter, a combination which he alone, of all living men, was entitled to wear! Needless to say, the Garter was removed and all was well."
30. The Flower of Progress who leads this effort is Mr. Goldbury—a typically Gilbertian conceit in its allusion to buried gold, but also anti-Semitic in attaching a Jewish-sounding name to someone specializing in shady business deals.
31. Knapp, *American Musical and National Identity*, 65.
32. Regarding the exoticism of *The King and I* and its basis in the other properties listed, see Knapp, *American Musical and National Identity*, 261–268.
33. Michael Rogin, "New Deal Blackface," argues that Hollywood's engagement with minstrelsy during the first two decades of synchronized sound represented "a nostalgic longing for an imaginary southern past" encouraged by the great depression and World War II.
34. Regarding nostalgia generally, see Boym, *Future of Nostalgia*. Many authors address minstrelsy's basis in nostalgia, from differing perspectives. Lott, *Love and Theft*, for example, following Austin, "*Susanna*," grounds the nostalgia

of minstrelsy as exemplified by the sentimental songs of Stephen Foster in the broader tradition of "home" songs such as "Home! Sweet Home!" (171–173, 179) and relates it to white longings attendant on western expansion (190–193, 203–207). Toll, *Blacking Up*, argues that the nostalgia of minstrelsy displaced a similar nostalgia, prewar, regarding American Indians, conceived as innocents (165), whereas, postwar, the nostalgia became centered on plantation life itself (187, 245).

35. The standard text on Orientalism is Edward Said's *Orientalism*.
36. This mode of nostalgia was new only in its degree and specific manifestation. As Toll (*Blacking Up*, 155) observes, minstrelsy had become nostalgic regarding its own past already by 1857.
37. Regarding the Nicholas Brothers' animosity toward Robinson, see Stearns and Stearns, *Jazz Dance*, 183; and Knapp, *American Musical and Personal Identity*, 92.
38. Regarding the "Bojangles" number generally and its relationship to Robinson in particular, see Decker, *Music Makes Me*, 74 and 247–249.
39. For additional discussion of this number along these lines, see Knapp and Morris, "Filmed Musical," 138–139.
40. Decker, "On the Scenic Route," 482–483. Decker's detailed account of the planning and filming of *Holiday Inn* complicates the screen evidence of "Abraham" considerably, and he uses his research to argue effectively against specific claims by Knight, *Disintegrating the Musical*, and Rogin, *Blackface, White Noise*, both of whom habitually use "Abraham" as an easily read marker for consistent Hollywood practices (Decker, "On the Scenic Route," 483–489). In Decker's contrasting summation, "'Abraham' is qualitatively unlike any other blackface number Hollywood made" (481). Specifically, there was much trouble taken over the precise language of Louise Beavers's insert; alternatives considered for the word "darkies" included "black folks," "we folks," and "our people," with "negro" appearing in the published sheet music (482). While Decker suggests that Astaire "avoided" a planned sequence in *Holiday Inn* in which he would dance with "pickaninnies," citing parallel suggestions and planned sequences from other films that were never realized (484), he elsewhere delineates Astaire's sustained strategies for integrating musical numbers by including blacks in the same frame with him; see chapter 9 of Decker, *Music Makes Me*. Among many other discussions regarding Hollywood's treatment of blacks, see especially Woll, *Hollywood Musical Goes to War*, 121–130.
41. Decker, "On the Scenic Route," 480–481. As Decker notes, Crosby's lips are not exaggerated as would be typical of minstrel makeup, although he lapses occasionally into minstrelsy's mannerisms and dialect.

42. Reynolds's appearance, grotesque as it is, has a direct model in Rosetta Duncan, who performed Topsy with her sister in *Topsy and Eva*, a Broadway musical from 1924 (Decker, "On the Scenic Route," 481).

43. This device of "accidental" racial crossover is as old as minstrelsy. See Lott, *Love and Theft*, regarding a skit from 1833 (Thomas D. Rice's *O Hush! or, The Virginny Cupids*) in which a bootblack hiding in a cupboard falls out covered in flour, whereupon he is accused of being "trash . . . a runaway from de nullifying States" (133).

44. *Judy Garland Database* quotes Roger Edens, regarding the failure of early preview audiences to respond enthusiastically to the minstrel-show sequence: "We tried to figure out why. As it turned out we realized there was no shot of Mickey and Judy making up in blackface. . . . And it was a very good lesson: if you ever are going to show someone in disguise, you better show them putting it on. So we did a retake showing Mickey and Judy getting into blackface so that the audience could tell it was them. And then the number went like a house on fire." Edens was the musical arranger on both films, newly composing some music for the minstrel show sequences, including the key numbers "My Daddy Was a Minstrel Man" and "Mr. Bones and Mr. Tambo" in the first and (probably) "Blackout over Broadway" in the second.

45. There is a residue of popular belief that Mr. Interlocutor did not traditionally appear in blackface, but there is no clear evidence for such a practice and much to argue against it, at least during the main span of minstrelsy. Lott rehearses the controversy in a note (*Love and Theft*, 264n6) after summarizing the development of the dynamic between this character and the end men as follows: "Seated in a semicircle, the Emmett troupe placed the bones and tambourine players at either end of the band, and though originally all were comic performers, these two endmen began to assume chief importance in most minstrel companies, particularly after the addition of the interlocutor—genteel in comportment and, popular myth notwithstanding, also in blackface" (140). According to Toll (*Blacking Up*, 63–64n63) and 152–154), the interlocutor may sometimes have appeared in whiteface during the 1890s, as a deliberate departure and as "part of the general use of whiteface in the minstrel show" at that time. One oddity resulting from the last-minute fix to the minstrel sequence in *Babes on Broadway* (see previous note) is that Richard Quine is shown blacking up with the others, although, as Mr. Interlocutor, he does not appear in blackface during the sequence that follows.

46. The "sooty" routine is offered, for example, as "a typically demeaning, rapid-fire minstrel joke" by Van Deburg, *Slavery and Race*, 41. Van Deburg cites Paskman and Spaeth, *"Gentlemen, Be Seated!,"* 29, as the source for the routine as he gives it.

47. The one exception is the dance solo by Ray McDonald in *Babes on Broadway*.
48. See "Film Review: *Babes on Broadway*," *Judy Garland Database*.
49. In *Babes in Arms*, Rooney performs "Ida, Sweet as Apple Cider" (Eddie Munson and Eddie Leonard) with "On Moonlight Bay" (Percy Wenrich and Edward Madden); his banjo solo in *Babes on Broadway* is based on Stephen Foster's "Old Folks at Home" and Ray Henderson's "Alabamy Bound." Garland performs Eubie Blake and Noble Sissle's "I'm Just Wild about Harry" with Rooney in *Babes in Arms*; in *Babes on Broadway*, she sings Harold Rome's "Franklin D. Roosevelt Jones" as a solo number and, with Rooney, Lewis F. Muir and L. Wolfe Gilbert's "Waiting for the Robert E. Lee." Garland's makeup changes for her concluding numbers with Rooney follow the convention in older minstrelsy of men performing in blackface and women in brownface; thus, Garland lightens up when her character switches from her drag Mr. Tambo to a young woman in a dress.
50. See chapter 5 in Baur, "Let Me Make the Ballads," especially his discussion of "Shoo Fly" (198–226).
51. On the affinity between musicals and camp, see Clum, *Something for the Boys*: "The gay voice in the musical's spectacle and presentation speaks with some irony, some awareness of its artificiality. In discussing that gay voice one must discuss camp, an overtheorized but crucial term that explains many of the links between musical theater and gay culture. At their best, and sometimes their worst, *musicals are camp*" (7, emphasis mine). I make the same claim from a somewhat different vantage point in the final section of this chapter.
52. Sontag, *Against Interpretation*, 282. Ross, "The Uses of Camp," suggests that Sontag's motivation for downgrading intentional camp was a fear that it might allow the creator and not the critic to take "full credit for discerning the camp value of an object or text" (145).
53. Sontag, *Against Interpretation*, 278.
54. Dyer, "Judy Garland and Camp," 111.
55. Wilde, *Complete Works*, 335.
56. Wilde, *Complete Works*, 375 and 325.
57. I discuss this wider field of campy operettas in Knapp, "Straight Bookends." For a fascinating collection of journalistic accounts of Wilde's excursion to the United States, see Hofer and Scharnhorst, *Oscar Wilde in America*. My discussion below of what I term "pirate camp" derives from Knapp, "Musical Faces."
58. Specifically, Ralph's madrigal "The Nightingale" and the Captain's folklike "Fair Moon, to Thee I Sing." For more on this topic, and on *Pinafore* more generally, see Knapp, *American Musical and National Identity*, 34–46.
59. Regarding this process of association, see Sinfield, *Wilde Century*.

60. This is probably most evident in the United States. An adaptation of *H.M.S. Pinafore* in 2001 by Mark Savage and the Celebration Theater in Los Angeles, *Pinafore!* was revelatory regarding how effective a gay reading of the show could be once the veneer of Victorian respectability is stripped away. See Knapp, *American Musical and National Identity*, 7 and 321n20.
61. An exception to this is *The Pirates of Penzance*, which I discuss later in relation to pirate camp. After a successful revival of the show with modernized orchestrations in New York City's Central Park (Joseph Papp and the Public Theater, 1980), with Kevin Kline, Linda Ronstadt, Rex Smith, George Rose, Tony Azito, and Patricia Routledge (broadcast on television in 1980 and released on DVD by Kultur in 2002), the production moved to Broadway for a two-year run, with Estelle Parsons replacing Patricia Routledge as Ruth. The success of the revival led to two fairly successful films, one of them attempting to incorporate an abbreviated version of the operetta as a fantasy within a film set in contemporary US America (*The Pirate Movie*, directed by Ken Annakin, 1982, discussed briefly below), and the other a modest reworking of the Papp production as originally cast but with Angela Lansbury as Ruth (*The Pirates of Penzance*, directed by Wilford Leach, 1983).
62. For a more extensive accounting of this line of influence see Knapp, "How Great Thy Charm."
63. As I put it in Knapp, *American Musical and National Identity* (13), "To some extent, the musical becomes camp the moment it actually becomes *musical*, for the first notes that sound under the dialogue are like a knowing wink to the audience, a set of arched eyebrows that serves as quotation marks around whatever is ostensibly being expressed, whether musically or dramatically. The element of camp in a musical thus shifts sudden attention to the performed nature of the drama, and in particular to the actual performer, thereby providing a more direct channel of communication between the performer and whoever in the audience may note and relish the artificiality."

    Regarding the mode of acting required in stage musicals, see Clum, "Acting"; and Deer and Dal Vera, *Acting in Musical Theatre*.
64. Gilbert and Sullivan, *Patience*, 56.
65. Gilbert and Sullivan, *Patience*, 45. What remains somewhat hidden within these obscure references is Bunthorne's point: that the application of chemistry drains the poetry out of nature, a position diametrically opposed to the embrace of modern chemistry in the dragoons' recent list song, "If You Want a Receipt," which consists of a list of "all the remarkable people in history" (27), followed by the instruction to "Take of these elements all that is fusible, / Melt them all down in a pipkin or crucible, / Set them to simmer and take off the scum, / And a Heavy Dragoon is the residuum!" (30–31).
66. Gilbert and Sullivan, *Patience*, 53–54.

67. Gilbert and Sullivan, *Patience*, 74.
68. Gilbert and Sullivan, *Patience*, 163–164.
69. Gilbert and Sullivan, *Patience*, 56.
70. Gilbert and Sullivan, *Patience*, 50. Because there is no accompaniment during Bunthorne's first two lines of recitative, it is easy enough—and surely intended—for him to underscore the absurdity by peering out at the audience between the opening question and its answer, "I am."
71. Gilbert and Sullivan, *Patience*, 54; for the third refrain, "mystic" becomes "flowery."
72. Gilbert and Sullivan, *Patience*, 53. Queen Anne reigned over England and Scotland from 1702 until her death in 1714, whereas Josephine was empress of France from 1802 until 1810, when Napoleon divorced her.
73. The *Oxford Dictionary of Music* (ed. Michael Kennedy) defines "galant" as "Courtly. 18th-cent. term to describe elegant style (Fr. *Style galant*; Ger. *Galanter Stil*) favoured by, for example, J. C. Bach, the Stamitzes, and early Mozart."
74. Gilbert and Sullivan, *Patience*, 138.
75. Gilbert and Sullivan, *Patience*, 154.
76. Other instances of 6/8 occur in the operetta, but at a much slower tempo.
77. Sinfield, *Wilde Century*. As Sinfield relates, neither Wilde's principal accuser, the Marquess of Queensberry, nor his own lawyer initially believed the strong evidence against him (1–2).
78. See Knapp, "Musical Faces," for a more extensive discussion of the roots and development of pirate camp.
79. Broadwell, "Swashbucklers on Stage"; see also Burwick, *Playing to the Crowd*, especially chapter 7.
80. Gilbert and Sullivan, *Pirates of Penzance*, 202.
81. Regarding the hunt and horse topics, see Monelle, *Sense of Music*, 38–40 and 41–65; regarding the former, see also Monelle, *Musical Topic*, 33–110.
82. Berlioz, *Lélio*, 28–30 (translation mine).
83. Gilbert and Sullivan, *Pirates of Penzance*, 22–23.
84. Gilbert and Sullivan, *Pirates of Penzance*, 24–25.
85. A variant ending, still used occasionally, reprises Major Stanley's "I Am the Very Model of a Modern Major-General" rather than "Poor Wandering One!" as the finale.
86. Regarding similar rhythmic transformations, see Monelle, *Sense of Music*, 45–47.
87. Among many writings about the Hays Code and its effects, see Leff and Simmons, *Dame in the Kimono*; and M. Bernstein, *Controlling Hollywood*.
88. See Knapp, *American Musical and Personal Identity*, 189–195.
89. Broadwell, "Swashbucklers on Stage," 1–16, makes intriguing connections between the pirate theme in *The Pirates of the Caribbean* ("He's a Pirate,"

composed by Klaus Badelt) and both "Come Away, Fellow Sailors" from Henry Purcell's *Dido and Aeneas*, composed three centuries earlier (1689), and a prominent "cavalry charge" cue in *Gladiator* (2000), composed by Hans Zimmer and Lisa Gerard.

90. Brett Farmer (*Spectacular Passions*, 99–100) details the mainstream critical view of *The Pirate*, referring to Sennett, *Hollywood Musicals*, 229–232: "Sennett . . . finds *The Pirate*, in particular, 'too extravagant,' 'florid,' 'gaudy,' 'strain[ing] a little too hard,' 'never tak[ing] itself seriously'—in short, it's a 'hothouse flower, beautiful to look at and admire but also too delicate to survive the years.'" Regarding the musical camp dimension of *The Pirate*, especially of Conrad Salinger's arrangements, see Stephen Pysnik's "Camp Identities," especially 142–242, and "Musical Camp"; the former also documents how deliberately *The Pirate* was conceived from the beginning in camp terms, citing Minnelli and Arce, *I Remember It Well*, 164.
91. This choral overlay is probably the contribution of Kay Thompson, who did the vocal arrangements for the film. For another discussion of this passage, see Pysnik, "Camp Identities."
92. Fulda's original name for Macoco was Estornudo (Sneeze). I wish to thank Stephen Pysnik for bringing this earlier alteration of the character's name to my attention (private communication, October 15, 2012).
93. "Black" was a common nickname/descriptor for pirates, most famously Blackbeard (Edward Teach, 1680–1718), Black Bart (Bartholomew Roberts, 1682–1722), Black Sam (Samuel Bellamy, 1689–1717), and Black Caesar (d. 1718, reputedly an African tribal chief).
94. Dyer, "Judy Garland and Camp" 111. Farmer, *Spectacular Passions*, 107–108, pushes this observation further (with an assist from Freud); see also Cohan, *Incongruous Entertainment*, 176 and 180–181.
95. Pysnik, "Camp Identities."
96. Pysnik, "Camp Identities," explores a quite different set of examples of campy arrangements and scoring from the film.
97. This contrasts with her earlier disappointed reaction to Don Pedro's aversion to travel, which Richard Dyer terms "the exact reversal in tone of Dorothy/Garland's line at the end of *The Wizard of Oz* or Esther/Garland's at the end of *Meet Me in St. Louis*" (Dyer, "Judy Garland and Camp," 110–111). The sharpest contrast between *The Pirate* and the other two films lies in their endings: in *The Pirate*, she joins Serafin's troupe, whereas she is happy to be safely back at home at the end of *The Wizard of Oz*, and fights throughout *Meet Me in St. Louis* to sustain her known home life.
98. Cf. Tinkcom, "Working Like a Homosexual," 122: "Camp becomes an important way for thinking about Minnelli's efforts inasmuch as it shaped his work on the films' visual style."

99. To be sure, Minnelli must share credit in much of this with cinematographer Harry Stradling, art directors Cedric Gibbons and Jack Martin Smith, set decorator Edwin B. Willis, and costume designer Tom Keogh. Nevertheless, what matters most here is the governing sensibility, which is clearly Minnelli's; we know this not only from a manifest consistency across these aspects of production in *The Pirate* but also from his extended work as a director. Minnelli's affinities for and competence in the visual realm were developed prior even to his stage directing career, since his previous jobs had included billboard painter, window dresser, costume designer, set designer, and color consultant.

100. The authors of the numbers performed in the "Ghost Theater" sequence are as follows:

    1. Edmond Rostand (English translation by Howard Thayer Kingsbury)
    2. George M. Cohan
    3. music by Harry Lauder, words by Harry Lauder and J. D. Harper
    4. music by Maurice Scott, words by R. P. Weston and Fred J. Barnes
    5. Edmond Rostand
    6. George M. Cohan

101. This number, along with most of her performance in *The Pirate*, amply supports Richard Dyer's contention that Judy Garland "is not a star turned into camp, but a star who expresses camp attitudes" (Dyer, "Judy Garland and Camp," 107).

102. For other ways in which the final duet version of "Be a Clown" stands somewhat apart from both *The Pirate* and film-musical conventions, see Feuer, *Hollywood Musical*, 39–41 and 83–84.

103. Regarding the importance of Anglophone cultures to the history of camp discourse, and possible derivation of the term from the French *se camper*, see Cleto, introduction, 10–11. The quoted lyrics are from "If You're Anxious for to Shine," in Gilbert and Sullivan, *Patience*, 53–54.

104. This English ecumenical spirit is grounded, legally, in the Thirty-Nine Articles ratified by Parliament in 1571 during the reign of Queen Elizabeth, particularly Article 34, which opens, "It is not necessary that Traditions and Ceremonies be in all places one, and utterly like; for at all times they have been divers, and may be changed according to the diversities of countries, times, and men's manners, so that nothing be ordained against God's Word." (I thank Mitchell Morris for pointing out to me the relevance of the Articles to this part of my argument.)

105. Regarding the claim that camp has historical and sustaining roots in the larger category of "urbane," I wish to thank Mitchell Morris (private communication, June, 2012). This harboring category allows one to withhold the label of "camp" until a later date, and to locate it more centrally, even exclusively, within closeted gay cultures for crucial decades of the twentieth

century. I argue here for a historically longer, more diverse application of the term, on the basis of its connection to either overt, self-conscious theatricality (already narrower than the category of "urbane"), or an intensified shared appreciation of overt theatricality even if it is (seemingly) unaware of its affective extremity. These are frequently features of urbane communities, but not the defining characteristic of urbanity.

106. This kind of trickster figure probably had its origins in what Ann Douglas terms "the fooling techniques of black culture, the 'puttin' on the ole massa' routines of mimicry and role-playing developed in the days of slavery," which minstrelsy put "at the heart of American entertainment" (Douglas, *Terrible Honesty*, 76).

107. See Lott, *Love and Theft*, 123, regarding minstrelsy's regulation of sympathetic treatment of resistance and regression: "If the black threat became too grave, audiences merely amplified the insult. . . . The desperate racial ambivalence that minstrelsy's audiences shared, in other words, *depended* on ridicule to counter the sort of attraction or fear we have repeatedly witnessed." Dialect, too, has a complex legacy, including its contributions to the ragging rhythms that characterized Tin Pan Alley in its early phases, which may be understood to rebel at one stroke against proper, grammatical English and proper (or conventional) musical syntax (see Furia, *Poets of Tin Pan Alley*, and chapter 9 of Douglas, *Terrible Honesty*). In this lineage, dialect begets ragtime, which enforces a displacement in musical reception from contemplation to dance.

108. Regarding the early importance of this showpiece "lecture" in minstrel shows, see Mahar, *Behind the Burnt Cork Mask*, 25, where he notes (based on programs from 1843–1848) that during this early period "lectures are focused almost exclusively on phrenology, which is unexpected given the range of topics available for parody during the period." Elsewhere, Mahar notes that "seventy-two books on the subject [of phrenology] were published between 1825 and 1855" (70). Allied with phrenology were nineteenth-century claims regarding women's intellectual inferiority to men based on skull size and shape, and similarly based twentieth-century claims that Jews were inferior to "Aryans" (the latter term a notorious and spurious appropriation of a racial category by the Nazis).

109. Mahar, *Behind the Burnt Cork Mask*, 72; Levison, *Black Diamonds*, 140–143 (Lecture 43). The entire lecture is available online at http://utc.iath.virginia.edu/minstrel/miesjchat.html, accessed September 1, 2012.

110. The New York African Free School, generally deemed a success, added a second building in 1820. A variety of factors—chief among them disputes over curricula and the nature of black advocacy, external political unrest, population shifts, and the establishment of private black schools—led to declining enrollments around 1830, and the schools were integrated into the public

school system in 1835. For more on the African Free Schools, their operations, and the politics surrounding them, see Rury, "New York African Free School."

111. *Bamboozled* imagines, as a television show, *The New Millennium Minstrel Show* (with black performers in blackface), initially proposed in bitter sarcasm by a pretentious black television writer (played by Damon Wayans), but becoming a surprise hit after blacks in the live studio audience seem to give whites permission to enjoy it. In the end, the weight of the tradition proves too heavy a burden for the show to carry, as both its star performers (Savion Glover and Tommy Davidson) and outsiders begin to see the show as a hateful reversion to a painful legacy, and as a betrayal of those damaged by that legacy and its persistent latter-day echoes. For more on *Bamboozled*, see Knapp, *American Musical and Personal Identity*, 79–94, where I discuss it in tandem with *Stormy Weather* (1943); and chapter 10 of Taylor and Austen, *Darkest America*, which contextualizes the film within the history of reactions to minstrelsy and its legacy.
112. Morris, *Persistence of Sentiment*, 207.
113. Gilbert and Sullivan, *Pirates of Penzance*, 149.
114. Gilbert and Sullivan, *Pirates of Penzance*, 205.
115. Gilbert and Sullivan, *Pirates of Penzance*, 69 and 111. "Unbounded domesticity" is itself a wittily oxymoronic descriptor.
116. Specifically, Dyer, "Judy Garland and Camp," claims it uniquely of a piece with Judy Garland's camp sensibilities: "Only *The Pirate* seems to use Garland's campness in a sustained fashion in its play with sex roles and spectacular illusion, two of the standard pleasures musicals offer" (110). See also Cohan, *Incongruous Entertainment*, 177: "*The Pirate* most completely and most provocatively realizes the camp informing Kelly's performing style as well as Garland's."
117. See Knapp, "Getting Off the Trolley," where I consider *The Wizard of Oz* (1939), *Meet Me in St. Louis* (1944), *Bagdad Cafe* (1987), and *Pane e tulipani* (*Bread and Tulips*; 2000). The term "divorce trope" is an inverted parallel of my term "marriage trope," which refers to a common plot device in musicals wherein "the central conflicts are resolved through the coupling of the principals, whose marriage . . . both symbolizes the resolution of larger conflicts and finds resonance in the community so established" (158–159; see also Knapp, *American Musical and National Identity*, 9; Knapp, *American Musical and Personal Identity*, 10; and Altman, *American Film Musical*, 50).

    Another way to read the "divorce trope" is, from a gay perspective, as a "coming out" scenario—which, indeed, *Bagdad Cafe* approximates, from a lesbian perspective. Regarding the heteronormative ending of *The Pirate*, Farmer (*Spectacular Passions*, 109) argues that "gay spectators of *The Pirate* seeking to clear a space for the articulation of queer fantasies—or fantasies of queerness—can refuse any simple notion of heterosexual containment"; see as well his earlier discussion of "Mack the Black" (105).

118. Knapp, "*Selbst dann bin ich die Welt.*"

119. Regarding nineteenth-century US America's negotiation between musical idealism and entertainment or socially based music, see Baur, "Let Me Make the Ballads," especially chapters 3 and 4 (the latter reelaborated as Baur, "Music, Morals, and Social Management"). Baur, "Of Conductors," locates a particular pivotal point in these developments in the concertizing strategies of conductors Louis Jullien and Theodore Thomas.

120. Horowitz, *Wagner Nights.*

121. Regarding this aspect of *The Jazz Singer* in particular, see chapters 1–2 of Most, *Making Americans.* Regarding the associated concept, often expressed as "the show must go on," see Most, "Birth of Theatrical Liberalism," and, regarding the basis of this and associated concepts in Jewish culture, see Most, *Theatrical Liberalism.*

122. Regarding the relationship between idealism as expressed in musicals and German Idealism, see chapter 4 in Knapp, *American Musical and Personal Identity,* and Knapp, "Performance."

123. As quoted above, "It is in the recognition of illusion that camp finds reality," and, from Dyer ("Entertainment and Utopia," 20): "[Entertainment that engages utopianism] does not, however, present models of utopian worlds. . . . Rather the utopianism is contained in the feelings it embodies. It presents, head-on as it were, what utopia would feel like rather than how it would be organized. It thus works at the level of sensibility, by which I mean an affective code that is characteristic of, and largely specific to, a given mode of cultural production."

124. McMillin, *Musical as Drama,* 2.

125. Knapp, *American Musical and National Identity,* 13; this passage is quoted more fully in note 63.

126. Regarding the category of "authentic," and the relationship of this category to the musical, see Wollman, *Theater Will Rock,* especially 24–41 and chapter 5; see also Knapp, "Performance."

127. Baur, "Of Conductors," details how this reverent attitude was imposed, bodily, under the influence of Theodore Thomas.

5 | "POPULAR MUSIC" QUA GERMAN IDEALISM

1. Exceptions to this exclusionary tendency include the pioneering Charles Hamm, most succinctly in Hamm, "Modernist Narratives and Popular Music" (see below). More aggressively revisionist are Elijah Wald, *How the Beatles Destroyed Rock 'n' Roll*; and Mitchell Morris, *Persistence of Sentiment.* In

setting the stage for his "alternative history," Wald writes, "In the creation of the [jazz and rock] canons, certain artists and styles have been examined in exhaustive detail while others have been ignored, often with little regard for which were more popular or more respected in their time. I understand the value of those canons . . . but because they account for such an immense proportion of the writing on American popular music, it has become hard to see beyond, around, under, and through them and to make sense of the broader picture into which they fit" (*How the Beatles Destroyed Rock 'n' Roll*, 4).

2. Hugh Barker and Yuval Taylor's *Faking It* provides the most extensive exploration of this relationship to date. Pursuant to the previous note, they write, early on: "[The] quest for authenticity has inspired countless musicians to make heartfelt and often groundbreaking music. . . . On the other hand, some great music—including entire genres such as rockabilly, Bubblegum, and disco—has been scorned as inauthentic. At times, the need to 'keep it real' has limited the kinds of music that musicians aspire to make and that critics and listeners appreciate" (xi).
3. In Knapp, Morris, and Wolf, *Oxford Handbook*, 408–421.
4. Charles Taylor offers mostly compatible views on the modern grounding of authenticity in the eighteenth century in chapter 3 of *The Ethics of Authenticity*.
5. Berman, *Politics of Authenticity*, xv; Berman identifies the source for this mode of authenticity to be the Existentialism of Heidegger and Sartre (among others), of which more below.
6. Among many writings about the intertwining of politics and rock and roll, see especially George Lipsitz's "Land of a Thousand Dances." Regarding authenticity as a category in rock criticism, based in Existentialism and the enduring profile of rock as oppositional and rebellious, see Mazullo, "Authenticity in Rock Music Culture."
7. Hunter, "To Play," 372–373.
8. Leistra-Jones, "Staging Authenticity." Regarding the reception of Liszt, both favorable and unfavorable, see S. Bernstein, *Performing Music*, especially chapters 3–5.
9. C. P. E. Bach, in his influential *Versuch über die wahre Art das Clavier zu spielen* (Essay on the True Art of Playing the Clavier, originally published in two parts, 1753 and 1762), argues that a presentational mode that aligns performer with the music being performed must be both authentic and theatrical, so that it may convey something essential about the music to an audience: "Since a musician cannot move us unless he himself is moved, it follows that he must be capable of entering into all the affections which he wishes to arouse in his listeners; he communicates his own feelings to them and thus most effectively moves them to sympathy. . . . We see and hear it"

(from the introduction to the first part, as translated by Piero Weiss, in Weiss and Taruskin, *Music in the Western World*, 272).

10. Arguably, the objectifying impulse of many within the "authentic" performance movement (also with important roots in the 1960s, a movement that is now more often termed "historicist" or "historically informed" than "authentic") places that mode of authenticist performance outside my quasi-religious formulation of how notions of authenticity work within performance traditions. But even within that movement the aura of religiosity lingers to the extent that it may overwhelm and subsume the objectifying stylistic component of the movement. The once-controversial writings of Richard Taruskin that I cite near the beginning of chapter 1 have helped effect a shift in how notions of authenticity have operated within the historical performance movement during the past twenty years or so; see particularly Taruskin, *Text and Act.*
11. See, for example, Daniel Beller-McKenna, *Brahms and the German Spirit.*
12. For the ties connecting Kierkegaard and later Existentialists to German Idealism, particularly as developed by Hegel, see Stewart, *Idealism and Existentialism.*
13. See, for example, Adorno, *Jargon of Authenticity*, an extended screed against Existentialism's appropriation of "authenticity."
14. Burkholder, *Charles Ives.*
15. Ives, *Essays before a Sonata.*
16. Burkholder, *All Made of Tunes.*
17. The extent to which these composers' actual biographies matched this paradigm matters less here than popularizing constructions. Thus, just as contemporary resistance to Beethoven receives much play in program notes, so do Mahler's experiences as a converted Jew from the provinces operating in an increasingly anti-Semitic Vienna, even though the role anti-Semitism played in eclipsing Mahler's posthumous reputation during the Nazi era was more relevant to his later reemergence.
18. Trilling, *Sincerity and Authenticity.*
19. Regarding the increasingly disembodied orchestra, see chapter 1; regarding the capacity of Wagner's orchestra to project deep inwardness, see Knapp, "*Selbst dann bin ich die Welt.*"
20. The distinction arises already in Kant's 1784 essay *Idee zu einer allgemeinen Geschichte in weltbürgerlicher Absicht* (*Idea for a Universal History from a Cosmopolitan Perspective*), where he locates morality exclusively in *Kultur*, whereas *Zivilisation* can claim only honor and decorum.
21. While it has been a subject of contention what these words refer to (see Hinton, "Not 'Which' Tones?"), they channel the energy of the movement's second *Schreckensfanfare*, which follows immediately after the second variation

of the theme devolves into developmental passagework, with a concomitantly greater level of abstraction.

22. Regarding Beethoven's deployment of this trope, see Sipe, *Beethoven.*
23. Regarding the association of youth with "popular music," see Frith, "Youth and Music."
24. Arguments about the relative authenticity of black and white jazz, and concerning folk music traditions, for example, predated the 1960s by several decades in US America; the latter arguments, in fact, have their roots in eighteenth-century Europe, as noted in chapter 1, although the folk music revival was itself built mainly on newly composed music in a style that imitated a folk-based tradition and advanced a political agenda, deriving a degree of perceived authenticity from both.
25. Racial politics and dance provide two main threads that weave in and out—with more than a few surprising twists (and shouts) along the way—of Wald, *How the Beatles Destroyed Rock 'n' Roll.*
26. See Abbott and Seroff, *Ragged but Right*, regarding the role of black minstrel performers in the transition to early ragtime, blues, and jazz.
27. Kernfeld, *Story of Fake Books.* The phrase "faking it" appears regularly in the literature on authenticity in popular music, most recently and prominently in the title of Barker and Taylor's *Faking It.*
28. The standard text here is Henry Louis Gates's *Signifying Monkey.* Alongside the apparent paradox of an authenticity based on faking it is another, entailed within the interracial dimension of blacks performing for whites, captured eloquently in Paul Laurence Dunbar's poem "We Wear the Mask" (Dunbar, *Lyrics of Lowly Life*):

    We wear the mask that grins and lies,
    It hides our cheeks and shades our eyes,—
    This debt we pay to human guile;
    With torn and bleeding hearts we smile,
    And mouth with myriad subtleties.

    . . . .

    We smile, but, O great Christ, our cries
    To thee from tortured souls arise.
    We sing, but oh the clay is vile
    Beneath our feet, and long the mile;
    But let the world dream otherwise,
    We wear the mask!

    This paradox may also dissolve if we imagine that the mask, derived in part from minstrelsy, does not occlude the authentic *something* that emerges perforce in African American musical performance. For related reflections, see Lhamon, *Raising Cain*; and Harell, *We Wear the Mask.*

29. As Elijah Wald notes in *Dozens*, "signifying" is also one of the terms applied to the titular game of trading insults associated with African American males, characteristically centered on sexually maligning the opponent's mother. As Wald also documents, there is a strong history for relating "the dozens" to some jazz practices ("cutting" and other forms of one-upmanship or mockery); these may in turn be traced to dancing competitions dating back to early minstrelsy, and in parallel to other musical traditions that enact competitions between performers.
30. Ken Burns's *Jazz* helped institutionalize the notion that jazz is America's classical music, by endorsing such formulations as consultant Wynton Marsalis's claim that "Ellington is our Mozart." The "America's classical music" claim was in any case already a common trope of introductory accounts of jazz, including Grover Sales's *Jazz*, and Billy Taylor's "Jazz." For a dissenting view, see Jon Pareles's "Don't Call Jazz America's Classical Music."
31. Panassié, *Real Jazz*; and Hodeir, *Jazz*.
32. Guthrie Ramsey's *Race Music* demonstrates how this fault line can impart an intractable yet intricately nuanced quality on a personal level, through examining his own strong identification with black musical cultures.
33. The first of these questions conflates different categories associated with the term "classic": being of a certain vintage and having a high intrinsic value. The second question suggests a more significant overlap between market forces and transformative folk-music processes than may actually obtain, especially given that what constitutes the musical "product" in the first instance, and the music that is subjected to folk-based transformations in the second, are not conceptually the same kind of thing. This is especially true from a neo-Marxist perspective; cf. Hamm's "second narrative of authenticity" ("Modernist Narratives and Popular Music," 23–27).
34. This was, to be sure, exploitative; see Douglas's *Terrible Honesty*, 282–288.
35. This appropriation of a "primitive" race to serve as a symbol for an aesthetic stance may well derive from minstrelsy and its reception in Europe, which found the Americas to be a rich source for the primitive, a habit of reception that also paved the way, especially in France, for an enthusiastic reception of jazz.
36. For one demonstration of how evocations of the primitive can contribute to claims of authenticity, see "Where Did You Sleep Last Night?: Nirvana, Leadbelly, and the Allure of the Primeval" in Barker and Taylor, *Faking It*, 1–27.
37. In a verse long suppressed for being too "communist," Guthrie cheekily denies the legitimacy of private property: "There was a big high wall there that tried to stop me; / Sign was painted, it said 'private property'; / But on the back side it didn't say nothing; / That side was made for you and me" (1940). "If I Had a Hammer" (1949) barely disguises part of the Soviet symbol of "hammer and sickle" as the "hammer of justice," which is paired with the US

American Liberty Bell (the "bell of freedom") in a "song about love between my brothers and my sisters / All over this land."

38. Elijah Wald's *Dylan Goes Electric!* complicates this scenario considerably, setting right many misconceptions about Dylan's role as the central figure in the emergence of folk rock.
39. Philip Auslander's *Performing Glam Rock*, chapter 5, argues that the expanded role of women and of the feminine more generally in glam rock came with a price tag, since its augmented theatricality and role playing impaired rock-based claims to authenticity.
40. Regarding the camp dimension of country music, see chapter 7 of Morris, *Persistence of Sentiment*. Regarding the complicated dance between country music and authenticity, see Peterson, *Creating Country Music*.
41. Besides those works cited in the previous note, see (in examples drawn from my home academic department's PhD dissertations of the past decade alone) Lester Feder's "Song of the South"; Olivia Mather's "Cosmic American Music"; Stephanie Vander Wel's "I Am a Honky-Tonk Girl"; Marcus Desmond Harmon's "Harris/Cash"; and Graham Raulerson's "Hobo in American Musical Culture."
42. The term "hickface" was coined by Robert Walser (personal communication, 2001).
43. Regarding the presumption of authenticity in African American music, see Ronald Radano's *Lying up a Nation*, in particular his jaundiced version of the narrative that "has more or less determined the way we hear performances across a range of genres, from blues to jazz to hip-hop": "The story goes something like this. Black music garners its strength and power from the integrity of a greater African-American culture forged under circumstances of enduring racial oppression. The qualities so often affiliated with black music—its soulfulness, its depth of feeling or 'realness,' its emotional and rhythmic energy, its vocally informed instrumental inflections—grow directly out of the depths of social tragedy only to rise up miraculously as the voice of racial uplift" (xii).
44. Isherwood, "From *The World in the Evening*," 51.
45. The adjective "positive" is still necessary here, as a caveat, since camp is still widely understood as a pejorative category, even in academia. Thus, at a recent international academic conference (June 2014), a presenter discussed the camp orientation of a popular television show under the rubric of "musical irony," explaining later, and in all seriousness, that he had avoided the term "camp" so as not to cast aspersions on the subjects of his work.
46. The campy personae of Waller and Callaway are on full display in the 1943 film *Stormy Weather* (directed by Andrew Stone).
47. Cf. Berman, *Politics of Authenticity*, 45–53, whose discussion of Montesquieu's *Persian Letters* (1721) probes this kind of distinction in cross-cultural terms,

within an argument regarding the greater potential for authenticity within the free sociality of modern urban life in Europe.

6. MUSICAL VIRTUES AND VICES IN THE LATTER-DAY NEW WORLD

Quoted in "Oscar Wilde in Omaha," *Omaha Weekly Herald*, March 24, 1882, 2; as given in Hofer and Scharnhorst, *Oscar Wilde in America*, 99.

1. Dyer, "Entertainment and Utopia," 20. See note 123 in chapter 4 for a more extended quotation.
2. Both of these names derive from French, as a token of affectation, but the surname "de Bris" also suggests a career in ruins ("debris"), or perhaps even circumcision (from Yiddish). More fancifully, "de Bris" may remind us of the "Frenchified trash" Haydn complained he was forced to write in *The Seasons* (1801) by his librettist, Gottfried van Swieten, who wanted more of the kind of descriptive music that had been a recurring feature in many of Handel's oratorios and in their earlier *The Creation* (1798), but which by century's end was considered old-fashioned. While this connection between *The Producers* and Haydn cannot itself be taken seriously, it serves to remind us that, just two years into the new century, the shift in Haydn's receptive environment had already begun, and that the relative lack of success of his second Handel-inspired oratorio was already being blamed on his failure to accommodate music's new calling: to eschew describing the world we know in order to reach for the metaphysical. Haydn's complaint refers to a passage that imitated the croaking of frogs, which he wanted to remove from the piano score; see Landon, *Collected Correspondence*, 197.
3. In the 2001 Broadway musical derived from the film, a slanted mirror made this effect visible.
4. Although bands appeared in symbolic formation since at least the early twentieth century, the style of moving formations that became popular on football fields during the 1960s (often televised) is usually credited to the innovations of bandleader William C. Moffit; see his *Patterns of Motion* (1964, with two follow-up books published in 1965 and 1970).
5. For more on camp's gay foils and heterosexual beards during this period, see Knapp, "Straight Bookends."
6. Regarding camp's broader heterosexual frame, see Knapp, "Straight Bookends."
7. Locke and Hoffmann, "Beethoven's Instrumental Music," 127–128.
8. Morris, "Musical Virtues."
9. Signal among these are Bonds, "Haydn and the Origins of Musical Irony"; Webster, *Haydn's "Farewell" Symphony* and "Haydn's Symphonies"; Wheelock, *Haydn's Ingenious Jesting with Art*; Sisman, "Haydn's Career"; and Lowe, *Pleasure and Meaning*.

Bibliography

Abbott, Lynn, and Seroff, Doug. *Ragged but Right: Black Traveling Shows, "Coon Songs," and the Dark Pathway to Blues and Jazz.* Jackson: University Press of Mississippi, 2007.

Adorno, Theodor. *The Jargon of Authenticity.* Translated by Knut Tarnowski and Frederic Will. Evanston, IL: Northwestern University Press, 1973. Originally published as *Jargon der Eigentlichkeit: zur deutschen Ideologie* (Frankfurt am Main: Suhrkamp Verlag, 1964).

———. *Mahler: A Musical Physiognomy.* Translated by Edmund Jephcott. Chicago: University of Chicago Press, 1992. Originally published as *Mahler: Eine musikalische Physiognomik* (Frankfurt, 1960).

Allanbrook, Wye Jamison. *Rhythmic Gesture in Mozart: "Le nozze di Figaro" and "Don Giovanni."* Chicago: University of Chicago Press, 1983.

Allen, Reginald. *The First Night Gilbert and Sullivan.* New York: Heritage Press, 1958.

Alpers, Paul. "Schiller's Naive and Sentimental Poetry and the Modern Idea of the Pastoral." In *Cabinet of the Muses: Essays on Classical and Comparative Literature in Honor of Thomas G. Rosenmeyer,* edited by Mark Griffith and Donald J. Mastronarde, 319–331. Atlanta: Scholars Press, 1990.

Al-Taee, Nasser. *Representations of the Orient in Western Music: Violence and Sensuality.* Farnham, UK: Ashgate, 2010.

———. "The Sultan's Seraglio: Fact, Fiction, and Fantasy in Eighteenth-Century Viennese 'Turkish' Music." PhD diss., University of California, Los Angeles, 1999.

Altman, Rick. *The American Film Musical.* Bloomington: Indiana University Press, 1987.

Anderson, Emily, ed. and trans. *The Letters of Mozart and His Family.* 3 vols. 3rd ed. Rev. Stanley Sadie and Fiona Smart. London, 1938; New York: W. W. Norton, 1985. Originally published in London, 1938.

Angermüller, Rudolph. "Haydns *Der Zerstreute* in Salzburg (1776)." *Haydn-Studien* IV (1978): 85–93.

Applegate, Celia. *Bach in Berlin: Nation and Culture in Mendelssohn's Revival of the "St. Matthew Passion."* Ithaca: Cornell University Press, 2005.

———. "How German Is It? Nationalism and the Idea of Serious Music in the Early Nineteenth Century." *19th-Century Music* 21 (1998): 274–296.

Applegate, Celia and Pamela Potter, eds. *Music and German National Identity.* Chicago: University of Chicago Press, 2002.

Auslander, Philip. *Performing Glam Rock: Gender and Theatricality in Popular Music.* Ann Arbor: University of Michigan Press, 2006.

Austin, William W. *"Susanna," "Jeanie," and "The Old Folks at Home": The Songs of Stephen C. Foster from His Time to Ours.* New York: Macmillan, 1975.

Avcioglu, Nebahat. *Turquerie and the Politics of Representation, 1728–1876.* Farnham, UK: Ashgate, 2011.

Babbitt, Milton. "Who Cares If You Listen?" In *Contemporary Composers on Contemporary Music,* edited by Elliott Schwartz and Barney Childs, 243–245. New York: Da Capo Press, 1978. Originally published in Chicago, 1967.

Babuscio, Jack. "Camp and the Gay Sensibility." In *Gays and Film,* edited by Richard Dyer, 40–57. London: British Film Institute, 1977. Reprinted and expanded as "The Cinema of Camp (AKA Camp and the Gay Sensibility)," in *Camp: Queer Aesthetics and the Performing Subject: A Reader,* 117–135 (Edinburgh: Edinburgh University Press, 1999).

Bakhtin, Mikhail M. *Rabelais and His World.* Translated by Hélène Iswolsky. Cambridge, MA: MIT Press, 1984. Originally published Moscow: Khudozhestvennaya Literatura, 1965.

Barker, Hugh, and Yuval Taylor. *Faking It: The Quest for Authenticity in Popular Music.* New York: W. W. Norton, 2007.

Baur, Steven. "'Let Me Make the Ballads of a Nation and I Care Not Who Makes Its Laws': Music, Culture, and Social Politics in the United States, c. 1860–1890." PhD diss., University of California, Los Angeles, 2001.

———. "Music, Morals, and Social Management: Mendelssohn in Post–Civil War America." *American Music* 19, no. 1 (spring, 2001): 64–130.

———. "Of Conductors, Orchestras, and Docile Bodies: Concert Culture as Embodied Experience in Gilded Age America." Unpublished paper, Society for American Music Annual Meeting, Cincinnati, March 2011. (I thank the author for sharing this paper with me in advance of publication.)

———. "Rhythm, Percussion, and the Performance of Social Class in the Blackface Minstrel Show." Unpublished paper, IASPM-Canada Conference, Dalhousie

University, June 13, 2009. (I thank the author for allowing me to quote from this paper.)
Beckerman, Michael. "Dvořák's 'New World' Largo and *The Song of Hiawatha.*" *19th-Century Music* 16 (summer 1992): 35–48.
———. *New Worlds of Dvořák: Searching in America for the Composer's Inner Life.* New York: Norton, 2003.
Beghin, Tom, and Sander M. Goldberg, eds. *Haydn and the Performance of Rhetoric.* Chicago: University of Chicago Press, 2007.
Beller-McKenna, Daniel. *Brahms and the German Spirit: Nationalism and Religion in the Music of Johannes Brahms, with Special Emphasis on the Large-Scale Sacred Choral Works.* Cambridge, MA: Harvard University Press, 2004.
Bent, Ian. "Heinrich Schenker, Chopin and Domenico Scarlatti." *Music Analysis* 5, nos. 2/3 (July–October 1986): 131–149.
Berlioz, Hector. *Lélio, ou le Retour à la vie.* Edited by Charles Malherbe and Felix Weingartner. *Hector Berlioz Werke,* Serie V, Band 13. Leipzig: Breitkopf & Härtel, 1900–1907.
Berman, Marshall. *The Politics of Authenticity: Radical Individualism and the Emergence of Modern Society.* New York: Atheneum, 1970.
Bernstein, Matthew, ed. *Controlling Hollywood: Censorship and Regulation in the Studio Era.* New Brunswick, NJ: Rutgers University Press, 1999.
Bernstein, Susan. *Performing Music and Language in Heine, Liszt, and Baudelaire.* Stanford, CA: Stanford University Press, 1998.
Beveridge, David. "Dvořák and Brahms: A Chronicle, an Interpretation." In *Dvořák and His World,* edited by Michael Beckerman, 56–91. Princeton, NJ: Princeton University Press, 2001.
Blasius, Leslie David. *Schenker's Argument and the Claims of Music Theory.* Cambridge: Cambridge University Press, 1996.
Blume, Friedrich. *Classic and Romantic Music: A Comprehensive Survey.* Translated by M. D. Herter Norton. New York: W. W. Norton & Company, 1970. Originally published in *Die Musik in Geschichte und Gegenwart: Allgemeine Enzyklopädie der Musik,* edited by Friedrich Blume (Kassel: Bärenreiter-Verlag, 1958 and 1963).
Bonds, Mark Evan. *Absolute Music: The History of an Idea.* New York: Oxford University Press, 2014.
———. "Haydn, Laurence Sterne, and the Origins of Musical Irony." *Journal of the American Musicological Society* 44, no. 1 (1991): 57–91.
———. "Haydn's 'Cours complet de la composition' and the *Sturm und Drang.*" In *Haydn Studies,* edited by W. Dean Sutcliffe, 152–176. Cambridge: Cambridge University Press, 1998.

———. "Haydn's False Recapitulations and the Perception of Sonata Form in the Eighteenth Century." PhD diss., Harvard University, 1988.

———. "Listening to Listeners." In *Communication in Eighteenth-Century Music*, edited by Danuta Mirka and Kofi Agawu, 34–52. Cambridge: Cambridge University Press, 2008.

———. *Music as Thought: Listening to the Symphony in the Age of Beethoven*. Princeton, NJ: Princeton University Press, 2006.

———. "Replacing Haydn: Mozart's 'Pleyel' Quartets." *Music and Letters* 88 (2007): 201–225.

———. "Rhetoric versus Truth: Listening to Haydn in the Age of Beethoven." In *Haydn and the Performance of Rhetoric*, edited by Tom Beghin and Sander M. Goldberg, 109–128. Chicago: University of Chicago Press, 2007.

Botstein, Leon. "The Consequences of Presumed Innocence: The Nineteenth-Century Reception of Joseph Haydn." In *Haydn Studies*, edited by W. Dean Sutcliffe, 1–34. Cambridge: Cambridge University Press, 1998.

———. "The Demise of Philosophical Listening." In *Haydn and His World*, edited by Elaine Sisman, 255–288. Princeton, NJ: Princeton University Press, 1997.

———. "The Patrons and Publics of the Quartets: Music, Culture, and Society in Beethoven's Vienna." In *The Beethoven Quartet Companion*, edited by Robert Winter and Robert Martin, 76–109. Berkeley: University of California Press, 1994.

Bowie, Andrew. *Aesthetics and Subjectivity: From Kant to Nietzsche*. 2nd ed. Manchester, UK: Manchester University Press, 2003. Originally published in 1990.

Boym, Svetlana. *The Future of Nostalgia*. New York: Basic Books, 2001.

Brandenburg, Sieghard. "The First Version of Beethoven's G Major String Quartet, Op. 18 No. 2." *Music & Letters* 58, no. 2 (1977): 127–152.

Brinkmann, Reinhold, and Christoph Wolff, eds. *Driven into Paradise: The Musical Migration from Nazi Germany to the United States*. Berkeley: University of California Press, 1999.

Broadwell, Peter. "Swashbucklers on Stage: Musical Depictions of Pirates and Bandits in English Theater, 1650–1820." PhD diss., University of California, Los Angeles, 2011.

Brodbeck, David. *Defining "Deutschtum": Political Ideology, German Identity, and Music-Critical Discourse in Liberal Vienna*. Oxford: Oxford University Press, 2014.

———. "Dvořák's Reception in Liberal Vienna: Language, Ordinances, National Property, and the Rhetoric of *Deutschtum*. *Journal of the American Musicological Society* 60 (2007): 71–131.

Brown, A. Peter. "Haydn's Chaos: Genesis and Genre." *Musical Quarterly* 73 (1989): 18–59.

Burkholder, J. Peter. *All Made of Tunes: Charles Ives and the Uses of Musical Borrowing.* New Haven, CT: Yale University Press, 1995.

———. *Charles Ives: The Ideas Behind the Music.* New Haven, CT: Yale University Press, 1985.

Burnham, Scott. "Haydn and Humor." In *The Cambridge Companion to Haydn,* edited by Caryl Clark, 61–76. Cambridge: Cambridge University Press, 2005.

Burns, Ken. *Jazz.* Ten-part documentary. PBS. 2000. With CD release *Ken Burns Jazz: The Story of America's Music.*

Burwick, Frederick. *Playing to the Crowd: London Popular Theatre, 1780–1830.* New York: Palgrave Macmillan, 2011.

Caldwell, A. E. "La Malinconia: Final Movement of Beethoven's Quartet Op. 18, No. 6: A Musical Account of Manic Depressive States." *Woman Physician* 27 (1972): 241–248.

Carpani, Giuseppe. *Le Haydine, ovvero Lettere sulla vita e le opera del celebre maestro Giusseppe Haydn.* Milan: Candido Buccinelli, 1812.

Carter, David. *Stonewall: The Riots That Sparked the Gay Revolution.* New York: St. Martin's Press, 2004.

Chafe, Eric. *Tonal Allegory in the Vocal Music of J. S. Bach.* New York: Oxford University Press, 1991.

Chantler, Abigail. *E. T. A. Hoffmann's Musical Aesthetics.* Aldershot, UK: Ashgate, 2006.

Chauncey, George. "The Double Life, Camp Culture, and the Making of a Collective Identity." In *Gay New York: Gender, Urban Culture, and the Making of the Gay Male World, 1890–1940,* 270–299. New York: Basic Books, 1994.

———. *Gay New York: Gender, Urban Culture, and the Making of the Gay Male World, 1890–1940.* New York: Basic Books, 1994.

Chua, Daniel. *Absolute Music and the Construction of Meaning.* Cambridge: Cambridge University Press, 1999.

———. "Haydn as Romantic: A Chemical Experiment with Instrumental Music." In *Haydn Studies,* edited by W. Dean Sutcliffe, 120–151. Cambridge: Cambridge University Press, 1998.

Clark, Caryl, ed. *The Cambridge Companion to Haydn.* Cambridge: Cambridge University Press, 2005.

Cleto, Fabio, ed. *Camp: Queer Aesthetics and the Performing Subject: A Reader.* Edinburgh: Edinburgh University Press, 1999.

———. "Digging the Scene: A Bibliography of Secondary Materials, 1869–1997." In *Camp: Queer Aesthetics and the Performing Subject: A Reader,* edited by Fabio Cleto, 458–512. Edinburgh: Edinburgh University Press, 1999.

———. "Introduction: Queering the Camp." In *Camp: Queer Aesthetics and the Performing Subject: A Reader*, edited by Fabio Cleto, 1–42. Edinburgh: Edinburgh University Press, 1999.
Clum, John M. "Acting." In *The Oxford Handbook of the American Musical*, edited by Raymond Knapp, Mitchell Morris, and Stacy Wolf, 309–319. New York: Oxford University Press, 2011.
———. *Something for the Boys: Musical Theater and Gay Culture*. New York: St. Martin's Press, 1999.
Cockrell, Dale. *Demons of Disorder: Early Blackface Minstrels and Their World*. Cambridge: Cambridge University Press, 1997.
Cohan, Steven. *Incongruous Entertainment: Camp, Cultural Value, and the MGM Musical*. Durham, NC: Duke University Press, 2005.
Collins, Randall. *The Sociology of Philosophies: A Global Theory of Intellectual Change*. Cambridge, MA: Harvard University Press, 1998.
Crawford, Richard. *The American Musical Landscape*. Berkeley: University of California Press, 1993.
———. *America's Musical Life: A History*. 2nd ed. 2001. Reprint, New York: W. W. Norton, 2005.
Dahlhaus, Carl. *Between Romanticism and Modernism: Four Studies in the Music of the Later Nineteenth Century*, translated by Mary Whittall, 103–120. Berkeley: University of California Press, 1980. Originally published in Munich, 1974.
———. *The Idea of Absolute Music*. Translated by Roger Lustig. Chicago: University of Chicago Press, 1989. Originally published in Kassel, 1978.
———. "Issues in Composition." In *Between Romanticism and Modernism: Four Studies in the Music of the Later Nineteenth Century*, translated by Mary Whittall, 40–78. Berkeley: University of California Press, 1980. Originally published in Munich, 1974.
———. "Musical Prose." In *Schoenberg and the New Music*, translated by Derrick Puffett and Alfred Clayton, 105–119. Cambridge: Cambridge University Press, 1987. Originally published in 1964.
———. *Nineteenth-Century Music*. Translated by J. Bradford Robinson. Berkeley: University of California Press, 1989. Originally published Wiesbaden: Akademische Verlagsgesellschaft Athenaion and Laaber: Laaber-Verlag, 1980.
———. *Realism in Nineteenth-Century Music*. Translated by Mary Whittall. Cambridge: Cambridge University Press, 1985. Originally published Munich: R. Piper, 1982.
———. "The Twofold Truth in Wagner's Aesthetics: Nietzsche's Fragment 'On Music and Words.'" In *Between Romanticism and Modernism: Four Studies in the Music of the Later Nineteenth Century*, translated by Mary Whittall, 19–39.

Berkeley: University of California Press, 1980. Originally published Munich, 1974.
Decker, Todd. *Music Makes Me: Fred Astaire and Jazz*. Berkeley: University of California Press, 2011.
———. "On the Scenic Route to *Irving Berlin's Holiday Inn* (1942)." *Journal of Musicology* 28, no. 4 (fall 2011): 464–497.
Deer, Joe, and Rocco Dal Vera. *Acting in Musical Theatre: A Comprehensive Course*. London: Routledge, 2008.
di Giovanni, George. *Freedom and Religion in Kant and His Immediate Successors: The Vocation of Humankind, 1774–1800*. Cambridge: Cambridge University Press, 2005.
Dolan, Emily I. "Haydn, Hoffmann, and the Opera of Instruments." *Studia Musicologica* 51 (2010): 325–346.
Douglas, Ann. *Terrible Honesty: Mongrel Manhattan in the 1920s*. New York: Farrar, Straus and Giroux, 1995.
Duberman, Martin. *Stonewall*. New York: Dutton, 1993.
Dunbar, Paul Laurence. *Lyrics of Lowly Life*. New York: Dodd, Mead, and Company, 1896.
Dyer, Richard. "Entertainment and Utopia." In *Only Entertainment*, edited by Richard Dyer, 17–34. London: Routledge, 1992.
———. "Judy Garland and Camp." In *Heavenly Bodies*, 178–186. New York: St. Martin's Press: Macmillan, 1986. Reprinted in *Hollywood Musicals: The Film Reader*, edited by Steven Cohan, 107–113 (London: Routledge, 2002).
Edwall, Harry R. "Ferdinand IV and Haydn's Concertos for the *Lira organizzata*." *Musical Quarterly* 48 (1962): 190–203.
Edwards, George. "Papa Doc's Recap Caper: Haydn and Temporal Dyslexia." In *Haydn Studies*, edited by Dean Sutcliffe, 291–320. Cambridge: Cambridge University Press, 1998.
Elias, Norbert. *The History of Manners*. New York: Pantheon Books, 1978.
Farmer, Brett. *Spectacular Passions: Cinema, Fantasy, Gay Male Spectatorships*. Durham, NC: Duke University Press, 2000.
Fay, Amy. *Music Study in Germany: From the Home Correspondence of Amy Fay*. London: MacMillan, 1886.
Feder, Georg. "Similarities in the Works of Haydn." In *Studies in Eighteenth-Century Music: A Tribute to Karl Geiringer on his Seventieth Birthday*, edited by H. C. Robbins Landon and Roger Chapman, 186–197. New York: Oxford University Press, 1970.
Feder, J. Lester. "'Song of the South': Country Music, Race, Region, and the Politics of Culture 1920–1974." PhD diss., University of California, Los Angeles, 2005.

Feuer, Jane. *The Hollywood Musical*. 2nd ed. Bloomington: Indiana University Press, 1993.
Fink, Robert. "Going Flat: Towards a Post-Hierarchical Music Theory." In *Rethinking Music*, edited by Nicholas Cook and Mark Everist, 102–137. Oxford: Oxford University Press, 1999.
Finscher, Ludwig. "Die Theorie des Streichquartetts." In *Die Entstehung des klassischen Streichquartetts: Von den Vorformen zur Grundlegung durch Joseph Haydn*, 277–301. Vol. 1 of *Studien zur Geschichte des Streichquartetts*. Basel: Bärenreiter Kassel, 1974.
Forbes, Elliot, ed. *Thayer's Life of Beethoven*. Princeton, NJ: Princeton University Press, 1967.
Forkel, Johann Nikolaus. *Über Johann Sebastian Bachs Leben, Kunst, und Kunstwerke*. Edited by Walther Vetter. Berlin: Henschelverlag, 1966. Originally published Leipzig, 1802.
Frith, Simon. "Youth and Music (1978)." In *Taking Popular Music Seriously*, 1–29. Aldershot, UK: Ashgate, 2007. Excerpted from *The Sociology of Rock* (London: Constable, 1978).
Furia, Philip. *The Poets of Tin Pan Alley: A History of America's Greatest Lyrics*. New York: Oxford University Press, 1990.
Gans, Herbert. *Popular Culture and High Culture*. New York: Basic Books, 1974.
Garratt, James. "Haydn and Posterity: The Long Nineteenth Century." In *The Cambridge Companion to Haydn*, edited by Caryl Clark, 226–238. Cambridge: Cambridge University Press, 2005.
Gates, Henry Louis, Jr. *The Signifying Monkey: A Theory of African-Ameican Literary Criticism*. Oxford: Oxford University Press, 1988.
Gay, Peter. *The Naked Heart*. New York: W. W. Norton, 1995. Vol. 4 of *The Bourgeois Experience: Victoria to Freud*.
Geiringer, Karl. *Joseph Haydn and the Eighteenth Century: Collected Essays of Karl Geiringer*. Edited by Robert N. Freeman. Warren, MI: Harmonie Park Press, 2002.
———. "The Portrait of Haydn over the Course of Time." In *Joseph Haydn and the Eighteenth Century: Collected Essays of Karl Geiringer*, edited by Robert N. Freeman, 9–18. Translated by Therese Ahren-August and Robert N. Freeman. Warren, MI: Harmonie Park Press, 2002. Original essay published as "Das Haydn-Bild im Wandel der Zeiten," *Die Musik* 24, no. 6 (1932): 430–436.
Geiringer, Karl, and Irene Geiringer. *Haydn: A Creative Life in Music*. 3rd ed. Berkeley: University of California Press, 1982. Revised and enlarged from Karl Geiringer's texts of 1946 and 1961.

Gilbert, William S., and Arthur Sullivan. *The Complete Plays of Gilbert and Sullivan*. New York: W. W. Norton & Company, 1976. Originally published Garden City, 1941.

———. *Patience; or Bunthorne's Bride*. Performing edition [piano vocal score with dialogue]. Melville, NY: Belwin Mills, 1970.

———. *The Pirates of Penzance; or, the Slave of Duty*. Performing edition [piano vocal score with dialogue]. New York: G. Schirmer, 2002.

Gloag, Kenneth. "The String Quartet in the Twentieth Century." In *The Cambridge Companion to the String Quartet*, edited by Robin Stowell, 288–309. Cambridge: Cambridge University Press, 2003.

Goehr, Lydia. *The Imaginary Museum of Musical Works: An Essay in the Philosophy of Music*. Oxford: Oxford University Press, 1992.

Gramit, David. *Cultivating Music: The Aspirations, Interests, and Limits of German Musical Culture, 1770–1848*. Berkeley: University of California Press, 2002.

Griffel, Margaret Ross. "'Turkish' Opera from Mozart to Cornelius." PhD diss., Columbia University, 1975.

Grim, William E. "The Coining of the Term 'Sturm und Drang' and Its Use in Music Historiography." In *Haydn's "Sturm und Drang" Symphonies: Form and Meaning*, 6–35. Lewiston, NY: Edwin Mellen Press, 1990.

Haimo, Ethan. *Haydn's Symphonic Forms: Essays in Compositional Logic*. New York: Oxford University Press, 1995.

Hamm, Charles. "Dvořák in America: Nationalism, Racism, and National Race." In *Putting Popular Music in Its Place*, 344–353. Cambridge: Cambridge University Press, 1995.

———. "Modernist Narratives and Popular Music." In *Putting Popular Music in Its Place*, 1–40. Cambridge: Cambridge University Press, 1995.

———. *Music in the New World*. New York: W. W. Norton, 1983.

Hammermeister, Kai. *The German Aesthetic Tradition*. Cambridge: Cambridge University Press, 2002.

Hanslick, Eduard. *Vom Musikalische-Schönen: Ein Beitrag zur Revision der Aesthetik der Tonkunst* [On the Musically Beautiful: A Contribution towards the Revision of the Aesthetics of Music] (Leipzig: Rudolph Weigel, 1854). Translated by Geoffrey Payzant. Indianapolis, IN: Hackett, 1986.

Harell, Willie J., ed. *We Wear the Mask: Paul Laurence Dunbar and the Politics of Representative Reality*. Kent, OH: Kent State University Press, 2010.

Harmon, Marcus Desmond. "Harris/Cash: Identity, Loss, and Mourning at the Borders of Country Music." PhD diss., University of California, Los Angeles, 2011.

Harrison, Bernard. *Haydn: The "Paris" Symphonies*. Cambridge: Cambridge University Press, 1998.

Hartman, Geoffrey. *The Fateful Question of Culture*. New York: Columbia University Press, 1997.
Haydn, Joseph. *30 berühmte Quartette*. Frankfurt: Peters, 1918.
———. *Concerti mit Orgelleiern*. Edited by Makoto Ohmiya. Munich, 1976. Vol. 6 of *Joseph Haydn Werke*. Edited by Georg Feder.
Head, Matthew. "Haydn's Exoticisms: 'Difference' and the Enlightenment." In *The Cambridge Companion to Haydn*, edited by Caryl Clark, 77–92. Cambridge: Cambridge University Press, 2005.
———. *Masquerade and Mozart's Turkish Music*. London: Royal Musical Association Monographs, 2000.
———. "Music with 'No Past?' Archaeologies of Joseph Haydn and 'The Creation.'" *19th-Century Music* 23, no. 3 (spring 2000): 191–217.
Hecker, Max, ed. *Briefwechsel zwischen Goethe und Zelter, 1799–1832*. 4 vols. Bern: H. Lang, 1970.
Hefling, Stephen E. "The Austro-Germanic Quartet Tradition in the Nineteenth Century." In *The Cambridge Companion to the String Quartet*, edited by Robin Stowell, 228–249. Cambridge: Cambridge University Press, 2003.
Henrich, Dieter. *Between Kant and Hegel: Lectures on German Idealism*. Edited by David S. Pacini. Cambridge, MA: Harvard University Press, 2003.
Hepokoski, James, and Warren Darcy. *Elements of Sonata Theory: Norms, Types, and Deformations in the Late Eighteenth-Century*. Oxford: Oxford University Press, 2006.
Hickman, Roger. "Haydn and the 'Symphony in Miniature.'" *Music Review* 43 (1982): 15–23.
Hinton, Stephen. "Not 'Which' Tones? The Crux of Beethoven's Ninth." *19th-Century Music* 22, no. 1 (summer 1998): 61–77.
Hitchcock, H. Wiley. *Music in the United States: A Historical Introduction*. 3rd ed. Englewood Cliffs, NJ: Prentice Hall, 1988.
Hodeir, André. *Jazz: Its Evolution and Essence*. Translated by David Noakes. New York: Grove Press, 1956. Updated from *Hommes et problems du jazz*, 1954.
Hoeckner, Berthold. *Programming the Absolute: Nineteenth-Century German Music and the Hermeneutics of the Moment*. Princeton and Oxford: Princeton University Press, 2002.
Hofer, Matthew, and Gary Scharnhorst, eds. *Oscar Wilde in America: The Interviews*. Urbana: University of Illinois Press, 2010.
Hoffmann, E. T. A. *E. T. A. Hoffmann's Musical Writings: Kreisleriana, The Poet, and the Composer: Music Criticism*. Edited by David Charlton. Translated by Martyn Clarke. Cambridge: Cambridge University Press, 1989.
Holloway, Robin. "Haydn: The Musician's Musician." In *Haydn Studies*, edited by Dean Sutcliffe, 321–334. Cambridge: Cambridge University Press, 1998.

Horowitz, Joseph. *Wagner Nights: An American History*. Berkeley: University of California Press, 1994.
Hubbs, Nadine. *Gay Modernists, American Music, and National Identity: The Queer Composition of America's Sound*. Berkeley: University of California Press, 2004.
Hughes, Rosemary. *Haydn String Quartets*. Seattle: University of Washington Press, 1969. Originally published London: British Broadcasting Corporation, 1966.
Hunter, Mary. "The *Alla Turca* Style in the Late Eighteenth Century: Race and Gender in the Symphony and the Seraglio." In *The Exotic in Western Music*, edited by Jonathan Bellman, 43–73. Boston: Northeastern University Press, 1997.
———. "Haydn's London Piano Trios and His Salomon String Quartets: Private vs. Public?" In *Haydn and His World*, edited by Elaine Sisman, 103–130. Princeton, NJ: Princeton University Press, 1997.
———. " 'To Play As If from the Soul of the Composer': The Idea of the Performer in Early Romantic Aesthetics." *Journal of the American Musicological Society* 58, no. 2 (2005): 357–398.
———. "The Quartets." In *The Cambridge Companion to Haydn*, edited by Caryl Clark, 112–125. Cambridge: Cambridge University Press, 2005.
Isherwood, Christopher. "From *The World in the Evening*." In *Camp: Queer Aesthetics and the Performing Subject: A Reader*, edited by Fabio Cleto, 49–52. Edinburgh: Edinburgh University Press, 1999. Originally published New York: Random House, 1954.
Ives, Charles. *Essays before a Sonata*. Edited by Howard Boatwright. New York: Norton, 1961. Originally printed 1920.
Jahn, Otto. *Life of Mozart*. Translated by Pauline D. Townsend. 3 vols. London: Novello, Ewer, 1882.
Jones, David Wyn. "Beethoven and the Viennese Legacy." In *The Cambridge Companion to the String Quartet*, edited by Robin Stowell, 210–227. Cambridge: Cambridge University Press, 2003.
———. "The Origins of the Quartet." In *The Cambridge Companion to the String Quartet*, edited by Robin Stowell, 177–184. Cambridge: Cambridge University Press, 2003.
Josephson, David. "The German Musical Exile and the Course of American Musicology." *Current Musicology* 79 and 80 (2005): 9–53.
Judy Garland Database. Accessed April 6, 2012. http://www.jgdb.com/babes.htm.
Katz, Jonathan Ned. *Gay/Lesbian Almanac*. New York: Harper & Row, 1983.
Kennedy, Michael, ed. *The Oxford Dictionary of Music*. 2nd ed. rev. Oxford University Press, 2007–2012. Accessed May 19, 2012. http://www.oxfordmusiconline.com/subscriber/article/opr/t237/e4102?q=galant&hbutton

_search.x=0&hbutton_search.y=0&hbutton_search=search&source=omo_t237&search=quick&pos=1&_start=1#firsthit.
Kerman, Joseph. "Beethoven Quartet Audiences: Actual, Potential, Ideal." In *The Beethoven Quartet Companion*, edited by Robert Winter and Robert Martin, 6–27. Berkeley, Los Angeles, and London: University of California Press, 1994.
———. *The Beethoven Quartets*. New York: Alfred A. Knopf, 1967.
Kernfeld, Barry. *The Story of Fake Books: Bootlegging Songs to Musicians*. Lanham, MD: Scarecrow Press, 2006.
Kimber, Marian Wilson. "The 'Suppression' of Fanny Mendelssohn: Rethinking Feminist Biography." *19th-Century Music* 26, no. 2 (fall 2002): 113–129.
Kittler, Friedrich A. *Discourse Networks, 1800/1900*. Translated by Michael Metteer and Chris Cullens. Stanford, CA: Stanford University Press, 1990. Originally published 1985.
Knapp, Raymond. *The American Musical and the Formation of National Identity*. Princeton, NJ: Princeton University Press, 2005.
———. *The American Musical and the Performance of Personal Identity*. Princeton, NJ: Princeton University Press, 2006.
———. "Getting Off the Trolley: Musicals *contra* Cinematic Reality." In *From Stage to Screen: Musical Films in Europe and United States, 1927–1961*, edited by Massimiliano Sala, 157–172. Vol. 18 of *Speculum Musicae*. Turnhout, Belgium: Brepols, 2012.
———. "'How Great Thy Charm, Thy Sway How Excellent!': Tracing Gilbert and Sullivan's Legacy in the American Musical." In *The Cambridge Companion to Gilbert and Sullivan*, edited by David Eden and Meinhard Saremba, 201–215. Cambridge: Cambridge University Press, 2009.
———. "The Musical Faces of Pirate Camp in Hollywood (Part I)." *Music and the Moving Image* 7, no. 2 (summer 2014): 3–33.
———. "Music, Electricity, and the 'Sweet Mystery of Life' in *Young Frankenstein*." In *Changing Tunes: The Use of Pre-existing Music in Film*, edited by Phil Powrie and Robynn Stilwell, 105–118. Aldershot, UK: Ashgate, 2006.
———. "On the Inner Dimension of Heroic Struggle in Beethoven's *Eroica*: A Mahlerian Perspective (And What That Might Tell Us)." *Beethoven Forum* 11 (2004): 41–89.
———. "Performance, Authenticity, and the Reflexive Idealism of the American Musical." In *The Oxford Handbook of the American Musical*, edited by Raymond Knapp, Mitchell Morris, and Stacy Wolf, 408–421. New York: Oxford University Press, 2011.
———. "Reading Gender in Late Beethoven: *An die Freude* and *An die ferne Geliebte*." *Acta musicologica* 75, no. 1 (2003): 45–63.

———. "'*Selbst dann bin ich die Welt*': On the Subjective-Musical Basis of Wagner's *Gesamtkunstwelt*." *19th-Century Music* 29 (fall 2005): 142–160.
———. "The Straight Bookends to Camp's Gay Golden Age: From Gilbert and Sullivan to Roger Vadim and Mel Brooks." In *Music and Camp*, edited by Christopher Moore and Philip Purvis. Middletown, CT: Wesleyan University Press, forthcoming.
———. "Suffering Children: Perspectives on Innocence and Vulnerability in Mahler's Fourth Symphony." *19th-Century Music* 22 (spring 1999): 233–267.
———. *Symphonic Metamorphoses: Subjectivity and Alienation in Mahler's Re-Cycled Songs*. Middletown, CT: Wesleyan University Press, 2003.
———. "A Tale of Two Symphonies: Converging Narratives of Divine Reconciliation in Beethoven's Fifth and Sixth." *Journal of the American Musicological Society* 53 (2000): 291–343.
Knapp, Raymond, and Mitchell Morris. "The Filmed Musical." In *The Oxford Handbook of the American Musical*, edited by Raymond Knapp, Mitchell Morris, and Stacy Wolf, 136–151. Oxford: Oxford University Press, 2011.
Knapp, Raymond, Mitchell Morris, and Stacy Wolf, eds. *The Oxford Handbook of the American Musical*. Oxford: Oxford University Press, 2011.
Knight, Arthur. *Disintegrating the Musical: Black Performance and American Musical Film*. Durham, NC: Duke University Press, 2002.
Koegel, John. *Music in German Immigrant Theater, New York City, 1840–1940*. Rochester, NY: University of Rochester Press, 2009.
Krafft-Ebing, Richard von. *Psychopathia Sexualis: Eine Klinisch-Forensische Studie*. Stuttgart, Germany: Enke, 1886.
Kramer, Lawrence. *Classical Music and Postmodern Knowledge*. Berkeley: University of California Press, 1995.
———. "The Harem Threshold: Turkish Music and Greek Love in Beethoven's 'Ode to Joy.'" *19th-Century Music* 22, no. 1 (summer 1998): 78–90.
———. "Haydn's Chaos, Schenker's Order; Or, Hermeneutics and Musical Analysis: Can They Mix?" *19th-Century Music* 16, no. 1 (summer 1992): 3–17.
———. "The Kitten and the Tiger: Tovey's Haydn." In *The Cambridge Companion to Haydn*, edited by Caryl Clark, 239–248. Cambridge: Cambridge University Press, 2005.
———. *Musical Meaning: Toward a Critical History*. Berkeley: University of California Press, 2002.
———. "Music and Representation: The Instance of Haydn's *Creation*." In *Music and Text: Critical Inquiries*, edited by Steven Paul Scher, 139–162. Cambridge: Cambridge University Press, 1992.
———. *Music as Cultural Practice, 1800–1900*. Berkeley: University of California Press, 1993.

Kramer, Richard. "Haydn's *Chaos* and Herder's *Logos*." In *Unfinished Music*, 153–170. Oxford: Oxford University Press, 2008.

La Grange, Henry-Louis de. *Gustav Mahler*. Vol. 2, *Vienna: The Years of Challenge (1897–1904)*. Oxford: Oxford University Press, 1995.

Landon, H. C. Robbins. *The Collected Correspondence and London Notebooks of Joseph Haydn*. London: Barrie and Rockliff, 1959.

———, ed. *Haydn: Chronicle and Works*. 5 vols. Bloomington: Indiana University Press, 1976–1980.

Landon, H. C. Robbins, and David Wyn Jones. *Haydn: His Life and Music*. Bloomington: Indiana University Press, 1988.

Larsen, Jens Peter. "Sonata Form Problems." In *Handel, Haydn, and the Viennese Classical Style*, translated by Ulrich Krämer, 269–279. Ann Arbor: University of Michigan Research Press, 1988. Originally published in *Festschrift Friedrich Blume* (Kassel: Bärenreiter, 1963), 221–230.

LaRue, Jan. "Bifocal Tonality in Haydn Symphonies." In *Convention in Eighteenth- and Nineteenth-Century Music: Essays in Honor of Leonard G. Ratner*, edited by Wye J. Allanbrook, 59–73. Stuyvesant, NY: Pendragon Press, 1992.

Leff, Leonard J., and Jerrald Simmons. *The Dame in the Kimono: Hollywood, Censorship, and the Production Code from the 1920s to the 1960s*. New York: Grove Weidenfeld, 1990.

Le Guin, Elisabeth. "A Visit to the Salon de Parnasse." In *Haydn and the Performance of Rhetoric*, edited by Tom Beghin and Sander M. Goldberg, 14–35. Chicago: University of Chicago Press, 2007.

Leistra-Jones, Karen. "Staging Authenticity: Joachim, Brahms, and the Politics of *Werktreue* Performance." *Journal of the American Musicological Society* 66, no. 2 (2013): 397–436.

Lessing, Gotthold Ephraim. *Hamburg Dramaturgy*. Translated by Helen Zimmern. New York: Dover, 1962. Originally published as *Hamburgische Dramaturgie*, edited by Otto Mann (Stuttgart: Alfred Kröner, 1958).

Levine, Lawrence W. *Highbrow/Lowbrow; The Emergence of Cultural Hierarchy in America*. Cambridge, MA: Harvard University Press, 1988.

Levison, William H., ed. *Black Diamonds*. Upper Saddle River, NJ: Literature House, Gregg Press, 1969. Originally published as *Black Diamonds: or, Humor, Satire, and Sentiment Treated Scientifically by Professor Julius Caesar Hannibal: In a Series of Burlesque Lectures, Darkly Colored*, in *"The New York Picayune"* (New York: A. Ranney, 1855).

Levy, Beth E. "From Orient to Occident: Aaron Copland and the Sagas of the Prairie." In *Aaron Copland and His World*, edited by Carol J. Oja and Judith Tick, 307–349. Princeton, NJ: Princeton University Press, 2005.

Lhamon, W. T., Jr. *Raising Cain: Blackface Performance from Jim Crow to Hip Hop*. Cambridge, MA: Harvard University Press, 1998.

Lipsitz, George. "Land of a Thousand Dances: Youth, Minorities, and the Rise of Rock and Roll." In *Recasting America: Culture and Politics in the Age of Cold War*. Edited by Lary May. Chicago: University of Chicago Press, 1989.

Locke, Arthur Ware, and E. T. A. Hoffmann. "'Beethoven's Instrumental Music': Translated from E. T. A. Hoffmann's *Kreisleriana* with an Introductory Note." *Musical Quarterly* 3, no. 1 (1917): 123–133.

Locke, Ralph, and Cyrilla Barr. *Cultivating Music in America: Women Patrons and Activists since 1860*. Berkeley: University of California Press, 1997.

Lockwood, Lewis. *Inside Beethoven's Quartets: History, Performance, Interpretation*. Cambridge, MA: Harvard University Press, 2008.

Lott, Eric. *Love and Theft: Blackface Minstrelsy and the American Working Class*. New York: Oxford University Press, 1993.

Lowe, Melanie. "Falling from Grace: Irony and Expressive Enrichment in Haydn's Symphonic Minuets." *Journal of Musicology* 19 (2002): 171–221.

———. *Pleasure and Meaning in the Classical Symphony*. Bloomington: Indiana University Press, 2007.

Macdonald, Dwight. "Masscult and Midcult." In *Against the American Grain*, 3–75. New York: Random House, 1962.

MacIntyre, Alasdair. *After Virtue: A Study in Moral Theory*. 2nd ed. Notre Dame, IN: University of Notre Dame Press, 1984.

———. *A Short History of Ethics: A History of Moral Philosophy from the Homeric Age to the Twentieth Century*. 2nd ed. Notre Dame, IN: University of Notre Dame Press, 1998.

MacIntyre, Bruce C. *Haydn: "The Creation."* New York: Schirmer, 1998.

Mahar, William J. *Behind the Burnt Cork Mask; Early Blackface Minstrelsy and Antebellum American Popular Culture*. Urbana: University of Illinois Press, 1999.

Mahling, Christoph-Hellmut. "Performance Practice in Haydn's Works for *Lira Organizzata*." In *Haydn Studies: Proceedings of the International Haydn Conference, Washington, D.C., 1975*, edited by Jens Peter Larsen, Howard Serwer, and James Webster, 297–302. New York: W. W. Norton & Company, 1981.

Martin, Robert. "The Quartets in Performance: A Player's Perspective." In *The Beethoven Quartet Companion*, edited by Robert Winter and Robert Martin, 110–141. Berkeley, 1994.

Mather, Olivia. "'Cosmic American Music': Place and the Country Rock Movement, 1965–1974," PhD diss., University of California, Los Angeles, 2006.

Mathew, Nicholas, and Benjamin Walton, eds. *The Invention of Beethoven and Rossini: Historiography, Analysis, Criticism*. Cambridge: Cambridge University Press, 2013.

Mazullo, Mark. "Authenticity in Rock Music Culture." PhD diss., University of Minnesota, 1999.

McCaldin, Denis. "Haydn as Self Borrower." *Musical Times* 123 (1982): 177–179.
McClary, Susan. "The Blasphemy of Talking Politics during the Bach Year." In *Music and Society: The Politics of Composition, Performance, and Reception*, edited by Richard Leppert and Susan McClary, 13–62. Cambridge: Cambridge University Press, 1987.
———. "Constructions of Subjectivity in Schubert's Music." In *Queering the Pitch: The New Gay and Lesbian Musicology*, edited by Philip Brett, Elizabeth Wood, and Gary Thomas, 205–33. New York: Routledge, 1994.
———. *Conventional Wisdom: The Content of Musical Form*. Berkeley: University of California Press, 2000.
———. *Feminine Endings; Music, Gender, and Sexuality*. Minneapolis: University of Minnesota Press, 1991.
———. "The Impromptu That Trod on a Loaf: How Music Tells Stories." *Narrative* 5, no. 1 (January 1997): 20–34.
———. "A Musical Dialectic from the Enlightenment: Mozart's Piano Concerto in G Major, K. 453, Movement II." *Cultural Critique* 4 (fall 1986): 129–69.
———. "Narrative Agendas in 'Absolute' Music: Identity and Difference in Brahms's Third Symphony." In *Musicology and Difference; Gender and Sexuality in Music Scholarship*, edited by Ruth A. Solie, 326–44. Berkeley: University of California Press, 1993.
———. "Narratives of Bourgeois Subjectivity in Mozart's 'Prague' Symphony." In *Understanding Narrative*, edited by Peter Rabinowitz and James Phelan, 65–98. Columbus: Ohio State University Press, 1994.
———. "Pitches, Expression, Ideology: An Exercise in Mediation." *Enclitic* 7 (1983): 76–86. Reprinted in *Reading Music: Selected Essays* (Aldershot, UK: Ashgate, 2007).
———. "Terminal Prestige: The Case of Avant-Garde Music Composition." *Cultural Critique* 12 (1989): 57–81. Reprinted in *Keeping Score: Music, Disciplinarity, Culture*, edited by David Schwarz, Anahid Kassabian, and Lawrence Siegel, 54–74. Charlottesville: University Press of Virginia, 1997.
McClelland, Clive. *Ombra: Supernatural Music in the Eighteenth Century*. Lanham, MD: Lexington Books, 2012.
McLamore, Laura Alyson. "Symphonic Conventions in London's Concert Rooms, circa 1755–1790." PhD diss., University of California at Los Angeles, 1991.
McMillin, Scott. *The Musical as Drama*. Princeton, NJ: Princeton University Press, 2006.
McVeigh, Simon W. *Concert Life in London from Mozart to Haydn*. Cambridge: Cambridge University Press, 1993.
Melton, James Van Horn. "School, Stage, Salon: Musical Cultures in Haydn's Vienna." In *Haydn and the Performance of Rhetoric*, edited by Tom Beghin and Sander M. Goldberg, 80–108. Chicago: University of Chicago Press, 2007.

Meyer, Eve R. "*Turquerie* and Eighteenth-Century Music." *Eighteenth-Century Studies* 7, no. 4 (summer 1974): 474–488.
Minnelli, Vincente, and Hector Arce. *I Remember It Well*. Gardent City, NY: Doubleday, 1974.
Mirka, Danuta. "Metre, Phrase Structure and Manipulations of Musical Beginnings." In *Communication in Eighteenth-Century Music*, edited by Danuta Mirka and Kofi Agawu, 83–111. Cambridge: Cambridge University Press, 2008.
Moffit, William C. *Patterns of Motion: Master Planning Guide*. Winona, MI: Hal Leonard Music, 1964.
Monelle, Raymond. *The Musical Topic: Hunt, Military and Pastoral*. Bloomington: Indiana University Press, 2006.
———. *The Sense of Music: Semiotic Essays*. Princeton, NJ: Princeton University Press, 2000.
Morris, Mitchell. "Musical Virtues." In *Beyond Structural Listening?: Postmodern Modes of Hearing*, edited by Andrew Dell'Antonio, 44–69. Berkeley: University of California Press, 2004.
———. *The Persistence of Sentiment: Essays on Pop Music in the 70s*. Berkeley: University of California Press, 2012.
Most, Andrea. "The Birth of Theatrical Liberalism." In *After Pluralism: Re-Imagining Models of Religious Engagement*, edited by Courtney Bender and Pamela Klassen, 127–155. New York: Columbia University Press, 2010.
———. *Making Americans: Jews and the Broadway Musical*. Cambridge, MA: Harvard University Press, 2004.
———. *Theatrical Liberalism: Jews and Popular Entertainment in America*. New York: New York University Press, 2013.
Nathan, Hans. *Dan Emmett and the Rise of Early Negro Minstrelsy*. Norman: University of Oklahoma Press, 1962.
Necker, Suzanne. *Mélanges extraits des manuscrits de Mme Necker*. Paris: Charles Pougens, 1798.
Nelson, Thomas K. "The Fantasy of Absolute Music." PhD diss., University of Minnesota, 1998.
Neuwirth, Markus. "Does a 'Monothematic' Expositional Design Have Tautological Implications for the Recapitulation? An Alternative Approach to 'Altered Recapitulations' in Haydn." *Studia Musicologica* 51 (2010): 369–385.
Newcomb, Anthony. "Narrative Archetypes and Mahler's Ninth Symphony." In *Music and Text: Critical Inquiries*, edited by Stephen Paul Scher, 118–136. Cambridge: Cambridge University Press, 1992.
———. "Once More between Absolute and Program Music: Schumann's Second Symphony." *19th-Century Music* 7 (1984): 233–250.

———. "The Polonaise-Fantasy and Issues of Musical Narrative." In *Chopin Studies*, vol. 2, edited by John Rink and Jim Samson, 84–101. Cambridge: Cambridge University Press, 1994.
———. "Schumann and Late Eighteenth-Century Narrative Strategies." *19th-Century Music* 1 (1987): 164–74.
Nichols, Thomas Low. *Forty Years of American Life*. 2nd ed. London: Longmans, Green, 1874. Originally published 1864.
Nowatzki, Robert. *Representing African Americans in Transatlantic Abolitionism and Blackface Minstrelsy*. Baton Rouge: Louisiana State University Press, 2010.
Obelkevich, Mary Rowen. "Turkish Affect in the Land of the Sun King." *Musical Quarterly* 63, no. 3 (1977): 367–389.
Özkirimli, Umut. *Theories of Nationalism: A Critical Introduction*. 2nd ed. New York: Palgrave Macmillan, 2010.
Panassié, Hugues. *The Real Jazz*. Translated by Anne Sorelle Williams. Adapted by Charles Edward Smith. New York: Smith & Durrell, 1942.
Pareles, Jon. "Don't Call Jazz America's Classical Music." *New York Times*, February 28, 1999.
Paskman, Dailey, and Sigmund Spaeth. *"Gentlemen, Be Seated!" A Parade of the Old-Time Minstrels*. Garden City, NY: Doubleday, Doran, 1928.
Pasler, Jann. *Composing the Citizen: Music as Public Utility in Third Republic France*. Berkeley: University of California Press, 2009.
Pasles, Chris. "Wigglesworth, Philharmonic Follow Beethoven's Lead." *Los Angeles Times*, February 7, 1998, F4. http://articles.latimes.com/1998/feb/07/entertainment/ca-16346 (accessed May 20, 2017).
Peattie, Donald Culross. "Beethoven—He Set Music Free." *Reader's Digest* 67, no. 401 (September 1955): 122–126.
Pederson, Sanna. "A. B. Marx, Berlin Concert Life, and German National Identity." *19th-Century Music* 18 (1994): 87–107.
Peterson, Richard A. *Creating Country Music: Fabricating Authenticity*. Chicago: University of Chicago Press, 1997.
Pickering, Michael. "'A Jet Ornament to Society': Black Music in Nineteenth-Century Britain." In *Black Music in Britain: Essays on the Afro-Asian Contribution to Popular Music*, edited by Paul Oliver, 16–33. Milton Keynes, UK: Open University Press, 1990.
———. "Mock Blacks and Racial Mockery: The 'Nigger' Minstrel and British Imperialism." In *Acts of Supremacy: The British Empire and the Stage, 1790–1930*, edited by J. S. Bratton, Richard Allen Cave, Breandan Gregory, Heidi J. Holder, and Michael Pickering, 179–236. Manchester, UK: Manchester University Press, 1991.

———. "White Skin, Black Masks: 'Nigger' Minstrelsy in Victorian Britain." In *Music Hall: Performance and Style*, edited by J. S. Bratton, 70–91. Milton Keynes, UK: Open University Press, 1986.

Pollack, Howard. *Aaron Copland: The Life and Works of an Uncommon Man*. New York: Henry Holt and Company, 1999.

Proksch, Bryan. *Reviving Haydn: New Appreciations in the Twentieth Century*. Rochester, NY: University of Rochester Press, 2015.

Pysnik, Stephen. "Camp Identities: Conrad Salinger and the Aesthetics of MGM Musicals." PhD diss., Duke University, 2014.

———. "Musical Camp: Conrad Salinger and the Performance of Gayness in *The Pirate*." In *Music and Camp*, edited by Christopher Moore and Philip Purvis. Middletown, CT: Wesleyan University Press, forthcoming.

Radano, Ronald. *Lying up a Nation: Race and Black Music*. Chicago: University of Chicago Press, 2003.

Ramsey, Guthrie P., Jr. *Race Music: Black Cultures from Bebop to Hip-Hop*. Berkeley: University of California Press, 2003.

Ratner, Leonard. *Classic Music: Expression, Form, and Style*. New York: Schirmer Books, 1980.

Raulerson, Graham. "The Hobo in American Musical Culture." PhD diss., University of California, Los Angeles, 2011.

Richter, Jean Paul. *Vorschule der Ästhetik: Kleine Nachschule zur ästhetischen Vorschule*. Edited by Norbert Miller. Munich, Germany: Carl Hanser Verlag, 1963.

Riggs, Robert. "'On the Representation of Character in Music': Christian Gottfried Körner's Aesthetics of Instrumental Music." *Musical Quarterly* 81 (1997): 599–631.

Rogin, Michael. *Blackface, White Noise: Jewish Immigrants in the Hollywood Melting Pot*. Berkeley: University of California Press, 1996.

———. "New Deal Blackface." In *Hollywood Musicals: The Film Reader*, edited by Steven Cohan, 175–182. London: Routledge, 2002. Reprinted from Michael Rogin, *Blackface, White Noise: Jewish Immigrants in the Hollywood Melting Pot*, 177–191 (Berkeley: University of California Press, 1996).

Rosen, Charles. *The Classical Style*. New York: W. W. Norton, 1971.

Ross, Andrew. "The Uses of Camp." In *No Respect: Intellectuals and Popular Culture*, 135–170. New York: Routledge, 1989.

Rothenberg, Sarah. "'Thus Far, but No Farther': Fanny Mendelssohn-Hensel's Unfinished Journey." *Musical Quarterly* 77, no. 4 (winter 1993): 689–708.

Rubin, Joan Shelley. *The Making of Middlebrow Culture*. Chapel Hill: University of North Carolina Press, 1992.

Rury, John L. "The New York African Free School, 1827–1836: Conflict over Community Control of Black Education." *Phylon* 44, no. 3 (1983): 187–197.

Russo, Vito. *The Celluloid Closet; Homosexuality in the Movies*. Rev. ed. New York: Harper & Row, Publishers, 1987. Originally published 1981.

Said, Edward. *Orientalism*. 2nd ed. New York: Vintage Books, 1994.

Sales, Grover. *Jazz: America's Classical Music*. Da Capo Press, 1992. Originally published 1984.

Sandrow, Nahma. *Vagabond Stars: A World History of Yiddish Theater*. Harper & Row, 1977.

Savran, David. *Highbrow/Lowdown: Theater, Jazz, and the Making of the New Middle Class*. Ann Arbor: University of Michigan Press, 2009.

Saxton, Alexander. "Blackface Minstrelsy and Jacksonian Ideology." *American Quarterly* 27, no. 1 (1975): 3–28.

Schenker, Heinrich. *The Masterwork in Music*. Vol. 1, *1925*. Translated by Ian Bent, William Drabkin, Richard Kramer, John Rothgeb, and Heidi Siegal. Cambridge: Cambridge University Press, 1994. Originally published Munich: Drei Masken Verlag, 1925.

Schiller, Friedrich. *Schillers Werke: Nationalausgabe*. Edited by Herbert Meyer. Vol. 22. Weimar, 1958.

Schroeder, David. *Haydn and the Enlightenment: The Late Symphonies and their Audience*. Oxford: Oxford University Press, 1990.

Scott, Derek B. "Blackface Minstrels, Black Minstrels, and Their Reception in England." In *Europe, Empire, and Spectacle in Nineteenth-Century British Music*, edited by Rachel Cowgill and Julian Rushton, 265–280. Aldershot, UK: Ashgate, 2006.

Sennett, Ted. *Hollywood Musicals*. New York: Henry H. Abrams, 1981.

Sinfield, Alan. *The Wilde Century: Effeminacy, Oscar Wilde, and the Queer Moment*. New York: Columbia University Press, 1994.

Sipe, Thomas. *Beethoven: "Eroica Symphony."* Cambridge: Cambridge University Press, 1998.

Sisman, Elaine. "Haydn's Career and the Idea of the Multiple Audience." In *The Cambridge Companion to Haydn*, edited by Caryl Clark, 3–16. Cambridge: Cambridge University Press, 2005.

———. "Haydn's Theater Symphonies." *Journal of the American Musicological Society* 43, no. 2 (1990): 292–352.

———. "Rhetorical Truth in Haydn's Chamber Music: Genre, Tertiary Rhetoric, and the Opus 76 Quartets." In *Haydn and the Performance of Rhetoric*, edited by Tom Beghin and Sander M. Goldberg, 281–326. Chicago: University of Chicago Press, 2007.

Smaczny, Jan. "Nineteenth-Century National Traditions and the String Quartet." In *The Cambridge Companion to the String Quartet*, edited by Robin Stowell, 266–287. Cambridge: Cambridge University Press, 2003.

Small, Christopher. *Musicking: The Meanings of Performing and Listening.* Hanover, NH and London: Wesleyan University Press, 1998.
Smith, Ruth. *Handel's Oratorios and Eighteenth-Century Thought.* Cambridge: Cambridge University Press, 1995.
Smither, Howard E. *A History of the Oratorio.* Vol. 3, *The Oratorio in the Classical Era.* Chapel Hill: University of North Carolina Press, 1987.
Snarrenberg, Robert. *Schenker's Interpretive Practice.* Cambridge: Cambridge University Press, 1997.
Solomon, Maynard. *Beethoven Essays.* Cambridge, MA: Harvard University Press, 1988.
———. *Mozart: A Life.* New York: HarperCollins, 1995.
———. "Some Images of Creation in Music of the Viennese Classical School." *Musical Quarterly* 89 (2007): 121–135.
Somfai, László. "' . . . *They Are Full of Invention, Fire, Good Taste, and New Effects*': Two Compositional Essays in the 'Erdôdy' Quartets Op. 76." *Studia Musicologica* 51 (2010): 317–324.
Sontag, Susan. "Against Interpretation." *Evergreen Review* 8 (December, 1964): 76–80, 93. Reprinted in *Against Interpretation and Other Essays*, 3–14 (New York: Dell, 1966).
———. *Against Interpretation* [*and Other Essays*]. New York: Dell, 1966.
———. "Notes on Camp." *Partisan Review* 31, no. 4 (fall 1964): 515–30.
Staffordshire Sentinel: "*Utopia Limited*: Gems of the New Opera." October 9, 1893. Accessed March 29, 2012. http://diamond.boisestate.edu/gas/utopia/reviews/review.html.
Stearns, Marshall, and Jean Stearns. *Jazz Dance: The Story of American Vernacular Dance.* New York: Da Capo Press, 1994. Originally published Perseus Books, 1968.
Steinberg, Michael P. *Listening to Reason: Culture, Subjectivity, and Nineteenth-Century Music.* Princeton, NJ: Princeton University Press, 2004.
Stewart, Jon. *Idealism and Existentialism: Hegel and Nineteenth- and Twentieth-Century European Philosophy.* London: Continuum, 2010.
Stowell, Robin, ed. *The Cambridge Companion to the String Quartet.* Cambridge: Cambridge University Press, 2003.
———. "Traditional and Progressive Nineteenth-Century Trends: France, Italy, Great Britain and America." In *The Cambridge Companion to the String Quartet,* edited by Robin Stowell, 250–265. Cambridge: Cambridge University Press, 2003.
Strausbaugh, John. *Black Like You: Blackface, Whiteface, Insult, and Imitation in American Popular Culture.* New York: Penguin, 2006.
Strunk, Oliver, ed. *Source Readings in Music History.* Rev. ed. Ruth A. Solie. Translated by Oliver Strunk. 7 vols. New York: W. W. Norton & Company, 1998.

Sutcliffe, W. Dean. "Haydn, Mozart and Their Contemporaries." In *The Cambridge Companion to the String Quartet*, edited by Robin Stowell, 185–209. Cambridge: Cambridge University Press, 2003.

Taruskin, Richard. "Facing Up, Finally, to Bach's Dark Vision." In *Text and Act: Essays on Music and Performance*, 307–315. New York: Oxford University Press, 1995. Originally published *New York Times*, January 27, 1991.

———. "How the Acorn Took Root." In *Defining Russia Musically: Historical and Hermeneutical Essays*, 113–151. Princeton, NJ: Princeton University Press, 1997.

———. "Nationalism." In *Grove Music Online*. Edited by Laura Macy. Accessed August 27, 2006. http://www.grovemusic.com.

———. "'Nationalism': Colonialism in Disguise." *New York Times*, Sunday, August 22, 1993. Reprinted in *Repercussions* 5 (1996, published 1998): 5–20.

———. *The Oxford History of Western Music*. Vol. 2, *The Seventeenth and Eighteenth Centuries*. Oxford: Oxford University Press, 2005.

———. *Text and Act: Essays on Music and Performance*. New York: Oxford University Press, 1995.

Taylor, Charles. *The Ethics of Authenticity*. Cambridge, MA: Harvard University Press, 1991.

Taylor, Timothy D. *Beyond Exoticism: Western Music and the World*. Durham, NC: Duke University Press, 2007.

———. "Peopling the Stage: Opera, Otherness, and New Musical Representations in the Eighteenth Century." *Cultural Critique* 36 (spring 1997): 55–88.

Taylor, William ("Billy"). "Jazz: America's Classical Music." *Black Perspective in Music* 14, no. 1 (winter 1986): 21–25.

Taylor, Yuval, and Jake Austen. *Darkest America: Black Minstrelsy from Slavery to Hip-Hop*. New York: W. W. Norton & Company, 2012.

Temperley, Nicholas. *Haydn: "The Creation."* Cambridge: Cambridge University Press, 1991.

Tibbetts, John C., ed. "Appendix A: Newspaper and Magazine Articles." In *Dvořák in America: 1892–1895*, 355–384. Portland, OR: Amadeus Press, 1993.

Tinkcom, Matthew. "'Working Like a Homosexual': Camp Visual Codes and the Labor of Gay Subjects in the MGM Freed Unit." *Cinema Journal* 35, no. 2 (winter 1996): 24–42. Reprinted in *Hollywood Musicals: The Film Reader*, edited by Steven Cohan, 115–128 (London: Routledge, 2002).

Todd, R. Larry. *Fanny Hensel: The Other Mendelssohn*. Oxford: Oxford University Press, 2010.

Toll, Robert. *Blacking Up: The Minstrel Show in Nineteenth-Century America*. New York: Oxford University Press, 1974.

Tomlinson, Gary. "Italian Romanticism and Italian Opera: An Essay in Their Affinities." *19th-Century Music* 10 (summer 1986): 43–60.

Trilling, Lionel. *Sincerity and Authenticity: The Charles Eliot Norton Lectures, 1969–1970.* Cambridge, MA: Harvard University Press, 1972.

Van Deburg, William L. *Slavery and Race in American Popular Culture.* Madison: University of Wisconsin Press, 1984.

Vander Wel, Stephanie. "'I Am a Honky-Tonk Girl': Country Music, Gender and Migration." PhD diss., University of California, Los Angeles, 2007.

Wagner, Richard. *Richard Wagner: Dichtungen und Schriften.* Edited by Dieter Borchmeyer. 10 vols. Frankfurt: Dieter Borchmeyer, 1983.

———. *Richard Wagner's Prose Works.* Translated by William Ashton Ellis. 8 vols. London: Routledge & Kegan Paul, 1893. Reprinted by New York: Broude Brothers, 1966.

Walbrook, Henry M. *Gilbert and Sullivan Opera: A History and a Comment.* London: F. V. White, 1922. "Gilbert and Sullivan Archive." Accessed March 29, 2012. http://diamond.boisestate.edu/gas/books/walbrook/chap15.html.

Wald, Elijah. *The Dozens: A History of Rap's Mama.* Oxford: Oxford University Press, 2012.

———. *Dylan Goes Electric!: Newport, Seeger, Dylan, and the Night That Split the Sixties.* New York: HarperCollins, 2015.

———. *How the Beatles Destroyed Rock 'n' Roll: An Alternative History of American Popular Music.* Oxford: Oxford University Press, 2011.

Walter, Horst. "Über Haydns 'Charakteristische' Sinfonien." In *Das symphonische Werk Joseph Haydns,* edited by Gerhard J. Winkler, 65–78. Eisenstadt, Germany: Burgenländisches Landesmuseum, 2002.

Waterman, David. "Playing Quartets: A View from the Inside." In *The Cambridge Companion to the String Quartet,* edited by Robin Stowell, 97–126. Cambridge: Cambridge University Press, 2003.

Watkins, Holly. *Metaphors of Depth in German Musical Thought: From E. T. A. Hoffmann to Arnold Schoenberg.* Cambridge: Cambridge University Press, 2011.

Weber, William. "Mass Culture and the Reshaping of European Musical Taste, 1770–1870." *International Review of the Aesthetics and Sociology of Music* 25, nos. 1/2 (1994): 175–190.

———. "Musical Idealism and the Crisis of the Old Order." In *The Great Transformation of Musical Taste: Concert Programming from Haydn to Brahms,* 85–121. Cambridge: Cambridge University Press, 2008.

———. *Music and the Middle Class: The Social Structure of Concert Life in London, Paris, and Vienna.* New York: Holmes & Meier, 1975.

Webster, James. "*The Creation,* Haydn's Late Vocal Music, and the Musical Sublime." In *Haydn and His World,* edited by Elaine Sisman, 57–102. Princeton, NJ: Princeton University Press, 1997.

———. “The D Major Interlude in the First Movement of Haydn’s Farewell Symphony.” In *Studies in Musical Sources and Styles: Essays in Honor of Jan LaRue*, edited by Eugene K. Wolf and Edward H. Roesner, 339–380. Madison, WI: A-R Editions, 1990.

———. “Haydn’s Aesthetics.” In *The Cambridge Companion to Haydn*, edited by Caryl Clark, 30–44. Cambridge: Cambridge University Press, 2005.

———. *Haydn’s “Farewell” Symphony and the Idea of Classical Style: Through-Composition and Cyclic Integration in his Instrumental Music*. Cambridge: Cambridge University Press, 1991.

———. “Haydn’s Symphonies between *Sturm und Drang* and ‘Classical Style’: Art and Entertainment.” In *Haydn Studies*, edited by W. Dean Sutcliffe, 218–245. Cambridge: Cambridge University Press, 1998.

Weiss, Piero, and Richard Taruskin, eds. *Music in the Western World: A History in Documents*. New York: Schirmer Books, 1984.

Wheelock, Gretchen. *Haydn’s Ingenious Jesting with Art: Contexts of Musical Wit and Humor*. New York: Schirmer Books, 1992.

Wilde, Oscar. *The Complete Works of Oscar Wilde*. Introduction by Vyvyan Holland. New York: Harper & Row, 1989. Originally published London: William Collins Sons, 1966.

Willson, A. Leslie, ed. *German Romantic Criticism*. Translated by Margaret R. Hale. New York: Continuum, 1982.

Wolf, Stacy. *A Problem Like Maria: Gender and Sexuality in the American Musical*. Ann Arbor: University of Michigan Press, 2002.

Wolfson, John. *Final Curtain: The Last Gilbert and Sullivan Operas*. London: Chappell, 1976.

Woll, Allen. *The Hollywood Musical Goes to War*. Chicago: Nelson-Hall, 1983.

Wollman, Elizabeth. *The Theater Will Rock: A History of the Rock Musical, from “Hair” to “Hedwig.”* Ann Arbor: University of Michigan Press, 2006.

Woolf, Virginia. “Middlebrow.” In *The Death of the Moth, and Other Essays*, 176–186. London: Hogarth Press, 1942.

Index